INSIDER

RV Raman is the bestselling author of *Fraudster*, and was the head of KPMG's Consulting Practice and the co-head of their Risk Advisory Services. He was also a Partner with A.T. Kearney and Arthur Andersen. Over a career spanning three decades and four continents, he has advised several banks, financial institutions, regulators, stock exchanges and corporates on matters of strategy, operations and risk management.

He currently teaches business strategy at IIM Trichy, mentors young entrepreneurs and advises select clients. He lives in Chennai, and can be reached through his website www.rvraman.com. *Insider* is the second novel in his corporate thriller series that explores white-collar crime in India.

Praise for *Fraudster*

'RV Raman...has taken life in the corporate corridors he has known only too well, and turned it into something teeming with compelling stories.' – *New Indian Express*

'Raman goes the Christie way in this excellent closed-room mystery that keeps us guessing till the very end even when the clues are out in the open.' – *Statesman*

'If art imitates life, then we all need to be very worried. RV Raman's novel, *Fraudster* is an insider's account of the less than salubrious side of the corporate world.' – *Deccan Chronicle*

INSIDER

RV RAMAN

hachette INDIA

First published in 2016 by Hachette India
(Registered name: Hachette Book Publishing India Pvt. Ltd)
An Hachette UK company
www.hachetteindia.com

SRD

ISBN 978-93-5195-031-8

Hachette Book Publishing India Pvt. Ltd
4th/5th Floors, Corporate Centre,
Sector 44, Gurgaon 122003, India

Typeset in 10.5/14 Minion Pro by SÜRYA, New Delhi

Printed in India by Manipal Technologies Limited, Manipal

FSC
www.fsc.org
MIX
Paper from
responsible sources
FSC™ C104740

Prologue

Germany, July 2011

The Indian watched the German from the corner of his eye. He would soon step out of the server room for a smoke break, time enough for the Indian to patch in the last block of code he had surreptitiously been inserting into his client's high-security system.

Indranil, a freelance computer programmer from Kolkata, had concluded on his second day in Germany that the brawny German was a guard masquerading as a programmer. The desks had been so arranged that he could see Indranil's screen at all times, but Indranil couldn't see his. By the second day, the conspicuous absence of keyboard sounds from the German's desk had spoken loudly. Indranil was being watched.

His suspicions had been aroused as soon as his jet lag wore off. Why had he been called to a data centre deep in the German hinterland? Even Einbeck, the closest town, was a quiet little place, miles from anywhere. Given the data centre's high-capacity linkages to the internet, Indranil could have worked on the project from India itself. Why haul him all the way to Europe?

He had no answer.

None of the people at the data centre spoke English, but his host had not skimped on hospitality. Everything Indranil needed had been provided. As an added incentive, a two-day yacht trip off the Baltic coast was on offer if he completed his work ahead of schedule.

Spurred on by the thought and with no other way to spend his time here in the German wilderness, he had worked through most of his waking hours. On the side, however, he had begun unravelling the mystery of the remote data centre. He had learnt that it hosted applications for several companies, including a Swiss bank, a British retailer and an MMORPG game.

After a week, he had discovered enough to realize that his client was involved in something suspicious. His hacking skills had led him to three other Indians logged into the server, who were working on different parts of the software. The client had broken up their project into parts and got freelancers to work on each piece in isolation, presumably so that no single person knew what the entire software actually did. Sheer chance, aided by his hacking skills, had allowed Indranil to see more than he ought to have.

Another week later, he had figured it out and had decided to covertly embed software that he could later exploit. There was enough redundant code in the system in which to hide his own cryptic and recursive code. It would be very difficult for someone else to find and remove it.

He had paced it perfectly too. His project was almost done and he had just one more day to go. The last blocks of his illicit code would be in place once the German stepped out for his cigarette. Indranil would be on his yacht trip by the next evening and his client would be none the wiser. By next week, he would be back in India.

As soon as the German picked up his cigarette packet and left the room, Indranil's fingers flew over the keyboard. Two windows popped up on his screen and his right hand gripped the mouse. The first window opened the file he had copied earlier from his pen drive to the computer. He transferred a block of code from it to the second window. Even as he saved the modified file, he opened another window and copied another block of code into it from the first window. Then again, as the last block went into a third file, he finally closed the windows and executed a command to compile the three modified files.

Three minutes later, he was finished. He sat back in relief as his pounding heart gradually calmed down.

It was done!

The German's smoke break lasted much longer than usual and there was a new tension in his bearing when he returned. He spoke little over dinner that night and his expression was pensive as he sat beside Indranil on the four-hour drive to Lübeck and the coastal town of Travemünde the next morning. Something had evidently happened during the smoke break, but Indranil couldn't gauge what it was.

The forty-foot yacht turned out to be smaller than the one he had fantasized about. The two cramped cabins and the saloon could just about accommodate five men. Indranil was to share a cabin with his German friend of four weeks, while two other Indians shared the second cabin. The fifth, the pilot of the hired yacht, would use the saloon.

One of his fellow Indians – a representative of the client – was Pramod, a swarthy middle-aged man with an enured face. The other was a diminutive young man named Anil. Jovial, gay and appropriately loud for a stag party, Pramod was clad in Bermuda shorts and a floral open-necked shirt. He soon proved to be the live wire of the evening, cracking jokes, both lewd and subtle, belting out popular Bollywood numbers and generally putting the others on the yacht at ease.

By the time the leisurely autumn sun finally went down five hours from the coast, the second bottle of scotch was half-empty and Anil was quite drunk. Indranil made a startling discovery before the other man's words began slurring and his speech became incoherent: Anil was one of the other three freelancers who had worked on the software.

Even as Pramod liberally poured the scotch into Indranil's and Anil's glasses, he was filling his own and the German's with ice. The German had grown very quiet, throwing occasional glances at Indranil. Twice, when he had caught those glances, Indranil was unable to fathom the man's expression. And that bothered him.

Suddenly, the penny dropped: *Pramod was planning something treacherous in the Baltic waters!*

Either he had discovered Indranil's deceit or had decided to dispose of the programmers who had built his software. Another flash of insight seared Indranil's mind: Pramod had deliberately used freelancers, because they were easier to get rid of than full-fledged employees of software companies.

Oh God! What had he gotten himself into?

Indranil's inebriation receded in an instant. He excused himself and went below deck as Anil began to sing drunkenly. In the toilet, Indranil switched on his mobile phone and waited.

Damn! There was no signal!

He had no specific plan in mind, but if he could catch a signal, he might be able to call someone or send a text message. He cursed the endless expanse of water around them.

Meanwhile, Anil had suddenly stopped singing.

As Indranil pocketed his phone, wondering what he should do, he heard a strangled cry, followed by a thud. His blood ran cold. He waited, not daring to move.

There was nowhere to hide on the yacht!

A couple of minutes passed in silence. Then he heard a splash and the yacht rocked gently. Fear gripped his heart and he began to sweat. Footsteps came down the stairs…and passed the toilet door. He opened the door just enough to catch a glimpse of his German friend entering his cabin.

Realizing that he couldn't stay in the toilet any longer without arousing suspicion, he trudged up to the deck. Should he grab a couple of life jackets and jump into the sea? How cold was the water? Would he freeze to death? He rejected the idea. In any case, he stood a better chance in a one-on-one with Pramod before the German returned.

When he reached the deck, Pramod was waiting for him with a gun held casually in his hand. They stared at each other. No words were necessary, but Indranil asked the question, anyway.

'Where is Anil?'

'Sleeping it off in his cabin. He passed out.'

A lie. Only the German had gone down the stairs.

'What now?' Indranil asked, backing away behind the deckchairs.

'We part company.' Pramod's smile was mirthless. 'Those deckchairs won't stop bullets, you know. And the water is pretty cold.'

'Why are you doing this?' Facing death, Indranil's fear had evaporated and the beginnings of a plan started taking shape.

'Just playing safe.'

'Safe?' Indranil shook his head slowly, his gaze fixed on the other man. 'Killing me would be the most unsafe thing you could do right now.'

'Really? Let's see.' The hand holding the gun rose, pointing the weapon at Indranil's chest.

'And hasty too.' Unlikely courage came to his aid. He gazed steadily into the gunman's eyes. 'Hear me out. What can possibly thwart you in the middle of the sea?'

The gun wavered for a moment and paused, its muzzle still pointing at Indranil's heart.

'Your software will do unexpected things unless I log in periodically and reset it,' Indranil continued before Pramod could decide. 'Things you wouldn't like.'

'Such as?' Pramod's eyes had become alert; his interest was aroused.

Indranil told him and watched the smile vanish from the other man's face. His expression had hardened.

'You're bluffing!' he hissed. His flinty eyes had narrowed to slits.

'Am I?'

It was all or nothing now. The time for Indranil's final gambit had arrived. He *had* to appear confident. He *had* to be bold. He summoned up the courage to step out from behind the deckchairs and sit down on one. He switched to Hindi and spoke uninterrupted for the next five minutes. Neither the German nor the pilot came up to the deck. Indranil's heart was thudding when he finished, but he tried to keep a poker face.

This was the crux. Had Pramod bought his story?

Without taking his eyes off Indranil, Pramod reached behind and unclipped a satellite phone from his belt. The gun continued to point at him…

▪

Four days later, a short report appeared in the *Times of India*:

Indians missing at sea

> Two software programmers from India are among the five men reported missing after the yacht they were holidaying on capsized in the Baltic Sea off the northern coast of Germany. A group of four men had set out on Friday with a crewman for a weekend pleasure trip. While German naval search and rescue helicopters have traced debris from the wreck, they failed to spot any survivors. The Indian embassy in Berlin is in touch with the German authorities.

Chapter 1

MUMBAI, OCTOBER 2015

Dusk fell unhurriedly on the proud glass-and-chrome towers of midtown Mumbai's emerging business district. A handful of men sat in the penthouse office of the tallest tower – the nerve centre of an unheralded 'finance company'. Shielded by the most advanced technology money could buy, they moved small fortunes every day between private financial empires and capital markets.

The Asian financial markets had long since closed and the men had concluded their European deals for the day. The US markets would open shortly. Now was the time to take advantage of the brief lull and enjoy a moment of leisure.

High on the tower's dark smoked glass, brightly lit chrome lettering proclaimed the presence of Purple Country's offices fourteen floors below. Unlike the veiled operations in the penthouse, Purple Country was anything but obscure. In fact, visibility was its lifeblood.

The spectacular rise of this young online company that catered to the entertainment needs of the well-heeled was the envy of those associated with the burgeoning luxury industry. From bespoke off-the-grid getaways to green vacations that clients could subsequently brag about to their envious audiences, from private movie screenings to discreetly arranged clandestine escapades, from limited-edition customized accessories to exclusive shopping expeditions, Purple Country delivered them all with minimal fuss and no hiccups.

The real boom had come when the company had taken its business online early in 2013 and added 'customizable affordable luxury' items and 'responsible luxury' tags to its offerings. It had created an exclusive online community, membership to which could only be procured by invitation. Demand for invitations naturally skyrocketed and the rich and the aspiring elite alike flocked to Purple Country.

Almost overnight, the first company of its kind tapped deep into the potential of the seven-billion-dollar Indian luxury market. As the industry rapidly grew to double its size in three years, Purple Country reaped handsome rewards by becoming the one-stop shop for a hitherto untapped niche segment of the population comprising the wealthy, time-starved business elite.

The market rewarded it in no small measure. In the two years since it went public, its share price had risen tenfold, pushing its market capitalization towards the one-billion-dollar mark. While some online retailers boasted of larger, dizzying valuations, this was one of the rare online companies to turn in real profits, year after year, and to successfully go public.

Shashi Kurva, its CEO, was pleased that evening. He had just received word of winning the prestigious 'CEO of the Year' award from a leading TV channel. The news had come on the heels of another honour: the advertising industry had selected Purple Country as India's most vibrant new brand.

At the open door of his cabin stood Carol, his secretary and right-hand person in the relentless drive that had seen Purple Country's revenues and profits soar. Five foot two, with rich brown-black hair and dark eyes that tilted ever so slightly upwards, she cut a striking figure. The bright young woman had been with Shashi for seven years now, having moved with him from a luxury hotel chain to Purple Country.

Assembled behind Carol's elegant frame was a cluster of employees.

'Come, Shashi,' she said, her eyes twinkling. 'Step out for a moment. The guys want to congratulate you.'

Shashi went out to pump hands and field demands for a party. He was a short man, no taller than five foot three, but his lean build and broad shoulders more than made up for his lack of height. His bow legs and light tread suggested athletic prowess in days gone by. Thick black hair, flecked with grey, set off a pair of alert, intense eyes that missed little. The burning drive in those eyes that had helped him excel at sport and prevail in brawls in his youth had remained with him in full measure as he took on the corporate world.

He shook hands now with the many people surrounding him, keenly aware that not everyone who congratulated him meant it. Some eyes were glazed, a few expressions sullen; these were employees who resented his unrelenting pressure to extract performance. But he didn't let that bother him. His mandate had been clear: triple revenues and double profitability. And he had done better than that. Much better.

Almost everyone in the crowd – including the disaffected employees – had benefited from the company's rise. Even relatively new recruits had stock options worth a lakh or two to their name, while more senior staff members were way ahead, a few with even a crore or two. Barun Sen, the company secretary and longest-standing employee, now enjoyed the security of a four-bedroom flat in Kolkata, thanks to Purple Country stock options. Carol, whose unshakeable faith in Shashi had impelled her to invest most of her bonuses in the company's shares, had built up a nice nest egg even before she'd turned thirty.

Unlike unlisted companies, where the value of illiquid stock options was just a number, the employees of Purple Country could actually sell their shares in the market and get the feel of *real* cash.

Some, like Barun, had done so, but many of his colleagues were still holding on to their shares, expecting their value to rise further. One way or the other, Purple Country had transformed many a life.

'Another bit of news!' shouted an erudite-looking man in metal-rimmed glasses, waving his mobile phone in the air.

Amit Khanna was the CFO.

'Our market cap has just touched a billion dollars!' As corroboration, he pointed to the screen of his phone, which showed Purple Country's current share price.

The room burst into spontaneous applause; clapping and whoops rent the air.

'Party!' someone shouted.

The rest took up the refrain: 'Pa-arty! Pa-aarty!'

'Yeah, yeah!' Shashi grinned in agreement. 'But not today; we have a board meeting tomorrow. We'll do it next weekend.'

A roar of approval greeted the announcement.

'The billion mark!' he shouted over the din, pumping his hands in the air. He was among the shortest men in the crowd. 'We've been waiting for this day and it has arrived! *Now* we shall party – and party hard! It will be a night to remember!'

As another roar erupted, Shashi returned to his cabin, gesturing to Barun and Amit to join him.

'Congratulatory emails are coming in, Carol,' he observed, waiting for his two colleagues to arrive. 'Looks like news of the "CEO of the Year" award is already on TV. Could you respond to the emails, please? Log into my mailbox and thank each person individually. They need to see it coming directly from me, not from my secretary.'

'Got it, Shashi. Two TV channels and three newspapers have requested interviews. What should I say?'

'Yes to all. Next week in our office. We must use every media opportunity we can get to promote the brand – in as unobtrusive a manner as possible, of course.'

'Our logo in the background, coffee served in Purple Country mugs, our letter pads and coasters laid out – things like that?'

'You got it.'

One of the first things Shashi had done after taking over as the CEO in 2011 was to refocus the business exclusively on the wealthy. By trying to cater to everyone, he had argued, the company was casting its net too wide and diluting its impact. He had changed Purple Country's raison d'être, reorienting it to serve the moneyed elite, and ruthlessly jettisoned anything that didn't fit that purpose.

To cap it off, he had created the vibrant new Purple Country brand, changing the company name and choosing purple as the dominant colour after extensive market research. Over one long weekend, everything about the company – its logo, interiors, stationery, furniture and a host of small things – had changed from a dull blue to a bold combination of purple, orange and yellow.

That had been the fun part for the employees. What came next was relentless, unending work, which had culminated in the steady rise of their stock-options value. Even as dozens left the company, unable to cope with the increased workload, the share price, which had been below par, rose to ₹52 in two years. In the next couple of years, it had surged further to an incredible ₹514.

As Barun and Amit joined him now in his cabin, Shashi got down to business.

'Have you reviewed the wording of the resolutions to be passed tomorrow, Barun?' he asked.

'Yes, Shashi.' Despite living in Mumbai for over 20 years, 50-year-old Barun still retained traces of his Bengali accent. 'I've made a couple of changes – '

He stopped abruptly. His close-set eyes had darted to the door as it opened. Shashi looked up impatiently. Carol came in and closed the door quietly behind her.

'What is it, Carol?'

'Two men to see you – '

'Impossible, Carol! You know I can't meet anyone today. I must prepare for the board meeting tom – '

'I know, Shashi. But this seems…important. Besides, those men are pretty adamant.'

'I don't care, Carol. They'll just have to come back next week.'

Shashi turned away from her and brought his attention back to Barun. Carol stood motionless for a few seconds, her eyes fixed on him. Then she turned abruptly and went out, closing the door firmly behind her. Moments later, the intercom rang.

'What – ?' Shashi began irritably, but Carol cut him short.

'I'm sorry, but I couldn't speak freely in front of Barun and Amit. Please hear me out. It's important.'

'Go on,' Shashi said quietly, quelled by Carol's perseverance and the urgency in her voice.

Her tenacity and perceptiveness had proved invaluable on more than one occasion in the past. That was one of the reasons, apart from her sheer efficiency, why Shashi had brought her along when he moved to Purple Country. She was more than a secretary.

'Two men are here,' Carol continued. 'One is from SEBI and the other, I suspect, is from the CBI or some such agency. They say they have come for an investigation and they won't be fobbed off.'

'Investigation? What investigation?'

'I have no idea. But I think you should see them.'

'Why?'

'They look quite determined. And I feel they are what they claim to be. The SEBI man – S.K. Varma – is from the Investigations Department. I have his card. The other man didn't offer one.'

'Hmm…okay. Give me a few minutes. Then send them in.'

Shashi hung up and brought his attention back to the two men seated before him.

'You were talking about the changes you made to the resolutions for tomorrow,' he said to Barun. 'Anything I should be aware of?'

'Not really. Just a few changes in the wording to comply with legal requirements. Nothing to do with content.'

'Okay. Amit?' He turned to the CFO.

'No changes since we reviewed it yesterday. All in order.'

'Any changes to the draft numbers since we sent out the board notes?'

'One minor change. Nothing material.'

'Okay, I'll see you guys at eight o'clock tomorrow morning.'

Amit stared at him, surprised. 'But what about your presentation? I thought we were to discuss the points for it now.'

Shashi shook his head. 'Some people are waiting to see me. Let's touch base at breakfast tomorrow before the meeting.'

Barun and Amit picked up their papers and left the room.

Moments later, Carol ushered in two strangers.

'Please take a seat, gentlemen,' Shashi said, once they had shaken hands and he had glanced at the SEBI identity card Varma flashed. 'I really can't spare the time for this meeting, but my secretary thought I should see you. I have a board meeting scheduled for tomorrow morning and I must prepare for it.'

'We're aware of that,' Varma said. He was a bearded man with unremarkable features. 'I suppose you are passing your half-yearly accounts?'

Shashi nodded. 'Among other matters.'

'Will you be beating market expectations?'

Shashi stared back at him. 'That's a strange question for a SEBI man to ask before the announcement of results.'

'Perhaps *I* can ask it,' the second man said.

He had introduced himself as Kashyap. The man had light brown eyes. The goatee that seemed to elongate his already lean face was immaculately trimmed; its edge was a smooth, unbroken curve.

'And where are you from?' Shashi enquired.

'Does it matter? I am working with Mr Varma. Please

understand that we are trying to handle this matter as quietly and discreetly as possible.'

Shashi glared at Kashyap, who countered with a smile of feigned politeness.

'So, will you be beating your last guidance?' Kashyap persisted. 'We have a reason to ask, as you will soon find out.'

'Yes. We've done better than the guidance issued in July.'

'Just as we expected. Do you know why?'

'Tell me.'

'An unusual number of your company shares were bought yesterday and today.'

'So? Ours is a well-traded stock.'

'I am not talking about the usual market trades. A single person bought shares worth over four crores in two days.'

Shashi blinked. That was a lot of shares! 'I still don't get it.'

'He had made similar trades one day before your first-quarter results three months back.'

'And?'

'And sold the shares at 17 per cent profit after the results were announced. He bought Purple Country shares on three occasions in the past eight months and sold them at hefty profits within a few days. The first occasion was when you acquired Serenity.'

Serenity Private Limited was a time-share holiday company that Purple Country had acquired early that year. The deal had been a closely guarded secret, one that no outsider could have known about.

'The timing of these trades has been perfect,' Kashyap continued. 'So perfect, it's uncanny.'

Shashi stared at him. Carol's hunch had been right; the man had to be from the CBI, the Economic Offences Wing or some such agency. Kashyap returned his stare, his eyes unflinching.

'So what are you trying to say?' Shashi asked slowly, picking his words with care. 'Someone knew about our results and the acquisition beforehand and bought our shares before the price went up?'

'So it would seem.'

'But how?' Shashi frowned.

'Surely you don't need me to tell you that?'

Shashi fell silent.

'If your results are better than the last guidance,' Kashyap went on, 'the share price is likely to jump significantly.'

Shashi nodded.

'Now, consider the most recent trade. Four crores' worth of shares will yield him a clean ₹40 lakh in just three days if the share price goes up by 10 per cent. Not bad at all!'

Shashi rose from his chair and went to the window. He gazed out, unseeing, registering nothing. After a few moments, he turned back.

'Are you sure of this, gentlemen?' he asked softly.

'We wouldn't be here otherwise,' Kashyap said.

'It would appear – prima facie– that someone with access to privileged information is using it to trade on the company's stocks.'

'Not only that,' Kashyap added. 'Increasing volumes suggest that the confidence in that information has steadily risen with each success. This trader now has the confidence to put over four crores at risk.'

Shashi's face had lost colour. 'Who is he?' he asked softly.

'It is usually difficult to discover the identity of the ultimate beneficiary, but we have identified him in this case.'

'Have you traced his relationships and contacts?

'We have.'

'Then finding out if he has insider contacts in this company – employees, directors, auditors – should be a relatively straightforward matter. That should lead you to the person who may have leaked information to him.'

'That is why we are here. We have established a connection with a person in the company.'

Shashi leaned forward and stared intently at the man he now strongly suspected to be from the Economic Offences Wing. EOW was the most likely agency to join SEBI in such an investigation.

'Who?'

Kashyap paused for a second before replying, sitting back and crossing one leg over the other without taking his eyes off Shashi.

'You.'

Chapter 2

Shashi's face turned red. He half rose from his chair, his fists clenched, and glowered at Kashyap.

'Is this your idea of a joke?' he hissed.

'This is no joke, I assure you.'

'Are you suggesting that I – '

'I am suggesting nothing,' Kashyap said flatly. 'I am here to tell you this and –'

'Do you know that I own 2 per cent of the company's shares?' Shashi snarled, rising to his full height. What providence had taken away in stature, it had given back as aggression. 'And have the option to buy an additional 3 per cent at the price it was at four years ago?'

'I do –'

'Do you know what the share price was when I took over? Below par! Nine rupees something. It is now ₹514 and the market cap is a billion dollars. We are the *only* online company in this space with a billion-dollar valuation *and* a profit record. You think I would risk that?'

'Perhaps not. I also realize that ₹40 lakh shared between two people is far from insignificant for a few hours' work.'

'You dare accuse me of insider trading?'

'We are not accusing you of anything, Mr Kurva,' Varma cut in. 'Please calm down. Your passion for the company is known to us. As is the fact that it has seen spectacular success after you took charge. We know that your promoter and your board swear by you, even if you are not popular with some of your employees.'

Partly assuaged, Shashi sat back in his chair, but continued glowering at the two men.

'We are here to inform you about our investigation,' Varma continued in a soft voice, 'and ask if you might be able to offer any clues as to how information could have leaked from your company.'

Shashi shook his head. 'I can't think of anything right now. This is a bolt from the blue. I need time to think.' He turned to Kashyap. 'Who is this trader you say is related to me?'

'Vivek Tola.'

'Vivek! He's my brother-in-law.'

'Your wife and his wife are sisters, right?'

'Yes.'

'Then,' Kashyap said, 'I need to ask you a few questions.'

Shashi glared at him.

'For the record, have you, knowingly or unknowingly, passed privileged information to Vivek Tola?'

'No!'

'Not even indirectly?'

'No.'

'Or through your wife?'

'No!' Anger flared in Shashi's eyes. 'Don't bring her into this!'

'When did you last speak to Vivek Tola?'

'I don't know...he and I never did it hit off. He's a sharp financier and broker – not the kind I hang out with.'

'Still, you do speak to him, don't you?'

'We can't choose our relatives, but we have to be civil to them. I spoke to him on his birthday...and wished him on his anniversary too. Apart from those two occasions, I don't think I've spoken much to him in the past year.'

'How about family functions?'

'Yes, those of course...I would have met him on and off. At a wedding or a birthday, perhaps.'

'In that case, you may have spoken to him recently?'

'Perhaps. I can't recall now.'

'Mr Kurva, are you willing to cooperate with the investigation?'

'Of course! I have no reason not to.'

'That is one of the reasons we are here. We need to look at your call records and financial transactions. We do have the authority to demand them, anyway, but if we did so, word of our investigation might spread. If you cooperate with us, the enquiry can be conducted more discreetly.'

Shashi nodded. 'I will speak to my bankers,' he said. 'I can write to Vodafone and MTNL also, if you wish.'

'Thank you. I have taken the liberty to prepare those letters for you to sign.'

Kashyap slid some papers across the table. A few minutes later, the two men left Shashi's office.

Shashi sat back, overwhelmed by the sudden turn of events. What a roller coaster of a day it was turning out to be! The emotional high created by the news of the two awards and the market cap hitting a billion dollars, followed by the jolt of being brought rudely back to earth by the two visitors. He wondered for an instant if he should call Barun and Amit to discuss the development, but quickly dismissed the idea. After all, you never knew who was involved. The fewer people he shared this with, the better.

But he had to discuss it with *someone* – especially since he was a potential suspect. He should not be perceived as trying to suppress such a development. He picked up his mobile and called A.K. Gupta, the chairman of the board.

'Hello?'

'Good evening, Mr Gupta. Shashi here. Could I have a word with you? Something has come up.'

'Sure.'

Shashi quickly summarized the situation.

'What did you tell them?' Gupta asked, once Shashi had finished.

'Nothing, apart from assuring them that I had not leaked information in any way.'

'What would you like to do now?'

'First, I would like to inform the board about this matter tomorrow. Then I'll carry out an internal investigation to find out how information could have leaked out.'

'Hmm…Why don't you speak to Mr Saldana first?'

M.A. Saldana was another director on the board and a corporate lawyer by profession. Considered one of the experts in company law, he was widely sought after.

'See what he has to say before taking action,' Gupta suggested. 'Call me back or conference me if you wish.'

Shashi hung up and called Saldana, who answered after two rings.

'Yes, Shashi?'

'Something dicey has come up. Mr Gupta suggested that I speak to you.'

'Shoot.'

Shashi summarized the situation for the second time in five minutes.

'You want to talk to the board about it?' Saldana asked.

'Yes.'

'If you bring it up as a part of the board meeting, it will be minuted. And minutes become permanent records for anyone to call for. It's better to tread cautiously till we have a better handle on this matter. Insider trading is serious.'

'What do you suggest?'

'Why don't you bring it up *after* the board meeting? We can ask the company secretary to leave the room. Then the discussion becomes a private one.'

'Okay. I'll tell the chairman.'

'I hope you haven't said much to the investigators, Shashi?'

'No. Oh, I agreed to cooperate and gave them access to my phone and financial records.'

'Good. I'll see you tomorrow morning.'

Shashi hung up, his thoughts in disarray. Insider trading was far too serious a matter to be taken lightly. More so if SEBI was investigating it. He had better begin investigating the Vivek Tola angle immediately. He packed his laptop and papers and came out of his office, calling his driver on the mobile.

'Leaving?' asked Carol, her elegant eyebrows arched. 'You haven't done your presentation yet.'

'Don't think I can now. I need to go.'

'Problem, Shashi?' Carol rose from her seat and approached him, her brow furrowed.

'Yeah.' Shashi nodded. 'It's a pretty mess.'

'Anything I can do?'

'Just make sure that everything is in place for breakfast tomorrow and the meeting after that.'

'I'll take care of it. Call me if you need anything. Oh, Kamna called just now. She said your mobile was busy and she wanted to know if you were having dinner at home.'

'Thanks. I'll call her from the car.'

Leaning back in the car seat after speaking to his wife, Shashi let his thoughts wander. How much temptation there was in the corporate world! The higher you rose, the more of it you had to handle. One of the reasons he had left his previous employer was the organization's thin moral fabric. Although nobody had been caught red-handed, casual after-office gossip had been suggestive. Rubbing shoulders with celebrities and twenty-something cricketers who had got rich quick only seemed to worsen matters. Shashi had left in disgust.

But insider trading was new to him. He had heard friends argue for and against it, but he was clear in his mind that it was wrong. If the law did not sanction it, there was nothing further to be said. He had never given it much thought. And now that he had come face to face with it, he felt queasy. The very thought of someone within his *own* team practising deceit to this extent was sickening. That he may have actually shaken hands with the traitor today made him feel contaminated, dirty. Instinctively, he wiped his right hand on his trouser leg.

He held himself to the highest standards of propriety and expected the same of everyone in his team. Insider trading was simply unacceptable. In his mind, it was grounds for instant dismissal, however important the person may be in the company hierarchy.

But first, he had to find him. Or her.

Chapter 3

Kamna, her mother firmly believed, was born under an unfortunate configuration of stars. A day after the baby arrived, the family astrologer had lamented that at the time of her birth, the planets that mattered were all inauspiciously positioned. Had Kamna held on for just 17 minutes more before she made her appearance, he claimed, her horoscope would have been the envy of all.

'Leave it to me,' Kamna's father, a wealthy jeweller, had grunted that evening.

By the next day, little Kamna had acquired a fresh birth certificate that reflected a more acceptable time of birth. The astrologer was told that the previous one had been an administrative error on the hospital's part. Without a word, he had drawn up Kamna's horoscope based on the new time of birth.

But this deception, Kamna's mother would insist in private, did not change the fact that the girl was star-crossed. That is what made her such an oddball, with her passion for the abstract eclipsing her interest in things material. Why else, she asked, would a girl, whose absorption in the movement of clouds and ocean waves made her lose track of time, be loath to even glance at a multi-carat diamond necklace that her peers would have drooled over?

In later years, it would become a source of embarrassment and despair for the wealthy Anjumal family that their younger daughter thought nothing of showing up at social functions, be it a birthday party or a wedding, in faded jeans and a nondescript cotton kurti. While her cousins swanned around, showing off several lakhs worth of jewellery on their expensively cared-for selves, Kamna would sit in a quiet corner, lost in an esoteric book or engaged in animated conversation with her elder sister, Chaaya.

Unlike her sibling, Chaaya was deemed 'normal' by their mother. With a healthy interest in jewellery, fine designer apparel and Bollywood, she was ready to impress her various chachis, mamis and aunties with her polished manner and silver tongue. By the time she was twenty-one, she could have been mistaken for a Bollywood celebrity herself – a fetching young classic beauty. Inevitably, Chaaya was in great demand among ladies who had eligible sons of marriageable age. And her mother lost no time in seizing the opportunity when feelers for a prospective matrimonial alliance were sent by a wealthy business family.

Kamna's situation was different. Though attractive in her own right, few of the Anjumals' social peers showed any interest in her. Her quirkiness, her mother was convinced, always came in the way. And by the time Kamna's twenty-ninth birthday came around, her mother had reason to be seriously worried.

The family was, therefore, enormously relieved when Kamna announced one day that she was going to marry 35-year-old Shashi Kurva, a high-flying corporate executive. It was at one of Purple Country's exclusives that they had met a year back, when Shashi's forceful personality and Kamna's unconventional ways had drawn them irresistibly to each other.

Kamna's mother was delighted. That her to-be son-in-law was a salaried employee, rather than the owner of an enterprise, and that he was from outside their community were minor shortcomings that would be overlooked or forgiven. After all, he was not bad-looking, carried himself well and was an ex-Air Force officer's son to boot. More importantly, he wasn't exactly poor. His company was now coming up in conversation at most parties. So Kamna's mother got down to making arrangements for the wedding with as much haste as enthusiasm, lest her unpredictable younger daughter suddenly change her mind.

Kamna didn't, but to her mother's dismay, refused to wear the extravagant bridal ensemble chosen for her that would have been appropriate for someone of her social stature. In desperation, her mother drew Shashi aside and tearfully enlisted his help.

'*Hamari izzat ka sawal hai, beta,*' she wept. '*Kamna ko tu hi samjha sakta hai.*'

'Do it just this once, Kamna,' Shashi had urged his fiancée. 'Do it for your mother, as a sort of parting gift when you leave home. You know how important such things are to her.'

Kamna had reluctantly agreed to wear one outfit of her mother's choice for the wedding ceremony and another for the reception. That she had given them both away to her maid's ecstatic daughter the very next morning remained a closely guarded secret of which her mother hadn't the faintest inkling. But having successfully enlisted Shashi's help in getting her daughter to cooperate, Kamna's mother had now become his staunch supporter.

After the wedding, every piece of Kamna's bridal jewellery found its way into capacious bank lockers, where they would remain undisturbed.

Now two years later, Kamna looked as youthful as she had during her wedding. But her usually clear brow was furrowed today as she waited for her husband to return home.

Shashi's call had been brief, but she had sensed that something was amiss. All he had said was that he was on his way home, but he had sounded distracted. That alone would not have troubled her; he was often preoccupied on his way home. But today, there was a disturbing note of despondency in his voice, something she rarely sensed in him.

The Shashi she knew was full of vigour and spirit. Never in the three years that they had been together had she known him to back down from a confrontation or a problem. He believed in taking the bull by the horns, even if it ended in a fracas, as many of his student-day arguments apparently had. She smiled fondly, recalling some of his animated descriptions of the fist fights he had been embroiled in.

She suspected he had mellowed over the years. The tales Carol had narrated from the time they were working with a luxury hotel chain had been indication enough. He had been a star performer there too, but had really come into his own after he moved in as the CEO of Purple Country.

She leapt up from the sofa when the doorbell rang and wiped her face clean of anxiety. If Shashi was feeling low, the best tonic for him would be her cheerfulness.

'Hi. How come so early?' she asked, as Shashi came in through the front door. 'Tomorrow's meeting cancelled?'

'No, it's on. Got to go early in the morning.'

The brevity of his reply and the tired look on his face were enough to confirm her fears. She sensed deep uneasiness in him.

'Problem, Shashi?' she asked softly.

'Yeah. Difficult day.'

'Go wash up. I'll fix you a drink.' She ruffled his hair playfully. 'For a change, we can have dinner together.'

She went into the kitchen, humming to herself, knowing that her show of chirpiness would help ease his tension a little. She quickly mixed two drinks and returned to the hall. While Shashi put away his shoes and bag, she switched on the music system and played some instrumental lounge music, choosing Chopin's compositions that she knew would help her husband relax.

'Have you spoken to Vivek lately?' he asked, once they were seated with drinks in hand.

Kamna was taken aback that he had begun the conversation by bringing up her brother-in-law, but managed to conceal her surprise.

'On the phone?' she asked. 'Not for weeks now.'

'And we haven't met him for months either, have we?'

'Nope. Wait…we did meet him at Panditji's granddaughter's wedding last month.'

'That's right. I'd forgotten. But you and Chaaya speak often, don't you?'

'Every other day. Why?' She wondered where this was headed.

'Do you ever discuss Purple Country?'

Kamna shook her head and smiled. 'Why would we want to waste our time talking about such boring stuff?' she teased.

'What *do* you talk about?'

'Oh, sisters have a lot to say to each other, you know. Especially after Mamma passed away, Chaaya has nobody to confide in. Vivek has no time for her. And our cousins and her so-called friends are all solid bitches. All they can do is gossip.'

Shashi fell silent, staring absent-mindedly into the glass in his hand. Kamna waited patiently.

'Have you ever spoken about Purple Country's performance or shares to Chaaya?' he asked suddenly.

'Not that I can recall. I have no interest in this stuff, Shashi. You know that the stock market bores the heck out of me.'

Never having wanted for anything and having seen everyone around her flaunt their wealth unabashedly, Kamna had developed a curious disinterest in and even disdain for money early in life. In this matter, she was the antithesis of her sister.

'You know what insider trading means, don't you?' Shashi asked.

Kamna nodded. 'That's when an employee uses confidential information to trade in his own company's shares. There was a high-profile case – Goldman Sachs, wasn't it? – in the US a few years back. There have been some in India too.'

'I wanted to discuss it with you – '

'*Me?*' Kamna blinked in surprise. 'You must be joking! I won't be able to make any sense of it, Shashi! Frankly, I don't think I have the brainpower for it.'

'Of course you do!' her husband said warmly. 'If you're intelligent enough to compose classical music pieces, no less, and paint the way you do, the stock market would be a breeze for you!'

Kamna's paintings had been receiving critical acclaim for a couple of years now and were sought after in the art market. And her musical compositions, featuring both classical forms and fusion, would have been popular, had she not ignored Bollywood's overtures.

'You know that Purple Country has been doing better than expected for the last couple of years, right?' Shashi asked.

'How could I not?' Kamna grinned broadly. 'You won't let me forget it for a moment!'

But her teasing didn't seem to register with her husband.

'Every time we announced our results,' he continued, 'our share price would jump – sometimes by 10 per cent, sometimes by 20. When this happened, everyone who held our shares became wealthier to an extent, depending on how many shares they held.'

'So if I know beforehand that the price is going to jump,' Kamna observed, 'I can buy your shares and profit.'

'And how would you know it beforehand?'

'If you told me, I suppose?'

'Exactly! If I – or anyone else in Purple Country – leaked the information before the results were announced. You could then make a killing overnight by buying the share before the announcement and selling it soon after.'

'I should think that happens pretty regularly, given our insatiable greed.'

'It does, Kamna, but it's against the law.'

'But why?' She frowned, unable to understand the logic underlying his argument. 'It's *your* company, right? *You're* the one who's worked so hard to make it succeed. So why can't *you* profit from it?'

At a loss for words, Shashi gaped at her for a moment. 'Because it's the *law*,' he said finally, throwing up his hands in exasperation.

'The law is an ass! It won't let you profit from your hard work, but someone else who has the information can. How stupid is that! But this happens all the time, Shashi – even a dumbo like me knows that. How often have I heard Papa buying or selling shares based on such information.'

'But that still doesn't make it legal, Kamna.'

She stared at him for a moment, not grasping what he was getting at. 'So which is the greater crime?' she asked. 'Leaking the information or buying shares?'

'I don't know...both are illegal.'

'If it's illegal, you would be stupid to buy shares in your name. You would use some other name that cannot be traced back to you.'

Shashi blinked and his face broke into a smile that softened his features. Kamna's heart gave a little leap as a glimmer of happiness returned momentarily to his face.

'For someone who knew little about the stock market a minute ago, that was a remarkably quick and astute insight.'

Kamna smiled back happily. 'You forget, I am a jeweller's daughter!'

'Your father traded in shares? I didn't know that he had played the stock market too. I knew him only as a wealthy jeweller and assumed that he ploughed back his profits into precious metal and real estate.'

'He always said that it was an easy way to make money. All you needed was the right information.'

Shashi's expression grew serious. Worry creased his face once again.

'Let's get back to what we were talking about – buying shares in another name. What if shares are bought in a name that can be traced back to me?' he asked.

'Too bad. Stupid you, I guess.'

Shashi drained his glass and looked up at her. His eyes had a tormented expression.

'Kamna, Vivek has been trading in Purple Country shares for the past eight months. Just before and after the quarterly results.'

'Vivek? So?'

'He's related to me.'

For a moment, she didn't grasp the implication. When she did, her heart skipped a beat and her eyes widened in shock. *So that's what the problem was!*

'Do they –' she choked on her words. 'Good Lord! Do they suspect that you…*you* passed information to him? To *Vivek*, of all people?'

Shashi nodded. Kamna couldn't remember when she had last seen him so despondent. A chill ran down her spine.

'My God, Shashi!' She hurried to his side. 'Is that why you came home early?'

He nodded. 'And to ask you if there is any way information could have inadvertently been passed to him. I have to face the board tomorrow.'

Chapter 4

'Good morning, gentlemen,' Gupta said at nine o' clock sharp the following morning. 'Mr Dheerajbhai has been unavoidably delayed, but we have a quorum.'

One of the doyens of corporate India and a highly successful serial entrepreneur, Dheerajbhai was the founder of Purple Country and its single largest shareholder. Among his gifts was the ability to judge people with unerring accuracy and assign them roles in which they were bound to flourish. It was he who had plucked Shashi from his former position at the luxury hotel and resort chain.

Three years after the incorporation of Purple Country, Dheerajbhai's foray into the travel and entertainment sector had been languishing for want of direction and leadership. A third of the company's net worth had already been eroded and the organization was in danger of sliding further downhill. What it needed, Dheerajbhai had declared to the board, was an energetic leader with a vision and the courage to realize it, no matter what. Seniority didn't matter. The younger, the better, he had insisted, as long as competence wasn't compromised.

Dheerajbhai had been as intrigued by Shashi's obsession with delighting customers as by his impatience with internal corporate hierarchy. He saw mirrored in the younger man his own inability to suffer fools and put up with incompetent bosses. He particularly approved of Shashi's brutal – even irreverent – candour and the fact that everyone knew exactly where they stood with him.

Saldana and Gupta had enthusiastically supported him and, within a week of meeting Shashi, they had made him an offer. Within a month of welcoming him on board, the staid, lacklustre brand had been replaced by a vibrant, colourful new one – Purple Country. As little as a month later, it was developing a character of its own as it rode towards success on the shoulders of a brand-new management team.

'Let us start our meeting,' Gupta went on. 'We have three investment proposals and the HR subcommittee's report to consider, in addition to the quarterly accounts and regular business. We'll begin with the investment proposals and leave the HR report till the end.'

He was about to continue when two office boys entered, carrying trays laden with beverages and snacks. Gupta turned to the company secretary with a frown.

'Could we please ask them to just leave the trays and go?' he said. 'We can help ourselves. It's best not to have anyone other than board members in the room during a meeting.'

Barun nodded hastily and rose to his feet. A minute later, the office boys had left and the meeting resumed. Gupta nodded to the CFO.

Amit presented the three investment proposals one by one. To the questions put to him subsequently, he answered crisply and with minimal help from Shashi. Once the proposals had been cleared, Amit tabled the quarterly accounts and took the board through it. By 10.30 a.m., the major financial items on the agenda had been cleared.

Gupta conducted the rest of the meeting quickly and efficiently. In another hour, the meeting was over.

'The board meeting is concluded,' he announced. 'Minutes will be circulated by Barun, as usual. He will confirm the date for the next board meeting within the next two weeks.' He closed his binder and nodded to Barun and Amit. 'If you will excuse us, gentlemen? We have another discussion that is not a part of the board meeting. Thank you.'

Barun and Amit stood up in surprise, gathered their papers and left the room after throwing a quick glance at Shashi. When the door had closed behind them, Gupta spoke again.

'Shashi requested a meeting with this group. He has something to tell us. Since we have another hour to go before lunch, we should be able to accommodate him if you gentlemen have no objections.' He waited for the others to nod their consent before turning to Shashi. 'The floor is yours.'

'Thank you, Mr Gupta,' Shashi began, rising from his place and positioning himself behind his chair. He preferred to stand while addressing the board. 'And thank you, gentlemen, for your time.'

He stood erect in his starched white shirt and navy blue tie, his hands resting lightly on the back of his chair as he looked directly at the men around the table.

'You may have noticed that I did not make my customary presentation on our company's strategic outlook,' he said. 'As you know, I usually wait to prepare it on the evening before our meetings so that I can take into account the most current developments before presenting my perspective. I did not make it this time, because something unexpected came up last evening. A man from SEBI and another from some investigative agency turned up in my office.'

He now had the full attention of his audience. He began summarizing the events of the previous evening. He was barely into his third sentence when Sudakar, one of the independent directors on the board, stopped him with a gesture and turned to Gupta.

'Mr Chairman, I take it that this is not a part of the board meeting?'

Something in his voice made Shashi uneasy. He gazed at Sudakar in apprehension as Gupta nodded.

'The issue that Mr Kurva has raised is a very grave one,' Sudakar continued.

The fact that he had referred to Shashi as 'Mr Kurva' instead of using his first name, which he invariably did at such meetings, didn't augur well.

'An allegation of insider trading, even a hint of it, must be treated with the utmost seriousness. I am, therefore, rather surprised that this was not included in the board's agenda.'

Gupta, a veteran director of numerous boards, wore a non-committal expression as he prepared to respond. But before he could do so, Shashi spoke up.

'Mr Chairman, may I respond to Mr Sudakar?'

Gupta nodded and Shashi turned to Sudakar.

'It was my suggestion, Mr Sudakar, and the chairman graciously accepted it. I fully agree that we must treat this matter with the utmost seriousness. But while I wanted to inform the directors about the matter without delay, there is little that I have to say at the moment, since I have not had the opportunity to conduct an investigation. As my intent was to seek your counsel on the way forward, I thought it best to ask for an informal meeting.'

A lengthy silence followed as Sudakar considered Shashi's explanation. He glanced at the other two independent directors who were staring at him.

'I see,' he said finally and turned to Saldana. 'What is your counsel, Mr Saldana?'

'I have no objection,' Saldana replied. 'The matter, as you say, is a serious one. I would tend to be cautious and not create documentation till an investigation is carried out.'

'When you say documentation, do you include board minutes?'

'Yes, I do.'

Sudakar contemplated the table's polished teak surface as he absent-mindedly shuffled his papers. The others waited. Then he looked up and addressed Gupta.

'I am not comfortable with the situation, Mr Gupta. If I am told about this matter informally, I am in no position to act as a board member. I then find myself in a situation where I am aware of the problem, but unable to act upon it. My views on the matter go unrecorded and that is not a tenable situation for an independent director. I don't know what the other independent directors feel about it, but if I am to be made aware of this issue, it must be done in a formal manner.'

Shashi groaned inwardly as Gupta turned to the other two independent directors.

'I concur with Mr Sudakar,' said one.

The other remained silent.

'Your position, of course, is understandable,' Gupta said slowly. 'I had looked upon us as a team and thought it best to talk about it openly and offer Shashi the best counsel we could.'

'We will, Mr Chairman. But an independent director has some specific responsibilities too.'

'Fair enough. We will formalize the proceedings if you so wish. What would you prefer as the way forward?'

Sudakar seized the opportunity.

'Now that we have been told informally, I suggest that we make it formal. Let us reopen the board meeting and continue.'

'If we make this a board meeting, Barun will be privy to it, Mr Sudakar,' Shashi protested. 'I had hoped to start the investigation confidentially, without any employee coming to know of the matter. After all, we don't know who could be involved.'

'One employee already knows about it,' Sudakar countered, without looking at him.

Shashi flinched as if he had been slapped. His features froze and he resumed his seat without another word. His armour of confidence was crumbling rapidly; the fact that he was the prime accused had hit home hard. For a fleeting moment, he considered offering his resignation in protest. Hardly had the thought formed than the fighter in him intervened. Purple Country was more his company than Sudakar's. He would stay and fight. But now was the time for prudence. He turned to Gupta.

'I will do whatever the board feels is appropriate, sir,' he said. 'Shall I step out while you take the decision?'

'Please stay, Shashi.' Gupta was visibly angry now. 'There is no decision to be taken. If I do not extend the board meeting now, the net of suspicion will spread to more people.' He looked around the table with deliberation. 'Does anyone have objections to reconvening the board meeting?'

The faces in the room remained non-committal, the voices silent. Gupta turned to Shashi.

'Could you call Barun in, please?'

A couple of minutes later, the proceedings resumed and all eyes turned to Shashi. This time, he did not rise from his chair and prepared to take up from where he had left off.

'If I may speak before Shashi resumes,' Sudakar butted in, oblivious to the atmosphere of veiled hostility around the table, 'I suggest that he start again from the beginning so that Barun can record his statement verbatim. I would also like the minutes to show that I asked for the reopening of the board meeting.'

Gupta nodded curtly and Shashi carefully repeated what he had said earlier, but briefly and without the slightest enthusiasm. He had the air of a man being forced into a charade, but he was also speaking slowly so that Barun could record his words. When he had finished, he sat back in his chair.

'What did you tell the man from SEBI?' Sudakar asked.

'I offered to assist in the investigation in any way I could.'

'What would that entail?'

'I have given them access to my bank records, other financial transactions and my phone records.'

'How about your wife's?'

Barun cast a shocked glance at Sudakar. A few others around the table frowned. Shashi's expression was unreadable.

'I am prepared to do whatever is required without demeaning myself or my wife, Mr Sudakar. I see no need to bring her into this.'

'I see…And how do you plan to investigate this matter?'

'My plans are irrelevant now,' Shashi snapped. 'Now that I seem to be the prime suspect.'

'Now don't take it personally, Shashi – '

'Pardon me for interrupting, Mr Sudakar. It has just been pointed out that I am merely another employee. I await the board's directions. I can step outside if you gentlemen wish to discuss your options.'

'Do you have any suggestion, Mr Sudakar?' Gupta cut in sharply. 'I presume you are in agreement that the matter needs to be investigated?'

Sudakar nodded, but remained silent.

'Given the concerns expressed,' Saldana interrupted, 'one condition suggests itself. For the investigation to have credibility, it must have board oversight. You may wish to appoint a board subcommittee.'

'I agree,' Gupta said. 'Any suggestions on the composition?'

'It should, perhaps, be headed by an independent director.'

Gupta turned to Sudakar. 'I suggest a three-man subcommittee under your chairmanship, Mr Sudakar. If you have the time, that is.'

'Okay. I would like to include a lawyer. I would be delighted if Mr Saldana could join the subcommittee.'

'I can. The third member could be another independent director so that they are in the majority.'

'Excellent!' Sudakar said, looking at the other two members of the newly appointed subcommittee. 'Can we meet tomorrow morning? Saturday?'

'Let's make it Monday,' Saldana said.

'Agreed!' Sudakar smiled broadly.

'Thank you, gentlemen,' Gupta said. 'The board meeting now stands concluded. Shashi, Barun, I suggest that you refrain from discussing this matter with others in the company for the time being.'

'I will do better than that, sir,' Shashi said. 'I'll remove myself from the premises till Monday. I'll stay away for longer if necessary.'

'Does Carol know about this matter?'

Shashi shrugged. 'She's the one who ushered the two men into my office.'

'Can you ensure that she keeps it confidential too?'

Shashi nodded, gathered his papers and left the room without a backward glance. He stopped briefly in his office to pack his things and put a gag order on Carol. He asked her to cancel all meetings for the day and headed home, his face set in grim lines.

The board had told him not to speak about the matter to employees of the company. He would respect it by staying away from the office. But that didn't prevent him from doing his own digging outside. He was walking a thin line by interpreting the board's instructions literally. But then, he had far more to lose than anyone else; he was the prime suspect, after all.

On the way out, he called Vivek Tola.

Chapter 5

Clean-shaven, portly and a few inches taller than Shashi, Vivek Tola swaggered down the short aisle outside his cabin and pushed open the door to the trading room. This was the nerve centre of his stockbroking business, where his traders bought and sold shares on behalf of the company and its clients. None of the four traders or the two clerks in the room looked up from their computer screens as Vivek entered. Three of the traders were speaking into their desk phones; one of them also held a mobile to his other ear.

An air of noisy haste pervaded the room as each man tried to execute his orders as swiftly as possible. A few minutes' delay might see a share price changing by half a per cent and that could mean a loss – or gain – of several lakhs for a client. With the volume of transactions Amethyst Financial Private Limited handled, crores could be made or lost in a short time. Timing was key.

October was the month the second-quarter results came in and made share prices jump or skid, depending on the results vis-à-vis market expectations. Those who had read the tea leaves right would make a killing, as would those who enjoyed the advantage of prior information. Vivek had just spent an hour on the phone. Now was the time to monetize the hard work.

'RS!' he called to the only trader who was not on the phone. 'How many of Spark Lloyd are you buying?'

'Fifty thousand at ₹329,' the trader replied. 'It's around ₹331 now. Waiting for it to fall to ₹329.'

'Buy, man. Buy!'

'At ₹331? It'll fall – '

'No!' Vivek hollered. A thick gold chain glinted from under his collar as he shook his head vigorously. 'The results will be out any time now. Buy now! I want two lakh shares more.'

'Okay. Two lakh of Spark Lloyd at ₹331.20 – '

'I said two lakh *more*, RS!'

'Yes sir! Two lakh fifty at ₹331.20.'

'Start selling once it crosses ₹360.'

'It's *falling*, sir. It was at ₹335 when the market opened. It's lost 1 per cent.'

'It'll move back up before lunchtime.'

Vivek glanced at his writing pad as he turned to another trader who had just got off the phone.

'BK! Short PTR Industries for six crores.'

'*Six crores?*' The trader cast an incredulous glance at his boss. 'We've already shorted PTR for ₹70 lakh. Six crores will blow the risk limit.'

'Just do it, BK. I'll cover the risk. What's the exposure to FLC Bank? We are long, right?'

'Right. Two crore twenty.'

'Continue holding it. Results are due on Monday. RS, BK, tell me when the trades are done.'

Vivek turned and sauntered out. On the way to his room, he tore off the top two sheets from his writing pad and fed them into a shredding machine. Just then, his phone rang and he looked at the caller's number in surprise.

'Hi Shashi!' he said, his voice concerned, as he pushed open the door to his cabin. '*Kya haal hai?* Hope all's well?'

When was the last time Shashi had called him on his mobile? If he ever had? Kamna was the one who usually called about family-related matters and that too on the landline at home. Did this rare call from Shashi indicate some sort of a crisis?

'All's well, thanks.' Shashi's voice was neither warm nor unfriendly. It was matter-of-fact. 'I was wondering if we could meet up today.'

'Sure,' Vivek found himself saying, feeling more surprised than ever. 'Would evening work for you? Trading hours are usually packed for me.'

'Yeah, evening will be fine. What time? And where?'

'Seven o'clock at my favourite bar? Kamna too – or only you?'

He was meeting someone at 6.30 p.m. at a five-star hotel nearby; someone who had helped in two highly profitable deals earlier in the week. A profit of three crores had come into the bank overnight and it was time to thank the man properly. But that wouldn't take more than half an hour.

'Only me,' Shashi clarified. 'Seven o'clock is fine.'

'Anything in particular you want to talk about?'

'Just wanted to pick your brains on something. See you in the evening.'

Vivek frowned as he hung up. Shashi had been polite as usual, but there was something deliberately vague, even a little evasive, in the way he had answered the last question. And he'd hung up in a hurry. Why? Vivek sat at his desk, fiddling with one of his several Mont Blanc pens and wondering what Shashi might want of him. He felt sure that it was not a personal matter nor even a family-related one. The tone would have been different then.

After a full minute, he shook his head and resumed his work. There was no point wasting time over a mystery that would be cleared up in a few hours. Meanwhile, there was money to be made before the day's trading ended.

▪

Vivek was already in the bar lounge of the five-star hotel at Nariman Point that evening when Shashi arrived. He was alone at a table near the glass wall of the bar lounge that overlooked the street outside and the sea beyond, his mauve silk shirt stretching over his ample torso. He lumbered to his feet on noticing Shashi, lifting his considerable bulk off the chair and welcoming him jovially, all three of his chins shaking with the effort.

'Great to see you, *yaar*!' he said loudly, embracing his brother-in-law with an exaggerated show of warmth. 'You corporate guys are always so busy that it's nearly impossible to meet you. Come, come, sit down!'

His platinum bracelet, initialled 'VT' in large letters, clinked as he waved a pudgy hand at an eager waiter. Clearly, Vivek was an important customer here.

'What's your poison today?'

'Do you have Ballantine's?' Shashi asked the waiter.

'Yes sir. 17 years.'

'That's great. Large one, please. On the rocks.'

As the waiter scurried away, Vivek unleashed on his brother-in-law a charming spell of bonhomie, accompanied by loud guffaws that made Shashi feel a little self-conscious. He had come here for a quiet chat and the way Vivek was attracting unwanted attention from the tables around them made him a tad uneasy. He forced himself to respond to the other man's efforts with a cordiality he didn't feel. His instinct told him that Vivek did not mean a word of the charade he was putting up; he was simply doing it for the benefit of others in the lounge. One had only to look into his dark, beady eyes to detect the complete absence of mirth. Vivek's decibel level fell as they settled down and once the waiter had served their drinks and set down bowls of potato wafers and roasted peanuts before them, he dropped the pretence altogether.

'What can I do for you, Shashi?' he asked. 'I confess I was a little surprised when I got your call.'

'I wanted to talk about the stock market and could think of no one better than you to discuss it with.'

'Sure. At your service.' Vivek's chunky fingers, each one bedecked with a gem-studded ring, busied themselves with the peanuts.

'You're primarily a broker, are you not?'

'Broker, yes. But we also advise clients on investments, buying and selling.'

'Yes, of course. Do you finance your clients too?'

'Uh-huh. That's where the real money is, my friend.'

'But you also take risks by lending.'

'I don't take on clients who can't repay. They may need time to repay, on occasion, but nobody runs away with my money.'

'How do you ensure that?'

'I have my ways.' The smile on Vivek's chubby face was benign. 'Firstly, I am careful about whom I take on as a client. Secondly, it's a small world – nobody can run away for long. *Kahaan jaaoge, yaar?*'

'You only lend money, right? You don't use your money to buy shares on a client's behalf.'

Vivek shook his head vigorously till his jowls wobbled.

'That would be foolish. Complete *bewakoofi*.'

'Do you trade too?'

'Of course. Why? Want tips?'

Shashi shook his head slightly. 'Just wanted to understand how you decide what to buy or sell and when.'

'There's a lot of information sloshing around in the market that you can pick up if you keep your ears open.'

'What kind of information?'

'Well, what analysts and "experts" say, what company executives volunteer and, of course, rumours – a whole lot of rumours.'

'What kind of rumours?'

'Oh, all kinds.'

'Other than the rumours, is the information you get legit?'

'Who cares? Information is information. Reliability and timing are all that matter. Not the source or the legality.'

'Are the rumours reliable?'

'Some are…if you know what to heed. By the way, why are you asking me all this? Are you planning to invest? I can handle it for you. No commission from family!' Vivek grinned. 'Or give me one crore and I will double it for you every two years, like I do with Chaaya's family trust. If you don't have it, I'll lend it to you on special terms.'

'Not right now, thanks. But tell me, what shares do you buy and sell?'

'Many, *yaar*! It changes every day.'

'Depending on rumours?'

Vivek's face had lost some of its geniality. 'I thought you wanted to talk about the market, not about me.'

A waiter deposited a bowl of pretzels on the table. Two pieces disappeared into Vivek's mouth.

'What did you buy this week, Vivek?'

'Why do you want to know?

'Purple Country?' Shashi persisted, ignoring the question.

'I don't remember…Wait! That's your company, right?'

Beads of sweat had formed on Vivek's brow. He picked up two more pretzels and popped them into his mouth.

'You bought Purple Country shares yesterday. Worth over four crores. Why?'

'It's a good company and its CEO is great!' Vivek's grin was half-mocking.

'Come on, Vivek. Tell me.'

'Listen. *I* made no trades yesterday.'

'This is serious, Vivek. What information did you have that made you buy so many shares?'

'What makes you think I bought your shares?'

'A SEBI man came to see me last evening.'

Vivek's hand, which was moving towards the pretzels again,

froze into stillness for a moment. He picked up his glass instead and drained it. An alert waiter came up and Vivek nodded silently to him. He wolfed down the snacks laid out on the table as he waited for the man to return. Soon, his fingers were gripping a full glass.

'What did the SEBI man say?' he asked.

'That you've been buying Purple Country's shares for the past few quarters and selling them at – '

'Buying and selling is what brokers do. I'm a broker, am I not?'

'And make huge profits in two to three days? They believe you have information the market doesn't.'

Vivek set his glass down with a thump. Heads turned in his direction, but he didn't seem to care. All pretence of cordiality had evaporated. His gaze, as it rested on Shashi, had turned frosty.

'Listen, *brother*,' he growled. 'I don't know if you realize how close to an allegation that sounds – market people don't make or take such comments lightly. But I am willing to overlook it, simply because you aren't market savvy.' He signalled to the waiter for the bill and handed him his credit card. 'Look, I'm not even accepting that I bought your company's shares and I don't give a damn what SEBI says. They can go stuff their heads up some garbage chute, for all I care! What I buy or sell is none of their bloody business. And as far as you and I are concerned, let's not mix personal and business matters.'

Shashi stared at Vivek for a moment. The other man glared back at him.

'This *is* personal, Vivek!' he exclaimed in frustration. '*Very* personal. I'm being suspected of insider trading. Do you realize that?'

'Screw them. They can't prove a thing. This isn't the US, where circumstantial evidence can be used. Even there, they had the evidence of phone calls. There's nothing of the kind here; we haven't spoken to each other for months. I don't even have your email ID.

There is *no* link between us. If the SEBI guys are so sure of their case, let them press charges. The case will fall apart on the first day itself.'

'It may not matter to you, but it's my reputation that's at stake!'

Vivek shrugged and rose. 'Who cares, bro?'

He swaggered out without a backward glance, leaving Shashi seething.

▪

An agitated Shashi turned pensive after dinner as he switched on the desktop computer in his study and sat back, waiting for it to boot up.

He was now certain that Vivek had been trading in Purple Country shares. That much his meeting had confirmed, even if Vivek hadn't admitted it. But how had he obtained inside information from Purple Country? That too for eight months! How had he known about the Serenity acquisition in advance? Very few people, apart from the board members, had known about it – only he, Barun and Amit.

Vivek had been confident that SEBI had no legal case against him. Shashi had to agree with him; with no direct evidence of information passing from Shashi to Vivek, it was difficult to build a case of insider trading.

Surely, SEBI knew that too? Then why had they confronted him about Vivek's trades? What were they hoping to achieve? Shashi's mind wandered back to the meeting with Varma and Kashyap. Was he missing something? Shashi himself seldom traded in shares. The few he had were long-term investments made years ago; he hadn't sold a single share in the past decade. Neither had Kamna.

Kamna! His eyes narrowed. What had Vivek said about Chaaya's family trust? He leapt to his feet and went to find his wife in the kitchen, instructing the cook about lunch the next day.

'Vivek said something about a family trust. Do you know anything about it?'

'It must be the one Papa had set up for Chaaya and me – the Anjumal Trust.'

'The one that holds his bequest to you and Chaaya?'

Kamna nodded as she piloted Shashi away from the kitchen and the cook's ears. 'It has only the financial instruments – shares, bonds and mutual funds. The properties are in our individual names.'

'Shares?' Shashi whispered, as a sinking feeling came over him. 'Who takes care of the trust? I mean, who administers it?'

'Papa's lawyers. But Anthony is the one who looks after day-to-day matters.'

'Anthony? He's little more than a clerk, isn't he? He's a good man, but he isn't equipped to make investment-related decisions. Who – '

Shashi bit off his question as Kamna set down the glass she was drinking from and spun around. Her face was white as chalk and her eyes wide. Instinctively, he knew the answer to his unarticulated question.

'Vivek,' Kamna croaked. 'Vivek manages the investments of the trust.'

Shashi felt as if he had been punched in the solar plexus.

I will double it for you every two years, like I do for Chaaya's family trust. Those had been Vivek's exact words.

No investment manager could double money every two years unless he was a wizard...or a crook! Had Vivek been using inside information from Purple Country to grow the money in the Anjumal Trust? If so, Shashi was in deeper trouble than he had imagined! His wife benefiting from insider trading of Purple Country shares was an *entirely* different matter from his sister-in-law's husband doing the same.

Kamna too seemed to have realized it. She was now standing close to him and holding his hands in her own.

'Do you...' He cleared his choked throat. 'Do you know what shares the trust bought and sold?'

'There should be reports in my email.' Kamna strode purposefully to the study. 'Anthony sends monthly reports that I don't even glance at. Chaaya is the one who monitors it all.'

Five minutes later, they were staring at a bunch of emails on the computer.

'*₹203 crore!*' Shashi gasped. 'Kamna, I had no idea you had so much…'

But Kamna wasn't listening. She was furiously scanning the attachments to Anthony's emails. She sat back a few minutes later and shook her head.

'The attachments are only one-page summaries,' she said, as Shashi studied one. 'They don't have the details of share trades.'

The first column, titled 'listed company shares', was followed by four columns of numbers. The second column showed the market value to be a little over ₹147 crore, and the last column showed an annualized growth rate of 40 per cent.

'Vivek wasn't lying!' he said softly. 'A 40 per cent growth rate means a doubling of money every two years.' He turned to his wife. 'Can you get the list of shares traded?'

Kamna nodded. 'I'll call Anthony in the morning.'

'Does he work on Saturdays?'

'Monday, then.'

Chapter 6

The doorbell chimed a little past ten the next morning. The housekeeper-cum-cook opened the door to find an attractive young woman in weekend clothes standing there.

'Hi Carol,' Kamna said, peeking from behind the housekeeper to see who had come. 'A pleasant surprise!'

'Hello Kamna.' Carol sounded uncertain. 'I'm not interrupting anything, am I? I wanted to talk to Shashi.'

'No, no. Come right in. He's in the drawing room.'

'Carol!' Shashi's eyebrows shot up as she came in. 'What brings you halfway across town on a Saturday morning? Come, sit. Like some tea?'

Carol's pretty face was clouded as she sat down and accepted the tea Kamna poured out for her. Faint lines creased her brow and her entire bearing was one of unease as she struggled to say what she had come for.

Finally, she looked up and blurted out, 'What's the problem, Shashi? You left immediately after the board meeting.'

'Should there be a problem?'

'Shashi, please! I've been with you long enough to know something went horribly wrong yesterday. It started the evening the SEBI man came, didn't it? I've been worried sick. You've never reacted like this before to any crisis.'

She looked anxiously from Shashi to Kamna, until her boss dropped his gaze and sat back, letting out a long sigh.

'Yes,' he said softly. 'There *is* a problem. But I'm not sure I should drag you into it.'

'I'm a part of everything you do!' Carol leaned forward earnestly. 'I see all your correspondence, I answer your calls, I send out your memos – everything! I am your *confidential* secretary, Shashi.'

'Yes, Carol. Still – '

'I *want* to know Shashi, unless...' She glanced at Kamna and lowered her gaze. 'Unless it's personal.'

'It's personal in a way, but it has more to do with Purple Country.'

He frowned as he weighed the matter in his mind. On the one hand, the board had directed him not to mention the matter to company staff. On the other, Carol already knew about the visit and Gupta had assumed that she was aware of SEBI's investigation.

Carol was right too; she was his confidential secretary, after all. He trusted her more than he did anyone else in the company. In the seven years she had been with him, there had been any number of instances when he had placed his faith in her without reservation. As the sales head of the organization they had both worked for earlier, he had even asked her to hide a very sensitive letter in her handbag. He had feared that the letter, which contained commercial terms that he wanted to keep out of a rival's reach, was the target of a mole inside the company. And then there was the time they had pulled off a coup by winning over the top three corporate accounts from a major competitor. Carol had maintained tight confidentiality during the three-month-long process. Just one small indiscretion on her part could have killed the deal.

More recently, when he was reshaping Purple Country's management team as the new CEO, she was the only one to know who was about to be fired and who was being hired. She had been similarly indispensable during the Serenity acquisition. And of course, there were the signed blank cheques that he always left with her for much of the seven years they had been together.

Now, when he needed eyes and ears inside the company during his self-imposed exile, who better than her fitted the bill?

'Okay,' he said. 'I'll tell you about it. But this is as confidential as it gets.'

Kamna rose, unsure if she should be a part of the impending conversation.

'No, Kamna, please stay,' Shashi urged. 'I'd rather you heard all of it.'

'Sure?' she asked.

'Absolutely.' Shashi nodded and turned to his secretary as Kamna sat down again. 'Carol, it seems I am being suspected of insider trading.'

'What insider trading?' His secretary sounded perplexed.

'They suspect I passed on privileged information to outsiders, who used it to make super profits in the stock market.'

'What nonsense!' Carol cried indignantly. 'What *utter* crap!'

'They say they have evidence.'

'Bullshit! They're making it up.' Carol's faith seemed unshakeable. 'You wouldn't – *couldn't* – do something like that!'

'You're sure?'

'Of course I am! You may be aggressive in business, but you wouldn't do something unprofessional like this. You wouldn't do anything to hurt Purple Country; it's precious to you. Besides, you wouldn't do something so *stupid*!'

Shashi grinned for a moment.

'Thanks for your vote of confidence. Nevertheless, what I just said is true. Somebody related to me seems to have traded in Purple Country shares and made a packet. Not once, but *thrice*.'

Carol's eyes widened, her gaze travelling back and forth between Shashi and Kamna.

Kamna nodded. 'It's true,' she said.

'It must be a coincidence, then,' Carol countered valiantly, unwilling to give in.

'That's what we're hoping. Shashi passed no information to him. As far as we can tell, SEBI has no such evidence.'

'But his reputation...'

'That's the problem,' Shashi interrupted. He then went on to tell her what had happened at the board meeting. 'With Sudakar all but accusing me and with him heading the investigating subcommittee, I'm not sure what lies in store.'

Just then, the doorbell chimed again. It was Barun. He saw a visibly distraught Carol and swallowed the words on the tip of his tongue.

'Hi Barun. What brings you here?' Shashi asked.

'This.' Barun pulled out an external hard drive. 'A copy of all the Outlook mailboxes in the company. Thought I would make a copy before any traces could be erased.'

'How did you get all the mailboxes? I thought they weren't accessible to anyone but the IT administrator?'

Barun smiled wryly. 'You forget I was the company's third employee. I've been involved in setting up every piece of the company's infrastructure. I don't think you want me to say more.'

'You keep it, Barun. I shouldn't; I'm a suspect.'

'Nonsense! Sudakar was just posturing, trying to act more independent than he really is. His position has gone to his head and his misguided professionalism is making him throw his weight around. He doesn't realize that he's hurting the company, but he'll come to his senses once he cools down. He knows better than to suspect *you*, of all people.'

Shashi shook his head. 'No, Barun. I think he was dead serious. In any case, I don't think the mailboxes would yield anything. A man who has been successfully passing on information for eight months wouldn't be using his office email ID.'

'It could be a woman too,' Carol interjected. 'Quite a few people have access to financial results before they're announced.'

'She's right,' Barun nodded. 'It wouldn't be difficult for anyone in the accounts department to see the results a couple of days before the announcement. The sales people would know about the revenues well before that.'

'And there are the secretaries,' Carol continued. 'I see the results at the same time you do. Minu, Amit's secretary, does too. As does the man at the photocopier. It's not inconceivable for office boys to steal or photograph papers if they so wished. Everyone has cameras in their mobile phones these days.'

'And there are at least a dozen people outside,' Barun added. 'The auditors, for one. There are four of them. Then there are the secretaries of board members too. They see the board papers days in advance.'

'And while we're on that topic,' Kamna interjected, 'let's not forget the board members themselves. Between employees and others, it appears that dozens of people have access to privileged information every quarter.'

'I guess that's true. But what about the Serenity acquisition, Barun? Only Amit, you and I knew about it before it was announced.'

'No, Shashi.' Carol shook her head. 'I knew about it too. There is very little you see that I don't. I wouldn't be surprised if Minu also knew of it. And the secretaries do gossip.'

'Outside the company,' Barun continued, 'the investment bankers and investors knew about the deal beforehand. As did the board members and their secretaries.'

'I'm not at all surprised,' Kamna reflected. 'I've overheard so many of Papa's conversations where he acted on inside information. It seemed such a normal, everyday thing that I didn't even pause to consider it until you told me about insider trading yesterday. I knew Papa used to buy and sell shares based on what he called "unofficial" information. I hadn't even stopped to think if it was illegal.'

'Barun!' Shashi suddenly spun around to face his company

secretary, his eyes shining. 'Can you get a list of the people who bought and sold Purple Country shares?'

'I can't get the share transactions themselves, but I can get the list of shareholders as of any date you wish. Our share registrar should have it.'

'Purple Country's shareholding at the end of each day?'

'That's right.'

'Great! Can you get the shareholding at the end of every working day for the past two years?'

'*Every* working day?' Barun's eyebrows shot up. 'That would be about 250 days a year, a total of 500 days.'

'Yes, it would! By comparing one day's shareholding with the next, we can generate a list of the people who bought or sold our shares that day.'

'Okay...But that list will only have transactions where delivery of the shares was taken into demat accounts. It will not include intra-day trades.'

'That's fine. I don't need intra-day transactions.'

'What details would you need?'

'Basic information only – date, price and quantity. And who bought or sold.'

Barun shook his head. 'You won't get price information.'

'Why not?'

'Share registrars don't capture the share price of each transaction. It's not relevant for them. That detail is available only with the stock exchange.'

'Hmm...' Shashi frowned and drummed his fingers on the sofa's armrest. 'Okay, get what you can. I'll use the average price for each day from the stock exchange website.'

'What do you have in mind?'

'I'd like to do some analysis to see if a pattern emerges.'

'Pattern?'

'Never mind. Can you get the data by Monday?'

Barun shook his head. 'I can try for Tuesday or Wednesday.'

'Get to it, Barun. Right away. This can be important. By the way, I'm not going to involve you in the analysis.'

'Why not?' Barun was indignant.

'I shouldn't be interfering with the subcommittee's investigation, remember? And you are a part of the subcommittee. I'm going to do my little analysis outside the office. Confidentially.'

Barun grinned. 'I see what you mean. Let Sudakar do his own investigation, eh?'

But Shashi's attention was already elsewhere as he glanced at the wall clock, his expression intent. 'What time is it in London now? Four and a half hours behind...it'll be a little after 6 a.m. I wonder if Tanu is up.'

'Send her a text message and see.' Kamna's features had gathered in a frown. 'But why?'

Shashi didn't answer. He was busy sending his text message. Barun moved away to make a call and Carol cast a quizzical look at Kamna.

'Tanu – Tanuja Kurva Fernandez – is Shashi's cousin,' Kamna explained. 'She works in London. Some kind of a data person – '

'She's an analyst, a data scientist,' Shashi interjected, putting down his phone. 'She works at Crystal Tower, a London-based analytics company that helps companies make sense of large amounts of data. If I remember right, she helps stock exchanges and regulators too.'

'She helps them make sense of data?' Carol asked. 'How?'

'Data scientists try to detect hidden patterns in mountains of data. They call it "big data". An electronics company, for instance, would be interested in knowing what kind of people are likely to buy certain kinds of gadgets at different stages of their lives. If they can figure that out from their data, they can then target specific age groups or specific occupations for specific products.

'Similarly, supermarkets would benefit from learning what categories of items are frequently bought together. That knowledge can then help them display such products close to each other or design sales promotions for related products. There is this classic example in the US of the link between diapers and beer. They found that young fathers who bought diapers for their babies were likely to buy beer as well. So they placed diapers and beer on adjacent shelves and boosted sales for both items. I'm hoping that Tanu can help us find patterns – '

Shashi broke off as his phone rang. 'Tanu!' He grinned and scooped it up.

'Hi Tanu. Did I wake you up?'

'Hi Shashi. No, I was up already.' A lively voice with a hint of a clipped British accent came through. 'What's up?'

Typical Tanu, Shashi thought. Straight to the point.

'You have a few minutes to talk, Tanu?'

'Sure.'

'You're still in the world of analytics, right?'

'Yup. That's the only world I know.'

'Did you mention the last time we talked that you'd done work for the London Stock Exchange?'

'I might have. LSE is a client of ours. So is NYSE. Why?'

'I wanted some professional advice from you.'

In the next few minutes, Shashi outlined the insider trading matter without mentioning the Purple Country connection.

'So I was wondering if you could help us conduct a preliminary investigation,' he said by way of conclusion. 'I'm trying to get the share registrar data of a company for the past two years.'

'I can, but not if the data is in Mumbai and I'm in London. You'll have to send me the data. I'll see what I can do outside office hours.'

'I don't want to send the data out, but I'll tell you what. Would you come down if I hired you to do it as a project?'

'I'd be delighted to, but it will cost you, Shashi.' Her voice was cautious. 'You don't need to, you know. I can do it on the side if it's not urgent.'

'Time is of the essence, Tanu. I need you here on Monday.'

'Monday!'

'Yes. Can you come? I'll make the arrangements.'

'I can't get away so soon, Shashi. I can try for…let's see… Wednesday at the earliest. And that too will be tight. In any case, we'll need a contract before I can travel.'

'I'll tell you what.' Shashi was relentless. 'Send me a draft contract in the next hour or two and we'll sort it out immediately.'

'What's the name of the company you want me to analyse?'

'Let's leave that out. I'd like to keep that under wraps.'

'Fair enough. I'll send you a draft contract by the end of the day.'

'Great! I'll now hand over the phone to my colleague, Carol. She'll work with you on the arrangements.'

▪

Five minutes after Carol and Barun had left, Shashi's mobile phone rang. It was an unknown number.

Shashi answered the call. 'Hello?'

'Mr Kurva?' The voice sounded muffled.

'Yes.'

'Good morning. How are you?'

Shashi's guard went up. He didn't recognize the caller, but there was something familiar about the voice.

'Who is this?' he asked.

'Kashyap.'

Shashi tensed. Why was Kashyap calling on a Saturday? More bad news?

'Yes, Mr Kashyap,' he said cautiously. 'What can I do for you?'

'I called to ask how your meeting with Vivek Tola went.'

'You had me followed?' Shashi snapped, a flicker of anger stirring within.

'Routine procedure, Mr Kurva. Surely you aren't surprised?'

'I shouldn't be, I guess,' he replied caustically. 'But I'm new to unsavoury circles.'

Kashyap brushed it off with a short laugh. 'So how did the meeting go?' he repeated.

'I'm not inclined to discuss that. Is there anything else you wish to ask?'

'For a man who claims that he doesn't hang out with Tola, you were very quick to meet him alone. The very next day at that!'

'So?'

'You did say that you were willing to cooperate with the investigation. If you've changed you mind, I'd like to know. At least we will know where we stand.'

Shashi took a deep breath and sat down on the settee. It wouldn't do to cross swords with SEBI and EOW. However unsavoury Kashyap might be, he had to accommodate him. But first, there was something he needed to find out.

'How can I cooperate with you when I don't know who you are?' he said.

'What do you mean?' Kashyap bristled.

'I know Mr Varma is from SEBI. I have no idea where *you* come from.'

'I went to your office with Varma, as you well know.'

'Yes, you did, but you could be his brother, for all I know. I'm sorry, Mr Kashyap. You must cooperate with me if you want the favour returned.'

A brief pause interrupted the conversation.

'Okay,' Kashyap finally said. 'I'm from the Economic Offences Wing.'

'EOW? Mumbai?'

'Yes.'

That was a small, if hollow, victory.

'Thank you. Now what do you want of me?' Shashi asked.

'Just tell me what happened at the meeting.'

'Nothing much. I confronted Vivek with what you had said. He denied it.'

'That's it? You lingered over your drink and Vivek had two. Surely, you exchanged more than that.'

Not only had Kashyap's man tailed him, he had also spied on his interactions with Vivek inside the bar.

'We began with pleasantries and I asked him about the stock market and his business. When I didn't get much out of him, I brought up the subject of his trading in Purple Country shares and mentioned your visit.'

'That's it?'

'That's the gist, yes.'

'What made him furious enough to walk out?'

'He resented my accusation.'

'He left you fuming too. Why?'

'He said he didn't give two hoots about the slur on my reputation. Or something to that effect. He insisted that he hadn't traded in Purple Country shares.'

'Hmm...he's technically right, you know.'

'What!' Shashi jumped to his feet. 'He didn't buy my company's shares?'

'That's right.'

'What game are you playing, Kashyap? You said Vivek had traded in my shares for eight months. What the f – '

'Hang on!' interrupted Kashyap. 'I said he was *technically* right.'

'What is *that* supposed to mean? He either bought my shares or he didn't.'

'He bought the shares through three firms.'

'Not as Vivek Tola?'

'No.'

'That's not the same as his buying shares in his own name!'

'He is the major shareholder in these firms. They are small, nondescript finance companies.'

'Kashyap, he and these firms are separate legal entities. They are not the same.'

'They are the same in spirit. That's what matters.'

Shashi was no longer listening. His anger had completely boiled over. Kashyap had deliberately misled him and he had fallen for it, hook, line and sinker. He had gone on to jeopardize his own reputation and destroy his peace of mind by taking it to the board. As a result, he was now the subject of an investigation within his own company – all because of Kashyap's chicanery.

'You bastard!' he shouted into the phone, making Kamna run up in alarm. 'You are screwing around with my life! You filthy swine! You…you…'

At a complete loss for words, he hung up. He sank back into the settee and buried his head in his hands, trembling with rage. Kamna sat down beside him and, without uttering a word, put her arms around him.

Minutes passed in silence and Shashi gradually regained his composure. He slowly narrated his conversation with Kashyap to Kamna.

Finally, after he had fallen silent, she asked in a gentle voice, 'How much of a difference does that make, Shashi? Is there a legal distinction between buying in your name and buying in the name of a company you partially own?'

'Honestly, Kamna, I don't know.'

'Would you like to ask someone? Isn't one of your board members a lawyer and your supporter?'

He nodded. 'Saldana.'

With a renewed spurt of energy, he rose from the settee, retrieved his phone and called Saldana. As usual, the lawyer answered the call on the second ring.

'Yes, Shashi?'

Shashi quickly summarized the conversation with Kashyap and asked him the question Kamna had posed.

'Hmm…It's difficult to give a straight answer to this one, Shashi. It will depend on a number of factors. For instance, they would have to establish that the share trades were carried out on Vivek Tola's explicit instructions. Mere ownership of the company is not sufficient, especially if it is part-ownership. Operational control needs to be proven.'

'How easy or difficult will that be?'

'It can be difficult. It depends on what happened in the firms before they bought the shares. Did Vivek give written instructions or verbal ones? Did he issue instructions at all? What if the share traders in the firms say that the decision was theirs and not Vivek's? Remember, Vivek has already had the opportunity to speak to his people.'

'Then does this make my position stronger, Mr Saldana?'

'I should think so. As long as there are no other trades that Vivek has made and no other beneficiaries close to you.'

Shashi's growing elation collapsed like a pricked balloon as his thoughts went to the Anjumal Trust. His knees went weak and he sank back on to the settee. His hands had turned clammy and his breathing was short. The fleeting moment of ecstatic relief had given way to despair and acute anxiety. *What if Vivek had invested the Anjumal Trust's monies in Purple Country shares?* There was no getting away from the fact that his wife was a beneficiary.

'Thank you, Mr Saldana,' he managed to say in a weak voice. 'I'll see you on Monday.'

As soon as he had hung up, the landline rang. Kamna answered it.

'One moment,' she said into the phone and turned to Shashi, with her hand covering the phone's speaker. 'Vivek wants to speak to you. He seems troubled.'

Without a word, Shashi took the phone.

'Hello?'

'Shashi?'

Vivek's voice was subdued and Shashi could hear the noise of traffic in the background. He glanced at the caller ID and saw that it was a landline number he didn't recognize.

'Ya. Where are you calling from?'

'A phone booth. Listen, Shashi. I need to talk to you. Can you come and see me at seven in the evening today?'

'Where?'

'Same place as yesterday. I'll take a table where we can speak more freely.'

'I'll be there. You're okay, Vivek? You don't sound – '

'I'm fine,' Vivek cut in. 'See you in the evening.'

The line went dead.

Chapter 7

Having entered the bar lounge, Shashi looked around the large room that was enclosed by two glass walls and a pair of wood-panelled ones. In a calmer frame of mind during this second visit, he was more receptive to the details of his surroundings. The wider stretch of glass wall on the far side offered an unimpeded view of the bay, making the tables arranged along its entire length the preferred seats in the lounge. Smaller tables, ideal for single patrons and groups of two, had been set up along the other glass wall to the left overlooking a busy street. There was little space to accommodate tables along the wall where the entrance to the lounge was located; a bar occupied most of its length and the washrooms too were lined up here.

Failing to find Vivek at any of the tables along the glass walls or in the middle of the room, Shashi glanced at his watch, wondering if he was early. He wasn't; the time was 7.05 p.m. At that moment, he heard Vivek call out to him. Trying to locate him, Shashi turned to his right and saw his brother-in-law seated at a small table tucked away in the corner where the two wood-panelled walls met. While the table Vivek had chosen was not far from the entrance, it was at a distance from most other tables – the best spot in the lounge for a private conversation.

Shashi glanced at Vivek as he took the other chair at the small table. His pink shirt was already damp under the arms and, unlike on the previous occasion, there was no joviality in evidence nor any trace of geniality either. Vivek was clearly ill at ease as he sat hunched in his chair with his back to the rest of the lounge. From his general appearance and manner, Shashi suspected that he had already downed a drink or two.

Withdrawn and distracted, Vivek silently gestured to a waiter to take Shashi's order. Once Shashi had ordered Ballantine's, his brother-in-law tapped his near-empty glass and held up two fingers, asking for two refills.

'Why did you – ' Shashi began, wanting to know why Vivek had called from a phone booth and not from his mobile, as usual.

But Vivek motioned for silence by briefly holding up his hand. It was clear that he didn't want to risk being overheard by the waiter. It dawned on Shashi why Vivek had asked for two pegs: he didn't want the waiter to interrupt them for a while.

Shashi nodded and fell silent. The next two minutes passed without either of them speaking, as they waited for their drinks to arrive and the bowl of assorted nuts to be replenished. Once the waiter had gone, Vivek gestured to Shashi's iPhone.

'Can you switch that off?' he asked quietly.

'Sure,' Shashi replied, surprised. 'Shall I put it on silent?'

'Turn it off, if you don't mind,' Vivek insisted. 'Don't want any device around that can record. I've done the same with my phone.' As if to corroborate his claim, he placed his iPhone alongside Shashi's.

Pretending to stretch, Vivek casually turned his torso and scanned the half-empty lounge. Most tables along the glass walls were taken, as were some in the middle of the lounge.

Shashi too cast his gaze across the lounge, wondering if Kashyap's men had followed him here today as well. If they weren't already here, they would be soon. His eyes followed the two men who had just walked into the lounge and taken a table at the centre of the room. A young couple entered and went to a small table near the glass wall. Neither the couple nor the men showed the slightest interest in Shashi and Vivek.

'Shashi, I have something to tell you,' Vivek began in an undertone. He was leaning forward, but his gaze was fixed on the table. 'What I'm going to say is for your ears only. If it gets around, I will completely deny it. Okay?'

So that's why he had wanted Shashi's phone switched off! Shashi nodded slowly as Vivek's troubled gaze flicked up to hold his own for a moment.

'Yesterday, you had asked me where I got my information from for trading in shares. I had said that there was a lot of information sloshing about, if you knew where to look. That is true. There is a fair bit of price-sensitive information floating around – sometimes about companies, sometimes about imminent government decisions and sometimes about interesting *benami* transactions of connected people. Some listed companies leak like broken buckets and several government ministries and departments are so porous, they're like sieves.'

He paused in obvious irritation as a waiter came up and deposited a plate of chilli cheese toast on the table.

'Complimentary, sir,' the waiter murmured and retreated.

'A lot of the information is misleading, often planted deliberately,' Vivek went on, pausing to pop two squares of chilli cheese toast into his mouth and chew. 'In fact, there's a lot more misinformation than authentic stuff doing the rounds. But with experience, you learn to distinguish between the two.

'Information is the currency in this business. Like I said the last time, the source and legality of information are irrelevant. Accuracy and timing are all-important. That helps me beat other traders. Really valuable information is held very close to the chest.'

He took a long swig from his glass, quickly cast his gaze around the room and continued.

'You asked me about Purple Country. Yes, there is inside information from Purple Country in the market. I don't know who is leaking it, I don't know whom it is leaked to, but I know that it exists. You must believe me when I say that *I* received no information from Purple Country.'

Vivek looked up into Shashi's face and held his gaze, trying to convince his brother-in-law of his sincerity.

Shashi was unmoved. 'You still traded in Purple Country shares,' he countered, not ready to be won over. 'Why would you risk crores if you didn't have price-sensitive information?'

'That's where experience comes in.' Vivek turned his gaze back to the table. 'As a broker, I buy and sell shares for a number of clients. I often lend them margin money too. I see them taking big risks with the money they've borrowed from me. These people are not fools, Shashi. Contrary to popular opinion, very few big players actually gamble. They *know* what they are doing.

'A few years back, I began mimicking the trades of one of my most successful clients, but with far smaller amounts than he risked. If he bought one lakh shares of Company X, I bought a thousand. When he sold his shares, I sold mine. I just followed him. And guess what? I found that my hit rate was high, very high. I made money almost every single time. Slowly, I increased the amounts I invested and profited handsomely. My claim that I can double money every two years is not an empty one.'

'I know,' Shashi nodded. 'I saw how the Anjumal Trust has performed.'

That brought a frown to Vivek's face. He seemed to consider a riposte, but changed his mind.

'So you see, Shashi,' he continued instead, 'you don't need inside information to succeed. If you know whom to follow and do it discreetly, your life is made.'

'By being discreet, you mean trading through small finance firms?'

Vivek nodded. 'For such transactions, no big player trades in his own name. He must retain the option of distancing himself from the trade, should the need arise.'

'Is that what happened with Purple Country?'

Vivek remained silent, apparently fascinated by the bowl of cashews in front of him. It dawned on Shashi that his brother-in-law was not going to acknowledge that he had traded in Purple Country shares.

'Who is this "big player" you follow?' Shashi asked. 'He can tell us where he gets his information about Purple Country from.'

Vivek looked up, an incredulous expression on his face. 'You actually want me to give you his name?'

'Yes.'

'And kill my golden goose?' Vivek suddenly sounded tired. 'The one thing I am not, Shashi, is a fool.' Two more squares of chilli cheese toast disappeared into his mouth.

'Then why did you tell me what you just did?'

'Firstly, to square up with you. Secondly, so that you can repeat this to your board if it helps you get off the hook.'

'But you will deny it.'

'Of course. But let your board know that there has been no passing of information from you to me. Let them also know that information is leaking, but through someone else – not you.'

'Why should they believe me?'

Vivek shrugged and picked up his iPhone.

'I'm sure you can be persuasive. See, you persuaded me – a hard-boiled trader – to disclose as much as I have.'

Shashi sat back and contemplated Vivek's bowed head. Was he telling the truth? He suspected not. Why had he called him all the way here just to tell him something he would publicly deny? Was he setting Shashi up for something? Quite possible. If so, what? He could think of nothing.

Suddenly, the truth struck Shashi – at least, what he thought was the truth. Vivek was trying to plant a story! If that was so, for whom was the story intended? The board? Unlikely. Vivek cared little for Purple Country, its board or its CEO. Who then? The answer came to him a moment after the question rose – SEBI! For some reason, the SEBI visit to Shashi's office had rattled Vivek.

One part of the story was true – no privileged information had passed between Shashi and Vivek. With the conviction stemming from that piece of truth, Shashi would tell the rest of the story with the same sincerity. That was Vivek's plan! At least, that was what Shashi thought was the plan. He decided to test it.

'There is no point my telling the board this cock-and-bull story,' he said aloud. 'It will only tarnish my reputation further.'

'Yourrr caall,' Vivek drawled, feigning nonchalance.

His words were beginning to slur. He also seemed to be wheezing a little. Shashi wondered how many drinks he had already downed before he joined his brother-in-law at the table.

'But I think it can get the SEBI men off your back.'

Vivek's tone seemed casual, but there was no denying the underlying tension. Shashi was now sure that his hunch was correct.

'Something is amiss, Vivek. I know it – '

'Nothing is amiss,' the other man said curtly, cutting Shashi off in mid-sentence. 'Don't worry.'

'Come on, Vivek.' Shashi leaned forward and continued softly. 'You called from a public booth. You took the trouble of getting out of your car so that you wouldn't have to use your mobile. Why?'

'That's got nothhingg to do with what wee arrre discussing.' Vivek's slur had become more pronounced. One corner of his mouth drooped below the other and he held his head cocked to one side. All the alcohol he had consumed was hitting him now. He was getting drunk.

Shashi sat back and studied him silently. Vivek's forehead

glistened with sweat as he sat back in his chair. A curious expression of surprise, mixed with dullness, had come over his face. Clumsily, he undid another button of his shirt and drained his glass. He had begun sweating profusely now and his skin had turned pale. He picked up another square of chilli cheese toast with an unsteady hand and managed to pop it into his mouth on the second attempt.

Vivek remained silent, his face devoid of expression, his gaze fixed on the table. His breathing was now laboured and shallow and dark patches of sweat stained his otherwise spotless silk shirt. He stared unseeingly at the table between them as his hands slowly turned over his iPhone a couple of times.

Suddenly, it slipped from his fingers and fell to the carpeted floor with a soft thud, but he did not move to pick it up. His hands had fallen to his lap and he seemed dazed.

'Vivek?' Shashi said softly.

His brother-in-law didn't respond, continuing to stare woodenly at the table. His head drooped, his chin resting on his chest. Shashi leaned forward and stared into his eyes. They seemed blind, unfocused. His face was paler still.

'Vivek!' he said again, this time with concern. 'Are you okay?'

When he didn't answer, Shashi reached out and touched the other man's arm. Vivek swayed to one side and collapsed in his chair. Shashi rose hurriedly and went to his side, grasping him by the shoulders and calling out his name repeatedly. Vivek slumped back against his chair. He was left staring at the ceiling as his head fell back.

'Is there a doctor here?' Shashi shouted hoarsely. 'Please! We need a doctor!'

A bearded man rose from a table nearby and rushed forward. 'I am a doctor. Stand back, please.'

Shashi did so and let the man through. Two waiters came running as the doctor examined Vivek. Shashi hurriedly picked up Vivek's iPhone from the floor and put it in his jacket pocket, lest someone step on it inadvertently.

'Ambulance!' the doctor called out within twenty seconds of examining the inert man. 'Call an ambulance!'

One of the waiters rushed out of the bar lounge as a fearful Shashi approached the doctor, who slowly straightened, then bent down again to sniff at something on Vivek's lips. He turned to Shashi, a frown creasing his grave face. His dark eyes bored into Shashi's.

'Doctor, what on earth – ' Shashi began, but the doctor cut him off.

'We have to get him *immediately* to a hospital. *Every* minute counts.'

Aghast, Shashi stared at Vivek's face. It seemed frozen, paralysed. The way he was slumped back in the chair suggested that he had no control whatsoever over either his limbs or his torso. Was he having a stroke? A heart attack? Then every minute *did* count! Shashi had to get word to Chaaya too.

He switched on his mobile phone and called Kamna.

▪

Midnight had come and gone, but no definite news had filtered through from the hospital's ICU. Shashi alternated between fidgeting in his chair and pacing the floor restlessly. His wife and sister-in-law sat close together. Kamna was trying to look calm and provide hope and emotional support to her sister, but Chaaya's face was a study in raging emotions. Anxiety, grief, fear and anger took turns to warp her expression even as her tears flowed unchecked. Shashi sensed she was expecting the worst.

He spun around at the sound of a door opening softly. One of the doctors attending to Vivek stepped out and gave Shashi a barely perceptible nod which suggested that he should follow him.

Shashi's heart sank as he realized that the doctor had beckoned to him surreptitiously to avoid attracting Chaaya's attention.

'He's fading,' the doctor announced the moment they entered his office. 'He's not breathing. In fact, nothing we have tried so far has worked. Respiratory paralysis. The prognosis is not good.'

'Is it a stroke?' Shashi asked. 'Or a heart attack? He seemed to be in great discomfort before he collapsed. And he was perspiring profusely.'

The doctor shook his head slowly. 'Neither. There is cyanosis, which is symptomatic of acute food poisoning. Are you sure he ate nothing other than what you listed for us?'

'Nothing. But as I said, I don't know if he had eaten anything else before I joined him.'

'Any seafood? Or something exotic?'

Shashi shook his head. 'He may have consumed a fair amount of alcohol.'

'No amount of alcohol can do this, Mr Kurva. I'm afraid – '

He broke off as the door opened and another doctor stepped in. One look at her face was enough to tell them what had happened.

'I'm sorry, Mr Kurva,' she said. 'We tried everything, but we couldn't help him. He's gone.'

Like a man in a dream, Shashi turned slowly and walked out of the doctor's office. How would he break the news to Chaaya?

As he turned to shut the door behind him, he thought he heard the lady doctor whisper to her colleague, 'The police are here.'

Chapter 8

Inspector Praveen Ranade gazed at the manager of the five-star hotel through his round, rimless glasses. The lanky, mild-mannered police officer in his early thirties looked more like a benign college lecturer than a detective. It was only when one looked carefully into his hard eyes did his experience as a detective become apparent. Even then, his bulldog-like tenacity would not have been in evidence.

His work did not bring him to this hotel often, but every time it did, the vastness of the atrium provoked the same response from him. What a waste of prime Mumbai space! The open floor could accommodate a couple of hundred cabins the size of his office and five such layers could be stacked, one on top of another, into the height of the atrium. That made it a thousand cabins in all! No wonder the hotel was expensive.

Most guests here would be business travellers, he guessed, staying at company expense. How many would spend their own money to stay there? Not many, but some might stay, on occasion, simply to make a statement. Some of Mumbai's elite, like the man who had died in the bar last night, made sure they were seen frequently at its restaurants and bar. Appearances were important.

Ranade pushed the thoughts away and brought his attention back to the matter at hand. The cause of Vivek Tola's sudden death had not yet been established, but the doctors who had attended to him suspected food poisoning. The inspector had not fully grasped their medical terminology, but he did understand that the symptoms were not consistent with cardiac arrest or any other natural cause of sudden death. On the contrary, there were sufficient signs to suggest unnatural death. That made it suspected homicide.

'Mr Tola may have died of food poisoning,' Ranade said to the nervous hotel manager sitting across the desk. Beside Ranade sat Sub-inspector Abdul, his assistant.

'If so, the food item that killed him must have come from outside the hotel.' The manager had clearly thought his position through. No hotel worth its salt, especially a five-star hotel, could afford to have its name even remotely linked with food poisoning. 'All the items served to him were served to several other guests too. Every single item.'

'Have you taken stock of all that he had consumed?' Ranade murmured.

The manager nodded vigorously as he pulled out a sheet of paper from his shirt pocket. 'I've looked at all the orders and made a list of the ingredients that went into them.'

'What about complimentary items?'

'Those too – assorted nuts, pretzels and wafers. They came from larger boxes or packets behind the bar. The Teachers whisky he drank came from a bottle that is still half-full. The Schweppes soda was from an unopened can served directly to the table. It is inconceivable that any of the items in question would affect Mr Tola, but nobody else.'

'Any meat or seafood that could have gone bad?'

'Out of the question.' The manager's tone was flat and brooked no discussion. 'We serve *nothing* but fresh meat. We have very strict norms about how long meat should be stored. In any case, Mr Tola consumed no meat.'

'Did everything he consumed come from the bar lounge?' Ranade asked, taking the sheet of paper from the manager.

'Yes.'

'Have you tallied your list with what was left on the table after Mr Tola died?'

The manager hesitated. Ranade looked up from the paper.

'Well? Did you?'

'No...The table was cordoned off on the doctor's advice.'

The doctor who had examined Vivek at the bar lounge had apparently insisted that the table remain untouched till the police came.

'He didn't want anything disturbed. But there really was no need, inspector; everything that reached the table had come from within the room.'

'Unless Mr Tola or his guest brought something with them?' Abdul asked.

'Exactly!' The hotel manager seized the opportunity. 'This is among the most reputable hotels in the country, inspector. We check every edible item thoroughly. With so many guests passing through the hotel and with many of them being allergic to various food items, we need to have a *pukka* system for checking.'

'What about the other things that could have contained poison?'

'What things?'

'Ice, for instance. Did Mr Tola take ice in his drink?'

'I...I am not sure. I will have to check with the waiter. Ice or water won't appear on the order slips.' The manager seemed shaken by the thought. 'But ice and water are bulk items too. They would have been served to other guests.'

'What about the glass Mr Tola drank from?' Ranade asked.

'I...how – ' the manager stammered.

'Would the waiter or the bartender be able to...' Ranade left the sentence unfinished as the manager turned pale.

'But why?' the man asked shrilly.

'You do check the background of the staff you employ, don't you?' Ranade countered the question with another.

'Yes, we do. I can get the records if you wish.'

'Please do. Can I see the two men now?'

'Certainly. They are waiting outside.' The manager paused and continued hesitantly, 'Do you suspect either of them – '

'It's too early to suspect anyone,' Ranade said crisply, cutting him off. 'We must cover all angles. I would like to see them one by one. If you could send in the bartender first, please?'

'He seems to have known that Vivek died of poisoning,' Abdul said quietly as the door closed behind the manager.

'Not surprising, Abdul. The loudmouth doctor who examined Vivek last night all but said so.'

'We will know soon enough.' Abdul glanced at his watch. 'The food items left on the table will be analysed shortly. The autopsy will be done by tomorrow.'

'I can't help but agree with the manager, Abdul. I would be surprised if we find poison in any of the bulk items. Unless the bartender had something to do with it, the poison must have found its way in *after* the items left the bar. That points to the waiter or – '

Ranade broke off as a knock sounded on the door. It opened a moment later. A large man of about forty stepped in hesitantly.

'I'm Samuel, the bartender here,' he said in a gravelly voice.

'Please come in, Samuel. Take a seat.'

Ranade took in the man as he approached the table and sat on the chair opposite him. Swarthy, he sported a long handlebar moustache that went all the way down to his chin. Uneasy eyes under a grizzled mane darted from Ranade to Abdul. Large hands clasped and unclasped nervously as he waited for the police officer to begin.

'Were you tending the bar lounge last evening, Samuel?' Ranade asked.

'Yes sir.'

'Tell me what happened.' Ranade smiled pleasantly and sat

back, trying to put the big man at ease. 'Take your time and try to remember everything that happened.'

'Not much to say, sir. The evening was still young when Mr Tola came in. It must have been a little short of 7 p.m. I didn't notice much, other than him having walked in, as the lounge had started filling up and my hands were full. Saturday evenings are busy times.'

'You do all the bartending on busy evenings?'

'No sir. There are two of us. Richard hadn't yet arrived when all this happened.'

'When does he usually come in?'

'Around half past seven – sometimes, a little earlier.'

'Okay. Go on.'

'Mr Tola ordered his usual drink – a couple of large Teachers 50 and soda. He was waiting for someone. The person came, maybe ten minutes later, and I served them the second order – two large pegs of Teachers for Mr Tola, and one Ballantine's for the other person. That's all I saw until the person with Mr Tola shouted for a doctor.'

'What happened after that?'

'A lot of chaos and confusion. The doctor said something about food poisoning and insisted that the table be cordoned off. The manager shut the bar lounge and we moved all the guests to the lobby lounge.'

'That's the long lounge just outside the entrance to the bar lounge?'

'Yes sir.'

'Okay. Going back to the drinks you served Mr Tola, tell me *exactly* how orders are taken and processed.'

'A waiter takes the order from a customer and writes it on an order slip. I take the order slip and put it in a small wooden box. Another person enters the order into the computer as and when he gets the time, in between helping me. Once I read the order, I take a fresh glass from the sideboard, pour the liquor into it and add anything else the order may require. A cocktail is a little more involved – I mix it in a different tumbler and transfer the cocktail to the glass. For margaritas, I prepare the glass separately.'

'Prepare the glass?'

'Rim the glass with salt. That must be done before the cocktail is poured in.'

'How do you select the glass for a certain order?'

'There are specific glasses for each drink – wine glasses, martini glasses, highball, flutes, tumblers, etcetera. They are either standing on the sideboard or hanging overhead. I pick the one I need and serve the drink.'

'What did you serve Mr Tola's whisky in?'

'An old-fashioned whisky glass – the lowball glass. It has a thick base and a wide brim.'

'From the sideboard?'

Samuel nodded.

'Now think carefully, Samuel. How do you select a particular glass – say, a lowball glass – from the sideboard.'

The bartender frowned as he ran through his usual routine in his mind. 'I take the nearest one, I guess…they are arranged in rows…I pick up one from the closest row…I think.'

'What happens after that? Do you add the ice?'

'No sir. Each customer decides how many cubes he or she wants. I just pour out the whisky and put it on the counter. The waiter takes it to the customer's table and offers ice, water or anything else that may be required.'

Ranade leaned forward and spoke softly, his eyes fixed on the bartender's face. 'Then at which stage could the poison have been introduced, Samuel?'

There was no missing the flint in the inspector's voice and gaze. Samuel was not the first man made to feel like a culprit by Ranade without being verbally accused of a crime.

Samuel broke out in a sweat and stammered, 'I don't know, sir. Honest to God, I have no idea! I will swear on my mother's grave. I have been thinking about it all night. It completely beats me. And Surendra wouldn't do anything wrong either.'

'Surendra?'

'The waiter who served Mr Tola.'

'Anything else you can tell us, Samuel?'

'No sir.' The bartender shook his head. 'I was busy and wasn't watching Mr Tola. Besides, the table he chose is not easily visible from the bar; it's in a corner. But you should watch the CCTV recording.'

'Does it cover the entire lounge?'

'It does. Several cameras were installed after 26/11. There are three in the bar lounge. They cover all corners, including the one Mr Tola was sitting in.'

'Thank you, Samuel. Would you send in Surendra, please?'

Surendra turned out to be a thin young man in his late twenties. If Samuel was nervous, Surendra was positively terrified. His hands trembled as he sat on the edge of the chair and waited for Ranade to speak.

'Don't be frightened,' the inspector said with a smile. 'I just want to ask some questions.'

The young man's eyes moistened in partial relief at Ranade's gentle tone. He swallowed and his voice was hoarse as he spoke haltingly in Hindi.

'Some people are saying that I gave Tola Saab the poison. The manager called people in my home town, asking about me. My father called me this morning to say that people in my town were spreading all kinds of rumours. People in the hotel are also looking at me strangely.' Surendra's palms came together in supplication. 'Saab, I swear I had nothing to do with his death. All I did was serve him like I always had, like I would any other customer.'

'Don't worry, Surendra.' Abdul placed a soothing hand on the agitated young man's shoulder. 'You have nothing to fear if you did no wrong. Now tell us what happened last evening.'

Gathering courage, Surendra recounted the events, largely repeating what the manager and Samuel had said. He concluded after five minutes by saying, 'I went to the table three times, sir. The first time was with Mr Tola's whisky, soda, nuts and pretzels – Mr Tola liked pretzels. The second time was with his second round of whisky and Ballantine's for his guest. The third time was with some more nuts and potato wafers.'

Ranade shook his head. 'You must have gone there at least one more time – to take the Ballantine's order. Am I right?'

'Y…yes sir,' the young man stammered, completely unnerved. 'I forgot. I must have gone four times. Sorry, sir.'

Ranade had his file open on his lap and was running his pencil down the list of items that had been left on the table after Vivek's death. While Surendra was speaking, he had marked off items with a small tick of his pencil. Now, as the waiter finished, the pencil tip hovered over the one entry that had not been ticked: chilli cheese toast.

'When did you serve the chilli cheese toast?' he asked casually.

Surendra looked at him in confusion. 'Chilli cheese toast?' he asked.

Ranade nodded.

'I didn't serve chilli cheese toast, sir. Mr Tola didn't order any.'

'Could he have ordered it through another waiter?'

'He could, sir. But that is unlikely. Even if he had, I would have known about it.'

'How?'

'The table number, sir. Mr Tola was at Table 13.' He blinked as if the link between the unlucky number and the client's death had just occurred to him. 'A single running tab is maintained for each table. Even if it had been ordered through another waiter, it would have appeared on Table 13's tab and I would have seen it. We checked it this morning too.'

'Okay. Where would chilli cheese toast be supplied from, had Mr Tola ordered it?'

'I would have placed a telephonic order with the kitchen and it would've been delivered to the bar. Then I would have served it to Mr Tola.'

Ranade dismissed Surendra after questioning him for another fifteen minutes. He then placed the file on the desk and pointed to the offending item on the list.

'Neither the manager nor Surendra mentioned the chilli cheese toast. But it was there on the table. Our photographs also show it clearly. You took them before the table was touched.'

'I wonder if it was ordered by another table, sir,' Abdul said slowly. 'What if a guest from another table had passed it to Vivek? The waiter wouldn't know and it wouldn't appear on Table 13's tab.'

'Possible. Go and check with the F&B manager while I make a phone call. Find out who ordered chilli cheese toast.'

As Abdul stepped out, Ranade called a number from his mobile.

'Ranade here,' he said. 'When are you starting the analysis of the items?'

'In a couple of hours. Why?'

'Can you do one item first? It's urgent.'

'Okay.'

'Check the chilli cheese toast for neurotoxins.' The doctors at the hospital had suspected that a neurotoxin might have been the cause of Vivek's respiratory paralysis and cyanosis. 'Call me immediately if you find anything suspicious in it.'

'Will do.'

'Can you check if some kind of powder is sprinkled on it?'

'Hang on a minute.'

Ranade waited impatiently as the man at the other end went away to inspect the chilli cheese toast. He was back in a couple of minutes.

'Nothing,' he said. 'It looks all right. The cheese on top has the kind of glaze you would expect from cheese that has melted and cooled.'

'No powder or crystals on the plate?'

'Nope.'

'Okay. Analyse it and call me once you finish.'

Ranade hung up and sat back with his pencil twirling between his thumb and forefinger – a long-standing habit that helped him think more clearly. It was evident that the chilli cheese toast had been delivered to Vivek's table surreptitiously. How? Where had it come from? And where had it gone before reaching Table 13? Even though there was no powder on it, he had a strong suspicion that the chilli cheese toast had been doctored. But how had it been done? Where? By whom? The first thing he would look for in the CCTV footage was whether any other customer in the bar lounge had approached Table 13.

He surfaced from his preoccupation as Abdul returned with news.

'Two orders for chilli cheese toast from the bar lounge,' he said. 'One at 6.45 p.m. and the other at 7.10. I have the table numbers.'

'Who were the customers at those tables?'

'Don't know yet. Will get the information soon. The manager is to give us the complete list of customers shortly.'

'Do you have the CCTV footage?'

'We'll get it on Monday.'

'Let's wrap up here. Oh! Ask the F&B manager for all the chilli cheese toast orders placed that afternoon and evening till 7.30 p.m.'

'*All* orders in the hotel, sir?'

'Everything. Room service, all restaurants, all kitchens. Do that while I make another call.'

Ranade picked up his mobile again and called a number from his file.

'Mr Shashi Kurva?' he asked, when the call was answered.

'Yes?'

'This is Inspector Ranade from the Mumbai Police.'

'Yes, inspector?'

'One quick question: do you remember what snacks were served at your table last evening?'

'Let me see…a bowl of assorted nuts…some pretzels…and a plate of chilli cheese toast, I think. Oh yes, and some wafers.'

'Sure?'

'I think so. Am I missing something? I can't recall anything else.'

'Do you remember in what order the items were served?'

'I'm not sure, inspector, but I think the nuts and pretzels were already there when I joined Vivek. The bowls may have been refilled later. The last item that came was the chilli cheese toast. Vivek ate a few pieces of it.'

'How many did you have?'

'None. I don't like cheese very much.'

'Then you wouldn't have ordered it. I suppose Mr Tola did?'

'He may have ordered it before I joined him. I don't think he ordered it after…Wait! I think the waiter said it was complimentary.'

'Are you sure, Mr Kurva?'

'Not really, inspector. It was not long before Vivek collapsed. Things are rather hazy in my mind. I hope you understand.'

'Sure. Do you know what happened to Mr Tola's phone?'

'It's with me, inspector. I'll give it to you when we meet.'

'Thank you, Mr Kurva. I'll call you later.'

A couple of minutes later, Ranade and Abdul stood at the entrance to the bar lounge, looking around. The table at which Vivek Tola had sat was about 20 feet away to their right, at the corner of the wall where the entrance was located and the other wood-panelled wall that was at right angles to it. Ranade walked up to the table and surveyed the bar lounge from there. Samuel had been right; the table was not visible from the bar.

He walked out of the bar lounge and stood outside the entrance, surveying the expanse of the atrium in front of him. Across a wide square of polished marble floor stood three lifts, beside which a short corridor led to the restrooms. To his right was the entrance to one of the hotel's popular restaurants. Running from there to his left was a wide lobby that led to the reception area and the hotel entrance.

Stretching alongside the lobby was a long, low area with three rows of small tables around which were grouped chairs or single-seater sofas. A few of the tables were occupied. To one side, near the middle of the long lounge, stood an L-shaped counter with a computer terminal at one end. Behind the counter that was laden with trays and cups stood two men.

A waiter was carrying two cups from the counter to one of the occupied tables. Another, bearing an empty tray, was walking down the broad steps behind the counter.

'The hotel staff claim they didn't serve the chilli cheese toast, but Shashi Kurva says the opposite,' Ranade murmured. 'The evidence bears out Kurva's version.'

'I'm told the two men had met here the previous evening and the meeting ended in some kind of disagreement. A waiter said that Vivek had walked out, leaving Kurva fuming.'

'There is a lot we are yet to discover, Abdul,' Ranade said quietly, studying the restaurant and the lobby lounge. 'Imagine the gall of a man who can kill someone in a bar full of people!'

Chapter 9

Ranade's phone rang as he entered his office on Monday morning. It was the man from the police lab whom he had asked to check the chilli cheese toast for neurotoxins.

'You were right,' the lab man said. 'Tetrodotoxin, also called TTX. It's a neurotoxin found in marine animals and one of the most notorious causes of food poisoning from seafood. Dozens die every year in places like Japan.'

'Seafood?' Ranade exclaimed in surprise. 'Are you sure?'

'Absolutely.'

'And you found it in the chilli cheese toast?'

'Yes.'

'What the hell was seafood doing in chilli cheese toast?'

'No idea, but there's enough toxin in the remaining squares of chilli cheese toast to kill two men.'

'Can you tell where exactly in the squares the poison was detected? You found nothing on the surface of the cheese.'

'Soaked in the bread under the cheese. There are no pieces of seafood there, Ranade, but the toxin is present in a very high concentration.'

'Injected?'

'Possible. There are holes in the melted cheese.'

'Then it is no accident, is it?'

'No.'

'What about the other items?'

'No TTX anywhere, apart from the chilli cheese toast. No traces in the drinks or in the other snacks.'

'Any doubts about your findings?'

'None. We tested twice. By the way, TTX is far, *far* more poisonous than potassium cyanide.'

'Hmm...How easy or difficult is it to get hold of this stuff?'

'No clue, Ranade.'

'Okay, thanks.'

The inspector hung up and looked enquiringly at Abdul, who had just walked in with three sheets of paper.

'The other lab reports have come in,' he said, dropping the sheets on the desk. 'Fingerprints on the chilli cheese toast plate are smudged and the two partial ones they could recover seem to be from the kitchen.'

'Any more information from the hotel?'

Abdul nodded. 'Chilli cheese toast seems to be a popular snack, sir. Twenty-two orders were placed between 4 p.m. and 7.15 p.m. – five for room service and the rest spread across four restaurants and lounges. It will be difficult to track them all, but we have all the customer details.'

'We may not need to track them all. How many were paid for in cash?'

'Good point, sir. Our man is unlikely to have used a credit card or ordered it for delivery to his room.' He counted entries from four sheets and looked up. 'Five.'

'Okay. Get the CCTV footage from the hotel. I'll go see Shashi Kurva now.'

Half an hour later, Ranade was ringing Shashi's doorbell. A short, neatly turned out man shooed away the housekeeper who had opened the door and confronted Ranade. He wore dark trousers with black socks, a white full-sleeved shirt and a red tie – elegant clothes that hung well on him. But for his missing shoes, he seemed ready to leave for work.

'Mr Kurva? I am Inspector Ranade from the Mumbai Police.'

Shashi's dark eyes bored into Ranade's and held his gaze for a moment before sweeping downward to take in the rest of him.

'Can I see an ID, please?' he asked in an even tone that was neither friendly nor hostile.

Here was a man who was used to doing things his way, thought Ranade, as he pulled out his identity card and handed it over. As Shashi studied it, the inspector took the opportunity to assess him. Erect, broad-shouldered and self-assured, Kurva seemed to be a man in control of himself. The large head suggested a person of superior intellect.

He must have been through a torrid 36 hours, but seemed none the worse for it. Ranade had expected him to be worn out and possibly distracted, but none of that was in evidence. The sub-inspector who had been at the hospital when Vivek died reported that Shashi seemed calm and in control. In addition to being the main support for his newly widowed sister-in-law, he had taken charge of matters as soon as the doctors confirmed his brother-in-law's death.

Ranade wondered how he had taken Vivek's death. Initial impressions were that he had not been on the best of terms with the deceased and had even quarrelled with him. But he had been very caring and tender towards Vivek's wife in her hour of distress. Like a brother, they had said, his arm around her shoulders as he led her to the car.

Ranade pushed away the thought as Shashi looked up from the ID. It wouldn't do to prejudge a potential suspect in a homicide case.

'Thank you, inspector,' Shashi said, returning the ID. 'Pardon me for taking the precaution, but I don't know you and you are not in uniform. Please come in.'

Ranade stepped into a drawing room done up in shades of rust, orange and dark brown. Drapes of ethnic design, sofas with earthy hues and woven coir floor mats created a distinctive setting highlighted by half a dozen tastefully chosen paintings. A large painting of a rustic little girl contemplating a glowing candle in the dark caught his eye as soon as he entered.

There were touches of modernity too. A large wall-mounted television set with a home theatre, a Bose music system and an adjustable recliner resembling a first-class airline seat – all a glossy black – stood out. Touchscreen-enabled controls on the recliner's armrest and on a small table beside it completed the impression of high-end technology at work. The drawing room, it seemed to Ranade, bore the imprint of two people – a refined, artistically inclined woman and a technology-savvy man.

When the inspector took a seat at Shashi's request and looked at him more minutely, it struck him that he might have misjudged the impact Vivek Tola's death had had on the man. In the natural light streaming in through the windows, Shashi's face looked drawn and dark circles were faintly visible under his eyes. So were the worry lines on his brow. He may have looked as though he was in control, but it was apparent to Ranade that the man had hardly slept the previous night.

'You'll pardon my abruptness, inspector,' Shashi began, 'but I need to get to my office as soon as possible. I have a crisis brewing there that needs my attention. When you called, I decided to stay back and meet you here, as this is a personal matter. So if you don't mind, can we get started? Here is Vivek's phone.' He placed an iPhone on the table in front of Ranade.

'Sure,' the inspector replied, picking up the phone. 'I needed to take a statement from you regarding Saturday evening.'

Shashi nodded and began giving an account of what had transpired at the lounge bar. Ranade listened to him carefully, noting that the man was precise in his narration, wasting little time on elaborate descriptions or empty words. He kept to the facts and finished his story within five minutes.

'I haven't yet told Vivek's wife or mine everything that I know, inspector,' Shashi admitted after he had finished. 'They're already reeling from the shock of his death. They do know that food poisoning was the cause, but I haven't shared my misgivings with them.'

'What misgivings?'

'How on earth could such a deadly poison get into him? Have they determined the cause yet?'

'Have you heard of tetrodotoxin, Mr Kurva?'

'Tetra *what*?'

'Tetrodotoxin or TTX. It's a neurotoxin found in marine animals.'

'Marine animals! What the f – '

'Did Mr Tola eat any seafood?'

'No, not as far as I could tell. We only had snacks and Vivek had several drinks.'

'What if I told you that the poison may have been in the chilli cheese toast?'

'Contaminated seafood in chilli cheese toast? That's ridiculous! You aren't serious?'

'Never been more serious in my life, Mr Kurva.'

Ranade watched as a range of emotions flashed across Shashi's face. This was no longer the CEO in control. This was now a bewildered family member, struggling to cope with a bizarre death.

'How could contaminated seafood get into chilli cheese toast?' Shashi murmured. 'The squares were so *small*. Even if a piece got in, how could it have been so deadly?'

'There is one other possibility, Mr Kurva.'

'What is that?'

‘The poison could have been deliberately put there.’

Shashi’s face was a picture of surprise and indignation. Ranade felt the man’s energy sweep over him.

‘Nonsense!’ he exclaimed. ‘Why the hell would someone put poison into chilli cheese toast?’ Shashi’s eyes searched Ranade’s face and quickly reassessed the situation. His voice dropped. ‘Are you *really* serious, inspector?’

‘It’s now a homicide case, Mr Kurva,’ Ranade said softly.

Shashi groaned and buried his head in his hands. ‘I guess Chaaya will need to be told soon?’

‘I’m afraid so.’

‘When?’

‘Sometime today. We will have to probe the motive.’

‘Murder?’ Shashi whispered. ‘But he sat there in front of me and consumed only what the waiter served. Nobody else came near us. How could anyone have killed him? And why would anyone want to?’

‘We don’t know yet, but we’ll find out. I believe he was upset when he met you on Friday evening. Anything you can tell me about it?’

‘I don’t know if it has anything to do with his death, inspector.’

‘Your meeting ended abruptly, I’m told. And in a quarrel. Is that right?’

Shashi’s head jerked up and he stared at Ranade. As realization dawned, the colour drained from his now-haggard face.

‘You…you suspect *me*?’ he whispered, his voice breaking.

‘It’s too early for suspicions, Mr Kurva.’ Ranade’s gaze was steady, taking in Shashi’s reactions. ‘But I must explore all possible avenues.’

‘But he was my brother-in-law! How could I ever do such a thing to Chaaya and her kids?’

Once again, his affection for his sister-in-law had surfaced. Ranade remained silent, watching Shashi’s face. He read turmoil in its expression, as incredulity gave way to confusion, dismay and, finally, anger. He sat back and glared at Ranade, his colour slowly rising.

'So that's why you came here to see me!' he muttered through clenched teeth. 'I'm your prime suspect! Then nothing I say will be of any use; you won't believe me.'

Ranade shook his head slowly. 'You'll be surprised at how much of what you said I accept as true. You're perhaps unaware of how difficult it is to conceal or feign emotions.'

Shashi's laugh was bitter. 'Is it, inspector? Do you know that theatre was my passion for many years? I'm choosing to tell you about it, because you'll find out sooner or later; I may as well earn some brownie points by being upfront. Acting is not difficult, inspector. It comes naturally to me.'

'Can we return to what I was asking? What was your quarrel with Mr Tola about?'

'I may as well tell you, I guess.'

Shashi took a deep breath and related the details of his meeting with Varma and Kashyap and of his subsequent confrontation with Vivek. He mentioned that Kashyap's men had followed him and witnessed his spat with his brother-in-law. Then he told the inspector about Vivek's call on Saturday from a phone booth.

'Something was obviously bothering Vivek,' Shashi mused. 'I don't know why he called from a public phone booth, of all places. I wonder if he suspected that his line was being tapped. He was distracted and uneasy when we met on Saturday evening. He seemed so distraught that my first thought was that he might be having a heart seizure or a stroke.'

Ranade quickly assimilated what he had heard. So Shashi was in trouble with SEBI! That was the crisis he had mentioned. With that realization, the inspector felt a new respect for the other man. Shashi was fighting battles on two fronts and still managing to stay in control. Now a third battle had just erupted with him being regarded as a murder suspect. Yet he was maintaining his cool. Ranade wondered how many men could do that in his situation.

'Tell me about your conversation with Mr Tola on Saturday evening,' he urged.

Shashi gave him an account of the conversation and concluded by saying, 'I'm not sure how much of what Vivek said is true. He could have been planting a story, of course, but if he was, I couldn't for the life of me figure out why.'

Ranade quizzed him for another fifteen minutes and then closed his notebook.

'I appreciate your telling me all this voluntarily, Mr Kurva. You do realize, don't you, that prima facie, you have a motive – '

'Not only that,' Shashi cut in. 'I had the opportunity too…that is, if I were stupid enough to kill him in front of dozens of people the day after we quarrelled. Come on, inspector, credit me with *some* intelligence.'

'I am not – '

'Also, think through the motive, inspector. What would I gain by killing Vivek? Especially after I learnt that Purple Country shares were not purchased by him, but by firms where he was a shareholder. I know enough of the law to realize that when Vivek and I met that evening, my position was stronger than I had first assumed.'

'Mr Kurva – '

'And as far as my reputation is concerned, there is no quicker way to demolish it than kill my brother-in-law in an open bar.' Shashi stood up, his eyes boring into Ranade's. 'I will not insult *your* intelligence, inspector. Think this through and you will realize that this prima facie bullshit you refer to holds no water.'

Chapter 10

What a terrible three days! Shashi couldn't remember a worse time in his life. First the SEBI bombshell, followed by Sudakar's pointless aggression at the board meeting. Then the shock of Vivek's callousness regarding Shashi's fate, followed by Kashyap's audacity. And finally, the ultimate disaster – Vivek's death. Poor Chaaya! Shashi's eyes moistened as he thought of her forlorn wail on learning of her husband's death. She had clung to Shashi and wept her heart out. There was nothing he could offer by way of comfort. Rarely in his life had he felt so helpless. The thought of Chaaya's fatherless kids had been especially numbing.

And on top of all that, he was now a prime suspect for murder! How much worse could things get? He picked up his office bag and made for the front door. He had just opened it when his mobile rang. It was Carol calling.

'Yes, Carol? I'm just leaving for office.'

'One moment, Shashi.' Her voice was edged with anxiety. 'Barun wants to talk to you.'

'Shashi,' he heard Barun say, 'have you seen the papers?' His voice was low, urgent.

'Not yet. The last two days have been a nightmare. I'll go through them in the car. Why?'

'Your name's been dragged through the muck by the business newspaper you hate. They're hinting that you had something to do with Vivek Tola's death.'

'What!'

'Listen to what they say: "...the nature of Mr Tola's death and the speed with which it overtook him suggest that it may have been caused by a fast-acting poison." Here's some more: "The only other person at Mr Tola's table was his brother-in-law, Shashi Kurva. People at the bar allege that the two men had met there the previous evening and parted after an acrimonious exchange of words. Mr Kurva is the CEO of Purple Country Ltd. Repeated calls to his residence went unanswered." They hold you guilty without actually saying so, Shashi. The share price has dropped 20 per cent in less than an hour.'

'Of course calls weren't answered!' Shashi cried. 'We were at Vivek's house all day. The family is utterly devastated!'

'But that's not what I called about, Shashi,' Barun continued quickly. 'The investigating subcommittee has taken note of the news report and the shit has hit the fan.'

'What happened?'

'Sudakar wants you suspended – '

'What!'

'But Mr Saldana intervened to remind him that suspension on the basis of mere conjecture would leave the company open to being sued by you. But Sudakar wanted you out. Shit! I've gotta run. Carol will – '

The line went dead.

'Hello!' Shashi shouted, wanting to know more, but to no avail.

He turned back from the front door and dropped his office bag on a sofa. Carol would call back. Thirty seconds later, his mobile rang again.

'What happened?' Shashi asked, as soon as he answered the call.

'Barun had to cut it short,' Carol explained in a low voice. 'He had come out of the boardroom on the pretext of taking a printout. Then Sudakar came looking for him and he had to rush back. He's left a copy of the printout for me to read out to you before I shred it.'

'Go on.'

'It's a note from the subcommittee to the chairman. It says: "In view of Mr Shashi Kurva's possible role in the insider-trading matter under investigation by the subcommittee and the speculation in the media about his involvement in Vivek Tola's death, it is recommended that Mr Kurva absent himself from the company's offices until such time as the matter is resolved to the company's satisfaction. It may be recalled that Tola was identified by SEBI as the person who had traded in the company's shares and benefited considerably from the aforesaid transactions. He was suspected to have been in possession of inside company information." The letter is signed by Sudakar.'

Shashi had gone numb. 'Anything else?' he heard himself ask.

'No. It's a short note. Barun said that it had already been emailed to Mr Gupta. The hard copy is to be given to him when he comes in.'

'The chairman is coming to the office?'

'Sudakar requested him to do so. Uh-oh…here he is…walking straight into the boardroom. He doesn't seem pleased. What should I do now, Shashi?'

Shashi's mind moved into high gear. 'Get off the phone and shred the letter immediately,' he ordered briskly. 'We don't want Barun getting into trouble. Stay at your desk, keep your eyes and ears open and call me if anything happens. I'll stay put at home for now.'

He hung up and flung himself on to a sofa, his thoughts churning.

Sudakar! Why ever had Dheerajbhai brought the moron on the board? He had always been a bit of a nuisance, quick to pounce on anything that could potentially tarnish his precious 'independent director' image. But it was usually for the sake of appearances, rather than anything else. Never before had he put the company at risk.

But this time, it was different. Didn't it occur to Sudakar that he would hurt the company by suspending its CEO? Such an action could wipe off a chunk of the market cap. Was he doing this merely to demonstrate his powers as an independent director? Or did he genuinely believe that Shashi was guilty of insider trading? Granted, insider trading was a big red flag for an independent director.

Whatever the reason, Sudakar had daggers drawn and Shashi would do likewise. He would not back down; the fighter in him had stirred. His mind went back to the news article. What if Kamna or Chaaya had seen it? He hadn't told them about the TTX angle. He had to do that soon.

His mobile rang again.

'Shashi,' Carol said, 'Mr Gupta wants you to join him for an early lunch at the Grand Central.'

'Parel?' He glanced at his watch. 'When?'

'Twelve-fifteen. Shall I confirm?'

'Yes. Did he say why?'

'No.'

Ten minutes later, having read the offending newspaper article, Shashi sat back in the car's rear seat and gazed unseeingly through the window as his chauffeur navigated through dense traffic.

How quickly things changed! He had been a hero not four days ago. He had been declared CEO of the Year and his brand had made it to the top. TV channels had been queuing up to interview him.

He smiled wryly, wondering if they still wanted to interview him. Perhaps they did, but for an entirely different reason. He asked himself how long it would be before some TV channel crucified him in the public trials that went under the name of talk shows. He pictured some anchor somewhere rubbing his hands in glee. Reporters and cameramen might well be waiting for him when he returned to his flat. And how long before someone unearthed the insider trading angle?

His thoughts turned to Vivek. Who would have wanted to kill him? He couldn't get the image of Vivek's last few minutes in the bar lounge out of his mind. His brother-in-law had been ill at ease, even scared. Of what? Of whom? Had he been silenced by the same person or group of people so that he wouldn't divulge names? Did that cock-and-bull story about a big player have some truth to it, after all? Was there more to it, then, than was immediately apparent?

If there was, the logical thing to do now would be to meet Varma and tell him what Vivek had said. He had to find out more about his brother-in-law's dealings. Kashyap's men had been in the bar lounge when Vivek died. They might have seen something.

He decided to go to SEBI after the meeting with Gupta.

A short while later, he was sitting at a corner table with Gupta and another man clad in black trousers, a white shirt and a grey jacket – Dheerajbhai. He was a slight man with thinning hair and pale skin that revealed his aversion to sunlight. But the five-foot-two frame belied a pugnacity that could be detected even from a fleeting glance at the deep-set eyes under greying brows.

The founder and the largest shareholder of Purple Country, though high on Forbes India's Top 50 list, was a man who stayed out of the public eye, preferring to let his professional CEOs represent his companies. His skill lay in making the right investments and getting the right people to run his companies, the day-to-day operations of which he seldom interfered in. While Purple Country had been one of his smaller assets when he created it, Shashi knew it was close to his heart.

An astute businessman, Dheerajbhai had chosen to enter the e-commerce space with a niche offering. While most e-commerce players had wooed the masses with the hope of attracting millions of customers and stratospheric valuations, Dheerajbhai had targeted a small but wealthy segment of luxury-goods buyers. That meant that he neither needed to spend a fortune on marketing and advertising nor finance huge discounts to attract customers.

Not having to burn cash as other e-commerce players did,

he didn't need money from private equity firms. His aversion to having venture capitalists on the board was well known, as was his disapproval of the valuation game they played. Their short-term orientation, he argued, hurt companies.

'I will be Purple Country's father,' he was reported to have said. 'I don't want it to be the bastard of a dozen venture capitalists.'

By not having to dilute his stake, he had remained the single largest shareholder. And once he felt the 'child' had grown up sufficiently, he took it public and listed it.

'I was delayed in Paris on Friday and couldn't make it to the board meeting,' he began. 'Unfortunately, Rohit couldn't make it at short notice.'

Rohit was Dheerajbhai's son, who occasionally represented his father at board meetings.

'I would have put an end to this nonsense right away.'

'Sudakar is an independent director, Dheerajbhai,' Gupta said quietly. 'He must be given space. The last thing we want is an issue of governance.'

'I understand, Mr Gupta. But at what cost? He's ruining the company. We don't want a director running riot.'

'With due respect, Dheerajbhai, I had warned you about him. He likes to wear his independence on his sleeve.'

'I should have heeded your advice, Mr Gupta. Anyway, his term ends in a month. I'll ask Koel if she will join the board.'

'Koel?'

'Koel Handa, my cousin.'

'Cousin? Will she qualify as an independent director?'

'You bet.' Dheerajbhai smiled. 'She meets every criterion. Besides, as a woman, she would bring diversity to the board.' He broke a breadstick with his thin hands and growled, 'As far as Sudakar is concerned, I'll see to it that none of his directorships are renewed.'

'The man is a bull in a china shop.'

'Screw Sudakar!' Dheerajbhai turned his full attention to his CEO. 'Listen, Shashi, I want you to know that you have my confidence and my unstinting support. I don't believe this nonsense about you passing insider information to your brother-in-law. I know you well enough to be convinced that you are incapable of such an act. If information is being passed, it is by someone else. And I want you to find him.

'SEBI investigating our company is a very serious matter. It needs to be handled with discretion and Sudakar is certainly not the man for it. I think it is best if Mr Gupta as the professional, non-founder chairman takes it on. I would like you or your office to call the SEBI men who had visited and put them in touch with Mr Gupta's office. He will take it up from there.'

'Of course,' Shashi said.

He would be going to SEBI, anyway, after this meeting to find out if Varma or Kashyap could throw some light on Vivek's death. He would also speak to Varma about Gupta.

'Meanwhile,' Dheerajbhai continued, 'I want you to continue running the company. So does Mr Gupta and all other major shareholders. There's no question of your leaving. Am I clear?'

Shashi nodded. He knew that more was coming.

'But Mr Gupta is right,' Dheerajbhai continued. 'We don't want Sudakar telling the world that the promoters are thwarting him, an independent director. That will raise a stink which, coming on top of all that has happened, could wipe off half our market cap. We *must* be perceived to be supporting him; we have no option. It is imperative that we acquiesce to his request – couched as the subcommittee's request, if you please – to keep you away from the office.'

'Okay,' Shashi said cautiously. 'Shall I go on leave?'

'Exactly! You are voluntarily removing yourself from the office premises to facilitate an independent and fair investigation.'

'Who will run the business?'

'Rohit will be deputed for the duration of your leave. You will be back inside a month, I assure you. The heavens won't fall in a month.'

'Is Rohit willing?'

'Yes. It will be a kind of training for him in an executive role. Should do him a world of good too and keep him away from that birdbrain of an actress he's dating. He will do as you direct – if you wish to stay involved from the outside, that is.'

'But Dheerajbhai, I am not an easy person to work with – '

'Don't I know it, Shashi?' Dheerajbhai smiled broadly. 'But you have turned this company around. You took the share price from ₹9 to ₹514. As a shareholder, Rohit knows where his priorities lie. Egos won't come in the way, I assure you.'

'Mr Gupta?' Shashi turned to the chairman.

'I agree,' the elderly man said slowly. 'I can spend some time if needed.'

Shashi took a deep breath and nodded.

'Okay, let's do it.'

'Excellent!' Dheerajbhai's smile was more of a grin now. 'Send Mr Gupta an email right away and follow it up with a hard copy. When you're on holiday, put your mind to catching the bloody insider who is leaking information.'

'Are you sure you want me to track the person, Dheerajbhai?'

Dheerajbhai looked at him sharply. 'Of course. Why do you even ask?'

'Because I'm not supposed to interfere with the subcommittee's investigation.' He raised a hand to pre-empt a premature response. 'Having said that, I do want to conduct my own investigation. I can do it outside the office and without interfering with the subcommittee's inquiry.'

'How?' Gupta asked.

'By analysing data from our share registrar. Do I have your support?'

Gupta nodded. 'As long as you give Sudakar no reason to claim that you are jeopardizing his efforts.'

'I won't. I'm hiring a data scientist to help me with the analysis. We won't even work in the office. I'll brief you when I come up with tangible results.'

▪

An hour later, Shashi was waiting impatiently at SEBI for the receptionist to return. She had asked him to wait and had gone into the office. He had asked to see S.K. Varma and shown her Varma's card. That had been over five minutes ago.

His only lead to Vivek's killer was Kashyap's men, who had been in the bar lounge during the murder. They *must* have seen something. He didn't have Kashyap's card, but Varma would have his contacts. Meeting Varma had become critical now.

The receptionist presently returned and apologized. 'I'm sorry to have kept you waiting, sir. This way, please.'

She led him down a corridor, turned into an aisle and knocked at a door.

'Executive Director?' Shashi asked, studying the unfamiliar name on the door. 'This isn't Mr Varma's office, is it?'

'No sir. Mr Kulkarni asked to see you. He heads investigations.'

Hearing a 'Come in!' from inside, the receptionist pushed open the door and ushered Shashi into a room holding a large desk, several chairs, a couple of sofas and two long bookshelves. Behind the desk, polishing his glasses, sat an elderly, grey-haired man. Occupying one of the chairs at his desk was a man busy studying some papers. Ranade.

That confounded policeman, Shashi thought. Why did he have to be here now? That too in Kulkarni's office! Why was Kulkarni keen to meet Shashi in Ranade's presence? Had the inspector told him about Vivek? And that Shashi was his prime suspect?

'Come in, Mr Kurva,' Kulkarni said, waving him to a chair. 'Take a seat. I presume you know Inspector Ranade.'

'Thank you,' Shashi said, sitting down and ignoring Ranade. 'I came to see Mr S.K. Varma.'

'On what matter, may I ask?'

'He had come to my office to discuss a matter relating to trading of my company's shares.'

'You are the CEO of Purple Country, right?'

Shashi nodded.

'And what was this matter you speak of?'

'I would rather discuss it with Mr Varma. It's sensitive.'

'Was it about insider trading?'

Shashi threw Ranade a cold look. 'Yes.'

'Can you describe S.K. Varma for me, please?' Seeing Shashi frown, he smiled and lifted his hand off the table. 'Do humour me, please. It will all be clear to you in a moment.'

'A bearded man…perhaps in his early forties…no remarkable features that I can recall.'

'I see…' Kulkarni removed his spectacles and began polishing them. 'You see, Mr Kurva, the S.K. Varma whose card is with you retired three years ago. And as fate would have it, he passed away last year. There is no S.K. Varma in SEBI now.'

'What!' Shashi cast Ranade another glance. The man, he noticed, was studying him with an inscrutable expression. 'But he showed me his identity card!'

'Identity cards are not difficult to forge, Mr Kurva.'

'He spoke the way I would expect a SEBI officer to speak. He spoke knowledegably about the stock market and insider trading. It never occurred to me that he could be an impostor!'

Shashi's mind was in a whirl. If Varma wasn't from SEBI, where was he from? What was his interest in Purple Country? What connection did that have to Vivek's murder?

'The man who came to your office was, indeed, an impostor,' Kulkarni continued slowly. He gestured towards the police officer. 'Inspector Ranade came here half an hour back with the same question.'

Shashi looked from the inspector to Kulkarni and back.

'Any idea who this impostor might be?' he asked.

'Not yet,' Ranade answered. 'We'd just established that there was no S.K. Varma in any of the SEBI offices, when the receptionist came in with your card.'

'Why would someone want to impersonate a SEBI officer? What did he stand to gain?'

Kulkarni and Ranade gazed at him silently.

'Well?' Shashi asked, perplexed, looking for an answer.

'We were hoping you could tell us,' Ranade said.

'I haven't a clue. The audacity of it!' Shashi thumped his fist on the table. 'Damn it, inspector, he boldly walks into my office, sends me into a tizzy and gets me into trouble with Vivek, my board and you. How the hell would *I* know why he did it?'

'He also sent Mr Tola into a tizzy.'

'So?'

'Just a line of thought. Can you see any motive there?

'No.' Shashi frowned deeply. 'There was another man with him – Kashyap.'

'Do you have his card?'

Shashi shook his head. 'He didn't offer a card. He didn't even mention where he was from. Only when he called me the day before yesterday did I insist on knowing. He said he was from the Economic Offences Wing.'

'EOW, Mumbai?' Ranade asked.

'Yes.'

'There is no one by that name in the EOW, Mumbai. We work regularly with them. I know all the people there. Can you describe him?'

'A middle-aged man...sporting a goatee...had eerie light brown eyes.'

Ranade grimaced. 'Coloured contact lenses, I'd wager. Were the edges of his beard smooth?'

'I think so...so was Varma's beard, now that you mention it.'

'Disguise.'

'Wait!' Shashi said, sitting up and pulling out his mobile. 'I should have the number Kashyap called from. He called...let's see...it must have been at eleven or eleven-thirty in the morning... Here it is!'

He held out the mobile for Ranade to look at. The inspector took down the number and made a couple of calls. Five minutes later, he hung up and turned to Shashi.

'Dead end. It's a public phone booth in Ballard Estate.'

Chapter 11

Sitting in the rear seat of his car, Shashi steeled himself for the inevitable moment when he would have to tell Chaaya that Vivek had been murdered. He dreaded that no less than the prospect of having to inform her eventually about the finger of suspicion pointing at him. How would she react, he wondered, if she believed him to be the culprit? What argument would he use to defend himself? Would unpleasant scenes follow? Would the situation create a rift between Kamna and her sister?

He made an effort to pull himself out of the vicious maelstrom of negative thoughts that seemed to be engulfing him and chided himself for even entertaining them. There was little he could do to remedy the situation. He just had to tell Chaaya what he must and deal with her reaction when it came. He pushed emotion away and let the logical side of his mind take over, trying to dispassionately analyse the recent events. Stripped of sentiment and peripheral events, the crux of the matter was this:

Two impostors had boldly accused him of insider trading and made him confront Vivek. They had silently watched the confrontation from a distance. The next day, an unnerved Vivek had sought to make peace with Shashi. At that point, someone had killed him. In public. And with clinical accuracy.

What did that reveal? Pitifully little – and it was all entirely circumstantial.

First, this was a planned, organized affair, involving multiple individuals. It was not only about someone leaking Purple Country's privileged information to Vivek. There was something more to it.

Second, these men were resourceful and ruthless. They had executed their plan perfectly. The manner in which they had killed Vivek was chilling in its boldness and precision. Neurotoxin! God in heaven! Shashi shivered involuntarily.

But why had they killed Vivek? And why had they involved Shashi? If they wanted to kill Vivek, why hadn't they just done it? What role had Shashi inadvertently played in the murder? What had Purple Country got to do with all this? Had insider trading actually taken place, as the impostors claimed? Or was that too a consummate lie?

But the fact remained that Vivek had talked about privileged information from Purple Country floating around in the market. What was it that he'd said? '*...there is inside information from Purple Country in the market. I don't know who is leaking it, I don't know whom it is leaked to, but I know that it exists.*' Had Vivek lied too? As Varma and Kashyap had? Who could he believe in this smoke-and-mirrors affair? Shashi's head had begun spinning. He couldn't make head or tail of it.

Should he have discussed Vivek's observations with Kulkarni? That would have been dicey. A CEO speaking of insider trading in his own company! He would have to discuss that with Gupta first. Shit! He had forgotten all about Dheerajbhai's request to connect SEBI with Gupta's office. Perhaps it was for the best. They had better reassess the situation in light of Varma being an impostor.

He came out of his reverie and looked up as the car slowed to a stop; he had reached Chaaya's apartment block. He stepped out and made his way to the lift with leaden feet, his guts knotted in anxiety.

Fifteen minutes later, he was with Kamna and Chaaya in the study that had served as Vivek's home office. Exhausted by all they had been through, Chaaya's children were finally asleep, getting their much-needed rest. The comings and goings of people he didn't recognize had prompted Shashi to talk to Chaaya in the study, rather than in the drawing room where there would be no privacy.

Svelte, refined and understated, where Vivek had been corpulent, crass and loud, Chaaya was the very antithesis of her late husband. She had taken care to maintain her figure even after two children and wasn't perceptibly heavier than she had been earlier. When she spoke, it was in low, dignified tones. The words she chose were polite, measured. Never had Shashi known her to swear or bitch about anyone. She was one of the most agreeable people he knew and he had taken an instant liking to her when they'd been introduced for the first time.

He wondered for the umpteenth time how she had consented to marry someone like Vivek. Perhaps his late brother-in-law hadn't always been quite so repugnant. But from the time Shashi had known her, Chaaya's attitude to her husband had been one of fierce devotion, a fact Shashi found inexplicable. From what Kamna had said about their family, Vivek had not treated Chaaya particularly well. Yet she had never failed to stand up for him.

'Chaaya, I have something to tell you,' Shashi began, looking nervously into her bloodshot eyes. 'I didn't bring it up earlier because I wasn't sure of it myself.'

'That Vivek was killed?' Chaaya asked softly, her expression revealing a curious mixture of grief and hardness. But her voice was steady. 'That someone deliberately poisoned him?'

'You know?' Shashi gasped.

Chaaya was so composed and had taken the news with such equanimity that it threw Shashi off balance. It was almost as if she had expected it.

She nodded slowly. 'One of Vivek's partners showed me the news article that said he might have been poisoned.'

'Then…then you would have seen my name mentioned too in this context.'

She nodded again.

'Chaaya…I had nothing to do with it. You've got to believe me! You mustn't – ' Shashi broke off as a perplexed expression twisted Chaaya's face.

'Shashi!' she exclaimed. 'Don't be silly! Of course, you had nothing to do with it! I know better than to believe some silly newspaper report. They're just trying to sensationalize the situation by raking up as much muck as they can.'

Relief flooded Shashi's being and he sat back feeling weak, at a loss for words. His guts felt like a tightly wound watch spring that had suddenly been released. All his anxiety had been for nothing! He could almost laugh with relief! He glanced at Kamna. Her grave face sobered him down.

'But a part of what the paper said was true,' he went on. 'Vivek and I had a bit of a spat on Friday evening.'

'I know,' Chaaya nodded. 'Vivek said it was a minor matter – something about him buying shares of your company without your knowledge. He said he might have made a mistake.'

'Did he? I don't know what happened after that, but Vivek seemed worried when he called me the next day. And then you know the rest. It was a terrible shock.'

Chaaya nodded, her eyes reflective. 'I'm not entirely surprised that Vivek was killed,' she said, making Shashi's eyes swivel back to her in astonishment. 'Aghast, yes,' she went on. 'But not surprised.'

'Not surprised?' Shashi was flummoxed. He knew Chaaya wouldn't say such a thing lightly.

'Successful men have enemies and Vivek was no exception,' she continued. Was there a hint of pride in her voice? 'Besides, he dealt with large amounts of money. Crores. From the moment I was given the news, I suspected it was no accident. I knew it couldn't have been food poisoning.'

'Who?' Shashi was about to ask, but the word died on his lips as he sensed his wife's warning gaze on him. He glanced at her and lapsed into silence.

'Do you know, he always kept a loaded pistol on his bedside table?' Chaaya went on, her eyes contemplating some distant horizon through the window. 'On the night before he died, he slept with it under his pillow. He had appointed two bodyguards to accompany him everywhere since Wednesday. Something had made him wary, afraid.'

'Do you know what it could have been?' Shashi asked gently.

'We'll find out.' Chaaya's face had set in hard lines. 'Pandey Bhaiya is back in town. He knows who all had a bone to pick with Vivek.' Her face softened as her gentle eyes returned to Shashi's face. 'Did he really die the way you said he did, Shashi? Or is there something unpleasant that you've kept from me?'

Shashi shook his head. 'It was no different from the way I described it. I'm told once paralysis and numbness set in, there wouldn't have been any pain.'

'What do the police say?'

'A poison called TTX, put, most probably, in a snack – chilli cheese toast.'

'Vivek loved chilli cheese toast,' she whispered. Tears streamed down her face. 'Thank goodness you didn't have it too!'

'I don't like cheese, unless – '

'Oh yes, I forgot. Well, thank heavens for that!' She tossed her sister a quick glance. 'You need to be careful, Shashi. We still don't know who did this or why.'

'Oh, I forgot. Inspector Ranade from the police will be coming here.'

'Police? Here?' Chaaya sat up erect, her eyes flashing. 'Why?'

'To talk to you...' He paused, taken aback by her vehemence at the very mention of the police. 'Chaaya, the inspector needs – '

'They have to investigate, Chaaya,' Kamna intervened in a soothing voice, laying her hand on her sister's arm. 'They'll simply ask you a few questions and leave.'

'What questions?' Chaaya's consternation was growing rapidly.

'They will want to establish the motive for...you know...Vivek's death.'

'I won't tell them a thing!' Her face grew a shade paler as a thought struck her. 'Will they search the house? They *always* want to search the house.'

'I don't believe so. What do you think, Shashi?'

'I don't think they will search the house. But why should that matter, Chaaya?'

'Wait here,' she said sharply and hurried out of the room.

'Why is she so afraid of the police?' Shashi asked Kamna in a low voice.

'Their experience with the police has not been pleasant. Their house has been searched a number of times in the past and whenever a lone police officer paid a visit, it was invariably to chisel money off Vivek. Bakshish, they call it. Chaaya naturally regards the police with grave suspicion. She has no faith in them – nor in our legal system.'

'Wow! I didn't know that. That isn't normal, is it?'

Kamna shrugged. 'That was how it was in my family too. I remember one occasion when a police raid of our home was conducted over an entire week. Papa got wind of it beforehand and hid stuff.'

'Stuff?'

'Diamonds. He hid handfuls of diamonds in the flowerpots lining the balconies. He took them out of their packets and mixed them with the soil in the pots. There are stories about my grandfather dropping bags of gold into the well located on the grounds of our ancestral house in Jaipur, just minutes before the police arrived.'

Shashi was stunned. This was the first time that Kamna had spoken about her family's brushes with the law.

'But this is murder, Kamna!' he whispered. 'The police *have* to investigate.'

'I know. But Chaaya's feelings about them are too deeply ingrained to be wished away.'

'The motive lies somewhere in Vivek's dealings. Surely, she understands that? The police must be given access to Vivek's business transactions.'

'Shh! Let's not talk about it until we're home. The whole business with the police isn't for us to decide on. It's Chaaya's. For now, just accept that Vivek didn't trust the police one bit and nor does Chaaya. She will try and find the killer herself – '

Sudden realization dawned on Shashi. 'Pandey Bhaiya?' he whispered.

Kamna nodded. 'Remember, whatever Chaaya tells you is in *total* confidence. You are family to her. Don't even think of passing it on to the police. Understand?'

'But Kamna, how can I deliberately conceal evidence?'

She shrugged. 'Papa used to say that hearsay was not evidence. Your silence doesn't go against the law unless you witness something and suppress it.'

'That's not how I see it! Nor do you, as far as I know. I *cannot* conceal evidence!'

'Shh! We'll talk about that at home, okay? Meanwhile, remember that Chaaya trusts you implicitly and will confide in you. There is no worse crime you can commit than to be a snitch.'

'Snitch!' Shashi exclaimed, but decided not to contest it.

Over the three years he had known Kamna, she had not spoken much about her family. He knew that they were wealthy jewellers and that her father had taken up the business his own father had set up in Jaipur. She had told Shashi about the family moving to

Mumbai some 30 years ago. But their distrust of the police and the legal system was new to him. Kamna had never mentioned it before.

Of Vivek and his family, Shashi knew still less. While Chaaya and Kamna visited each other every week, their husbands hardly met outside family functions. While Shashi always looked forward to Chaaya dropping in, he could count on his fingertips the number of times he had visited them at home. He was now discovering new and disturbing things about the Tolas.

'By the way,' Shashi continued, 'why did you glare at me when I began speaking to Chaaya?'

'To even suggest that she may have suspected you is an insult to her, Shashi.'

'What!'

'You are family and she will trust you for that alone. Fortunately, she didn't take offence when you brought up the subject. Thanks to my repeating it to her often enough, she accepts that you aren't quite familiar with the ways of our family...and are different.'

The door opened and Chaaya gestured to Kamna to join her. Left alone, Shashi sat back and tried to sort out the tangle in his head. Things were happening too fast and he didn't seem to be in control of anything.

There was so much he didn't understand about Kamna's family – their way of thinking, the people they trusted – and those they didn't – and the secrecy shrouding their business dealings. And who was this Pandey Bhaiya Chaaya seemed to count so much on? That had sounded ominous.

After a moment of introspection, during which he pursued these different strands of thought in vain, he gave up and decided that the best way was to ask Kamna when they were alone again. A few minutes later, the door opened and the sisters came in, with Kamna carrying a black wooden box, which she put into a cloth bag.

'Come,' she said quietly to Shashi. 'Let's go before the police arrive.'

'What's in the box?' he asked in a low voice.

'Things that Vivek didn't want anyone – especially the police – setting their eyes on. Make sure you behave as if nothing is amiss. Just forget about this bag and remember not to bring up the topic in the car.'

Shit, he swore under his breath. Matters were spiralling out of control. Was he now becoming an accessory to the crime of concealing evidence? He wondered for a second if he should take a stand on the matter then and there, but his regard for Chaaya and his wife's loyalty to her sibling came in the way. Confused and alarmed, he followed Kamna out of the house.

As the chauffeur drove them home, they did not exchange a word. Kamna sat staring silently out of the window, her arm resting lightly on the cloth bag. Glancing at her, Shashi realized that he had never seen her usually amiable face set in such harsh lines. Her jaw was clenched, her eyes narrowed, her lips compressed. There seemed to be an air of steely determination about her that he hadn't seen before. At the same time, she appeared to be unnaturally, disconcertingly calm.

Something was changing in her; and that something had surfaced in the past couple of days. For the moment, she bore an unsettling resemblance to her late father, who could be utterly ruthless when he believed the situation demanded it. With trepidation, Shashi wondered what lay in store.

When they reached home, Kamna quietly put away the wooden box in her steel almirah and returned to the drawing room. In her hand was a small notebook.

'Kamna,' Shashi said more emphatically than he had intended, 'we have to talk about this. I *cannot* become an accessory – '

'I know,' she said quietly. 'That's why I brought this for you to see. Here, have a look at it.'

He opened the small, dog-eared notebook and flipped through the first few pages. They were filled with neat rows of incomprehensible strings of letters and numbers. Each row was written in one of three colours – green, blue or black. Most of the entries had been neatly struck out with a single line through the entire row. Some rows had red markings in the margin.

'What is this?' he asked.

'Code.'

'What sort of code? Looks like gibberish to me.'

'Far from it. Tell me, what was Vivek's business?'

'He was a broker.'

'And?'

'A financier?'

Kamna nodded. 'A financier has to keep records of how much money he lent to whom and on what terms. This is Vivek's record. An old one, from the look of it.'

'Why couldn't he keep records in a spreadsheet or a computer system?'

'And have the whole world know about his dealings?'

Shashi looked up with a perplexed air. This was getting murkier. 'Why not? What did he have to hide?'

Kamna let out a sigh and her face took on a tolerant expression.

'A humongous amount of money changes hands every day in this city,' she said. 'And not all of it is by account payee cheques. A lot of transactions are off the books. Their records have to be kept somewhere.'

'How do you know about this? I thought you cared little for the world of finance and money.'

Shashi was beginning to get a sinking feeling. The trepidation he had felt in the car had not been misplaced.

'I do. But I also come from a family of jewellers. Family proprietorships are run very differently from corporate businesses. How many of the jewellery trade's financial transactions do you think are shown in books of accounts?'

Shashi shrugged.

'Very little,' Kamna continued. 'A mere fraction. And what is shown is often fictitious and is worked backwards from how much sales they want to declare. They use an elaborate system of chits and codes to keep track of the vast amounts of money and gold that change hands every day. These, I am told, work as well as any computerized accounting system in the corporate world.'

Shashi stared mutely at his wife as the first glimmerings of insight into her family dawned on him. Now things were starting to make some sense. He recalled Chaaya saying that Vivek had dealt in crores of rupees. He had kept codified records, because large chunks of the transactions were outside the formal system of banks and taxes. Chaaya had also mentioned that Vivek had enemies and would sleep with his gun within reach. No wonder she had not been surprised by his murder.

If Vivek had been a part of a murky world that had its own way of keeping track of who owed how much to whom, they would have had their own laws, their own methods of enforcement too. Pandey Bhaiya! So that's where he came in!

Shashi's eyes returned to the dog-eared notebook and he studied the code with new interest. If each line represented a transaction, something in that line would also represent a name. Something other than the transaction amount and the terms. In which case, the clues to Vivek's killer lay somewhere in these pages.

'Can you read this code?' he asked Kamna.

'I won't.'

'Why not?' Shashi was struggling to understand the curious code of honour that ran in her family.

'Because it is Chaaya's property, not mine. It's not a line I will cross.'

'But – '

Kamna cut him off with a raised hand.

'You know how all of this family stuff works, Shashi?'

'Tell me.'

'Trust. It runs on trust. If trust within a family is betrayed, the whole system collapses. But blood is thicker than water. Some bonds can never be broken. If ever they are, retribution is swift and grim.'

Shashi's eyes widened and he recalled Chaaya's words. Understanding dawned. He was family to her; she trusted him implicitly. She would not suspect him of Vivek's murder unless there was a very strong reason for it. Newspaper articles didn't count. Whether he wanted it or not, he was a part of the mess. Shit!

If Chaaya trusted him so much, how much more must she trust her sister? Kamna was the person she was closest to. His sinking feeling returned as his thoughts went to the wooden box. *What was Kamna hiding from the police? That too in his house!*

He was Ranade's prime suspect and something related to Vivek's death was being hidden in his house. Bloody hell! Talk about culpability!

'We can't hide evidence in our home, Kamna,' he said, trying to sound resolute. 'This *must* go back to Chaaya's place.'

'Don't be silly! It can't be kept there. You know why.'

'Somewhere else, then. I don't want to be part of this deception.'

'Deception? We're helping Chaaya. She has nobody else!'

'Try and understand, Kamna.' Shashi tried to sound reasonable. 'I am suspected of aiding Vivek in insider trading. And of killing him after our spat in the bar. I cannot hide evidence in my house.'

'Is that so?' She snatched back the notebook from him and turned towards her room. 'I can keep my sister's things in my house. If it ever comes to that, I'll tell the police that I kept them here without your knowledge.'

'Listen, Kamna – '

'*You* listen, Shashi!'

Kamna had spun around and was confronting him, her words almost hissing through her teeth. He had never seen her like this.

'There are only two people in this world who matter to me – you and Chaaya,' she told him. 'Whoever killed Vivek has hurt both of you. Deeply. I will get back at them. Nothing else matters now, understand? *Nothing!*'

'But the police – '

'Screw the police! Pandey Bhaiya will find the killer. You and I will do everything to help him and Chaaya. Come, it's time to get back to her house and be with her before the police get there.'

'But – '

'*Shashi!*' Kamna's eyes were aflame with an emotion he didn't dare try to identify. 'You are like a brother to her. She needs you. She has nobody to lean on – just the two of us. And there are matters on which I'm not qualified to advise her. She'll need your help. Don't let her down!'

Kamna turned on her heel and strode away, leaving Shashi stunned. The feeling of dread deepened as he tried to sort out the dilemma in his mind. On the one hand, he didn't want to lie to Ranade or withhold anything from him. That would only deepen the policeman's suspicions. On the other, he was getting more deeply embroiled in Vivek's affairs. Try as he might, he could not seem to avoid learning more about his dubious dealings.

As for Kamna, this was a different woman from the one he thought he knew so well. The arty, easy-going woman he loved, the one who was quite indifferent to money and the things it could buy, was nowhere in sight. In her place was a cold, ruthless woman who had little regard for the law.

She had told him on their wedding night that she wanted to escape from a world where only money mattered; a world where right or wrong was defined by how much one gained or lost; a world where laws were impediments to be worked around. She had been afraid that if she lingered there for long, she too would become a part of the system she despised.

Kamna had wanted to leave it all behind, to not even refer to it in passing. She looked forward to a lifetime with a man who valued rectitude and loyalty. Once her parents had passed away, just a year after her wedding, she had left the business and her inheritance in Chaaya's capable hands. At last, Kamna was living the life she wanted.

But Vivek's murder and the attack on Shashi's integrity had awakened something in her. Something that frightened him, something that he didn't know how to deal with.

Swearing under his breath, Shashi picked up the house keys and followed his wife out to the car.

Chapter 12

Ranade got off his Qualis a couple of hundred feet from the upmarket apartment block he was heading for and slowly walked the rest of the way, taking in the scene. Abdul had told him that every floor of the building contained only one flat and Vivek owned four of its six flats, in addition to the penthouse.

Two Audis, one BMW and Vivek's black Jaguar stood among the pillars with some smaller cars. Several men stood chatting around a water cooler on the pavement outside the gate and a few more were strolling inside the compound. To Ranade's practised eye, a couple of them looked to be private security guards. Down the lane beyond the gate was a tiny temple, abutting the wall at the far corner of the compound. The small house of worship housed a single stone idol protected by a locked grille door.

As Ranade strolled up, a policeman approached and saluted him.

'What's been happening?' the inspector asked in Marathi.

'People have been coming and going, sir,' replied the policeman. 'Most stay for a short while and leave.'

'Is the prayer meeting over?'

'Yes sir. Finished in the morning.'

'Any visitors in the house now?'

'Only Madam's sister and brother-in-law. They've practically been staying here since Tola Saab died.'

'What's the story behind the water cooler?'

'Tola Saab had it installed three years back. It offers much-needed relief to passers-by on muggy days like this.'

Ranade nodded and made his way to the gate. His mental picture of Vivek Tola was gradually taking shape. If what Abdul had learnt from the police grapevine was true, Vivek had tons of unaccounted wealth and his own little band of strongmen. The successful and reportedly ruthless man had also taken care to build his image of a benevolent patron in the area where he lived. The water cooler was a part of his image-building efforts.

Crooks occupying high positions in the corporate world tended to boost their public image by getting themselves on the boards of charitable organizations and NGOs. Businessmen and politicians who looted the country bought peace with their conscience by dropping chunks of gold into Tirupathi's *hundi*s. Vivek had chosen his own way to elevate his standing in the community where he resided. The water cooler would not be the sole gift. There would been others too.

The security guard at the gate, having seen the policeman salute Ranade, did likewise and let him pass. A minute later, the inspector rang the bell placed discreetly on the wall beside the ornate teak door on the second floor.

'Madam *hai?*' he asked, as a liveried man opened the door.

'*Aap kaun?*' the man asked politely.

Ranade was not in uniform.

Before the inspector could answer, Shashi came up behind the man.

'Come in, inspector,' he said and opened the door wide. 'Please take a seat. You've come to see Chaaya, I suppose?'

'Thank you. Yes.'

Ranade stepped into a vast drawing room that looked like the suite of some exclusive seven-star hotel. A finely veined Italian marble floor, a false ceiling with concealed lighting, soft leather sofas, gilt trimmings and an exquisite Persian carpet left the visitor in no doubt about the extent of Vivek's wealth. Gleaming gold strands woven into heavy drapes complemented gilt-trimmed display cases full of priceless crystal figurines. But the object that struck Ranade as soon as he stepped in was a two-foot-high 'Om' symbol made of clear crystal. Concealed in and under the exquisite creation were tiny, virtually invisible LEDs that lent the artefact a mystical glow, as though it were not quite of this world.

Ranade stared at the crystal object, recalling that in Shashi's flat, the pride of place was occupied by a painting of a little girl with a candle. If Shashi's drawing room was about elegance and refinement, Vivek's seemed to be about an unabashed display of opulence. Ranade wondered what kind of a woman Vivek's widow was likely to be.

He took his place on a sofa and waited as Shashi disappeared into the corridor at the far end of the drawing room. A minute later, a woman clad completely in white came out from the lobby, followed by another .

'Namaste,' the first one said in a muted voice, joining her palms together. 'I'm Chaaya Tola. And this is my sister, Kamna, Shashi's wife.'

As Ranade rose and reciprocated with the same gesture, Chaaya waved him back to the sofa.

'Please be seated, inspector.' She sat on the sofa opposite him and adjusted her sari pleats. Kamna sat down beside her, while Shashi stood at a distance.

'May I offer you something?' Chaaya asked politely. 'Some tea or juice, perhaps?'

'Thank you.' Ranade adopted a soft, courteous tone. 'Just some water will do.'

Chaaya nodded to the liveried man and returned her attention to Ranade.

'First, may I offer my deepest condolences, Mrs Tola,' the inspector began. 'I am terribly sorry to impose myself on you at a time like this. I hope you understand.'

Ranade thought he detected a fleeting look of surprise on Chaaya's face as he spoke. It seemed to him that she had also relaxed a wee bit.

In the very brief interaction he had just had with her, the inspector was aware of a growing feeling of surprise within himself. He was not sure what he had expected, but he had not anticipated meeting a refined woman who spoke impeccable English in a modulated voice and displayed perfect manners. Perhaps the vulgar opulence of the drawing room had misled him. He realized, somewhat belatedly, that the drawing room was a reflection of Vivek's personality rather than Chaaya's. He had been the dominant one in their relationship.

'I do understand, inspector,' Chaaya responded. 'We must go through this. Please ask what you need to.' She turned as Shashi made to leave the room. 'Shashi, I'd rather you stayed. Please. I'm sure the inspector won't mind.'

Given no real choice, Ranade remained silent and studied Chaaya as Shashi took a chair placed along the wall. Her face was drawn and weighed down with grief. She seemed to be making an effort to hold herself together.

'You are aware that your husband died of poisoning, aren't you?' he began gently.

Chaaya nodded.

'We have reason to suspect that it was not an accident.'

'Shashi told me.' There was a tremor in Chaaya's voice now. 'Vivek may have been murdered.'

Ranade silently heaved a sigh of relief. This was always a difficult part of the procedure, but Chaaya had made it easier for him by being so direct. Even as he made a quick assessment of her character, he found himself admiring her fortitude. Although her shoulders were bowed with grief, she seemed to be in control of herself. She chose her words with care, aware of the image she projected. Everything about her manner was measured, thought through.

Which meant that she was not going to let her guard down in the presence of a policeman. Given who her late husband had been and what his business dealings involved, that was hardly surprising.

Ranade couldn't help thinking that Chaaya Tola was very different from Shashi, who had made no effort to conceal anything. Despite being the CEO of a very successful company, he had been quick to reveal his true feelings and quicker to pick up the cudgels and defend himself when he realized that he was being perceived by Ranade as the prime suspect. Even after this discovery which must have shaken him, Shashi had been far from secretive, sharing all the details about Varma's visit and the subsequent board meeting, although he knew full well that the facts he had disclosed to the inspector showed him in a bad light. There was a certain uncompromising honesty about him that Ranade found admirable.

But not so with Vivek Tola's widow. The inspector sensed that she would play a cat-and-mouse game with him, revealing as little as possible without giving him reason to suspect that she was holding something back. While these thoughts passed through his mind, the inspector noted with the seasoned police officer's detachment that Chaaya's face was remarkably attractive, its most striking features being a pair of intelligent eyes.

'Can you think of a reason why anyone would want your husband dead, Mrs Tola?' he continued.

Chaaya shook her head slowly, her gaze fixed on the carpet. Something between a sob and a shudder shook her shoulders.

'No,' she replied in a voice low enough to be a whisper. 'I don't have the faintest idea.'

'Did he have any enemies?'

'How could such a kind man have enemies, inspector?' Chaaya's red-rimmed eyes rose to meet Ranade's. 'Ask the people around the building. You saw the temple outside?'

Ranade nodded. 'And the water cooler too.'

'He installed it so that poor people could get clean, cool water to drink on a hot summer day. The temple, small as it is, feeds a dozen people every day. Vivek used to sponsor the Ganpathi pandal in this lane every year.'

'Was he a God-fearing man, Mrs Tola?'

Chaaya nodded and dropped her gaze. 'Puja every morning before breakfast.'

'What about his business, Mrs Tola? Did he have rivals?'

'All successful men have rivals, inspector. I don't think my husband was an exception. But not being directly involved in his professional dealings, I can't say for sure.'

'He ran a sharebroking business, didn't he?'

'A pretty big one.'

'He would have bought and sold shares for many people. Any…' He left the sentence hanging.

After a moment's pause, Chaaya lifted her gaze and fixed it on Ranade. He experienced a twinge of regret as he noted how frosty her eyes had become.

'I wouldn't know, inspector,' she said carefully. 'I'm sure you'll find all the records you need at the office. Abhishek Kumar, the general manager, will be there to help you. But if you are hinting at Vivek's argument with Shashi at the bar, let me assure you that it was a trivial matter.'

Ranade hid his surprise at her forthrightness. His regard for this gentle-mannered, yet firm, lady went up a notch.

'There is a suggestion that Mr Tola may have been involved in insider trading of Purple Country shares,' he continued. 'Would you be able to throw any light on that matter?'

'No, inspector, I would not.' She held his gaze, her own steady, unflinching. 'It was my husband who ran the business. I ran the house.'

'Did he ever mention anything about it? Even in passing? A hint, perhaps?'

'He was a broker who handled hundreds of transactions every day. He never mentioned them at home. I'm afraid I know nothing about the matter you refer to.'

It was becoming increasingly apparent to Ranade that she would say nothing further on the matter, even if she knew something about it. He decided to change the topic.

'Was there anything unusual in his manner in the past few days? Was he disturbed, angry, wary…?'

Chaaya shook her head.

'Anything at all, Mrs Tola, that seemed different, out of place?'

'I can think of nothing, inspector. I'll let you know if something occurs to me later.'

'Thank you for your cooperation, Mrs Tola. May I, once again, offer my condolences?'

Ranade threw a quick glance around as he turned to go. Shashi's face was expressionless, but Kamna's gaze, fixed on the inspector, was distrustful.

▪

Amethyst Financial Private Limited turned out to be a surprisingly cramped little affair on the ground floor of an office complex in Lower Parel. Beside the glass door on which the company's name was etched were four small brass-and-wood nameplates affixed to the wall, each bearing the name of a company. The premises, Ranade noted mentally, as he pushed the glass door open, apparently housed the registered offices of four other companies.

Beyond the glass door was a small reception area enclosed

entirely in glass, except for the wall to the right, which held an LED TV and a rack with twenty slots, each containing a business magazine or newspaper. To the left were two glass doors that led to small meeting rooms. Beside the receptionist's desk, another glass door opened into a hall accommodating several desks and cubicles along its length.

'May I help you?' the girl behind the desk asked, as Ranade stepped in through the main door.

'Mr Abhishek Kumar, please,' he replied. 'He is expecting me. Praveen Ranade.'

With Ranade was Daniel Paul from EOW, a dark, grizzled man in his fifties. They had decided not to mention that Daniel was from EOW, lest that discourage Abhishek from being forthcoming about commercial matters. It was best to let him assume that Daniel was Ranade's colleague from the Mumbai Police.

Just as the girl picked up her desk phone to call Abhishek, a middle-aged man hurried in from the hall beyond and greeted Ranade.

'Inspector Ranade?' he asked. 'This way, please.' He led them towards one of the meeting rooms. 'Chaaya Madam said you would be coming.'

'Can we have a look at the office before we talk?' Ranade asked, gazing through the glass wall behind the receptionist.

'Certainly.' Abhishek turned and led them through the glass door into the hall with small cubicles flanking the narrow aisle on one side. 'This is the main room, where most of the employees sit – analysts, relationship managers, accounts and admin.'

Ranade carefully surveyed the hall, taking in the files and stacks of papers occupying every inch of available space. Typical Mumbai office, he thought, cramped as hell. Computers fought for space on some desks. The wall to the left of the aisle was of frosted glass and held two etched-glass doors leading into private cabins.

'This is Mr Tola's office,' Abhishek said, indicating the first door, 'and that is mine.' He walked down the aisle and pushed open a wooden door. 'This is the trading room. Entry to it is restricted.' The room held half a dozen chairs facing computer screens. All but one were vacant.

'Very little activity?' Daniel asked, nodding at the near-deserted room.

'The markets closed fifteen minutes back. The traders have gone out for their tea-and-smoke break. When the market is open, this is the nerve centre.'

'Can we see Mr Tola's room too?'

'Certainly. I thought you would want to.'

Abhishek pulled out a key ring from his pocket as he hurried up the aisle and unlocked the door to Vivek's cabin. The small room held a desk crowded with papers and electronic gadgets, four chairs and a filing cabinet. Behind Vivek's chair was a small safe embedded in the wall.

'Who has access to the filing cabinet and the safe?' Ranade asked.

'I have the key to the filing cabinet, but not to the safe. Only Mr Tola used the safe.'

'Do you know what it contains?

'I do know that it has the securities and original documents relating to the collaterals given by borrowers. I'm not sure what else it contains.'

'Borrowers?' Daniel asked.

'We lend to some of our customers so that they can trade in the market. Short-term funds only.'

'How short term?'

'Usually, from three to thirty days. Mostly bridge funds or margin money. Shall we go to a meeting room? We'll have more privacy there.'

Ranade nodded and Abhishek shut the door to Vivek's room

and locked it. A minute later, they were in one of the small meeting rooms.

'How many employees do you have?' Ranade asked, studying the business card Abhishek had handed him. The name, 'Abhishek Kumar', ran across the top; below it was printed 'General Manager and CFO'.

'Eighteen employees, excluding me, and two office boys on contract. Four traders, a five-man analysis team, five client-service managers, three accounts staff and one admin.'

'As the GM, you run the company, I suppose?'

'Only some of the operations. Mr Tola took all the client- and investment-related decisions. He also handled trading matters. I look after accounts and some administration and also compliance and risk management.'

'How many clients do you have?'

'Oh, hundreds! Most of them are broking clients.'

'And borrowers?' Daniel asked.

'Not many. About half a dozen at any given time.'

'Do they owe you large amounts of money?'

'Sometimes. Loans usually range from five lakh to a crore.'

'How much is owed now?'

'Not much, actually. I'll have to check the records to give you the exact figure. But less than usual.'

'Anyone over a crore?'

'Well...' Abhishek fidgeted uncomfortably. 'That's confidential. People don't like to have their borrowings disclosed.'

Ranade gazed steadily at the reluctant GM. This was the first instance of a lack of cooperation on his part. 'This is a police investigation, Mr Kumar,' he reminded him gently. 'I can call for the information formally, if you so wish.'

Abhishek squirmed in his chair and seemed to make up his mind. 'Okay. One borrower has taken about five crores.'

'I thought you said the amount didn't exceed a crore,' Daniel pointed out.

'That is the normal range. This one is rather...unusual.'

'Who is this person?'

'Mr Navin Gokul. He's based in Pune.'

'What collateral did he give for five crores?'

Abhishek shifted in his chair again. 'Nothing.'

Daniel's eyebrows shot up. 'You seem to be contradicting yourself, Mr Kumar.'

'Well...as I told you, this is an unusual case.'

Daniel waited.

'You see...Mr Gokul was Mr Tola's partner in Aran Advisors Private Limited, his Pune venture. It is not my place to ask questions in such a case.'

'But you handle risk management.'

'I monitor exposure, limits and that sort of thing. The nature of the collateral was for Mr Tola to decide on. Of course, I did tell him that a collateral would be desirable in this case.'

'What did he say to that?'

'He said, "I don't need a collateral from Navin. I have enough." And that was the end of the matter.'

'Okay. Can you think of anything unusual that happened in the last week or two?' Ranade asked.

Abhishek shook his head.

'Any large deals, disagreements, arguments, defaults and suchlike?'

'Nothing. All was as usual, as far as I know.'

'Did – '

'Wait a minute!' Something had suddenly occurred to Abhishek. 'We got back five crores unexpectedly.'

'Where from?'

'From Aran Advisors. That was Mr Tola's contribution – the seed capital – to set up the company.'

'Why is it unusual?' Daniel asked.

'It's just that I had not known it would be coming. We had not factored it into our cash flow. Mr Tola had made one of his regular trips to Pune last week, but didn't mention anything about taking back his investment in the venture.'

'What is this Aran Advisors Private Limited?'

'A finance company that helps clients invest. It offers investment advice and facilitates trade through Amethyst Financial. It also manages portfolios for some clients. Mr Tola and Mr Gokul were the two partners who owned the venture. Mr Gokul runs the Pune office.'

'Okay.' Ranade shifted topic. 'Did anyone buy an unusual number of shares of a particular company?'

'I wouldn't know about the trades, inspector. But we maintain a record of all trades. Just to remind you, it is for clients only. All we do is execute the buy-and-sell orders they give.'

'Did any of them place an order in Purple Country shares?'

In response, Abhishek picked up the phone and asked someone to come in with his laptop. Thirty seconds later, a young man walked in.

'What was the name of the company you said?' Abhishek asked.

'Purple Country.'

The young man typed the words into his laptop and peered at the screen for a few seconds before shaking his head. 'Nothing on Friday.'

'Try the entire week,' Abhishek suggested. 'Last week, that is.'

The young man typed the words into the keyboard again and shook his head.

'When was the last order on Purple Country placed?' Abhishek asked.

'Four weeks back. 2,000 shares sold.'

Abhishek turned to Ranade and looked enquiringly at him.

'Can you show me Thursday's and Friday's orders?' the inspector asked.

The young man typed again and turned the laptop screen towards Ranade and Daniel. It showed a table listing twenty or so orders, along with several pieces of information.

Daniel reached out and scrolled down the table, which seemed to contain a large number of transactions. Clearly, the brokerage business was brisk. The data seemed to change randomly as he scrolled down, except for the first two columns that indicated the order time and sequence number. Just as he was going to stop, something caught Daniel's eye and he scrolled back up.

'There is a gap in the sequence number,' he said, pointing to an entry.

'That happens, on occasion,' Abhishek explained, not looking at the screen. 'Sometimes, the orders don't go through and are cancelled at the very last moment. These create gaps.'

'I don't understand.'

'This data that you see is from our internal system. The actual buying or selling of shares is done on a separate system – the stock exchange trading systems of the NSE or BSE.'

'Okay. So?'

'The orders from clients are first entered in our system and a sequence number is generated. Then the trader executes the order on the NSE or BSE trading system. But sometimes, if the price has changed too drastically or the required quantity is no longer available, the trader may not proceed with the order. In such cases, we have to delete the order that we had created on our system. But in the meantime, other orders would have been executed and the sequence number would have progressed. The cancelled order then becomes a gap in the sequence number.'

'I see. Does that happen often?'

'Sometimes, but not very frequently.'

'Can you give me the trade data for the past 10 days?'

'I'm sorry.' Abhishek shook his head firmly. 'Our terms protect client privacy. It is one thing to show you a sample on screen and quite another to hand over the data to you. If you still need to have it, we will have to follow the legal process.'

Abhishek nodded at the young man, who rose and left the room with his laptop.

'That just delays things, Mr Kumar,' Ranade murmured, as the door closed.

'I know, but unfortunately, I have no choice. Our clients have their rights too and we have signed non-disclosure agreements with them. If you were a client of ours, you wouldn't want us to give your data to someone else.'

'But this is a police investigation.'

'Even so, we must follow due process. I would be liable for breach of contract if I divulged information without proper cause. I could go to jail.'

'I can speak to Mrs Tola if you wish.'

'That won't help, inspector. I cannot go against the terms of the contracts. I can hand you the data only if I get a formal request.'

'Okay. I'll formally call for the last eight months' data. I suggest you begin preparing it.'

'Eight months!' Abhishek sat back, shocked. 'Why?'

'Can't disclose that now. I will also need information on borrowers.'

'That will take some time. We keep only manual records of borrowers.'

Ranade was surprised. 'Really?' he asked. 'In this age of computers and IT?'

'Mr Tola didn't trust computers with sensitive information. He was quite paranoid about it. When there were rumours last year that Apple's and Google's systems had been hacked, he had every password in the company changed. "Those are supposed to be the best systems in the world," I remember him saying. "If they can be cracked, so can ours. I know of a very high-security network that has been cracked. There is no IT system in the world that can't be broken into. Remember Snowden?" I suspect he was right.'

'I see. Can you think of any reason why someone would want to kill Mr Tola?'

Abhishek was silent for a moment. He seemed to be deep in thought. Then he shook his head slowly. 'All of us have been talking about that lately, but none of us can find a reason. It seems so... so strange, unreal.'

'Anyone who might have wanted him out of the way?'

'No one I can think of.'

'Any financial distress that you may be aware of? Or any complications?'

'None. The company is doing very well in this bull market. We have had a good time since the new government came to power.'

'What about Mr Tola? Personally?'

'I wouldn't know, inspector.'

'Don't you handle his income tax?' Daniel asked.

'No. Bipin S. Mehta and Company does that.'

'I saw four nameplates at the door. Whom do they represent?'

'Mr Tola's other companies. This is their registered office.'

'All proprietorships?'

Abhishek shook his head. 'Private limited companies. But Mr Tola was the dominant shareholder.'

'How about Amethyst Financial? Who are the shareholders?'

'Mr Tola owned 90 per cent. There are three minority shareholders. I can give you the details.'

'How did Mr Tola seem in the last few days before his death?' Ranade asked.

'I'm not sure, inspector.' Abhishek frowned and stopped.

The inspector waited patiently.

'I'm not sure, but he seemed...preoccupied on Friday. You know, it may just be my imagination, but he seemed rather pensive and edgy.'

'Anything specific?'

'Well...he locked himself up in his office for an hour or so and I heard the safe open and close. He usually locks the door when he opens the safe, but never for that long.'

After ten more minutes of questioning, Ranade and Daniel left.

'So, what do you think?' Ranade asked the EOW man once they were back in the inspector's Qualis.

'It seems to be a regular broking business.'

'But Abhishek wasn't aware of certain things despite being the GM.'

'That's often the case in proprietor-run firms,' Daniel explained. 'GM is just a fancy title for someone who is little more than a chief accountant and an admin guy rolled into one.'

'What about the gaps in sequence numbers?' Ranade asked. 'Is that normal?'

'His explanation seemed to hold water. I'll look into it later, but I think what he said was true. However, I can't help thinking that it's convenient too. We wouldn't know, would we, if they had deleted Purple Country trades?'

'That's what I thought too. And Navin Gokul? The Pune firm?'

'That requires investigation. Are you planning to go to Pune?'

'Yes, I am. That's why I took the address.'

'I'll join you.'

Chapter 13

Ranade and Abdul walked up a flight of stairs and entered a room that had a number of LED TVs mounted on a wall. Audiovisual equipment crowded the table and racks below and cables snaked all over the floor. A technician rose from his chair as they stepped in.

'I have synchronized the three cameras in the bar lounge into one screen,' he said, pointing to the large TV mounted at the centre of the wall. 'You will see the events simultaneously from three viewpoints.'

'No time lag between the three footages?' Ranade asked.

'None. The three windows are fully synchronized. You'll notice that the time display below each window matches the others to the second.'

'Excellent. Let's begin.'

The lights dimmed as the technician pressed a button and three windows flared to life on the large TV screen. All of them showed the same scene inside the bar lounge from different angles.

The top left window showed the bar lounge from one corner. An unoccupied Table 13 stood at the left edge of the picture. The view displayed in the top right window was from the corner diagonally opposite Table 13; it showed the table near the top edge of the picture. Table 13 was not visible at all in the third window, which was below the other two windows on the TV screen. Between the camera and Table 13 stood the bar, protruding several feet from the wall and blocking the view of the lounge entrance and the table. Displayed below each window was a digital clock reading 18.46.22.

The bar lounge was less than half-full and most of the early customers had taken tables by the glass walls. Samuel, the bartender, could be seen behind the bar with another man. Two waiters, one at the bar and the other at a table, were clearly visible in their white full-sleeved shirts and maroon sleeveless silk vests over dark trousers. Their white gloves stood out clearly in the small pictures.

'This is just before the deceased came in,' the technician said. 'Shall I begin playing?'

'Please.'

The figures on the screen sprang to life as the digital clock began counting forward. Half a minute later, a portly figure in a pink shirt and dark trousers walked in through the entrance and paused, looking around the room. A few seconds later, he seemed to make up his mind and went to the table at the corner to his right: Table 13.

'That's Vivek Tola,' the technician said.

Staring at the screen, the three men watched the waiter at the bar walk up to Vivek and talk to him for no more than thirty seconds before returning to the bar and writing something down on a slip of paper. Samuel took a glass from the sideboard and poured an amber liquid from a bottle he had selected from behind him. Then he placed the glass on the bar counter and returned the bottle to the counter behind him.

Meanwhile, the other man behind the bar brought out a can of soda from under the counter and produced two glass bowls of snacks. The waiter placed the four items on a tray and took them to Table 13.

'Should I fast forward to the moment before Kurva comes in or would you like to watch the events unfold in real time?'

'Fast forward,' Ranade replied. 'We'll replay it in full later.'

The technician speeded up the video till the clock showed 19.03

and brought it back to normal speed. At 19.04.51, a short man in jeans and a sports jacket walked in and looked around. He then turned, as if he'd heard Vivek calling out to him, and walked to Table 13.

'Shashi Kurva,' the technician prompted.

'No greetings from either of them,' Abdul murmured, as they watched Shashi take his seat at the table. 'No handshakes either.'

Ranade watched silently as a waiter came to the table and took the next order.

'They aren't speaking,' Abdul said. 'Strange.'

'They must be waiting for the waiter to serve and leave them on their own.' Ranade's voice was contemplative.

The two men on the TV screen remained silent for another couple of minutes while a waiter served them and withdrew. There was a brief exchange of words. Then the two men seemed to fiddle with their phones and set them down on the table before Vivek leaned forward and began talking.

Hardly a minute or two later, a waiter approached the table again. Vivek paused as the man served them something on a plate and withdrew.

'The chilli cheese toast!' Ranade rasped.

The clock showed 19.11.09.

Vivek leaned forward, picked up two pieces from the plate that had just arrived and popped them into his mouth before dropping the toothpicks with which they had been speared back on the table. Then he resumed speaking, with Shashi contributing very little to the conversation. When Shashi began to speak, Vivek helped himself to two more squares of chilli cheese toast.

For the next few minutes, the two men continued talking on and off, with Shashi staring fixedly at Vivek. The latter took another piece of chilli cheese toast and sat back in silence.

'Fifth piece,' Abdul observed quietly. 'He consumed a great deal of TTX, I must say.'

Both the men were now sitting back in their seats and Shashi seemed to be saying something. He then leaned forward and peered into Vivek's face. He reached forward and touched Vivek's shoulder. Vivek slumped to one side and Shashi leapt to his feet and went around the table to grasp him by the shoulders. As Vivek slumped further in his chair and his head fell back, an apparently agitated Shashi could be seen shouting. All faces in the room turned to him and a waiter ran up to the table. A few moments later, a guest from another table approached and bent over Vivek.

'The doctor.'

By this time, several men were crowding around the table. Little of either Vivek or the table was visible. Two men rushed in through the entrance and headed towards the table. Chaos reigned for the next few minutes before someone began ushering the guests out of the bar lounge.

'Okay, stop,' Ranade called out and turned to Abdul. 'So the waiter did serve the chilli cheese toast, as Kurva had claimed. It wasn't one of the customers from another table.'

'The poison must have been added before the plate was brought to the table,' Abdul observed. 'Kurva didn't touch it.'

'Yes, but the question is: did he know that it was doctored?'

'Either he knew or had a narrow escape. He couldn't have been closer to death at that moment. But Surendra did serve the chilli cheese toast, after all.'

'Did he?' Ranade mumbled. He frowned deeply and turned to the technician. 'Go back to the point where Vivek collapses and play the video backwards from there.'

They leaned forward as the video began playing in reverse from the moment Vivek was seen slumping in his chair. The men watched a slumped Vivek straighten up and Shashi sit back in his chair, talking. A waiter walking backwards came to the table and picked up the plate of chilli cheese toast.

'Slow motion!' Ranade called out and the technician halved the speed of the video. The waiter slowed his pace as he walked backwards.

'Stop!' Ranade yelled, sitting up in his chair. 'Did you see that? The waiter came through the entrance of the bar lounge! It was not Surendra at all; both he and the other waiter were serving other tables when this *third* waiter came in. It was another man wearing the same waiter's uniform, down to the white gloves. Now play it forward slowly. At quarter speed.'

They watched closely as a man dressed as a waiter entered the bar lounge, walked up to Table 13, placed the plate on it and left through the entrance.

'Stop,' Ranade said and sat back, glancing at the digital clocks on the TV screen. 'Someone walked in at 7.11 p.m. and served the poisoned chilli cheese toast. It would have been one of the twenty-odd orders placed that day.'

'This is footage from the cameras *inside* the bar lounge, sir,' Abdul said. 'We also have footage from four other cameras *outside*, in the atrium. I think two of them show the bar lounge's entrance from the outside.'

'Excellent, Abdul! Do you have them here?'

The technician was already rummaging through discs on his desk. A few minutes later, the TV flared to life again. Visible on the screen was the scene in the atrium outside the bar lounge.

'We'll have to play one camera at a time,' the technician said. 'Synchronizing multiple cameras will take some time.'

'No need to synchronize. One is good enough. Go to 7.10 p.m. and play forward.'

The video flickered forward at high speed as the technician's practised fingers operated the controls. It presently slowed to double speed and then to normal speed. The clock showed 19.09.47.

The scene before them was of the square area bordered by

the lobby and the lobby lounge to the right, the lifts below, the restaurant to the left and the bar lounge at the top. Only a part of the lobby and the lobby lounge were visible at the far right of the screen. A number of tables in the lobby lounge were occupied.

As Ranade and Abdul studied the scene intently, a waiter approached one of the tables at the end of the lobby lounge where a man was sitting. Without exchanging a word with him, the waiter picked up a white plate from the table and walked briskly towards the bar lounge. He disappeared through the entrance and returned twenty seconds later.

'Pause!' Ranade called out and the video froze.

The waiter's hands were empty and the clock showed 19.11.13.

'Play,' Ranade murmured and leaned forward, his eyes alert.

The waiter strode across the screen into the corridor flanked by the washrooms on one side. At the right edge of the screen, the man at the table rose and disappeared down the lobby.

'Stop and play backwards.'

They watched the footage at varying speeds for the next fifteen minutes, pausing and speeding up from time to time.

'So,' Abdul summarized at the end of it, 'two men came to the lobby lounge at 6.37 p.m. and took a table near the entrance to the bar lounge. They placed an order at 6.39 p.m. and – '

'Chilli cheese toast?' Ranade asked.

Abdul consulted his papers and nodded. 'An order of two coffees and two plates of chilli cheese toast...I will confirm the table number shortly.'

'Good. Continue.'

'The order arrived at 6.51 p.m. and the men bent over the plates several times after that. They also opened a small bag they had brought with them. The video image is not clear enough for us to decide what exactly they were doing. We can't make out if they doctored the chilli cheese toast there and then or simply replaced it with a poisoned one.'

'I'll synthetically enhance it,' the technician volunteered. 'Let's see if we can make out what they did.'

'At 7.05 p.m., one of them disappeared into the washroom. At 7.11 p.m., a man dressed as a waiter came out from one of the washrooms, delivered the plate to Vivek's table and vanished back into the washroom. The other man left the hotel at the same time.'

'Check the footage again,' Ranade said, rising from his chair. 'The man who posed as the waiter would have left the washroom dressed differently from the way he was when he entered it. See if you can catch his face from footages from the cameras in the lobby and the reception area. He must have passed close to at least one camera. Get photographs of the other man too, though I'm not sure how helpful they'll be; he seemed to have a cap pulled over his forehead.'

Chapter 14

Ranade and Daniel were already past Panvel on their way to Pune the next morning when the gloom of dawn lightened, giving way to daylight. Vivek had lent a considerable sum of money to Navin without a collateral. That, Abhishek had admitted, was unusual. Moreover, Vivek had recently pulled back his investment of five crores from Aran Advisors. Unexpectedly, according to Abhishek. There was evidently something more to the relationship between the two men than Abhishek was aware of or had owned up to. Abdul's investigations revealed that Vivek had called and visited Navin Gokul regularly. He had, in fact, made three calls to him on the day he died – twice in the morning and once around noon.

'I don't need a collateral from Navin. I have enough…' was what Vivek had said to Abhishek. What did 'I have enough' mean? Had he enjoyed some sort of a hold over Navin? Given the kind of ruthless man Vivek was, how had Navin taken that? Could there have been a possible motive for murder there?

Regardless, there seemed to be big money at stake here. Just like the banking scam Ranade had cracked some time ago. When he began investigating the death of FLC Bank's chairman, he had no clue that it would eventually lead to the exposure of a complex white-collar crime. Collusion and greed had led to an intriguing modus operandi, culminating in murder. His mind went back to the victims in that case. How different they had been from Vivek Tola!

That case had taught Ranade a great deal about the world of finance and the experience had helped him effectively handle instances of financial fraud that he would subsequently investigate. Perhaps, the Tola case would teach him about the stock market.

They reached Aran Advisors Private Limited at 10 a.m. and found it open. It was a small two-room office, with three desks and a couple of extra chairs. A girl looked up as the inspector stepped in.

'I'd like to meet Mr Gokul,' Ranade announced.

'He's not going to be in today. Can I help you?'

'Where can I see him?'

'Your name, sir?'

'I'm from the Mumbai Police.' Ranade showed her his ID. 'I need to meet him regarding a matter I am investigating. When will he be available?'

The girl got flustered. She rose hurriedly to her feet and pulled up chairs for Ranade and Daniel. Once they were seated, she took her place behind the desk and spoke in a low tone, her voice betraying nervousness.

'I don't know when he will be back, sir. He sent me an SMS saying he was going out of town and wouldn't be coming in today.'

'Does he have a secretary?'

'I'm the secretary. This is a small office; there are only three of us here.'

'And who are the other two?'

'Mr Gokul and the clerk.' She gestured towards a man arranging files on another desk.

'Perhaps you can help by telling us what this company does?' Daniel suggested. 'What's its business?'

'As the company's name suggests, we are investment advisors,' the girl explained. 'We provide equity advice to investors, mostly HNIs. And if our customers so desire, we also help them buy and sell in the stock market.'

'Do you have a trading desk here?'

'No sir. We send the orders to Amethyst Financial in Mumbai. They do the trades for us.'

'And who provides investment advice to your customers? Mr Gokul?'

'Yes, but the advice usually came from Mr Tola of Amethyst Financial.'

'I see...Then what does Mr Gokul do?'

'He runs the company, sir. He and Mr Tola were the owners.'

'You mentioned Mr Gokul sending you an SMS,' Ranade said. 'Could I see it, please?'

The girl picked up her mobile phone and brought up the text message: '*Going out of station for a few days. Will call you. I won't be accessible on the phone*'.

'Have you tried calling him?' Ranade asked, returning the phone to her.

'No sir.'

'Please try now.'

The girl picked up the desk phone and dialled a number. Ranade stared at the phone's LCD display and checked the number that came up there against the one in his notebook. She was indeed calling Navin's mobile.

'Not going through, sir,' the girl told him. 'Says it's switched off.'

She handed the receiver to Ranade so that he could listen to the message and confirm it for himself. The message in Marathi was followed by one in Hindi. Ranade disconnected and redialled the number. He received the same message again.

'Do you know where Mr Gokul has gone?' he asked, replacing the receiver.

The girl shook her head. 'He had said nothing about travelling.'

'Who books his tickets when he travels?'

'I do. But he didn't ask me to do so this time.'

'Is that usual?'

'No sir. But he has done that a couple of times before, when he had to travel at short notice. He booked his tickets online.'

'I see. You don't have any information other than the SMS?'

The girl shook her head.

'So, for all you know, he may still be in Pune.'

'But the SMS – '

'If you ignore the SMS?'

The girl shook her head mutely. A new anxiety had crept into her eyes.

'Please try calling his residence,' Ranade suggested.

She picked up the desk phone and dialled another number.

'It's ringing, sir,' she said after half a minute. 'No reply.'

'Nobody else at home? His wife – '

'He's a bachelor. A maid and a cook come in once a day.'

'Do you have their numbers?'

'Yes sir.'

'Call them, please.'

Daniel sat back and let Ranade drive what was now a police investigation into a person's whereabouts. Five minutes later, the inspector had made little progress despite the many phone calls made at his behest. The cook hadn't seen Navin after Friday night and knew nothing of his travel plans. Navin had apparently told him not to come in on Saturday, as he would be eating out. The maid had seen him on Saturday morning when she came in to clean, but had no other information. She had taken leave on Sunday.

Vivek had spoken to his business partner three times on Saturday, the day he had been killed. Navin had not been seen since. Was there a connection between the former's murder and the latter's disappearance? If so, what was it?

The SMS to Navin's secretary had been sent a little after 10 a.m. on Sunday. What if the SMS had been sent from his phone, but by someone else who had got hold of it? And where had it been sent from? Ranade pulled out his mobile and called Abdul.

'Abdul, track the location of Navin Gokul's mobile from Friday night onwards. Get the call records too.'

He then turned to the girl, who now looked positively scared.

'Do you know where Mr Gokul was on Saturday?'

'He had said that he was meeting friends that day and wouldn't be coming to the office.'

'In Pune?'

The girl seemed confused. 'I think so...I don't know.'

A pencil appeared in Ranade's hand and he began twirling it around his thumb as he assimilated the information. If Navin had been in Pune all through Saturday and well into the evening, he couldn't have killed Vivek. But what if he had been in Mumbai?

According to Abhishek Kumar, Vivek had unexpectedly pulled back his investment in Aran Advisors. Was that an indication that the relationship between the two business partners had soured? If so, it was conceivable that Navin might have wished Vivek harm.

But what if that was not the case? What if Navin too was a target of the same malice that had ended Vivek's life? Was Navin another victim? After all, he hadn't been seen or spoken to since Saturday morning, the day Vivek was killed. Ranade looked up at the girl across the desk.

'Does anyone else have his house keys?' he asked.

'No sir. Not as far as I know.'

'How far is his place from here?'

'Two kilometres.'

'Come.' Ranade rose briskly. 'Take us there.'

The girl gave the clerk hurried instructions and hastened out of the office behind the inspector. They climbed into the Qualis and made their way through traffic as the girl gave directions. Ten minutes later, they were standing in front of an upmarket block of flats. The frontage was a patchwork of lawn and flowerbeds, interspersed with arrangements of decorative rocks. Colourful fish swam lazily in a shallow pond. In one corner, a gardener was busy tamping down the soil around new plants.

With the girl leading the way, the men went up to the third floor and rang the doorbell of one of the flats. When it went unanswered, they rang it several times again and waited for over five minutes. There was no response. Ranade went downstairs and called the watchman.

'Gokul Saab's car is here,' the watchman said in response to a query, pointing to a blue Ford Ecosport. 'It was here all through yesterday as well.'

'Where is the nearest police station?' Ranade asked.

'Two streets away,' the watchman answered, his eyes alight with unseemly curiosity. 'I'll show you where it is.'

Ten minutes later, a sub-inspector and a policeman had joined Ranade. They spoke to the residents of the neighbouring flats, but gleaned no more information than they already had at their disposal. At Daniel's request, Ranade arranged for his driver to drop the girl and the EOW man back at her office so that the latter could continue with his enquiries into the commercial aspect of Aran Advisors.

Ranade called a local assistant commissioner of police he knew. He briefed the ACP on Vivek's murder, the calls exchanged between him and Navin and the latter's sudden disappearance on the day of the murder and suggested that they enter and search Navin's flat.

Fifteen minutes later, the ACP called back to say that he was organizing a warrant. He would soon send a local inspector, a photographer and a locksmith to Navin's flat.

As Ranade waited for them to arrive, Abdul called to say that Navin's phone had been switched off after the SMS was sent to his secretary and had not been switched on since. The SMS had been sent from Pune.

Later in the morning, Ranade and his team entered Navin's flat. The drawing room was large and well furnished, though unkempt. The inspector noted the lavish use of glass and the predominant shades of blue and black. The far end was taken up by a shiny black bar stocked with at least three dozen bottles. Beside the bar stood a fridge. The pride of place on the wall to Ranade's right was occupied by a large Sony Bravia TV. Mounted high on the wall were two long speakers. Against the opposite wall stood a long blue sofa on which newspapers and magazines lay carelessly tossed. Three doors led from the hall to the other areas of the flat.

Ranade's first feeling was that of relief. He had half-feared that he would find Navin dead in the flat. He stepped into the main bedroom and stood there, looking around him with a frown. The doors to the two wardrobes stood partly ajar and a muddle of clothes lay strewn around on the bed. A slight rectangular impression on the bedcover seemed to suggest that a small suitcase or strolley had been placed there earlier. One of the two drawers in the desk had been pulled out a few inches and the chair pushed back from the desk.

Navin, it appeared, had left home in a hurry. Once the photographer had done his work in the bedroom, Ranade walked across to the desk and picked up two files. One held Navin's credit card statements and the other, his bank statements. Ranade photographed several pages with his mobile phone and sent the photos to Abdul.

'Ask the banks to place alerts on the accounts. They must inform us immediately if any credit card or debit card is used. If an ATM is used, we need the video footage from the ATM kiosk. Also, get details of all transactions since Saturday.'

An hour's search yielded no clues to Navin's whereabouts, but just as they were leaving the premises, Abdul called.

'A credit card was used on Sunday to purchase a flight ticket,' he said. 'He took a 4 p.m. flight from Mumbai to Bengaluru.'

'Okay. The bird seems to have flown the coop. He must have gone by road to Mumbai and taken the flight.'

'There's more. He used an ATM in Malleswaram last evening to withdraw –'

'Malleswaram?' Ranade cut in.

'An area in Bengaluru. I've asked for the video footage.'

'Good. Send the footage to Pune as soon as it comes. I want his secretary to identify him. And send me the number of the concerned police officer in Bengaluru. I'll call him on my way back to Mumbai. We need to catch this bird.'

As his Qualis was speeding back to Mumbai an hour later, Ranade called Inspector Srinath in Bengaluru and briefed him on the case. He told him that Abdul would be sending all available details shortly and asked that Navin be traced. He suspected that the man might be staying in a hotel near the ATM.

'Malleswaram is full of hotels,' Srinath said. 'It'll take time.'

'If I were in hiding, I would not be out in public unless it was absolutely necessary,' Ranade said. 'I'm not surprised that he visited the ATM at 8 p.m. It would be dark then and that's a time when there are still a lot of people on the streets. Do you agree?'

'Yes.'

'Extending the logic, he would go to an ATM as close to the hotel as possible, assuming he is staying in a hotel. I would, therefore, start with hotels inside a small circle – say, half a kilometre wide – around the ATM and then go outwards.'

'What would you like us to do if we get him?'

'Detain him for questioning.'

■

Abdul looked up as Ranade entered the office after returning from his Pune trip. The gleam in the other man's eye told the inspector that he had found something important.

'It's just come in, sir,' Abdul said, pointing to half a dozen photographs on the desk. 'Video grabs from a camera near the hotel's reception area.'

Ranade walked over and gazed silently at the photographs of a bearded man of indeterminate age. They were a series of stills taken from above as the man walked under the camera. The man's hand was obscuring a part of his face in three of the photographs and in two of them, he was looking down at the floor. One photograph showed his eyes and other features more clearly and Ranade tapped it with his fingernail.

'Get the lab to enhance this. The beard is, most likely, a fake. Get them to erase the beard and create an image of the man as if he were clean-shaven.'

Ranade stood irresolute as Abdul picked up the phone and began speaking to the lab technician. Something was bothering him. He was missing something that should have been obvious. To whom would he show the photos? To the hotel manager, the bartender and the waiters in the bar lounge, for sure. Perhaps some other people in the hotel. Who else?

There was the off-chance of Shashi having taken in details of the waiter's appearance. Ranade would show him the clean-shaven version as well as the original photo. He felt he was closer to the thought that was trying to surface, but not quite there. What else? What was his subconscious trying to nudge him towards?

Suddenly, the thought popped into his conscious mind and he grinned. Of course!

'Abdul!' he called out. 'Have the lab make a third version of the photo with a smaller beard – a Frenchie. I want postcard-sized prints of the three versions.'

Three hours later, soon after sundown, Ranade was sitting across a small table from Shashi in Chaaya's house. On the table was the unaltered video grab that Shashi was looking at. The only other person present in the room was Kamna. Her expression was inscrutable.

'He doesn't seem familiar,' Shashi said shortly, staring hard at the image. 'I can't be sure, with so much of the face obscured by the beard.'

'It's a fake beard,' Ranade pointed out. 'Zooming the image reveals a clean edge at the boundaries. There's an abrupt change in the shade of the underlying skin as well. The change wouldn't have been so sharply distinct if the beard were natural.' He pulled out another photo and laid it beside the first one. 'This is how he might have looked without a beard. We can't be sure, as the clean-shaven look is computer-generated.'

As soon as Shashi looked at the clean-shaven version, there was a perceptible change in him. His eyes grew intent. He frowned deeply, unconsciously cocking his head to one side, then to the other, as he struggled to place the person in the photo.

'There's something familiar about this man,' he said slowly. 'But...but I can't seem to place him. I have a strange feeling of recognition when I look at that forehead, those eyes and even the nose...But where could I have seen him before?'

Ranade waited for a full two minutes as Shashi closed his eyes and sat back, then looked at the photo again, looked away and came back to it again and again. After a few minutes, he gave up.

'Can you leave this with me?' he asked Ranade. 'It may just come back to me.'

'Let me show you another version of the photo.'

The inspector pulled out the version with the French beard and laid it on the table. The man in the photo now had a neatly trimmed moustache and goatee.

Shashi's eyes widened.

'Kashyap!' he hissed.

Kamna was staring at him.

'Sure, Mr Kurva?' Ranade asked.

'Absolutely! This *is* Kashyap, the man who came to my office with the SEBI guy. We must show the photo to Carol, my secretary. She saw him too.' Shashi was overcome with excitement as he glanced at his watch. 'She's probably left the office by now, but I can send her the photo on her mobile.'

'Please do.'

Pleased, Ranade sat back as Shashi went about photographing the third image with his mobile. This was what the inspector had been hoping for. Based on nothing but his intuition and the proof that the men who had visited Shashi's office were impostors, he had built up expectations that Vivek's killer would turn out to be one of those very men.

'Inspector,' Kamna intervened, breaking into his stream of thought, 'would you like Chaaya to look at the photos too? In case she has seen this man somewhere else?'

Ranade looked at her in surprise for a moment. Then sheepishness took over.

'Of course, Mrs Kurva. Why didn't I think of that myself?'

He knew the answer – he had been too excited by the prospect of Shashi identifying the man in the photo to even contemplate the possibility of others recognizing him too.

'May I take them in to show her?' Kamna asked. 'She's not in any state to come out here.'

'Yes, of course!'

Ranade gathered up the three photos and handed them to Kamna, who went into the house. Soon afterwards, Shashi's phone rang.

'Carol,' he said, answering the call, 'I'll put you on speaker. Inspector Ranade is here. I would like him to hear what you have to say.' He touched a button on the screen. 'Go on, Carol. Did you have a look at the photo?'

'Yes, Shashi, I did.' The tinny voice from the mobile phone's loudspeaker was laced with suppressed excitement.

'Recognize the man?'

'Of course I do! He had visited the office with S.K. Varma of SEBI the day before the board meeting.'

'Ms Carol, this is Inspector Ranade. Are you sure you recognize him?'

'I'm quite sure, inspector. I remember the face well enough, as he was waiting across my desk for nearly ten minutes before I took them into Mr Kurva's office.'

'Do you recall seeing him anywhere else?'

'No…no, inspector. I don't think so. I had never seen this man before his visit to the office. Nor have I seen him since. I don't think I would have missed those eerie light brown eyes.'

'Thank you, Ms Carol. May I request you to not speak about this matter to anyone?'

'Of course. I understand.'

'Thank you. Now please delete the photo from your phone.'

Shortly thereafter, Kamna returned with the photographs and shook her head.

'Sorry, Chaaya doesn't seem to recognize the man in any of the photos.'

'That's okay, Mrs Kurva. Thank you.' Ranade put away the photos and looked up. 'Please don't mention this matter to anyone. I'd appreciate it if you could delete the photo from your phone too, Mr Kurva. We don't want anything to alert the killer.'

'Let me delete it in your presence, inspector,' Shashi volunteered, picking up his mobile. As Ranade looked on, he deleted the photo as well as his message to Carol. 'There, it's done.'

'Thank you.'

■

Hardly had Ranade's Qualis driven off from the apartment block's gates than Chaaya appeared in the drawing room.

'Has he left?' she asked.

Shashi turned from the window. 'Yes, he has and – ' He broke off and stared at the sheets of paper in his sister-in-law's hand. 'What's that?' he asked.

'Copies of the photos the policeman brought to show you.'

Shashi's gaze flew to Kamna's face. Their eyes locked for a moment. He instantly understood what had happened. On the pretext of showing Chaaya the photos, his wife had scanned them.

'They are photos of Vivek's killer,' Kamna said softly, her eyes imploring as she gazed at Shashi. 'It's vital information for us.'

'I have sent them to Pandey Bhaiya,' Chaaya added, making Shashi shift his stunned gaze to her.

'The inspector expressly warned us not to mention this matter to anyone,' he snapped. 'Not *anyone*! As a precaution, he even made us delete the photos from our mobiles. And you, you end up doing *this*!' His words ended in a shout.

Chaaya stepped back, shocked at his ferocity, and threw a questioning glance at her sister.

'I fail to understand why you can't let the police investigate the case without meddling in it!' Shashi continued angrily. 'Besides, do you have any idea how dangerous this man is? He has already killed once. He won't hesitate to do it again.'

'We're hardly preventing the police from investigating the case, are we?' Chaaya replied calmly. 'On the contrary, you have helped them, haven't you, by identifying the culprit?'

'Then why not let the police take it forward?' Shashi fumed. 'Why should you want to get into it?'

Chaaya took the time to settle down on a sofa before she replied. When she did, her face wore a look of cultivated patience.

'Look, Shashi. Vivek's murder is connected in some way to his business dealings. Is that a fair assumption?'

'Yes.'

'Then the killer is someone who had dealt with Vivek and had reason to kill him.'

'Yes. So?'

'So the police aren't likely to know, are they, the identities of all the people Vivek had dealings with? Whereas Pandey Bhaiya would know, for sure.' Chaaya was completely earnest in her justification.

'Then why don't we get Pandey Bhaiya to tell Ranade about all the people Vivek had dealings with?'

'You can't be serious!' Chaaya's face bore an expression of shock and she threw a glance at her sister. 'Let the police into our business affairs?'

'Why not?'

'Expose our business dealings to their scrutiny?' Chaaya's face had taken on an incredulous look. 'Shashi, have you any idea what you're saying? They will dig deeper and deeper until they find enough to blackmail me with. Instead of the meagre bakshish we pay now, I'll be coerced into paying – '

'I've come across all sorts of people and if my judgement isn't entirely skewed, Ranade seems quite above board,' Shashi said. 'Hardly the blackmailing kind, I would imagine. All he's interested in is finding the killer.'

'I agree that this policeman doesn't quite fit the mould of the others I have seen so far. He looks a decent sort. But you do realize, don't you, that the information we give him will not stay with him? He'll be obliged to share it with his colleagues in the course of the investigation.'

'Shashi,' interrupted Kamna, her face like thunder. 'After all that I told you – '

'Don't be cross with him, Kamna,' Chaaya said beseechingly, reaching for her sister's hand and pulling her down beside her on the sofa. 'He's only trying to protect me. Like a brother would.' She smiled at her sibling and an unspoken message passed between them. 'Don't worry about it. I'm not offended or anything. I realize that his background is different from ours and it influences his perspective on things.'

Hearing her sister's words, Kamna's eyes moistened.

'Shashi is a gem,' Chaaya continued. 'He's totally honest and speaks his mind. Which one of our relatives is like that, Kamna?'

Shashi, who was listening dumbfounded, finally found his voice.

'I didn't mean to offend you, Chaaya,' he began, his tone somewhat apologetic. 'I just – '

'But you didn't, honestly! Just go on being who you are, Shashi. I've trusted you implicitly from the time I first met you. The only favour I'm asking of you is that you not pass on any information to your policeman friend.'

Friend! Shashi scoffed inwardly. He got up, went to the window and stared out. The sinking feeling had returned. Far from being Ranade's friend, he was the inspector's primary suspect! Not only had he been unwittingly implicated in the insider trading affair and his brother-in-law's murder, if you please, but he could now be deemed guilty of concealing evidence as well for hiding Vivek's possessions in his own house! God alone knew how incriminating these might turn out to be.

As if that were not enough, copies of the photographs Ranade had shown him were now lying three feet away from him – despite the inspector's explicit instructions about maintaining confidentiality. He would be in one hell of a mess if the policeman found out what was happening behind his back.

Shashi's thoughts turned to Kamna's family. The past week had made it clear that they weren't quite what he would describe as 'normal'; at least, certainly not by his parameters of judgement. For one, they had an awful lot to hide. Somehow, they had evolved a peculiar worldview of their own, determined by their own notions of right and wrong. They neither respected nor feared the law. Consider, for instance, those bags of gold, gems and jewellery dumped into wells to evade the taxman's attention; those crores lent to individuals, with nothing but obscure codes in a notebook to show for it; those loaded guns kept under the pillow for the purpose of self-defence...Were these the sort of things 'normal' people did? And then there was this shadowy Pandey Bhaiya, whoever the hell he was. Chaaya seemed to trust him blindly.

How the sisters had changed in a matter of days! The refined, dainty Chaaya was out to find her husband's killer with this Pandey Bhaiya's help; out to exact revenge on her own, without police assistance. And Kamna! How could his loving, sensitive wife be so oblivious to the trauma she was putting him through? Didn't she know that she was making him run afoul of the law – a situation he hated? Could this possibly be the same girl who had been desperate to leave behind the trappings of wealth and position so that she could share a simple life of rectitude and loyalty with him?

Loyalty...Kamna's notion of it seemed to have changed drastically. Her blind devotion to her sister had swept aside any concern she might have had for rectitude.

No sooner had Shashi entertained the thought than he realized he was being harsh on her. This was a difficult time for Kamna, perhaps the most difficult she had ever endured in her life. Once it passed, she would come to her senses and be distraught at the thought of what she had forced upon him. The combined effect of Vivek's murder and the slur on Shashi's reputation had been too much for her to bear. It had temporarily warped her perspective. Something in her had snapped. This was a time when Kamna needed her husband's full support, not his censure. He had to help her cope.

For the first time in his adult life, Shashi was at a loss. The corporate world was so much easier to deal with. There, he could be distant, dispassionate, even ruthless. With cold detachment, he could put people in their place, even fire them if the situation so warranted, without sparing a thought for their feelings. In a worst-case scenario, he could quit and go elsewhere. But marriage was something else. How could he be cold or ruthless in dealing with his wife? Or with Chaaya, for that matter?

In the quagmire he found himself in now, Shashi was desperately seeking a stable middle ground to stand upon. In vain.

Chapter 15

A little after 10 a.m. the next day, Shashi switched on the TV. He went straight to the CNBC channel to check how the Purple Country stock was doing that morning. It was 36 per cent down from the weekend closing price before Vivek's death.

Traders in Vivek's stockbroking firm had claimed that the stock was under heavy selling pressure, with sellers dumping large volumes. Lakhs of shares were being offered by potential sellers, but there were few buyers. The huge mismatch had sent the stock price plummeting for two days running. Worse still, the trading volumes were very low – a mere fraction of the usual volume. That meant that potential buyers were waiting for the price to fall further before thinking of buying. It was further evidenced in the deep discount at which Purple Country's stock futures were trading.

The traders had also spoken of malicious rumours making the rounds; whispers about insider trading in the stock, with some going to the extent of implicating Shashi in Vivek's murder. Shashi, it was also alleged, had been banished from the company because he was guilty; a replacement was unlikely to be half as effective as he had been. Besides, could there be some truth in the reports that even the accounts had been fudged? How else had such a noticeable spurt in profitability been achieved in so short a span of time? No other e-commerce company had come even remotely close. The traders were convinced that those vicious rumours had been deliberately started.

Resigned to more hammering of the stock, a tense Shashi waited for the ticker at the bottom of the screen to reach the letter 'P'. And when it did, his fears were confirmed: Purple Country had fallen heavily for the third day running. The market cap had halved in just three days.

Shashi groaned and buried his face in his hands. How hard he had worked to build the company! Not just him; scores of others too. Long days, running into long nights, for years together. At the rate the stock was falling now, four years of hard work would be undone in two weeks flat!

He bristled at the unfairness of it. Unlike some unlisted e-commerce companies that boasted of multi-billion dollar valuations on the basis of spreadsheets and rosy business plans, Purple Country was a company that had made real profits, quarter after quarter. Unlike e-commerce giants that lost money hand over fist and had to raise funds every few months, his was a company that had withstood scrutiny by any yardstick. Not only were its profits real, it also paid sizeable dividends every year. Some start-ups never made profits and, as a result, saw their value fall once they were listed on the stock exchange. Purple Country had flown even higher after listing.

It was one of the very few online companies to be valued by the stock market itself and not by non-transparent investors whose interests were served by sky-high valuations. Purple Country's valuation was not a grand total at the bottom of a private equity fund's spreadsheet, with a hundred convenient assumptions. Its valuation was solid; it could be relied upon.

Or so he had thought.

How easy it was for hidden enemies to destroy their company's hard-won reputation simply by hinting that their accounts had been falsified! The nerve of it! And the iniquity! Shashi's blood boiled at the thought and at the realization that there was nothing he could do about it. How did one fight an invisible enemy?

His thoughts went to Carol. She had invested most of her savings in Purple Country shares. She had implicit faith in the company... and in him. She didn't come from a wealthy family and a part of her little nest egg was already eroded. He felt impelled to protect her interests.

Purple Country was his ticket to success too, to financial nirvana, if there was such a thing. Unlike his earlier jobs where he had had to work under the directions of others and fail because of their failings, Purple Country had given him the opportunity to drive a business the way *he* deemed fit. And it was at the helm of this company that he had realized his potential. He had every right to reap the rewards.

He strode up and down the room like a caged lion. The expression on his face was defiant. He would show them! Once Tanuja arrived, they would find clues from the share registrar data. He stopped in his tracks at the thought. Had Barun obtained it yet? Why hadn't he called? Shashi picked up the phone and called him.

'It came in last night, Shashi,' Barun told him. 'I have it with me now.'

'How large is it?'

'Two DVDs. About five hundred spreadsheets in one and a large ASCII file in the other. The IT guy at the share registrar was very helpful. Apparently, he has had similar requests before. In addition to generating spreadsheets showing the shareholding each day, he has merged spreadsheets into a single ASCII file. According to him, it will be far easier to generate a share transaction list from it. Handling five hundred spreadsheets would be cumbersome, he says.'

'Great! Give me a copy and put the original in the fireproof safe in the office.'

'Okay.'

'Do you know when Tanuja is arriving?'

'Late tonight, Carol said. She'll be picked up by the hotel car.'

'Anything else from your side, Barun?'

'Yes. The chairman is going to be on CNBC at noon. You probably know that the stock fell today as well.'

'Yeah, I know. How difficult it is to build, Barun! And how easy to destroy! Who do you think is behind this?'

'No idea. But we'll recover, Shashi. Don't you fear!' Barun's voice rang with unshakeable conviction. 'I was the third employee of the company and I know! There is too much substance in our company for it to be killed by mere rumours. The people who sell the stock today will be kicking themselves a month from now. The market may be fickle in the short term and be driven by sentiments. But not in the long term. Investors won't be fooled.

'You know, Shashi, the first few years of the company were nothing special. But things began changing once it became Purple Country. It's a different company now – strong, resilient and solid. Its strength comes from its people and performance – things that rumours can't destroy.

'Purple Country is my ticket to a comfortable retirement, Shashi. And yet, I am not worried. My stock options and the shares I already own are what my wife and I are banking on. I'm sure that is the case for others too. What we are seeing is only a blip. Purple Country will weather the storm.'

At noon, Shashi was in front of the TV once again. With him were Kamna and Chaaya. Gupta's interview started a minute after noon.

'Good afternoon, Mr Gupta,' the anchor said. 'Thank you for joining us. I'm sure things would be very busy at Purple Country right now. I really appreciate your sparing the time.'

'My pleasure, as always.'

Clad in a dark blue suit and a light blue tie, Gupta seemed completely at ease. Shashi marvelled at the man's poise and self-control. He looked just as he had after the Serenity acquisition, the day the stock had soared.

'Mr Gupta, your stock has fallen steeply for the third day in a row and there is nervousness in the market about it. Would you, at the outset, like to make a statement to your investors?'

That was exactly the opening Gupta needed. Shashi made a mental note to thank the anchor the next time he met her.

'Thank you, I will,' responded Gupta with a smile and a nod. 'Let me take a minute or two to outline what led to this misunderstanding.

'Our CEO, Shashi Kurva, was approached on Thursday last by a man claiming to be from SEBI. Since he had shown a SEBI identity card, we had no reason to doubt him. He said that SEBI was investigating an insider trading matter related to the company and he wanted to talk to Mr Kurva about it. Ostensibly, his reason was that the person who had allegedly benefited from the trades was a relative of Mr Kurva's.

'Mr Kurva extended his full cooperation, including offering the man his personal phone and financial records. As soon as the visitor had left, Mr Kurva called and briefed me. Fortunately, we had a board meeting the next day, during which we discussed the matter. I wish to stress the fact that Mr Kurva voluntarily shared the information with me and the other board members. I also want to point out that he did so immediately, as soon as the man had left his office.

'However, when Mr Kurva went to SEBI on Monday, he was told quite categorically that the man who had visited him was an impostor. No person of that name, designation or appearance existed in SEBI. Again, Mr Kurva informed me immediately about the developments.

'In the meantime, the board had already appointed a subcommittee to investigate the matter Mr Kurva had raised and the investigation was under way. In keeping with the spirit of the investigation, Mr Kurva recused himself. He voluntarily went on leave so that his presence in the office would not influence the investigation. I would also like to state that the subcommittee comprises two independent directors and a renowned lawyer. It has no employees or promoters.

'So, as far as the board and I are concerned, there has been no wrongdoing and Mr Kurva's actions have been in keeping with the highest standards of corporate governance. I would like to state further that these developments have had no repercussions whatsoever on the company's performance. Not one customer has left us and not one contract has been cancelled. It is, in every way, business as usual.'

Shashi sat back with satisfaction. Gupta had been convincing. He had neither oversold nor faltered. His choice of words and tone had been perfect. So perfect, in fact, that for a few seconds after Gupta had finished, the anchor was at a loss for words.

'Thank you, Mr Gupta,' she finally said. 'A statement cannot be more unequivocal than that; it certainly clarifies several issues. If I may, I have a couple of follow-up questions.'

'Sure.' Gupta was all courtesy.

'News reports suggest that the person who had allegedly benefited from trades in your company's shares was related to Mr Kurva and died under...um...suspicious circumstances. Can you comment on that?'

'I really can't say much, simply because I don't know much. I believe the police are investigating the death as a possible homicide, just as they are investigating the whereabouts of the impostor in an effort to discover his real identity. I am not privy to any details and none of the board members has met the police. Mr Kurva is in regular touch with the police. As far as the deceased's identity is concerned, yes, he was Mr Kurva's brother-in-law.'

'Is Mr Kurva still on leave?'

'Yes. He is spending all his time with his late brother-in-law's family. Understandably, they are devastated by the tragedy.'

'And your internal investigation? Is it continuing?'

'It is. We have given our independent directors full freedom to handle it as they deem fit. It is now up to them to decide when the investigation should draw to a close. Neither I nor the directors will interfere in the proceedings.'

'Thank you, Mr Gupta. That was very clearly put.'

'Could I add one thing, if I may?' Gupta asked.

'Certainly!'

'I would like to reassure our investors that there is absolutely nothing to be concerned about. The company's performance has not suffered in any way. Nor is Mr Kurva going away. He will be back once things settle down on his personal front. False rumours – that you have been gracious enough not to bring up – have reached my ears too. I ask our investors to lend no credence to them. I do not even want to dignify such rumours by mentioning them on TV.'

'Thank you, Mr Gupta. Thanks for giving us your time.'

'My pleasure.'

Shashi pressed the mute button and turned to Kamna. 'What do you think?'

'He handled it very well, I must say.'

Shashi nodded. 'It'll go down well with the investors. I hope the share recovers.'

Just then, his phone rang.

'Watched it, Shashi?' Barun asked. 'He was very good, wasn't he?'

'Yeah, he was.'

'Now, let me give you the bad news. Sudakar wants to initiate a forensic investigation.'

'Forensic investigation! Into what?'

'Into – hold your breath, Shashi – into the company's accounts –'

'What! How stupid can a man be? He is the head of the frigging audit committee, for God's sake!'

'Which is why he wants to do it, he says.'

'It makes no sense! No bloody sense!'

'Amit is furious. He wants to speak to you. Hang on.'

'Hello, Shashi?' Amit said. 'You've got to stop this foolishness. There is absolutely nothing wrong with the accounts and he bloody well knows that. He is a chartered accountant himself.'

'Why is he doing this, Amit? It makes no sense to me, but I'm not an accountant. What earthly reason could he have?'

'Nothing, apart from the rumours. The bugger is so bloody full of himself and his so-called professionalism that he wants to appear whiter than white.'

'Yes, but – '

'Purple Country is what *we* built, Shashi.' Amit's voice trembled with emotion. 'Sudakar has contributed nothing. He has no right to hurt Purple Country.'

'When did this happen?'

'Half an hour ago. We haven't told the chairman yet.'

'Tell him now. I'll speak to him too. The chairman has just won a battle. If we announce a forensic investigation now, the market will take it as an indirect acknowledgement of guilt. Mr Gupta's name will be mud and our stock price will go through the floor.'

▪

The insider sat alone in the refuge of his cabin, pretending to work. He had just watched Gupta's interview on CNBC and the entire office had watched it with him. The employees hadn't held back in abusing the one who had brought Purple Country to such a pass. Curses, voiced in language both crude and nuanced, had been hurled with abandon by those around him as he mutely watched the results of his handiwork, his treachery.

Purple Country, a serious, focused company, had put all its energies into the right things and had cared little for pretence or posturing. It had quietly, if aggressively, gone about its work, turning a deaf ear to critics and naysayers, ignoring competition that came from quarters eager to engage in mudslinging, never thinking to pause and boast about its remarkable achievements. The company was a lot like Rahul Dravid, his favourite cricketer.

This was the Purple Country he had betrayed. For money.

It was now hurting the way a living person with a grave injury would have hurt – badly. And *he* was the one who had conspired to inflict the mortal wound.

'Oh, why did I ever get into this thing!' he moaned inwardly, but he knew the answer.

In a moment of indiscretion, he had crossed the line between ambition and greed; a moment when impatience had got the better of him. On the one hand, he was hungry to make a lot of money quickly; on the other, he had failed to recognize Purple Country for what it was.

It was a little before his thirty-seventh birthday that he had succumbed to temptation. His career was progressing well; some had even commented on his stellar performance. But verbal acknowledgement and praise alone would no longer do for him; those periodic salary raises and bonuses did little to satisfy him, since his income didn't even come close to the kind of money he was aspiring to earn.

His friends in other companies were moving up faster in life than he was. They had moved into much larger flats, were driving bigger cars. He had begun to feel more than a twinge of envy as he observed their superior lifestyle. And he had started questioning his choices. Was he with the wrong company? Should he be moving out? The thought had gnawed at his heart deeply enough for him to share his concerns with an old friend.

It was at this vulnerable moment in his life that the man had approached him. The insider knew him only as 'Zeus'. He had not offered his real name or any clue to his actual identity. They had met in the dim private booth of a bar where the other man's bearded face was barely visible. Lightly tinted glasses had hidden his eyes.

'All you have to do is to give me information in time,' Zeus had said in a voice that didn't sound natural. 'You will be more than handsomely rewarded for your efforts.'

'And how do I pass the information on to you?'

'I have a foolproof method which ensures that the information can't be traced back to you. Just remember that you should desist from trading in Purple Country shares. As long as you abide by that rule, no court in the country can touch you.'

'In that case, in what way will I benefit?'

Zeus had replied in detail to his query and given him a week to decide. Three days later, the insider had agreed to the deal without consulting his wife, his habitual conscience keeper.

The insider now looked up and stole a glance through the pattern etched on his glass door. People had gathered in the aisles to discuss Gupta's interview. They were furious at the person who had apparently destroyed what they had worked so hard to build. He wondered what they would do to him if they knew he was the real culprit.

Gupta had done all he could to calm the troubled waters, but he wondered if that would be enough. There was more to this than met the eye. Someone somewhere was going after Purple Country hammer and tongs. Why? Who? Was it Zeus or someone else? What did Zeus plan to gain by driving down the share price?

And Sudakar! Had he gone mad? Why was he going after Shashi? *Shashi*, of all people! He was the one who had turned the ship around and made Purple Country what it was today. The insider felt anger rise in him and he squirmed at the conflict it generated in his mind. *He* had hurt the company far more than Sudakar had; yet, he felt righteous anger at the independent director. He felt like tugging at his own hair in frustration, but controlled the urge and contented himself with loosening his tie.

This was madness!

He took a deep breath and tried to get a hold on himself. What was done was done. He couldn't change the past, however much he might wish to. There was only one way forward. He had to cut himself free of this insanity, whatever the cost. Family and peace of mind were far more important than illicit money. And strangely, the Purple Country he had betrayed had become family to him.

But Zeus, he knew, wouldn't let him go easily.

▪

Inspector Srinath and two plainclothes officers entered the small hotel in Malleswaram while another stood casually on the pavement outside. It was one of the many budget hotels that catered to business travellers floating through Bengaluru every day. Set deep inside the labyrinth of 'main roads' and 'crossroads' that was Malleswaram, it was in a locality crowded with shops and a scattering of restaurants – an ideal place for a nondescript business traveller to go unnoticed.

After visiting close to two dozen hotels in the vicinity of the ATM, they had found a guest by the name of N. Gokul staying in this one. The only problem was that he had checked in on Monday and not on Sunday, as they had anticipated. They had now decided to make a positive identification.

Armed with the three photographs that Ranade had sent, Srinath approached the front desk and asked for the manager. The inspector had a quiet chat with him in the latter's office before displaying the photographs to him and the front-desk clerk.

'That's him,' the clerk said, tapping on one photo.

'Sure?' Srinath asked.

'Not 100 per cent, but I'm reasonably sure. Oh, wait a minute – we would have photocopied his ID.'

A couple of minutes later, they were looking at a copy of Navin Gokul's driving licence.

'He's in 221,' the clerk said. 'The key is not in its slot. So he should be in his room. He has hardly gone out since he checked in. Ordered only room service.'

Srinath and the two plainclothesmen went up the staircase and stood listening outside Room 221. Hearing no sounds from the room, Srinath nodded and the two plainclothesmen took up position on either side of the door. The inspector knocked.

No answer. He knocked again, a little louder this time. Still no answer. He knocked several times in vain and turned to glance at the manager who was watching them anxiously from a little way down the corridor.

'Do you have another key?' Srinath asked the man.

The manager nodded and brought out a key, which he inserted into the door before turning the lock. As soon as the door opened, he knocked loudly and announced, 'Housekeeping!'

Getting no response, he pushed the door open and stepped in, followed by Srinath.

The room was vacant.

Srinath checked the bathroom and found it unoccupied too. He then opened the cupboard. Empty as well; neither clothes nor toiletries. Closing the cupboard, he began examining the room and found a small strolley suitcase in a corner. There was nothing else in the room that could have belonged to a guest.

'Packed and ready to go,' the inspector commented. 'Prepared to fly at a moment's notice, if need be.'

'He has taken the room key with him,' the manager said. 'The room keys are attached to large brass squares to discourage guests from taking them out of the hotel.'

'We'll wait in the lobby,' Srinath told him. 'He may return any time. Does the hotel have a restaurant?'

'Yes, but he is not there. I checked.'

As they walked down the stairs and reached the lobby, they noticed a man in a blue shirt standing on the pavement just outside the hotel entrance. He was slim, of medium height and wore his hair long. In his hand was a shiny brass square with a key dangling from it. The manager froze as the clerk behind the desk gesticulated wildly to them.

'That's him!' the clerk exclaimed in Kannada.

The man outside turned and looked at the manager, seemingly frozen in his tracks, and the three men standing behind him. All four were staring at him. It must have been clear from their expressions that he was the target of their scrutiny. The man's eyes widened and fear leapt to his face.

Navin Gokul turned and ran, even as Srinath shouted at the sole plainclothesman waiting outside the entrance to stop him. Before the plainclothesman could act, Navin was already sprinting into the first lane he reached as he fled. He ran through it and took a left. In the next few minutes, out of sight of the policemen, he took several turns and plunged deep into a grid of 'main roads' and 'crossroads'. Along the way, he pulled out a new sweater from a shopping bag he was carrying and paused for a few seconds to put it on. His blue shirt was now concealed under a grey sweater. Job done, he jettisoned the shopping bag and slowed to a brisk walk. He flagged down a passing autorickshaw and climbed in.

Back at the hotel, a furious Srinath was unjustly berating the plainclothesman who had let Navin slip past. The inspector had just finished exchanging caustic words with the manager and the clerk for having unwittingly alerted Gokul. But it was too late to undo the damage. He called Ranade and sheepishly related what had happened.

'We can still catch him,' Ranade responded. 'My guess is that he will try to flee Bengaluru. And he is likely to head for the railway station or the airport, though I can't tell which.'

'The railway station, if he wants to go to a small town,' Srinath suggested. 'But he cannot go very far very quickly. If he takes a flight, on the other hand, he can go just about anywhere. What do you think?'

'Can't say. His chances of being seen by someone he knows will be lower in the hinterland, but he will also stand out as a non-Kannadiga.'

'Unless he pretends to be a tourist in Mysore or some other place.'

'Hmm...How far is the railway station from where you are?' Ranade asked. 'And the airport?'

'The station is about three kilometres away. But the airport is pretty far off – some thirty-odd kilometres.'

'Okay...And I suppose finding him at the station won't be easy. Besides, if he has taken a taxi or an autorickshaw, he'd almost be there by now.'

'Very likely.'

'Okay, then, let's take a chance.' Ranade came to a decision. 'Alert the police at the airport. I'll inform the banks so that I know straight off if he uses a credit card again to buy a ticket.'

Meanwhile, Navin had got off the autorickshaw along the way and taken a taxi. With nothing but his wallet and the clothes on his back, he was now on his way to the airport. Though he tried to maintain a deadpan expression, his darting eyes betrayed his fear. He glanced through the taxi's rear window from time to time, as if to make sure he wasn't being followed.

An hour and a half later, he was standing at the airport, looking up at the screen displaying the list of departing flights. After staring at it for a few minutes, his expression fraught with indecision, he seemed to make up his mind. Glancing quickly around him, he approached a ticket counter.

'Do you have seats on the next flight to Delhi?' he asked the salesgirl.

'6.15 p.m.? No sir. It's closed. I can put you on the waiting list for the 7.55 flight if you wish.'

'Wait list, is it?'

'Yes sir.'

'How about the Kolkata flight, then?'

The girl stared at him for a moment. 'You want to go to Kolkata or Delhi?' Her tone was even and her expression polite, but it was obvious that she was both intrigued and amused.

'Do you have an available seat on the Kolkata flight? The 7 p.m. flight.'

The girl tapped a few keys and nodded. 'Yes sir, we do.'

Navin slid his credit card across under the glass screen. 'Could you issue me a ticket, please? The same name as the credit card.'

'Are you sure, sir?'

'Yes.'

'You do want to fly to Kolkata?' Amusement had given way to disbelief. 'Not Delhi?'

'That's right.'

'Once I issue it, sir, you can't cancel without paying a cancellation fee.'

'Just do it, lady.'

Shortly thereafter, Navin entered the terminal building and approached the check-in counter. Elsewhere, phone lines were buzzing. The credit card company had just alerted Ranade and he, in turn, called Srinath.

As Navin cleared the security check fifteen minutes later, a policeman barged into the airline ticketing office. Making irate customers wait, he forced the ticketing girl to pull out the tickets that had been purchased recently. He gave her the credit card number and the transaction amount. Two minutes later, he was rushing out, calling Srinath on his mobile.

'He is taking the 7 p.m. Kolkata flight,' he announced. 'Arrival 9.25 p.m.'

'Stop him at the gate!' Srinath shouted back. 'Don't let the flight take off with him on board!'

In the meantime, Navin's flight had been called. He went straight to the departure gate and joined the moving queue of passengers. He gave the officer checking the boarding passes at the gate a cursory glance, failing to notice the stripes on his epaulette that distinguished him from the regular uniformed security guards who usually performed this duty. Beside the officer stood a flummoxed female security guard.

Once the officer had checked Navin's boarding pass and studied his face, he lifted his arm and made a small gesture before handing the pass back to him. When Navin stepped through the gate and began walking towards the aerobridge, two other men approached him.

'Mr Navin Gokul?' one asked.

'Yes?'

'This way, please.'

Chapter 16

Shortly after 9 a.m., Shashi rang the bell beside Tanuja's hotel room door. The woman who answered it was Kamna's age. Dressed in blue jeans and a T-shirt, she was just as tall and of a similar build. But unlike Shashi's wife, his cousin had wavy hair. She grinned and hugged Kamna before welcoming them both into her room. With exchanged greetings and pleasantries behind them, Kamna gestured to the small suitcase she had brought along. Tanuja's baggage hadn't arrived yet and Shashi's wife had brought some of her own clothes to tide her over until it did.

Five minutes later, Shashi was telling Tanuja about Vivek's death and briefing her on the details of the insider trading matter. For the first time since the whole sordid affair began, he was letting down his emotional defences. From the moment of Vivek's death, Shashi had been serving as Kamna's and Chaaya's emotional mainstay. He had been compelled to keep his vulnerable side hidden, his own emotional turmoil in check. Now, sitting in front of his favourite cousin, he let himself go.

He and Tanuja had grown up together in a joint family in Kerala before her parents moved to England. Both had been restless and adventurous children who wouldn't take 'no' for an answer. They were in the habit of ganging up against the adults and arguing with them until they got their way. If one was scolded for disobedience – a frequent occurrence – both would simply vanish outdoors into the vast greenery that surrounded their ancestral home and not return for hours.

Shashi now bared his heart to this cousin who had always been more like a sister to him. After unburdening himself, he gradually collected his thoughts and broached the subject for which he had asked Tanuja to come all the way down to India.

'I had a look at the data from your share registrar,' she told him. 'Demat account number, number of shares held, holding date – all the key information is there. We should be able to construct the day-by-day picture of who bought and sold Purple Country shares. All that remains is the share price, which the share registrars don't capture. As you suggested, I'll download the average price of the day from the stock exchange and use it. The results won't be precise, but they'll give us a pretty good indication of what's been happening.'

'You've already figured out how to do it?' Shashi asked.

'The data is fairly standard across the world, you know, and comprises just a handful of items. There isn't much variation, as there are few firms that build stock exchange systems. Only the codes, such as demat account numbers and share codes, vary. Share registrars adopt the same standards. Once I know the order in which they are laid out in the data file and how they are delimited, I'm set. In this case, it is even simpler, as all transactions relate to just one stock.'

'But we have only shareholding data. You'll need to extract the share transactions from it.'

'See my laptop blinking away?' Tanuja jerked her thumb towards the desk on which her laptop was open. 'That's what it's doing now.'

'Wonderful! What else do you need?'

'We need to talk about the analysis. Once we agree on what we're aiming to do, I can start the analysis.'

'Okay. From my perspective, I need to know if people have been buying and selling large quantities of shares around certain events,'

Shashi told her. 'I mean, events like quarterly announcement of results, after which the share price often jumps. There are a couple of other events like an acquisition we made. The price really leapt after that.'

'So you need to know if the same person has repeatedly bought shares before an event and sold them after at a significant profit, right?'

'Right. I guess I'll have to give you the dates of these events.'

Tanuja shook her head. 'Not necessarily. Barun had sent me the stock price data for the last two years. I've already examined it and have identified seven major events. The acquisition you mentioned is one of them. The price jumped between 8 and 20 per cent during these events, except for the acquisition, when it jumped 30 per cent. I've already got the dates.'

'There must be lakhs of transactions involved. How do you plan to handle it all? Will your laptop alone be enough for you to do the job?'

'That's another thing we need to agree on. You said you wanted to identify instances where a person made significant profit. What would qualify as "significant"?'

'Well – '

'₹5,000?' Tanuja cut in.

Shashi shook his head. 'Too low.'

'₹10,000? ₹15,000??'

'Hmm...This whole exercise is aimed at catching the big fish, not small fry. If there is systematic insider trading taking place, they must be making a lot more money. It wouldn't be worth the risk otherwise. Why would someone risk it for ₹15,000?'

'Right,' said Tanuja. 'So what is the threshold?'

'Say...one lakh rupees profit. Can we start with that?'

'Sure, let's start with a profit of a lakh of rupees in the first iteration. We can move that up or down in subsequent iterations.

As I said, the six of the seven events have yielded between 8 and 20 per cent profit. Let's take a conservative average of 10 per cent profit. Now, if 10 per cent profit equals one lakh, the trade must have been worth at least ₹10 lakh. Right?'

'Yup.'

'Okay, the first thing I will do is remove trades that are worth less than ₹10 lakh.'

'But a buyer or seller may have split it across multiple transactions.'

'Exactly! My software will take care of that by aggregating each demat account's transactions across a few days. The other thing I will do is focus on a time window around each event. The window will start three or four days before the event and end six or seven days after it.'

'Why different periods before and after?' Shashi enquired.

'That's often the pattern. It takes longer to sell, as the price is higher. Besides, there will be more sellers than buyers after a price jump.'

'Got it.'

'So, this is what I will do: I will first discard all transactions outside the seven event time windows. I will then remove transactions that don't add up to ₹10 lakh for a demat account number. These two filters alone will remove 90 per cent of the transactions or more. What will remain are a few thousand transactions; at most, ten thousand or thereabouts. These, I can handle on my laptop.'

'Brilliant, Tanu!' Shashi was delighted. 'How long will this take?'

His cousin grinned back at him. 'I've already done a part of it. I've stripped away the data that is not pertaining to the event time windows.'

Shashi couldn't help being impressed. Here she was, less than nine hours since she had landed, and she had already made progress.

'What will you do next?'

'I'll look for patterns. We have some routines that throw up patterns.'

'When do you think you'll have the patterns?'

'By evening – latest, by dinner.'

'Wow!'

'I'll have to crash after that; sleep deficit would have hit me by then. Oh, one more thing: in order to reduce the size of the data to manageable levels, I've had to remove the names and addresses from the share registrar data. I'll only use the demat code for the analysis. Based on the demat account number, we can add back the names and addresses after the analysis. My laptop can't handle five million records if they have names and addresses appended to them. Just removing them reduced the size to one-tenth.'

'Five million records?'

'Uh-huh. About 10,000 shareholders and 500 days. We'll do our analysis on the demat account ID.'

'Great, Tanu. Where would you like to work?'

'Is it okay if I work in my hotel room?'

'Sure it is. I was wondering if you needed any assistance.'

'I'd rather not be disturbed. Besides,' she said, grinning at Kamna, 'I'm not very sociable when I'm working.'

'Don't I know!' Shashi said.

'Do you want to pick up some clothes?' Kamna asked.

'I'll take up your suggestion and use the ones you've brought along. If I buy new ones now, I won't have space to take them back. Anyway, my luggage should arrive in a day or two.' She turned to Shashi. 'I suppose I'll have to make a presentation. When is that likely?'

'Tomorrow? If you get your patterns today, that is.'

'Okay. I travelled down in a business suit. I'll have it cleaned and ready for the presentation tomorrow.'

■

Shashi and Kamna returned to find an impatient Chaaya waiting for them. Dressed in a simple churidar suit that was likely to pass unnoticed, she was carrying a small black duffel bag in her hand.

'Can you come with me to the office, Shashi?' she asked, as soon as they had come in through the door.'

'Office?' Shashi was confused for a moment.

'Vivek's office,' she said quietly, her gaze moving to meet Kamna's. 'Abhishek from the office called. There's been a break-in.'

'When?' Kamna asked.

'Sometime during the night. He didn't want to inform the police till he had spoken to me.'

'Then you need to go there before the police are called in.'

'Exactly.' Chaaya nodded. 'Will you mind the house, Kamna? I need Shashi to accompany me.'

'Of course! Be careful.'

She needs someone she can trust, Shashi thought, following Chaaya out through the door and into the lift. *I am family. But what am I letting myself in for? How can I get out of this mess?*

They were silent as the lift reached the ground floor. Chaaya strode towards an Innova parked nearby and climbed in, with Shashi following her. Beside the driver sat another man. Shashi wondered if he was armed. Doubtless, he was a guard.

Not a word was exchanged between them as the Innova swiftly made its way to the office. The guard hopped off, opened the door for Chaaya and followed her as she stepped out and entered the office. Abhishek hurried to open Vivek's cabin door for her.

'What happened?' Chaaya asked him. 'Anything missing?'

'Nothing has been touched, madam,' he said softly. 'Nothing missing in the main office, as far as we can make out. But I don't know about Mr Tola's cabin. The main door and the cabin door were found unlocked in the morning.'

Abhishek pointed to the fresh scratches around the keyhole

of the cabin door. The frosted glass door had a metal panel in the left-hand corner, into which the lock was fitted. Once he, Chaaya and Shashi had entered the cabin, Abhishek shut the door.

'Mr Tola's desk has been searched, as have the filing cabinet and the cupboard. I cannot say if anything is missing.'

He went around the desk, moved the chair behind it and gestured silently to the safe in the wall. It was obvious that the intruder had made strenuous efforts to pry it open. The resultant scratches on its surface at several places were deep enough to have removed the paint. Around the safe's door were telltale marks where a sharp tool had apparently been inserted between the steel door and its frame to force it open. The intruder had not succeeded in achieving his aim.

Chaaya stared at the safe for a moment and then nodded towards Abhishek. He quietly left the cabin, after which she locked it from inside. Taking a pair of large keys from her duffel bag, she opened the safe, while an irresolute Shashi stood across the desk. She swivelled Vivek's chair around, sat down on it and began methodically examining the contents of the safe.

Though uncomfortable about a situation where he was being made a reluctant witness to the contents of Vivek's safe, Shashi could not help but notice them. Chaaya took out several papers and small files that she quickly scrutinized before placing them on the desk.

The next item was a small red box. As she opened it, Shashi's stunned gaze came to rest on dozens of large diamonds resting on the silk lining inside. After a pause, Chaaya shut the lid and put the box away in the duffel bag she had brought with her.

There was more to come: two bundles of papers, agreements, sale deeds and property titles, by the look of it. These too she placed on the desk after a careful scrutiny. Just as Shashi was concluding that Chaaya had emptied the safe, she reached in and pulled out the last item. It was a small notebook bound by an elastic band, very similar to the one she had given Kamna to hide in her flat.

'Put this away in your jacket pocket,' she murmured to Shashi, swivelling around in the chair to face him. 'Make sure you don't take it out till we are safely back home.'

As Shashi complied silently, Chaaya put the papers and files back into the safe and locked it. She swung the chair around again and examined all the drawers in the desk.

'There are expensive things in here,' she said in a low voice. 'Pens and watches the intruder could have taken, but hasn't. Maybe, he didn't want to risk being seen with them. There is a fair bit of foreign currency here too.'

She put all the items into the duffel bag. Five minutes later, she rose and picked up her bag.

'You have the notebook?' she whispered.

Shashi nodded.

'Don't let anyone even suspect that you have it. Behave normally, as you would if you weren't carrying it. Even in the car. Okay?'

Shashi nodded again. He hadn't spoken a word all through. Chaaya opened the cabin door and Abhishek came in.

'Nothing missing, as far as I can see,' she said. 'I'll keep the safe keys. You can inform the police about the break-in now.'

Two minutes later, they were in the Innova, heading to a bank.

'I'll be back shortly,' she told Shashi when they reached the bank. 'Can you stay in the car? I'll just drop off this stuff.'

She was back in ten minutes. She tossed the duffel bag casually into the rear of the car, as if she wanted to make it amply clear that it was now empty. Anyone who might have been keeping watch would assume that whatever she had brought from the safe was now secure in a bank locker. Why did she have to emphasize that point, Shashi wondered. For reasons of safety?

Shashi blinked as the penny dropped.

The intruder had been looking for something specific, but hadn't found it because it had been in the safe. Then Chaaya had transferred certain items from the safe to a bank locker with the intention of sending out a signal to anyone who might be surreptitiously keeping an eye on them that she was not taking home the object the intruder had been after.

But in actual fact, she was! She was taking home the small notebook now safely lodged in Shashi's jacket pocket. That was why she had cautioned him to act as if he wasn't carrying something so vitally important! That was why she had made him wait in the car. That was why she had made it so obvious that she had returned empty-handed from the bank.

Shashi found himself making a valiant effort to resist poking around in his pocket to feel the edges of the all-important notebook and stared silently out of the window, hoping that he appeared nonchalant to a possible observer. When they reached home, Chaaya left the empty duffel bag in the car, directing the driver to bring it up later, and strolled unhurriedly back to the house. She was continuing the charade even outside her apartment block!

But once inside, she dropped her mask and led him, along with Kamna, into the study, where Shashi silently handed her the notebook. For the next few minutes, she went through the notebook and dictated its contents to Kamna, who wrote down the details on a sheet.

'12 March, KSK, 5…17 April, TRH, 10…2 June, TKJ, 7…'

The list slowly lengthened till three-fourths of the sheet was covered with Kamna's jottings. Chaaya then took a calculator and added the last column.

'11 people, ₹73 crores,' she said slowly. 'I'll have to call them.'

She turned to the last page, where numbers stretching over several digits were noted against rows of initials. 'KSK', 'TRH', 'TKJ' and the other initials from the list were followed by a fifteen-digit number. Chaaya studied each figure and wrote down a ten-digit number she had constructed from each. They were mobile phone numbers.

'I'd better start calling them now,' she said, picking up her mobile.

Kamna rose to her feet and led Shashi out of the study, closing the door softly behind her.

'What was that about?' he murmured.

'Those are people Vivek had lent money to.'

'₹73 crores?'

Kamna nodded. 'Some of them are filmmakers and jewellers – I recognized some initials.' She smiled and glanced at Shashi. 'What did you think of the way those mobile numbers were recorded?'

'How did she manage to decipher them?'

'Remove the first, fourth, eighth, twelfth and fifteenth digits and reverse the order of the remaining digits.'

'Why this elaborate scheme? The notebook was in a safe, anyway.'

'A notebook can fall into the wrong hands at any time.'

'Including those of the police?'

Kamna nodded. 'Especially those of the police.'

'Why was the intruder looking for the notebook?'

Kamna shook her head, her brow furrowed. 'I don't know…If we can figure that out, we'll be closer to identifying the man behind Vivek's murder.'

'And Chaaya is calling the borrowers now to see if any of them sound suspicious?'

'The calls are also a way of letting the borrowers know that she is aware that they owed Vivek money and that she has now taken charge. She'll also try to judge from the way they talk to her if there was any acrimony between the borrower and Vivek or if there were repayment issues.'

'I see. What about this insider trading matter?'

Kamna turned and looked Shashi full in the face.

'Chaaya doesn't think it's relevant,' she said. 'From the financial angle, it's too small a matter to prompt anyone into killing Vivek.'

Shashi was taken aback. 'She told you that?'

Kamna nodded. 'Some ₹40 lakh, you said, right? Hardly a sum to kill for; Vivek dealt in crores. Besides, what is the connection between share trading and the notebook? Share trading is done with white money; it passes through banks and brokers. The notebook is about…er…unaccounted money.'

'In that case, Chaaya suspects that some borrower – '

'She thinks it must have been someone who had business dealings with Vivek,' Kamna cut in. 'A large sum of money is at stake, Shashi – crores, not lakhs. It must be someone who stood to lose or gain several crores.'

■

Ranade and Abdul sat across the desk from Navin in the windowless room. After taking him into custody, the Bengaluru Police had sent him to Mumbai by a late morning flight. Now in Mumbai Police's custody, Navin appeared calm as he asked why he was being detained. Ranade didn't answer the question.

'Why did you flee from the police in Bengaluru, Mr Gokul?' he asked, instead.

'I didn't know they were the police.' Navin's response was quick, assured. 'They weren't in uniform, as you know. A man could surely be excused for taking to his heels when four strange men start chasing him? So would you, inspector, had you not been a policeman yourself.'

Smooth answer. Navin had thought things through during his confinement.

'You didn't return to the hotel,' Ranade went on. 'Instead, you tried to flee the city.'

'Of course I did! Why wouldn't I? I was an outsider, while they were obviously locals. The dice was loaded against me. I would have been a fool to return.'

'Why did you leave Pune suddenly?'

'Personal reasons, inspector. Why do I need to answer such questions? You still haven't told me why you are detaining me.'

Ranade gazed silently at Navin. An average citizen would have been nervous and anxious at being detained by the police. He would have wanted to make phone calls, get in touch with his family to say that he was okay. Navin hadn't asked for permission to make a single phone call. He was playing his cards close to the chest, waiting to see what he could learn from the police before making a move. The answers he was giving to questions in Mumbai varied not a jot from the ones he had given in Bengaluru. Three rounds of interrogation had not yielded anything new. Navin had been doggedly consistent.

'I will tell you shortly, but after I've asked a few more questions,' Ranade told him. 'Where were you on Saturday?'

'At what time of the day?'

'Why don't you tell me about your whereabouts during the whole day?'

'I drove to Mumbai after breakfast and returned to Pune at around 7 p.m. After that, I was at home.'

'Meeting friends in Mumbai?'

'More business associates than friends. I had a lunch meeting at the Grand Hyatt.'

'Santa Cruz?'

Navin nodded.

'Can anyone corroborate that?'

'Yes. There were four of us at lunch. I'll give you the names and contacts. You could check with the hotel too; I paid with my credit card.'

Ranade knew that he had used the credit card at 2 p.m. at the Grand Hyatt. His phone's location had corroborated that too. It was after 2 p.m. that the details about Navin's movements had become hazy, veiled in mystery. Navin's phone had gone off the network and not reconnected until late at night in Pune.

'What did you do after the meeting?'

'I drove back to Pune.'

'Anyone with you? The driver?'

'No. I drive myself.'

'Did you stop on the way?'

Navin shook his head.

'Was there a problem with your phone?'

'It ran out of power.' Navin stared at Ranade in surprise. 'The battery ran out a little after I left the Hyatt. Now will you kindly tell me why you are asking these questions?'

Ranade gazed at him for another moment. Nothing he had said contradicted the evidence. But his mobile phone was off during the crucial period from 2.30 p.m. till after Vivek's death. Navin could have been anywhere. Now was the time for Ranade to open the topic of Vivek Tola.

'It's to do with a man by the name of Vivek Tola. Do you know him?'

'Yes, of course.'

'How do you know him?'

'He's my partner in the business I run.'

'Equal partners?'

'I run the business, but he has a larger share of the profits. His investment is more than mine. 80:20.'

'Are you aware that he's dead?'

'Yes. I saw it in the Sunday papers.'

'Just before you fled from Pune?'

Navin didn't answer.

'You left suddenly on Sunday morning,' Ranade said slowly, his eyes studying Navin's face. 'It was not planned. It was too late to catch a flight from Pune. So you drove down to Mumbai to do so.'

'How can you be so sure that it wasn't planned in advance?'

A touch of defiance.

'You didn't inform either your cook or your servant.'

Surprise once again surfaced on Navin's face, followed by a tinge of nervousness.

'Nor did you tell your secretary,' the inspector went on. 'In fact, you had meetings scheduled in Pune on Monday.'

Navin looked away, staring at the desk. Watching him in silence, Ranade sensed he was thinking rapidly and arriving at a decision. A minute later, Navin looked up and gave the inspector a nod.

'I'll tell you why I left suddenly,' he said. 'I ran away from Pune, because I feared for my life.'

Ranade waited. More was coming.

'Vivek had called me on Friday to ask a strange question. He wanted to know if anyone had been following me. Funnily enough, I had noticed two men – complete strangers – several times on Thursday. I had wondered about the coincidence of seeing the same men a number of times on the same day, but hadn't paused to consider if they might be following me.

'After Vivek's call, I strolled out of the office and noticed one of those two men again. And the second man was there when I left the office for a meeting later in the afternoon. I called Vivek and told him about it. He said that some men were following him too and that's why he had asked me if I'd noticed anything out of the ordinary. He didn't know who those men were nor why they were following him.

'Now put yourself in my shoes, inspector. Given what Vivek had shared with me, how do you think I would react when I found out the very next morning that he had been murdered? Yes, I admit I panicked. My first thought was about my own safety. I wondered if those men were planning to kill me too. It was a Sunday morning and I decided to leave Pune without telling anyone.

'Then imagine my shock and dismay, when strange men come looking for me at my hotel in Bengaluru. What was I to think? They weren't in uniform. I assumed the worst and fled.'

'I see... Why didn't you say so earlier?'

'What would you have wanted me to say, inspector? From what I had read in the papers, the murder had been boldly executed in a public place. Whoever arranged for it is certainly a powerful man. And powerful men have a lot of clout with the police.'

Ranade's eyebrows shot up. 'You thought that the police might actually be in collusion with the killers?'

Navin merely shrugged.

'Can you think of anyone who might have wanted Mr Tola dead?' Ranade continued.

Navin shook his head. His response had been instant. The inspector sensed he had anticipated the question.

'How was your own relationship with Mr Tola?'

'Pretty good.'

'Mr Tola pulled out five crores from the company, didn't he?'

'Yes. It was a part of our accumulated profits.'

'Any business confrontations or bad blood between the two of you?'

Navin shook his head. After saying his piece, he seemed to have decided to clam up. Ranade couldn't help but feel that his little speech had been rehearsed. Navin had wanted to be sure that he was being questioned in connection with Vivek's murder before actually speaking out. He had decided in advance what he was going to say.

Ranade interrogated him for another half an hour, going over some of the same questions he had already asked. He got nothing new. At the end, he asked the one question he had been holding back. It was a shot in the dark.

'You made a call a few days ago from a public phone booth,' he said quietly.

Panic leapt into Navin's eyes, but he quickly suppressed it. His face had gone a shade paler.

'Why did you use a public booth when you had several phones at your disposal?'

'You must be mistaken.' Navin's voice was firm. 'I made no calls from a phone booth.'

Chapter 17

The moment Shashi began checking his mail the next morning, his attention was arrested by a mail from Amit; its subject line said: 'Personal'. Experience had taught him that such mails were often about employee issues such as resignations. The mail was addressed to Gupta as well. Shashi opened it and began reading:

Dear Mr Gupta, Shashi,
I understand that the board's subcommittee is planning to initiate a forensic audit into the company's accounts. This decision, I am told by Mr Sudakar, is based on rumours circulating about falsified accounts.

As you know, a forensic audit is a rare event that immediately calls into question the integrity of the company's accounts. It is seen as a poor reflection on the company's CFO. From my perspective, I have found nothing to suggest that our accounts are incorrect and would appreciate a clearer explanation for our considering such a measure. In my view, it would be prudent for the board to consider if there is, indeed, cause for such a drastic step. However, I do recognize that this is the board's prerogative.

If, in its wider wisdom, the board does go ahead with a forensic audit, my position would become untenable.
Best regards,
Amit

Shashi read the email twice before calling Amit.

'Your mail is clear enough, Amit,' he began. 'Did you speak to the chairman about Sudakar's plan?'

'He was non-committal and promised to look into the matter. I heard nothing from him all of yesterday. I slept over it last night and decided that I couldn't possibly continue if the board does go ahead with the forensic audit.'

'Rather drastic, isn't it, Amit?'

'What would you do in my place, Shashi?'

He was right. Shashi would have done exactly the same thing. In the two years they had worked together, Amit's performance had been exemplary – not just as an accountant, but also as a finance person. Not only had he been instrumental in driving down the cost of borrowing, but was also the primary reason behind Purple Country acquiring Serenity at such a favourable price. Amit was a top-drawer CFO, someone Purple Country was lucky to have.

'Rest assured that the forensic audit will find nothing amiss,' Amit continued. 'Nothing. However, it will tarnish my reputation. My only defence would be to resign in protest and make public the reason for my resignation. I will, of course, wait till the audit is completed before I act. There is only so much one can take from an idiot of a director.'

Again, Amit was right. Why on earth was Sudakar behaving so recklessly? He was certainly smart enough to know that calling for a forensic audit now would cause the company much grief. Gupta's reassurances on TV had slowed the fall of the share price, but hadn't halted it altogether. It had fallen another 10 per cent on the fourth day, taking the cumulative fall in four days to 48 per cent.

Was Sudakar acting on his own? Or was someone else behind this? Was a rival using the independent director to damage Purple Country's image? Sudakar had broken all norms of directorial conduct. Of course, he may have something personal against Shashi that was making him go after the younger man once the opportunity presented itself. But to call for a forensic audit because of malicious rumours was sheer stupidity.

'Hold your horses, Amit,' Shashi advised him. 'You've made your position clear. Don't do anything further till I get back to you. I'm meeting the chairman this afternoon.'

▪

At noon, Shashi was present at the private lunch organized in a five-star hotel by Dheerajbhai for fund managers of mutual funds and other institutional investors. The week had seen Purple Country's market cap more than halve after five successive days of falling share price. The share was now trading at ₹253.

Clearly, there was malice at play, Shashi told himself. Far from abating, the rumours had turned more venomous. They had now taken a decidedly personal turn, casting slanderous aspersions on Shashi's character and the nature of his relationship with Chaaya. One way to deal with them was to let them play themselves out. Investors would eventually tire of them and Purple Country's consistent performance would prove the rumourmongers wrong.

As the promoter, Dheerajbhai had seen it appropriate to throw his weight behind Gupta. He had asked Shashi to join them, as his presence would help convey a strong 'business as usual' impression. Seeing merit in the argument, Shashi had reluctantly agreed and left it to Tanuja to complete the analysis.

The meeting began with Dheerajbhai reiterating what Gupta had said on TV and personally endorsing the latter's comments. He talked at length about the company's growing customer base, its enviable positioning vis-à-vis competition, its first-mover advantage and its continued delivery of profits and dividends. He went into the details of the business that had taken place since Vivek's death and demonstrated that neither business nor customer confidence had been eroded in the slightest way. He then invited questions and answered them in as forthright a manner as possible, with Gupta and Shashi frequently pitching in.

'SEBI is not investigating Purple Country for insider trading or any other matter,' Shashi said in reply to a direct question. 'As far as Mr Tola's death is concerned, the police are investigating it and it would be premature on my part to make any comments, other than to say that I am assisting the police to the extent I can. As far as I know, I am not being investigated. I intend to return from leave once matters stabilize in Mr Tola's home.'

After the three men had fielded a barrage of questions with obvious candour, Dheerajbhai ended the lunch meeting with a declaration that took the guests by surprise.

'If any of you wishes to sell your shares,' he said, 'let me know next week. We can arrange a block deal. At ₹253, the stock is a steal; I may as well take advantage of it myself.'

▪

A few hours later, Shashi and Tanuja, both clad in dark business suits, entered a conference room at SEBI. While Tanuja was setting up her laptop for the presentation, people began filing in, one by one, to take their seats. By the time her laptop and projector were in place, seven people were in the room, seated and waiting for the arrival of the seniormost person – Kulkarni, the executive director whom Shashi had met on Monday.

'Shashi,' Tanuja hissed, 'why are there so many people in here? A sensitive presentation like this one should be restricted to one or two people.'

'I don't know,' Shashi replied in an undertone. 'I don't even know who they are. Kulkarni is the only one I have met so far.'

As soon as the executive director entered, Shashi shook hands with him and drew him aside.

'What we are about to present is highly sensitive information,

Mr Kulkarni,' he explained in a low voice. 'It should be kept restricted to as few people as possible. Do we really need to have so many in the room?'

'Everything we do at SEBI is sensitive, Mr Kurva,' Kulkarni told him. 'These men handle confidential information every day. This is nothing new for them. I suggest we start the presentation; we don't have much time.'

Shashi realized there was little more he could do about it, for protocol was paramount in the way government offices functioned. Besides, it was apparent from Kulkarni's attitude that by allowing this meeting to be held, he was accommodating Shashi's request. Shashi decided not to push it, as he had another request to make of the executive director at the end of the presentation.

He began by introducing Tanuja and himself and saying that they had come to share insights from an analysis they had carried out. He went on to establish Tanuja's credentials as a data scientist who had worked with the LSE and NYSE. Just then, the door opened again and two men stepped in. Ranade and Daniel.

'We have done a preliminary analysis of data from our share registrar,' Shashi continued. 'We think you will find it interesting.'

With that, he handed the floor to Tanuja, who launched into the first slide of her presentation. It showed the jagged graph rising steadily from left to right. At seven places in between, the graph jumped sharply to varying degrees.

'This is Purple Country's share price movement for the past two years,' she said briskly, her clipped British accent bringing expressions of surprise to some faces. 'As you can see, the share price has climbed steadily from ₹52 to ₹514 in these two years. While there has been a steady upward trend, the price jumped rather significantly on seven occasions.'

Tanuja hit a key on her laptop and seven red boxes appeared around the seven places where the graph moved sharply upwards.

'We refer to these as "events". The price jumps during these events range from 8 to 20 per cent, except once, when it jumped 30 per cent.' She indicated one of the seven red boxes with her laser pointer.

'How long have these jumps taken?' Kulkarni asked.

'One to three days.'

'And the 30 per cent jump?'

'Two days.' She turned to face the others in the room. 'When we correlated these events with developments within Purple Country, we found that six of them corresponded to announcements of financial results and the seventh to an acquisition. Unsurprisingly, good financial results have made the share price jump. Any questions?'

The men in the room shook their heads.

'Now, let's take a look at the trading volumes,' she continued and went on to the next slide.

It showed an uneven graph resembling the skyline of a far-off, jagged mountain range on some alien planet. It was punctuated with tall, sharp spires rising amidst long, shallow valleys that ran for much of the graph's length.

She let the audience study the graph for a minute before hitting a key again. The seven red boxes sprang to life once more, enclosing seven of the tallest spires within them.

'These are the seven events I mentioned earlier,' she said. 'Trading volumes jumped very significantly during these events.'

'That's not abnormal,' Daniel interjected, speaking for the first time. 'Spurts in trading volumes often accompany price jumps. And they frequently occur around result announcements.'

'I agree,' Tanuja smiled. 'People invariably trade more at these times. Sellers try to book profit, while buyers look to invest in a promising stock. However...' She paused to emphasize her imminent disagreement, '...look at the profile of this spurt.'

She hit a key and went to the next slide, which showed the close-up of one of the spires.

'The trading volume has ballooned *before* the event. Normally, volumes rise *after* the price jump, not before.'

Daniel sat up, staring intently at the graph on the slide. 'Are you sure about this?' he asked.

'Absolutely.'

Two other men had also grown visibly excited. Kulkarni's eyes were on them.

'Is this the pattern during all seven events?' Daniel asked.

'Yes.'

'What is the relevance of this?' Kulkarni cut in.

Before Tanuja could respond, Daniel spoke up.

'A favourable announcement from a company increases interest in the stock, sir,' he explained. 'For example, if a company announces a better-than-expected quarterly result, some investors rush to buy it. Or if a company makes an acquisition that gives it an advantage, the price jumps and investors buy into the stock.

'In other words, sir, there is a cause-and-effect relationship between the two, where the announcement is the cause and the increased volumes the effect. The effect would follow the cause. But this analysis reveals quite the opposite! The effect is preceding the cause! People are buying large volumes of the stock before the financial results are announced. That can happen only if they are anticipating favourable results.'

'Are you suggesting that they had privileged information about the company's performance?'

'Precisely! Insider trading.'

Shashi intervened.

'One moment!' he said crisply, drawing all eyes to himself. 'Before we pass judgement, let's understand that what we are seeing here is an analysis of trades. These patterns are indicative, not conclusive.

'For insider trading to be established as a fact, we need to accomplish two essential things: first, we must prove that privileged information was passed from one party to another. Second, we must prove that the recipient acted on the information. What we are seeing here is neither. This is only a pattern that suggests insider trading as a possibility.'

'Ms Tanuja,' Kulkarni asked, 'have you seen such patterns before?'

'Yes. Thrice in New York and at least twice in London.'

'Did they indicate insider trading in those instances?'

'Yes, they did. But as Shashi said, they are indicative and will not stand in a court of law. To make that possible, we must get more details and redo this analysis with the actual transaction prices. For that, we will need stock exchange data. Now, if you permit me, I'll proceed with the presentation. There is more.'

'Please.'

Shashi watched Kulkarni with growing satisfaction. This was exactly what he had hoped for. The executive director was hooked and the interest of the audience had been aroused. That the suggestion of insider trading had come from one of SEBI's men was an added bonus. Shashi didn't have to convince them now. He suppressed a smile and turned to watch Tanuja.

'Now,' she said, 'I will turn to the analysis of the share-registrar data. We analysed the trades around these seven events, limiting our analysis to large trades. We searched for cases where a person or company bought the share before an event and sold it soon after. We found a large number of such cases.

'Then for each event, we added up all the share purchases made by a person or a company before the event and, similarly, added up their sales after the event. This is what we found.'

She hit a key and went to the next slide. It showed rows of data from a spreadsheet.

'Two hundred and twenty-seven cases of purchase before an event and sale immediately after the event. In almost all the cases, the buyer sold the entire purchase within two weeks of purchase.'

She paused to let her stirred-up audience study the slide, then switched to a spreadsheet. She slowly scrolled down to show them all the 227 rows.

'The average profit from these trades has been 17.2 per cent,' she continued, pointing to a highlighted figure at the bottom of the spreadsheet. 'And now, we go to our final finding.'

She brought up the next slide.

'When we analysed these 227 cases further, we found that they had been executed by 49 demat accounts. Some of them had traded during all seven events and some less often. But what is clear is that the people operating these 49 demat accounts have been systematically profiting from buying and selling Purple Country shares.'

A buzz of murmurs, rising to a crescendo of louder exchanges, erupted in the room as the SEBI men began speaking excitedly to each other. Only Ranade remained silent, gazing pensively at Shashi and Tanuja, twirling his pen between his thumb and forefinger. Tanuja returned to her seat and Shashi, having risen in anticipation, took up the discussion.

'Gentlemen!' he called and waited for the murmurs to subside. 'What you have seen is a preliminary analysis of the data we obtained from our share registrars. We couldn't use actual stock exchange transactions, because we don't have access to them. And since we couldn't get transaction prices, we have used daily average prices to estimate value. This is not precise and will not be accepted as evidence. As Tanuja said, we need to redo this with actual stock exchange transactions.

'Further, our data only includes the cash-segment transactions where delivery has been taken. It does not include futures and options, which is a more cost-effective way to profit from privileged information.

'And finally, we haven't yet determined the identities of the people behind the 49 demat accounts. We could have extracted them from the share registrar data, but that would have been time-consuming and we didn't have time to spare.'

'If you can give me the demat account numbers,' Daniel said, 'I will get you the details.'

'Thank you. I have the list ready.'

Shashi strode across and handed Daniel a CD and three sheets of paper. Once they identified the dubious traders, he would know which of his employees was leaking inside information.

He had also got Kulkarni sufficiently interested in the analysis. The next step would be to ask him for access to stock exchange data. He turned to the executive director and continued.

'One issue Tanuja didn't elaborate on is the trend of suspicious trading you have just seen. It has increased steadily over the past two years.'

'Who else knows about your analysis?' Kulkarni asked.

'Only our chairman, Mr Gupta. Nobody from Purple Country has been involved in the analysis. I have not been to the office this week and Tanuja has been working in the hotel.'

'I see...How long did this take you?'

'Two days.'

Kulkarni's eyebrows shot up. Shashi smiled and continued.

'She had done some groundwork in London, but she received the trade data as recently as yesterday morning. Once we get the names and addresses of these 49 demat accounts, we'll be able to complete our preliminary analysis. We can then rerun the analysis with stock exchange data, if you wish.'

Kulkarni turned and nodded at the others. They rose and filed out of the room, leaving Ranade and Daniel behind.

'This is Daniel from EOW,' Kulkarni said by way of introduction, gesturing towards the man Shashi did not know. 'He has been working with us for the past two weeks on a matter that is related to you in some way.'

'Me?' Shashi said, taken aback.

'We have been investigating your late brother-in-law, Mr Tola. We received an anonymous tip-off from someone who claimed that Mr Tola was indulging in insider trading and other illicit practices.'

'What!' Shashi couldn't contain his surprise. Of all the people in the world, Vivek! Was it just a coincidence?

'That's why I found it extremely interesting when you spoke the other day about possible insider trading in Purple Country. Inspector Ranade thinks he knows who the anonymous caller is, but is unable to prove it.'

Shashi turned to Ranade enquiringly.

'Navin Gokul,' the inspector said. 'Do you know him?'

'No,' Shashi replied. 'Do you want me to check with Chaaya?'

Ranade nodded and Shashi turned back to Daniel.

'When can I expect the account details of the 49 demat accounts?' he asked.

'You'll have them by tomorrow.'

'Excellent!' He turned to Kulkarni. 'Can we meet the day after? We'll share the final findings with you. We have some suspicions that can be confirmed only after we get the details of the demat accounts.'

Kulkarni nodded. 'Okay. I'll be able to tell you the specific time of the meeting in the morning.'

With the man's goodwill on his side, Shashi decided to press his advantage.

'Mr Kulkarni,' he said, 'I have a few ideas on further analysis that we can do after this one. But for that, I will need access to stock exchange data. Tanuja is going to be with us this week and the next. She can help us. And it won't cost you anything.'

Kulkarni gazed at Shashi for a long moment and nodded. 'Let's see what we can do.'

'But Shashi,' Tanuja cut in, 'I won't be able to analyse stock exchange data on my laptop. It can't handle the volume. I'll need a powerful computer and the appropriate tools.'

Kulkarni chuckled. 'I think we can be of some help there.'

▪

'Do you realize what a tight spot we're putting Shashi in?' Kamna asked Chaaya.

For the past two days, she had been brooding over the matter of broaching the topic tactfully without offending her sister. Knowing it would be difficult, she had nonetheless urged herself to go ahead; Shashi's plight was becoming increasingly difficult to witness.

Chaaya blinked in surprise. 'Are we?' she countered. 'In what way?'

'By involving him in Vivek's business affairs. Not only is Shashi being investigated for insider trading, he's a suspect in Vivek's murder, Chaaya! You do understand, don't you, that things will only get worse for him if he withholds information from the police? What's more, we made copies of the photograph Ranade had brought over for us to look at – that too after he expressly instructed us not to share it with anyone. Shashi will be in deep trouble if the inspector finds out about that.'

Kamna was dismayed to see that her sister's eyes had turned a shade colder.

'You don't want us to involve your husband in anything related to Vivek, is it?' Chaaya murmured. 'I see. I...I am so sorry, Kamna. I hadn't realized you felt this way about your own family.'

'No, no! That's not what I meant, Chaaya,' Kamna protested, feeling mortified. 'What I'm trying to say is that we must be careful about how we involve Shashi.'

'In other words, I shouldn't have taken him to Vivek's office? Is that what you meant?'

'Um...well...Oh God! How do I put it?' Cornered, she blurted out, 'Look, Chaaya, Shashi prefers not to be entrusted with information he cannot share with the inspector. For instance, he's aware of the contents of Vivek's safe at the office, but must keep that information from Ranade. Similarly, the notebook is potential evidence, both against Vivek's killer and the insider leaking privileged information from Purple Country. If Shashi withholds such information from the police, he will be incriminating himself further and getting into deeper trouble. And with that Sudakar after him, he can't afford to take such risks. We mustn't get him into a greater mess than he's already in. Please try and understand that, Chaaya.'

'But...but...' Her sister's eyes brimmed. 'What option do I have, Kamna? Other than you and Shashi, who else do I have to stand by me in a crisis like this?'

'I know! I understand!' Kamna murmured soothingly, her heart going out to her recently widowed sister. She sat down beside her now and took her hand comfortingly in her own. 'Well, what's done is done, I guess. But from now on, let's just think things through before –'

She broke off at the sound of a moving vehicle outside and went to the window to check. Full of remorse at the awkward way she had handled the issue and ended up upsetting her sister, Kamna was furious with herself. Trust her to botch it up! Her words had come out all wrong and she had hurt Chaaya's feelings. She was now impatient for Shashi to return, keen on learning how SEBI had reacted. He had mentioned over the phone that Tanuja had found clear indications of insider trading in Purple Country shares, but he had not shared the details with her.

Kamna peered out of the window. The sun had just set and

darkness was descending with the onset of dusk. It seemed denser, more opaque than usual, all-enveloping. It took her a moment to figure out why.

'The watchman hasn't yet switched on the lights outside,' she remarked to Chaaya, trying to change the topic that had caused her sister such pain.

'Sonu!' Chaaya called out.

The manservant instantly emerged from the lobby. '*Ji*, madam?' he murmured.

'Tell the watchman to switch on the lights outside,' she told him in Hindi. 'I fail to understand how he keeps forgetting. He's been working here long enough.'

'*Ji*, madam.'

Kamna watched Sonu open the front door. The moment he did, he seemed to freeze. Then slowly, he backed away from the open door as though something out there had terrified him. The corridor outside was dark. From that darkness emerged three men. They entered the flat boldly, silently, shut the door behind them and locked it. With them was the watchman, mute and trembling with fear.

With a shock, Kamna realized that the strangers were all armed. She stared at the elongated snouts of their pistols. Silencers. The men were in police uniform and one of them was wearing a cap like Ranade's. Between the cap, pulled low over the forehead, and the beard, little of the man's face was visible. The other two men had ski masks pulled over their faces.

Ordering the watchman to go and squat in a corner, the men spread out across the room. One moved close to the window and gestured with his pistol to Kamna, directing her to draw the curtains. Numb from shock, she came to her senses with a start and complied. Another man had taken up position behind Sonu, his pistol pressing into the servant's back. The third man, the one with the cap, was evidently the leader. He strode to the centre of the drawing room, where Chaaya stood in mute terror.

'Hand over the notebook,' he said in Hindi, adjusting his cap so that it didn't obstruct his vision. A bit more of his face was now visible.

'What?' Chaaya seemed confused. 'What notebook?'

'Your husband's notebook. The one you used to call people today.'

Chaaya hesitated, unsure and frightened. Kamna watched her pale face, trying to read her thoughts. The contents of the notebook were key to her picking up the threads of the shady half of Vivek's business dealings. But how had the men got to know of the notebook so quickly? The only people who could have guessed it existed were the ones Chaaya had called.

'Where are your children?' the leader asked in a soft voice.

The blood drained from Chaaya's face. It looked chalky white, like a ghost's.

'A…away,' she stammered, her words barely louder than a whisper. 'At a friend's place.'

They had actually gone to her cousin's house for the night.

The man turned and looked at Kamna. 'Your sister?' he asked Chaaya.

He gestured with his pistol and the man by the window jabbed his weapon into Kamna's ribs. She gasped and staggered back in pain.

Chaaya needed no more convincing.

'It's inside…the notebook,' she blurted out. 'I'll have to go and get it.'

'Be quick. I'm right behind you. So don't try anything smart. Remember that one gun is pointed at your sister and another at your servant. My men won't hesitate to pull the trigger.'

Chaaya disappeared into the lobby, with the leader following close behind. They were back in a minute, Chaaya walking ahead of the man in whose hand was clutched the notebook she had brought back home from Vivek's office safe.

Kamna focused her attention on the leader and studied his features intently. Could he be Kashyap? Did his face resemble the one in the photo Ranade had shown them? She decided after a couple of seconds that it did not. In that case, this was someone else. One more person who could lead them to Vivek's killer. She began studying his face in detail, trying to memorize every contour, every visible feature.

Presently, at a signal from him, the man standing close to Kamna backed away to the door. When the leader turned to the third man who was guarding Sonu, she scrutinized his profile, filing away as many details in her mind as she could. In response to the leader's gesture, the third man pushed Sonu towards the door, his pistol pressing into the small of his back.

The leader slowly backed towards the door, his eyes sweeping across the room from one side to the other as he scanned it carefully, giving Kamna the chance to examine his face from three angles – the front and in profile, from both sides.

'We're taking your servant along with us. We'll release him once we get away from here,' he said. 'Raise the alarm and you'll never see him again. No sounds, no phone calls, nothing. Understood?'

Unable to utter a word, Chaaya merely nodded. The men stepped backwards into the dark corridor outside and closed the door. Kamna dashed to the window and moved the curtain aside an inch. A minute later, Sonu, prodded by the three khaki-clad men, emerged from the building and climbed into a white Scorpio with them. Fifteen seconds later, the vehicle had driven off and vanished into the darkness.

Chapter 18

Shashi frowned, puzzled at the expression of extreme anxiety, verging on fear, with which Chaaya answered the door. Her general behaviour had been just as odd. She had opened the door a crack and peered out at him before unlatching the door chain. The watchman at the gate too hadn't seemed himself. Despite the look of intense relief on his face when he saw Shashi, the man had looked jittery and mumbled something unintelligible in response to his query.

'Thank God, it's you!' Chaaya whispered. She opened the door partially to let Shashi through, only to shut it quickly and lock it the moment he had stepped inside.

'What happened?' he asked, bewildered, surveying the hall for a clue.

Kamna was busy sketching on a sheet of paper and did not look up. The frown of concentration on her face told him that she was not to be disturbed. On the small table in front of her lay several pencils and some sheets of paper. The contrast between her single-minded focus on her sketching and Chaaya's tension perplexed him all the more. Something was amiss.

'They came and forcibly took away the notebook,' Chaaya blurted out, her voice shaking with pent-up fear.

'Who?' Shashi asked, staring at her.

'Three men,' she replied, her voice dropping as though the walls had ears.

'Anyone you know?'

Chaaya shook her head.

'Complete strangers,' she said in a hushed voice. 'Armed. Asked where the children were.' Her face crumpled at the thought of what could have happened if they'd been around, but she composed herself with some effort. 'They took Sonu away with them to ensure their own safety. Said they would release him later.'

'The notebook they took – was it the same one you had brought back from Vivek's office safe?'

Chaaya nodded. 'That's specifically what the men came for. Somehow, they knew I had it with me.'

'But how?' Shashi asked. 'Vivek's cabin has frosted glass all around. Nobody could have seen you take the notebook out of the safe. Nor could anyone have seen me putting it into my jacket pocket.'

'Remember those people to whom I had made calls yesterday? I had to look up their phone numbers in the notebook,' she said softly. 'One of them must have passed on the information.'

'I see.'

Shashi paused, absorbing what Chaaya had just told him. He took in the look of devastation on her face and was surprised that Kamna hadn't looked up once from her sketch nor made any effort to calm her sister down. He took Chaaya gently by the elbow and made her sit down on the sofa beside him.

'Now tell me in detail what happened,' he said gently.

As Chaaya narrated the sequence of events, her sister continued to sketch furiously.

'Sonu hasn't returned yet?' Shashi asked, when she had finished.

Chaaya shook her head, her wide, fearful eyes fixed on his face. 'I hope he's okay,' she said in a choked voice.

'Ah! It's done!' Kamna's voice suddenly cut into their exchanges. 'Have a look, Chaaya.'

They stood around the sofa to gaze at the four sheets of paper that Kamna had laid out on the small table before her. They were all portraits of the same man – bearded in the first two, clean-shaven in the others. In the first portrait and the third, he was facing the viewer; in the second and fourth, he was in profile.

'Ditto!' Chaaya exclaimed, pointing excitedly to the bearded faces. 'That's exactly how he looks! Kamna, you're a genius!'

'I know this guy,' Shashi muttered, picking up the sketch for a closer look. Anger rose in him as full recognition dawned. 'It's Varma!'

'The man who accompanied Kashyap to your office?' Kamna gasped. 'You're sure?'

'You bet! He's the SEBI impostor.'

Shashi drew out his phone and photographed the two sketches. While sending them to Carol, he glanced at the other two sketches. 'What about these?' he asked. 'The clean-shaven versions?'

'This is how I imagine he would look without his beard,' Kamna said, examining the drawings again. 'I had a good, hard look at the contours of his jawline, cheekbones and lips. I am fairly sure this is how he actually looks. That beard is fake, you know.'

Within a couple of minutes, Carol had sent her own confirmation of the man's identity; he was, indeed, Varma.

'We must inform the inspector about this,' Shashi declared. 'We'll need his help. Things have become way too dangerous.'

'No!' Chaaya cried. 'That's out of the question. If he comes to know about the notebook, he'll start asking awkward questions. One thing will lead to another and we'll be forced to disclose the details of Vivek's business dealings to him.'

'Okay, then –' Shashi began, but Kamna interrupted him.

'The watchman is already aware of what happened, Chaaya,' she reminded her sister gently. 'Word would have spread to several people by now. I'd be surprised if the watchman hasn't already told our driver. He was right here in the room after those men brought him in at gunpoint, remember? Sonu was present too. They both know what those men were after. The man – Varma – clearly asked for the notebook and took it away with him. Sonu and the watchman saw it all and overheard every word. It's only a matter of time before the police come to know – whether we choose to call them in or not.'

'But Kamna, they'll insist on knowing what the notebook contained!' Chaaya wailed. 'They'll want to know what was so important in it that had made those men desperate to retrieve it.'

'Yes, Chaaya, I understand.' Kamna's voice was gentle, soothing. 'Let's think this over a bit and decide what would be the safest reply to such questions.'

'Perhaps,' Shashi suggested, 'you could say you didn't know what it contained.'

'Will they buy it?' Kamna asked.

Shashi shrugged.

'Will they get to know about the phone calls Chaaya made to those eleven people?' Kamna persisted.

'We can't rule it out, I guess,' he replied, drawing out each word. 'All they have to do is look at Chaaya's call records.'

'Remember what Papa used to say, Chaaya?' Kamna asked. '"When you have to lie, stick as close to the truth as possible. Especially, the verifiable truth." You've heard him say that often enough.'

Chaaya nodded. 'Those men forcing their way into the flat and taking the book away is verifiable,' she mused. 'And the police could well find out that I did make those calls. They would, wouldn't they, Shashi?'

'The more I think about it, the more likely it seems,' he replied. 'Things are getting murkier and neither you nor I can throw much light on what's happening or why. It's safest to assume that the police will check all our call records. With a break-in and a larceny following so soon after Vivek's death, the police are unlikely to leave any avenue unexplored.'

'Let's sleep over it,' Kamna suggested. 'We have till tomorrow morning to decide. Let's also hand my sketches to Ranade tomorrow – '

'Oh!' Chaaya intervened, 'Pandey Bhaiya called. That man Kashyap is often seen around Sewri, he says. He's trying to find out where exactly in Sewri.'

'He discovered this in just three days?' Shashi asked, impressed.

'This kind of thing is right up his street, Shashi.'

'Shouldn't we keep Ranade posted about this?' he asked.

Chaaya shook her head firmly. 'No. I don't want him knowing about Pandey Bhaiya.'

'There's no way we can share Pandey Bhaiya's information with him, Shashi,' Kamna added. 'Ranade will ask straight off how he managed to identify Kashyap without knowing what he looked like. One thing will lead to another and he'll find out that we copied the photo he'd brought with him, despite his express instructions to keep it confidential. Then we'll be held guilty of deliberately compromising the investigation.'

They were skating on thin ice, Shashi realized. Dangerously thin ice. He had not yet lied outright to Ranade, but was getting close to that moment. He had already withheld a fair bit of information. Yet they were working together with SEBI on the analysis of share trades. Worst of all, he was hiding something from Ranade, although he didn't even know what it was that he was hiding. He *had* to find out what the black wooden box contained, the one that Kamna had brought over from Chaaya's house and put away in her steel almirah.

▪

'Why is insider trading considered such a big deal, Daniel?' Ranade asked, as they sat facing each other across the inspector's desk, sipping tea. 'So many people make money in the stock market in so many different ways. Why is insider trading singled out for special condemnation?'

'Information asymmetry, Ranade,' Daniel replied. 'An insider has more accurate information than the average market player. If he were to use that to trade, it would be unfair on the market players. And if such trading were allowed to continue unfettered, faith in the equity markets would be eroded and the markets would collapse.'

'But information asymmetry does exist in the stock market, doesn't it? While conducting proprietary research, big firms interview company executives and government officials. They then use the information gleaned to trade. They don't share it with the market.'

'You've touched upon what some consider a grey area. It's a thin line between proprietary research and insider information. A somewhat blurred line, to be honest. Do you know, some people actually advocate legalizing insider trading? Some of these guys are economists and writers.'

'Really? What is their argument in support of making it legal?'

'They have two or three. One is about the nature of free markets – markets are about information and share prices should reflect the latest available information. An efficient market uses the most up-to-date information to adjust a share price. By banning insider information, they say, you prevent the latest information from getting to the market. In Doug Bandow's words, we force people to trade today on yesterday's information.

'On the other hand, had insider trading been legal, the transgressions at Enron and other companies would have been exposed sooner. People inside these companies would have sent signals by dumping stocks or selling them short – critical signals would have reached the markets sooner, even if the information itself hadn't.'

'Interesting!' Ranade remarked. 'I didn't know there were big guns advocating legalization of insider trading.'

'Oh, there are!' Daniel continued. 'Some also argue in favour of legislation that will make insider trading a legitimate means for company employees to earn an income. That way, salaries can be kept low, making companies more profitable. It would benefit shareholders.'

'Really? So what's your take, Daniel?'

The other man grinned and shook his head. 'You and I only enforce the law, Ranade. We don't make it. If the law says it's illegal, it *is* illegal. Ours is not to question why…and that sort of thing.

'Having said that, I should point out that insider trading takes place in other areas. Like real estate. As soon as you come to know that your neighbour is selling his flat, you rush in to buy it before the information about its availability on the market becomes public. The same is true of the job market; as soon as you know there's a vacancy, you rush to pip others to the post.

'But leaving all these hypothetical situations aside, my problem with insider trading is that it is hard to detect and still harder to prove. For example, if you did *not* buy a stock because an insider had told you that the share price was likely to fall, wouldn't that be insider trading too? But there is no way to catch it. Even in the so-called regular cases, it is horrendously difficult to establish the information trail that led to insider trading.'

Daniel rose to his feet as Abdul walked in.

'I better get back,' he said. 'Thanks for the tea. See you tomorrow.'

'Any progress on tracing Kashyap?' Ranade asked Abdul, once Daniel had left.

For want of his actual name, they had taken to referring to the man by the alias he had used while masquerading as an EOW officer.

Abdul shook his head. 'We don't have leads that tell us where to look, sir. And we don't want to tip him off by being too open in our search.' He drew out some photographs from a cover and grinned broadly as he said, 'But we've had better luck in Pune.'

He spread four sets of photographs on the desk. Some were close-ups; others had been taken from afar. The pictures had caught four men from different angles and in various postures – standing, lounging, walking.

'Your hunch was right, sir,' Abdul continued. 'Two of these men are taking turns to keep a watch on Navin's house and office. They are usually alone, but they turn up together sometimes.'

Ranade studied the photographs at length. The close-ups were clear and would come in handy for identification. The high-resolution long shots provided credible evidence that could be used in court.

'Have you identified them?' he asked the other man.

'These two are thugs from a local gang,' Abdul told him, jabbing the photographs of two young men with his forefinger. 'The others are from Mumbai. They have been seen several times in Sewri. We don't know their names yet.'

'Ah! Look for Kashyap in Sewri. He would be connected to these men.'

Ranade sat back and picked up a pencil to twirl around his thumb. With a faraway look in his eyes, he began reviewing the case in his mind. Abdul drew up a chair and sat across the desk. The twirling pencil was a sign that Ranade wanted to think aloud.

'Let's see what we know so far,' the inspector began. 'Vivek was killed in a pre-planned manner, using TTX on chilli cheese toast. It is clear from the footage that the killer was Kashyap, but we don't know who is behind him.'

'Either Kurva was incredibly lucky that the killer chose a cheese dish,' Abdul commented, 'or he knew that the snack was poisoned.'

'Hmm...yes. There is a third possibility too. The killer knew of Kurva's aversion to cheese. If so, the killer knows him well and wants to keep him alive for some reason. Let's set that aside for the moment and discuss what we *do* know.'

'Yes sir. What about Vivek's insider trading?'

Ranade shook his head. 'We don't know for sure that Vivek traded in Purple Country shares. Assuming the guise of a SEBI man, Varma had *claimed* that Vivek had traded in them. Kurva *suspects* Vivek of trading in the shares through his company. But we have not established it as fact.'

'In that case, nothing regarding the insider trading affair has been established as fact.'

'Correct. For all we know, it may be a mirage, a fictional invention to mislead us and cast suspicion on Kurva.'

'Why would someone want to implicate him?'

Ranade shrugged. 'Who knows?'

'I would tend to agree with what Kurva told you earlier, sir. It would be very stupid of him to kill his brother-in-law a day after they had been seen arguing in public.'

Ranade remained silent, frowning and twirling the pencil.

'Besides, what does Kurva stand to gain from it?' Abdul went on.

'That is the biggest hole we have in the case, Abdul – the motive. Why was Vivek killed? It's a strange case. Opportunity, means and weapon are all clear. We also know who actually delivered the poison; we have video footage of the murder taking place. But we don't know why it was carried out. Was it something to do with the insider trading at Purple Country? Or something else?' He looked up at his deputy. 'What did you think of Vivek as a person?'

'An astute businessman?'

'An interesting man. On the one hand, he installs a water cooler for thirsty pedestrians and maintains a temple for people in the locality. Charitable acts, on the face of it. On the other hand, he has a reputation for ruthlessness, especially when it comes to money. With his coterie of henchmen and people in his pay who take care of the police and the taxman, he seems to have been a minor don in his own right. I'm told he had financed a couple of films too.'

'Such a man would have made enemies, sir.'

'Wouldn't he?' Ranade nodded. 'But Mrs Tola claims otherwise. What do you think of her?'

Abdul shrugged and shook his head.

'She's a fine lady,' the inspector continued. 'Remarkable poise and very attractive. A sharp woman too. Doesn't trust policemen. She isn't divulging even half of what she knows. She doesn't want me probing into her late husband's business affairs, that's for sure.'

'That's how they all are, sir. Too much black money floating around to let us come anywhere close.'

'And Navin Gokul? Is he telling the truth?'

'Not entirely, sir.' Abdul shook his head. 'He's holding back a good deal. We don't know where he was when Vivek was killed.'

Ranade nodded. 'The only thing we *do* know about Navin is that he fled from Pune on learning of Vivek's death. While the reason he offered for doing so seems plausible, there's more to his relationship with Vivek than meets the eye.'

'So we have very little by way of facts, sir. One: Kashyap killed Vivek by poisoning the chilli cheese toast. Two: Navin fled from Pune as soon as he learnt of Vivek's murder.'

'We know one more thing, but we don't know if and how it is connected with the case – the phone call from the public booth.'

'What phone call, sir?'

'Oh yes, I forgot to mention it. Kulkarni said that they were discreetly investigating Vivek Tola.'

'What for?'

'For potential illicit trades, including insider trading. You see, they had received an anonymous tip-off over the phone a few days ago. They investigated the call immediately and found that it had been made from a public phone booth in Pune that's roughly a kilometre from Navin's office.'

Ranade set down his pencil and rose.

'Come, let's talk to Navin once more. We don't have enough evidence to hold him any longer.'

Half an hour later, Ranade was sitting across the desk from Navin Gokul for the second time.

'Is there anything else you wish to tell me, Mr Gokul?' he asked.

Navin seemed brighter than he had been the previous day and more self-assured.

'Nothing, inspector.'

'Have you recollected anything about the call you made from the public booth?'

'I told you. I made no such call.' Navin looked Ranade in the eye as he spoke.

'Okay. You said you had fled from Pune, because you feared for your life. Do you feel safe enough to return now?'

'I must return sometime, I suppose. How much longer do you propose to detain me?'

'I could release you right away if that's what you wish. But if your fears about being targeted by Vivek's killer are well founded, you would be safer here in our custody.'

'I think I may have overreacted the day I heard about Vivek. His death came as such a shock that I panicked. I would like to return home as soon as possible.'

'Are you sure, Mr Gokul?'

Navin nodded.

'Your house and office are still being watched,' Ranade said slowly. 'Someone is waiting for you to return.'

Navin fell silent for a moment. His face betrayed nothing, except that he was thinking furiously. Presently, he threw up his hands and shrugged.

Chapter 19

Ranade gazed at Kamna's sketch in amazement. Thick with pencil strokes that seemed to create depth on a flat sheet of paper, it was far more realistic a portrait than any he had seen the police artists create. The face looked curiously alive, with details discernible only to an artist's trained eye. Unlike the police sketches he had come across in the course of his career, the portrait seemed to capture the emotions on the man's face.

'My compliments, Mrs Kurva,' he said in genuine admiration. 'I don't think I have ever seen a more realistic portrait. This will serve the purpose as effectively as a photograph would have. Perhaps you should join the force.'

Kamna smiled her thanks. 'I do hope it leads you somewhere, inspector,' she said. 'Those men must have been desperate to take such a chance.'

'Entirely my view too.' He turned to Chaaya who was sitting quietly beside her sister, taking in their exchanges. 'What was so important in the notebook to make those men that desperate, Mrs Tola?'

'I wish I knew,' Chaaya replied earnestly, her words tinged with helplessness. 'Unfortunately, I had just a brief look at its contents. I have no more than a sketchy impression.'

'And what did you see?'

'Just initials and phone numbers. Some were of people I knew

'I don't want to send you back into a situation where your life may be at risk, Mr Gokul, but I have nothing with which to hold you back,' Ranade continued deliberately. He had to make sure that Navin understood his position. 'But you could stay here longer if you wished. You will be protected.'

'Thank you, inspector. But as I said, I have to return sometime.'

For the next five minutes, Ranade spoke to Navin about the possible threats he could be facing, but the latter remained steadfast in his intent to return to Pune in the morning.

'Very well, then,' Ranade said. 'I'll sign your release right away. You can leave tonight or tomorrow morning. By the way, would you like to see Mrs Tola before you return to Pune?'

Abdul had brought in a cardboard box containing the things that had been taken from Gokul when he was detained. Navin opened the box and began transferring his belongings to his pockets as he replied.

'I have never met or spoken to Mrs Tola. I don't think she knows me.'

Why then, Ranade wondered, had Chaaya called him yesterday? There had been a missed call from her on Navin's mobile phone. Ranade rose and left the room to sign the release papers.

'Go to Pune early tomorrow morning, Abdul,' he directed after Gokul had departed. 'Navin's return to Pune is bound to stir things up. You will need to be quick. And make sure you're armed.'

and a few whom I didn't. Vivek must have had business dealings with them.'

'Only initials? No names?'

'That's right.'

'And what did you do after you had glanced through the notebook?'

'You see, inspector, I have to pick up the threads of my husband's business – now that he...he's no longer there – for our children's sake. So I called some of those numbers.'

'I see...Did you speak to all of them?'

Chaaya shook her head. 'Several, but not all.'

'Do you have the numbers you called, Mrs Tola?'

'I don't remember them, but they should be in the dialled numbers list in my phone.'

Ranade was vaguely puzzled by her unexpected cooperation, her sudden promptness in providing information, especially when he knew how much she distrusted the police. Surely, there was something illicit about this part of Vivek's business dealings? Why else had those names, marked by hard-to-identify initials and phone numbers, been jotted down in a notebook and hidden away in a safe?

'What did you discuss with the people you called?' he asked.

'Why do you want to know?' Chaaya's gaze was steady. 'What bearing does that have on your investigation?'

'Well, Mrs Tola, your calls prompted those men to invade your house and take the notebook away forcibly.'

Chaaya nodded.

'The motive for last evening's unfortunate incident is linked to your calls,' Ranade continued. 'The incident is, most likely, connected with Mr Tola's death.'

'Okay, I see your point. The calls were brief. The purpose was to inform those people that I was going to be looking after Vivek's business and would be in touch with them after I had taken stock. Meanwhile, they were to call me if they had anything to discuss. You see, inspector, I haven't yet had a chance to look at my husband's papers. But before I did that, I felt it was important for his clients to see that there was continuity.'

It was imperative for Chaaya to do that, Ranade thought, because Vivek had been a moneylender. It was critical for her to convince his borrowers that his widow was not only in charge now, but aware of the loans he had extended to them. So the all-important notebook must have contained details of Vivek's illicit loans – records that the EOW and the income tax authorities would love to get their hands on. Likelier than not, one or more of the listed borrowers did not want to pay up and had forcibly removed the notebook from Vivek's home to erase the loan record.

Ranade pushed aside the thought and resumed his discussion.

'Did you speak to someone called Navin Gokul?' he asked.

'Navin Gokul?' she repeated the name slowly, as though pronouncing it for the first time. 'I don't think so. Two of my calls went unanswered, though. One of those numbers had the initials "NKG" against it, I think.'

'Navin Kumar Gokul. That's right.'

'Who is he?' Chaaya frowned, apparently trying to place the name.

'Mr Tola's partner in Aran Advisors, his Pune venture.'

'Ah!' Chaaya's face cleared. 'I see. I didn't know his name. I don't think I have met him.'

Ranade nodded. That tallied with Navin's version and Chaaya sounded sincere enough. Unless some deep subterfuge was involved, both were speaking the truth.

'Was that the name you mentioned yesterday at the SEBI office?' Shashi interrupted. 'The anonymous tipster?'

Ranade nodded and quickly changed the topic. This was not something he wanted to discuss in Chaaya's presence.

'May I request you to hand me those phone numbers you dialled, Mrs Tola?' he asked.

Ten minutes later, he was walking out of the flat with two new avenues of investigation to explore – Kamna's sketch and the phone numbers.

At last, the case was gathering momentum.

▪

Ranade and Daniel were already in the small discussion room when Tanuja and Shashi walked in. Unlike the previous meeting, this one was being held in an unmarked office in BKC, a short distance from Kulkarni's office. The executive director had called earlier in the day and given Shashi the address of the computer centre that housed new high-end equipment to analyse market trades.

Hardly had Tanuja set up the laptop and the projector than Kulkarni joined them.

'Nobody else will be joining us,' he assured them. 'Keeping in mind the nature of the information that could potentially be revealed today, it's best that we restrict the group size.' He turned to Tanuja. 'We will show you our facilities after the meeting. If they meet your requirements – which I think they should – you can continue your analysis here. I have got you clearance to access the stock exchange and depository data.'

'NSE or BSE?' Shashi asked.

'Both. You'll have to sign a confidentiality agreement – both of you.'

'Sure. Can we start with the presentation? It's going to be a relatively short one.'

Kulkarni nodded and Shashi began as Tanuja took her seat.

'We had concluded the last meeting with a list of 49 demat accounts that had benefited significantly from trading in Purple Country shares,' he said. 'We saw evidence of each account purchasing shares just before an event and selling them at a profit immediately after. The average gain was 17.2 per cent and the average holding time was 6.3 days.

'Prima facie, it was clear that the people behind these forty-nine accounts had high confidence in the outcomes of each event, as they had risked large amounts of money. But we did not know their identities. With Mr Daniel Paul providing us with the names and addresses of these demat accounts, we now have the identities too.'

Shashi hit a key and brought up a spreadsheet on the screen. It showed names, addresses, dates, share volumes, share prices and profits. He quickly scrolled through the forty-nine rows without pausing on any one name.

'This list becomes more interesting when we start grouping these 49 accounts based on their addresses. We find that seventeen of these account holders are individuals and 32 are companies. Let's look at the 17 individuals first.'

He went to the next tab on the spreadsheet.

'When we compared the addresses of the 17 account holders and eliminated duplicates, we arrive at a list of 8 households. Each household had been using two or three demat accounts to trade in Purple Country shares. All have one account in the husband's name and another in the wife's. Some hold another jointly or in a child's name. There is only one exception, where the trader has used a single demat account.

'When we narrowed down the 17 individual demat accounts to eight households and aggregated the profits, we found that…'

Shashi went to the third tab of the spreadsheet and dramatically directed the laser pointer to the bottom of the screen.

'…the households had profited by ₹31 lakh on the average.'

'Who are these people?' Kulkarni asked.

'I'm not sure, although I do recognize a couple of names.' Shashi looked at Ranade and continued. 'That is something you can find out easily.'

'Certainly. I was going to ask for the spreadsheet.'

'Excellent! We have made copies for you on CDs.'

'Did you find any Purple Country employee on your list?' Kulkarni asked.

'No.' Shashi couldn't help smiling in relief. 'I confess I am pleased that there isn't a single employee on this list.'

'What about Vivek Tola?' Daniel asked.

Shashi shook his head. 'He isn't there either.' He looked at Ranade. 'You remember, inspector, Vivek had told me as much?'

'What had he said?' Daniel asked.

'That *he* hadn't traded in Purple Country shares.'

'Okay. These are the demat accounts held by individuals. What about the ones operated by firms? Mr Tola may have traded through a company.'

Shashi went to the next tab; he had arranged the tabs sequentially to match the order of the presentation.

'Unlike individuals, the firms are difficult to group. While a few of them share addresses, that alone may not be conclusive. We will need to look at the promoters of each firm to consolidate the list. Someone with easy access to promoter and shareholder details of these firms would be in a position to pierce the corporate veils.

'Even without aggregating related firms, the numbers are in a different league. While the average household profited by ₹31 lakh, the average firm – *each* of the 32 firms on an average – has profited by 1.87 crores. This is *before* aggregating the firms by promoter. If an average promoter uses four firms, he or she would have profited by seven or eight crores.'

'And these,' Tanuja added from where she sat, 'are only trades where share delivery was taken. These do not include derivatives.'

'I see the point you were making yesterday,' Kulkarni said, his pensive gaze resting on Tanuja. 'A trader can make a lot more money in derivatives than in outright share purchase.' He pointed at the screen and continued. 'If this is the position in share purchase, I wonder what an analysis of derivatives will throw up.'

Ranade cleared his throat awkwardly. 'Pardon me,' he said a trifle apologetically. 'Could you explain what you just said? I'm an ignoramus on derivatives trading.'

'It's like this, inspector,' Shashi answered. 'The traditional way to trade in the stock market is to buy and sell shares. When you buy a share, you pay the prevailing market price and the share is credited to your demat account. When you sell it, you get the full share price, and the shares go out of your demat account.'

'Okay.'

'Now, derivatives are contracts, not shares. Simply put, you enter into a contract to buy or sell shares on a certain date in the future, but you don't actually buy the share. As a part of the contract, you agree on the price at which you will buy or sell the share. Let's say that Purple Country is trading at ₹250 today. You can enter into a contract to buy the share at ₹275 on the last Thursday of this month. If you hold the contract till that day and the share price goes up to ₹300, you can still buy it at ₹275, even though the market price is ₹300. You stand to gain ₹25.'

'Got it. But I don't understand Mr Kulkarni's comment. How can a trader make more money in derivatives than in outright share purchase?'

'When you buy a share outright, you pay the full market price. Full 100 per cent. But when you trade in derivatives, you don't need to pay the full price. You need to pay only, say, 15 per cent of the market price when you enter into a contract. Only if you hold the contract until maturity do you have to pay the balance.

'Let's say that you have ₹10 lakh to invest. At ₹250 per share, you can buy 4,000 shares if you purchase the shares outright. But with the same ₹10 lakh, you can buy contracts for 26,667 shares if you take the derivatives route. And when the share price jumps by

10 per cent in a few days, the value of your contract too will jump by around 10 per cent. You can make *seven* times the profit if you take the derivatives route.'

'I see...This is most interesting! Thank you, Mr Kurva. For analysing derivatives trades, you need data from the stock exchanges.'

'Precisely! And Mr Kulkarni has just given us access to that.'

'Coming back to your analysis, Mr Kurva,' Daniel said, as Ranade sat back, 'do you recognize any of the firms?'

'Unfortunately, I do. The names of two of those firms are familiar. I saw their nameplates at Vivek Tola's office.'

'The small brass-and-wood nameplates beside the glass doors leading into his office?' Ranade asked, sitting up.

Shashi nodded. This was the part he had been hedging, hoping that postponing it would somehow solve the problem.

'To be honest, inspector, I was hoping I wouldn't find those names in our analysis; that Vivek had nothing to do with the trading of Purple Country shares. I wish it weren't that way, but I can't argue with data. It's now up to you to verify it. But please grant me this one request – I don't want to tell Chaaya as yet. She'll be absolutely devastated.'

An uncomfortable silence descended on the group as Shashi sat down heavily and stared at his fingernails. He had prayed that Vivek hadn't traded in Purple Country shares through his firms. His prayer hadn't been answered.

He was surprised at his own reaction. How much his attitude towards Vivek had changed in these few days! A week ago, he had gone to meet him with the intention of nailing him and bringing his transgressions out into the open. But now he was trying to defend him! He wondered idly what Sudakar was up to, when Kulkarni's voice shook him out of his musings.

'Let me show you the computing facilities,' he heard him tell Tanuja.

'They're excellent!' she gushed after fifteen minutes. 'You have all the tools I need.'

'We will reserve one of the rooms for you,' Kulkarni told her, 'so that you can work in privacy. You can start from Monday.'

'Can I work here at night too?'

'You'll certainly be safe inside the building, but I'm concerned about you travelling back home at a late hour. Especially after what I've heard from the inspector.'

'I'll try and be with her,' Shashi said.

'Even so, please don't travel at late hours,' Ranade said, his face grave. 'There has already been a break-in and a larceny in one week. Your analysis may well lead you to stumble upon something inconvenient for someone.'

Chapter 20

Dusk was falling. Chaaya drew the curtains and shut out the gloom. It was a few minutes to the time when those armed intruders had forced themselves into her flat last evening and terrorized them. The memory, fresh and unsettling and less than 24 hours old, brought the goosebumps out on her flesh. She sensed a tension in Kamna's unusual quietness too. And it made her nervous that Shashi was again at the SEBI office today.

Sonu had returned at about 10 p.m. last night, thankfully unharmed, but a nervous wreck. He had stayed indoors all day, reluctant even to run errands, although he didn't need to go far, just to the *kirana* shop a couple of hundred yards away. He had not uttered a word all day.

That Pandey Bhaiya had posted two men on the grounds of Chaaya's apartment block was, curiously enough, not as comforting for her as it ought to have been. The sense of vulnerability that had overwhelmed her after last evening's incident seemed to intensify as she saw it reflected in other members of the household.

That an unseen, nameless tormentor had chosen to target Chaaya and her family was a harrowing experience, coming as it did on the heels of Vivek's murder. She hoped her brother-in-law would come back soon. Shashi's forceful personality gave her a sense of stability; he was someone she could trust, lean on. She thought for the hundredth time how thankful she was for his honesty, his forthrightness; unlike most of her cousins or Vivek's, Shashi was not two-faced. Not having to second-guess his intentions or seek hidden meanings in his words was a huge relief to her exhausted mind. His booming voice and direct manner chased away the burden of oppressive silences.

But was Shashi okay with the way she was handling things? She had sensed that she was putting him in a bit of a spot by involving him in Vivek's business matters, but had been too caught up in her own grief to give it serious thought. Her sister had come out and said as much, forcing her to confront the truth. Chaaya realized that she wasn't being entirely fair to Shashi and certainly not after the support and care he had gone out of his way to provide her. But who else could she turn to? Who else could she trust wholeheartedly, the way she trusted him? She would make it up to him after all this was over. She didn't know how, but she would. He was the brother she had never had.

The stillness of the evening was shattered by the sudden ringing of her mobile phone. Chaaya jumped. The two sisters instinctively glanced at each other, fearful, but also a little thankful for the break in monotony.

Chaaya picked up the phone. It was from an unknown Mumbai landline.

'Hello?' she said.

'Mrs Tola?' The voice was low, gruff, unfriendly.

Chaaya felt herself tense. 'Yes?'

'You gave me the wrong notebook yesterday.'

'What?'

Chaaya's thoughts whirled as she tried to make sense of the caller's simple statement. Then it clicked into place. The man on the other end of the line was Varma! She thought the matter had ended with him barging into her home to take the notebook away. What now?

'The notebook you gave me last night,' he repeated. 'It was not from the safe.'

'It was!' Chaaya almost wailed. 'It was the one I brought back from the safe. You saw Vivek's jottings. It's his handwriting.'

'Did you bring any other notebook back with you?'

'No, I didn't! There –'

'What else was there in the safe?'

'Mostly papers.' Chaaya considered mentioning the diamonds and decided not to. Those men would take them away for sure. 'And some cash.'

'Foolish men die early. So do women who lie.'

'I'm telling the truth, I swear! You must believe me!'

'What did you put back in the bank locker?'

'The cash and some of Vivek's valuables.'

'What valuables?'

'Rolex watches and some high-end pens. That's all. Please believe me!'

'Don't play games, woman! Go back to the office and check the safe again. Look for another notebook.'

'But tomorrow is Sunday –'

'*You* are the new proprietor! Tell your manager to be at the office tomorrow.'

'Wh…what does the notebook you mention look like?'

'It's a small one. It may have the letters "SX" printed or written on it.'

'On the cover?'

'On the first page inside. Or a logo with the letters "SX" imprinted inside a ring. Bring any notebook you find in the safe.'

'What does the notebook contain? Tell me, so that I can be sure I have the right one.'

'It will have some phone numbers and the names of a few Greek gods.'

'Greek gods?' Chaaya was dumbfounded. 'Which Greek gods?'

'Zeus, Apollo, Ares. Understood?'

'I...I hope so.'

'Don't try any tricks. Remember, you are a lone woman with two small children. Be sensible. I'll call you tomorrow.'

The phone went dead.

Chaaya sank into a sofa and buried her face in her hands. She was trembling all over, too overcome with shock to cry. She gulped in lungfuls of air, as though she were finding it difficult to breathe. Kamna sat down beside her and enclosed her in a hug. The children stared at her, wide-eyed and unsure. Minutes passed as Chaaya tried to get a hold on herself. Then she lifted her head and spoke haltingly, repeating to her sister the conversation she had just had with the caller.

'It's okay, Chaaya,' Kamna said softly. 'Just do as he says and everything will be fine.'

'But what other notebook does he want? I haven't a clue! The one he took away had all the important information. It had details of the latest loan transactions. It was the one Vivek had been using.'

'There's another notebook in the black wooden box you gave me for safekeeping,' Kamna whispered to her.

Chaaya shook her head. 'That's an old one. Vivek copied the outstanding items into this new notebook.'

'Then could there be a *third* notebook? Not with Vivek's loan transactions, but something else? Something important?'

Chaaya turned to Kamna, her expression anxious. 'What else could a third notebook contain?'

Kamna shook her head. 'I don't know...Maybe something we don't know about? Maybe it has nothing to do with Vivek's regular business? Is it possible?'

'It's possible, I guess, but...' Chaya left the sentence unfinished.

'What if those men are not interested in Vivek's loan transactions at all? Varma said to look out for a notebook with phone numbers and the names of Greek gods.'

Chaaya's face was blank. 'I don't have a clue as to what he could mean, Kamna.'

'Do you know what's in the wooden box, Chaaya?'

'Not really…Vivek had followed the usual practice.'

It was a practice Chaaya's father had initiated. All sensitive items that could prove awkward if they fell into the wrong hands were stored together in one place so that in the eventuality of a raid on the house, they could be whisked away to a safe location. The practice had helped Chaaya's father through tough situations many times in his life. While he had used a briefcase for the purpose, Vivek had opted for a plain wooden box, which was less obvious to prying eyes.

'Should we go through the box's contents?' Kamna suggested. 'That may provide some answers.'

'But I have no intention of handing over anything from the box to those men. Whatever has been placed in it must be of vital importance.'

'We don't have to hand over anything to anyone, Chaaya. We can just have a look to find out what it contains. We don't even have to tell anyone about it.'

'But how are we going to manage that? How can we do it without arousing anyone's suspicion? If I visit your flat now or in the near future, those men will know right away that I've kept something of importance there.' Chaaya frowned. 'There's one option, but I'm not sure you'll approve of it.'

'What's that?'

'Shashi could go through the box's contents…if you're okay with it.'

Kamna was silent, thinking over her sister's suggestion for a long time. Then she spoke. 'I guess I'm okay…but I don't know how Shashi will feel about it.'

'Will you ask him, then? Please? We have no other option and Varma will be calling tomorrow. Nobody needs to know that Shashi went through the contents.'

'Okay. I'll ask him if he could go directly home from his SEBI presentation and have a look at what's in the box. There's no need for him to come back here tonight.'

'Thanks,' Chaaya whispered. 'He can call you once he has opened the box and been through its contents.'

▪

Ranade stepped out of SEBI and immediately returned Abdul's last missed call. Judging by the number of calls and messages he had received from his deputy while Shashi was making his presentation, it was clear that Abdul had been busy in Pune.

'Navin seems to be winding up the business, sir,' he told Ranade the moment he answered the call. 'He has given notice to his employees and landlords. His secretary says that he has been busy all day, calling clients and closing their accounts.'

'And why is he doing that?' Ranade asked.

'He says the business has become unviable after Vivek's death. Tola was apparently the one taking the investment decisions for the firm and its clients. Without him, the business has lost its core.'

'When is Navin closing it down?'

'Tuesday or, latest, Wednesday, sir.'

'The coming week?' Ranade was stunned. 'That soon?'

'Yes sir. He's in a hurry.'

'So that's why he was in such a rush to get back to Pune! He had panicked initially and fled to escape the goons. But now that he's had time to think about it, he's decided to shut shop and vanish from the scene.' A thought flashed through Ranade's mind. 'Has he given notice to the landlord of his flat too?'

'Yes sir. And he's selling his car as well. I suspect he's leaving Pune for good.'

'Not just leaving, Abdul. He's fleeing!' Ranade's mind was in high gear now. His fingers itched for a pencil to twirl. 'He's running away from the men who'd been following him. He had taken a sizeable loan from Vivek Tola. I wonder if he's planning to return it at all.'

'If he plans to evade those men as well as Mrs Tola, he may well try to disappear altogether. That's the only way he can escape the men.'

'Exactly! Tell me, if you were able to ferret out all this information, wouldn't others be able to do the same?'

'Very likely, sir. With two employees and several clients, he can't keep his departure a secret.'

'Not to mention his selling the car and vacating both the office and the flat. The landlords may be putting out advertisements shortly. How is he disposing of the contents of his flat? His furniture and so on?'

'He's paying his secretary to do it for him. He is paying her six months' salary and has asked her to close down the office and the flat for him. I suspect he's planning to vanish with just a suitcase sometime in the middle of next week.'

'He may not even take that suitcase, Abdul. Remember how he fled from the Bengaluru hotel? With just the clothes on his back. Meanwhile, we must assume that his pursuers are also aware of his plans. If they're the ones who killed Vivek, what do you think they will do now?'

'They'll complete their work – whatever that is – as soon as possible, sir.'

'Have they been watching him?'

'Like hawks. Both at the office and at his residence.'

■

Shashi had just finished briefing Gupta on their findings and on the meeting with SEBI, when Kamna's message arrived. He called her back and listened as she narrated what had happened. Not wanting to alarm Tanuja, who was sitting beside him in the car, he responded mostly in monosyllables and agreed to go home to check the contents of the wooden box.

In truth, he was relieved by Kamna's request. He had been itching to find out what the box contained, but had not wished to open it without her consent. With every passing day, the urge to explore its contents had been growing stronger. But the feeling that his wife would not approve of him meddling in Chaaya's most private affairs had held him back. He had never withheld anything from his wife since their marriage, but lately, he had been on the verge of breaking his own vow.

While the phone call from Kamna had resolved his dilemma, indecision had now given way to a sense of foreboding. He wondered what the box held and how much more the discovery of its contents would add to his already serious problems.

Now safely inside his flat, he checked to confirm if the front door was securely locked before approaching Kamna's steel almirah that stood in their bedroom. He paused for a moment before opening it, his eyes going automatically to the drapes at the windows to ensure if they were fully drawn. Satisfied, he opened the almirah and the locker inside. The black wooden box lay within.

His fingers shaking, Shashi pulled on a pair of latex gloves he had taken from the kitchen. The future turn of events being highly uncertain, he had decided not to leave fingerprints on the box that might be used against him as evidence. Kamna's prints would already be on it, but he could do little about that, other than wipe them off as best he could.

He reached into the locker, pulled out the black wooden box and placed it on the small table beside the bed. The plain, unmarked box was about a foot square and half a foot high, with a hinged lid and a small hasp to fasten it. A number lock secured it.

Using one of Kamna's silk scarves, he wiped the outer surface of the box thoroughly and repeated the exercise with his cotton handkerchief. Using the number she had given him, he unlocked the box and lifted the lid.

In one corner of the velvet-lined receptacle was a white iPhone. Beside it lay two satin pouches, one black and the other wine red. In the other half of the box, a long, flat jewellery box rested on a sheaf of paper folded lengthwise and held together with a silk ribbon.

He picked up the black satin pouch and opened it. Inside were five keys, each with a separate tag attached to it. Locker keys, by the look of them. He pulled one out and read its tag: 'HDFC L-24.'

The wine red pouch contained two elongated leather pouches, one bearing the logo of a Swiss bank embossed in gold, the other, the name of a European private bank. He didn't need to open them to know what they contained. The fact that Vivek had offshore accounts and lockers was a piece of information that Shashi would rather have done without, even though he had suspected it all along.

Feeling increasingly uneasy about the entire situation, he replaced the pouches and opened the jewellery box. For a moment, all he could do was gape, blinking in awe at the largest collection of diamonds he had ever set eyes on. Each of these sparkling gems was so large, it looked unreal. The smallest one weighed no less than three or four carats.

Shashi hastily snapped shut the jewellery box and picked up the sheaf of papers. While most of them were handwritten chits and notes, some were signed originals of agreements. He flipped through them, not recognizing any of the names – except one.

The document was an agreement between Navin Gokul and Vivek Tola, transferring 60 per cent of the former's holdings in the Pune firm to the latter as collateral for a loan of five crores. The agreement mentioned an exorbitant interest rate and specified a time limit for repayment of the loan, failing which the shares would irretrievably become Vivek's.

Shashi replaced the silk ribbon around the sheaf and was about to return it to its place, when he noticed a slit in the velvet base of the box. Next to it, partly covered by the two satin pouches, was a slight bulge. Something was hidden under the velvet lining.

He slid two fingers through the slit, pincered the flat object between them and tried to pull it out. It wouldn't budge. Something was getting in the way. Keeping his index finger under the velvet, he ran it around the flat object a few times before realizing what the problem was. Most of the object, which felt like a small leather-bound diary, was nestling inside a depression in the bottom of the box. Only a quarter of it protruded from the depression; hence the bump in the velvet base.

There was only one way to remove the diary. Shashi emptied the box, turned it upside down and struck the bottom with the flat of his palm. When the velvet bulged further under the weight of the freed object, he slid his fingers in again and pulled it out.

It was indeed a small notebook with a leather cover. With shaking fingers, he opened it.

On the first page was a small handwritten symbol – the letters 'SX' inscribed inside a thick circle. The next three pages had a list of fifteen-digit numbers, which Shashi now recognized as disguised mobile numbers. Above each number were initials comprising two or three letters and a two-digit number.

On the next page were three other numbers with 'Ares', 'Apollo' and 'Hermes' written above them. The last page had a single fifteen-digit number, above which was written 'Zeus'.

There was no longer any doubt. This was the notebook Varma was looking for.

Shashi reached for his mobile phone.

Chapter 21

Shashi was in a strange place. On a meadow under a purple sky at the twilight hour before dusk; a group of strange figures was dancing in the distance. With their long, thin limbs and blobs for heads, the figures looked too peculiar to be human. He stared at them as they drew nearer and saw that they were stick figures, the kind one found in cartoons. They were strangely familiar though, and he wondered why. With them were Chaaya and Kamna, playing haunting music on strange instruments.

He suddenly recognized the stick figures – the dancing men from Sherlock Holmes's story, 'The Adventure of the Dancing Men'; stick figures that resembled men, but were, in reality, a code. Each figure, with a unique combination of limb position and head, represented a letter of the alphabet.

Their Zulu-style dance was rudely interrupted when an armed Varma and Kashyap turned up and began shooting, downing five of the dancing digits. Chaaya fled and hid behind a tree, while Kamna urged the remaining ten digits to run to Shashi.

The ten digits did as they were told, rearranging themselves into a mobile number as they approached him. Finding no other place to hide, they leapt into Shashi's jacket pocket and took refuge in Vivek's mobile phone ensconced there.

Then came a terrible god in all his glory, with a shimmering thunderbolt in his right hand and fury blazing from his eyes. Zeus! Shashi fled, urged by the whimpering of the dancing men in his pocket.

But Zeus caught up with him in two long strides and paralysed him with one searing glance. With Shashi frozen, the god reached into his pocket and seized the phone with the dancing men.

Shashi woke up with a gasp and lay sweating in bed. The luminous wall clock displayed the time: 5 a.m. What was that dream all about? The dancing men were a disguised mobile number; that much was clear.

But that was not it...Something else had brought on the dream. Something had been bothering him all night; something he should have done, but had overlooked. What was it? A part of the dream was gnawing at the back of his mind. The memory of Chaaya deciphering the fifteen-digit numbers – the disguised mobile numbers – recorded in the notebook kept coming back to him. There was some connection between those disguised mobile numbers and Vivek's phone that he had missed. The thought, hovering below the surface of his mind, lay just beyond his grasp. What was it?

He rose and went about his early morning routine; he was to take the notebook back to Chaaya's flat first thing in the morning. While he was brushing his teeth, the subliminal thought surfaced abruptly, making him choke on a mouthful of rinsing water.

The phone in the wooden box!

In his excitement over discovering the hidden notebook, he had ignored the iPhone lying in the same box. If Vivek had taken care to place it in the box, it must be containing important information too!

Shashi hurriedly rinsed his mouth, pulled on the latex gloves, retrieved the wooden box and was about to switch on the phone, when instinct stopped him. What if there was a SIM card inside? If there was, it would connect to the network as soon as he switched on the phone. That would leave a trace with the telecom operator and might even alert someone somewhere.

He flipped the phone over and opened it as quickly as his latex gloves would permit. Once he had removed the SIM card and snapped the lid back in place, he switched it on.

At first glance, nothing appeared out of the ordinary. The home screen seemed normal and displayed no unusual icons. He navigated to the contacts and blinked in surprise. It was empty. No contacts! How was that possible?

He went to the 'recent calls' section and scrolled down. There were several calls, the last of which had been made on the night before Vivek's death. Whom did these numbers belong to? Were they the same numbers recorded in the notebook he had discovered the previous night? Shashi opened the notebook and picked up a writing pad and a pen.

Now what had Kamna said about the disguised phone numbers?

Remove the first, fourth, eighth, twelfth and fifteenth digits and reverse the order of the remaining digits.

He copied the first fifteen-digit number from the notebook in the pad, struck off the extraneous digits and wrote the remaining digits in reverse order. He compared the number on the pad with the calls on the phone. It did not match. He went to the second number in the notebook and repeated the exercise, with the same result. There were 17 rows of numbers in the notebook. Would he have to do this for each and every one of them or was there a simpler, more effective way? Thirteen numbers featured on one list. There were three on another page and a single one on the last page. The latter had a name against it, rather than initials – 'Zeus'. What if Shashi chose that number next?

He struck off the irrelevant digits and copied the remaining ones in reverse order. He placed the writing pad and the iPhone side by side and compared the numbers. They matched.

Vivek had spoken to Zeus – whoever that was – the night before he had been killed.

In the next ten minutes, Shashi decoded seven of the other

numbers and compared them with those on the recent calls list on the iPhone. He found four matches.

Shashi's heart was beating rapidly. He was now sure that the iPhone in the wooden box – Vivek's *second* iPhone – had been used exclusively for communicating with the people listed in the notebook. If so, he had better investigate the phone thoroughly when he had the chance.

Hands trembling, he copied the details of the recent calls and photographed them with his own phone. He then went to the messages and stared uncomprehendingly at them for a moment. They were junk promotional messages touting all manner of things – plots of land, data cards, work-from-home jobs, laptop-repair services and a whole range of such things.

'Ultrafast 4G data cards at affordable prices. 5, 10 & 15 GB plans. Call 8101817036.'

'Reliable, experienced call drivers. Half-day, full day, monthly. Arun 9305005072.'

'Laptop repairs. All brands. Reliable and quick service. Pick-up and drop available. 6210213107.'

Unrelated promotional messages that had little in common. Except that they all had a mobile number at the end. He scanned some of the mobile numbers. They seemed okay as far as he could tell, although he hadn't known that mobile numbers also began with '6'.

Why on earth would Vivek have wanted to keep junk messages? Or had he merely been indifferent to them? Since he hadn't sent or received messages through this phone, had he just ignored junk messages and not bothered to delete them? Puzzled, Shashi took a few photographs and returned to the home screen to check out the software on the phone.

After ten minutes, he concluded that the only app Vivek had installed was a suite of games. He launched the suite and discovered that it offered some simple games: chess, Space Invaders, Tertis and Reversi.

By 6.30 a.m., Shashi was sure that the iPhone had been used very sparingly and only for one purpose. The iPhone 4s, at least a couple of years old, still looked new. It had no scratches at the bottom as well-used phones tended to have.

He returned the phone to the box, kept the notebook outside and put the box back into the steel almirah.

At 7.15 a.m., he entered Chaaya's flat with the notebook in his pocket. He had sorted out his thoughts and was clear about one thing – they *had* to share his latest discovery with Ranade. But for that, he would have to convince Chaaya first.

'It seems to me,' he told her and Kamna after breakfast, 'that the motive behind Vivek's murder lies in some dealings that were outside the purview of his usual business activities. It doesn't seem to be connected with Amethyst Financial or the financing business he was personally operating outside Amethyst.

'However, the motive has everything to do with this.' He gestured to the notebook he had brought out from the black wooden box. 'And it is linked with Vivek's second iPhone. You must have seen him using it, Chaaya. What did he use it for?'

His sister-in-law shook her head, perplexed. 'I'd seen him use it occasionally, but thought it was a backup phone, in case his regular phone stopped working. He would take it out sometimes, late in the evening or at night. But I don't know what he used it for.'

'Did he make calls from it?'

Chaaya shrugged. 'I don't remember him making any.'

That meant Vivek had made calls when she wasn't around. Most of the calls had been made late in the evening or at night. Had Vivek deliberately kept these calls from his wife?

'Did he send or receive messages?' Shashi asked.

'I don't know, but I did hear some sounds coming from it from time to time. I think they were game sounds. Vivek used to play games on the phone; I'd seen him shooting aliens or playing cards on the phone. He said that it helped him relax before going to bed.'

'How often did you see that? Every day?'

'Once in a while. Maybe, a few times a month?'

'Do you see any link between that phone and those areas of Vivek's business activities you are aware of?'

'No…no, I can't. That's why I'm surprised. He kept me updated on all major aspects of his business dealings, both in Amethyst and outside. And I knew where all the important documents were kept. It was just a precaution, in case something unforeseen were to happen.'

'So you knew about everything but this notebook and the second iPhone?'

'So it seems.' Chaaya sounded hurt.

'What would you like to do now, Chaaya?' he asked gently. 'The answers to why he…died lie somewhere in the notebook and the second phone.'

'I can't decide, Shashi. What options do we have? These men seem to be cold-blooded and utterly ruthless. What do you think would be the right thing to do?'

'Well…one way to find out is to take Ranade into confidence about the latest development.'

'That would be risky, Shashi.'

'I know.' Now was the time to push, when she was wavering, caught in a state of indecision. 'If we don't get Ranade into this, we may never find the answers. The other option is to do nothing and wait for it all to die down.'

'Then we'll never get to the truth!' Chaaya protested. 'We will never know why Vivek died or who killed him.'

This was exactly the reaction Shashi had hoped for. The only way to persuade her to take Ranade into confidence was to present a less desirable option as the only alternative.

'That's true,' he said and fell silent.

Those were the only two choices: they either had to work with the police or let things be. There was no doubt that the men who had killed Vivek were ruthlessly efficient and would stop at nothing. It would be sheer madness for Chaaya to take them on, even with the mysterious Pandey Bhaiya's help. Besides, she knew neither what she was up against nor where to find those men.

There was no question of Shashi taking it on either – he was in enough trouble due to the deeds of others. Left to himself, he would have told Ranade everything in the hope that the police would track down the murderer. But it was not his decision to make. Chaaya – fragile, vulnerable and with two small children to bring up – had to choose between difficult options. If ever anyone had found herself caught between a rock and a hard place, it was Chaaya. He glanced up at her and saw indecision and desperation twist her features. She looked lonely and vulnerable despite Kamna's comforting hand clasping hers.

Shashi realized that his attitude to Chaaya had also changed in the past few days. He had always been fond of her, but had seldom visited her at home because of his aversion to Vivek. He and his brother-in-law had never quite got along; there had always been a disturbing undercurrent in the polite small talk they exchanged whenever they met socially.

Chaaya's helplessness following the murder and the unreserved trust she had reposed in him had changed matters. Despite the dilemma she had plunged him into, he saw her as a vulnerable woman in need of his support. Poor Chaaya! He had to help her in any way he could. Now was the time for him to weigh in and help her cut through her tangled thoughts. He leaned forward and spoke in a low, firm voice.

'Listen Chaaya, you have only two options, neither of which is easy. If you want to find Vivek's killer, you must tell Ranade about the notebook and the second phone. They are vital clues, without which the mystery may remain unresolved. Yes, I agree that you do run a risk by confiding in Ranade. But it appears that this second notebook has nothing to do with Vivek's regular business. To that extent, the risk is somewhat lessened.

'But if you take the other option and remain silent, the chances of finding the killer will be that much more diminished. Besides, you will be guilty of obstructing the law. That isn't a burden you want to carry when you have two small children to bring up. You wouldn't want to jeopardize their future.'

Chaaya nodded, her eyes searching Shashi's face. 'What would you do in my place?' she asked softly.

His response was immediate. 'I would tell Ranade,' he said, without hesitation. 'The children's welfare would be my highest priority. That means you must make sure you don't run afoul of the law or compromise their future in any way. Even if Vivek's assets are frozen by the authorities, there is sufficient money in the Anjumal Trust for you and the children to lead a comfortable life. My second priority would be to find Vivek's killer.'

'What about Varma? Should we tell him about the notebook? He'll take it away the moment he knows we have it.'

'Let's delay that decision for now. Let's go back to Vivek's office, just as Varma had directed you to. Meanwhile, if you do agree to share this information with Ranade, I have an idea.'

'What is it?'

'With the inspector's help, we can use the notebook as bait to lure and trap Varma.'

That seemed to strike a chord with Chaaya and the confusion and uncertainty on her face cleared.

'Yes!' she whispered, a spark of resolve brightening her eyes. She sat up straight and her chin lifted. 'I'm not going to let Vivek's killer go scot-free!' she said with determination, tears glinting in her eyes. 'Speak to the inspector, Shashi. Let's bait the shark!'

'Excellent!' Shashi felt lighter; a burden had lifted.

'Okay!' New energy seemed to radiate from Chaaya. Her eyes were intent with purpose as she stood up. 'When should we go to the office?'

'Any time the manager is available. That Varma fellow will be calling sometime today. I'll speak to Ranade while you talk to Abhishek.'

'Come, Kamna. Help me sort out my papers,' Chaaya said, striding purposefully towards her room.

Kamna paused to squeeze her husband's shoulder and whisper her thanks before she hurried after her sister. He allowed himself a fleeting smile and glanced at the clock before he reached for his mobile.

8.30 a.m. was as good a time as any to call Ranade.

▪

The inspector had just reached the outskirts of Pune when Shashi's call came through. He listened silently as Shashi told him about the phone call from Varma and his instructions to search Vivek Tola's office safe again in quest of a particular notebook.

'We haven't been to the office yet,' Shashi told him. 'But Chaaya searched Vivek's cupboard and discovered the notebook Varma's after. She also found another phone.'

Shashi then proceeded to describe the contents of the notebook and the phone.

'Did you check all the 17 numbers in the notebook against the phone's call list?' Ranade enquired.

'I stopped after I found four matches. I thought it was more important to speak to you as soon as possible. We need to find out whose numbers they are and you are best placed to do that.'

'What is the size of the notebook?'

'About four inches by three inches,' Shashi said. 'It's between half and three-quarters of an inch thick and has no more than fifty pages.'

'Plain or ruled?'

'Plain.'

'How is it bound?'

'Hardbound, with an imitation-leather covering. Brown. I can send you photos of it if you like.'

'At once, Mr Kurva. Your idea of using it as bait is an excellent one, but we can't use the notebook you have found. I'll have a similar one made – one with a tiny tracking device embedded in the leather binding.'

'Won't that be risky, inspector? What if this Zeus discovers it?'

'We have access to some very sophisticated technology, Mr Kurva. The device will look like a thick piece of cardboard or leather and will be no larger than a small stamp. It will be made in such a way that no one can guess it's there in the binding.'

'Okay. When –'

'I can have it delivered late this evening.'

'Then we'll have to find a way of keeping Varma at bay for now. He's sure to call today. We'll have to cook up a story to fob him off until we're ready. This is what I'll do.'

Shashi narrated what he had in mind.

'Good idea,' Ranade agreed, once Shashi had finished. 'It should work. But I'll need the original notebook so that I can have a forger copy the contents from it into the fake one.'

Shashi let out a chuckle. 'Don't bother about that, inspector. My wife's skills are not confined exclusively to sketching and painting. I'll wager that you won't be able to distinguish between my original handwriting and her forged version of it. Kamna will forge the notebook once your man delivers it and she'll do an excellent job of it.'

Ranade considered it for a moment. Chaaya's flat would be watched. Anyone sent there to pick up the notebook and deliver it to the police would be noticed and the obvious conclusions drawn by Varma's men. The proposition was a risky one. However, if Kamna could forge the notebook's contents, that would reduce the risk significantly. Her sketch of Varma had been uncannily lifelike. If her skill at forgery was even half as advanced, their purpose would be served.

Besides, both Abdul and he were in Pune and time was of the essence if they were to trap Varma. That meant that neither of them could see the forged notebook before it was given to Varma. He would have to rely on Shashi's judgement.

'Okay,' he agreed. 'You'll get a courier delivery this evening. Blue Dart or DTDC, most likely. Get Mrs Kurva to forge the notebook tonight and send me photos of her work as soon as she is done, no matter what the time is. If need be, I'll have a woman in plain clothes drop in to check it on my behalf.'

'Okay. We'll do that.'

'Once I clear the forgery, let Varma pick up the notebook tomorrow. We'll be ready.'

'Excellent!'

'Do you have the number from which Varma had called yesterday?'

'I'll text it to you as soon as I hang up.'

'Also send me photos of the phone numbers in the notebook. I'll start by locating Zeus.'

'Sure.'

'Please tell Mrs Tola to be careful. These men are utterly merciless. I have two plainclothesmen patrolling your street, but it's better not to run unnecessary risks.'

'I'll do that.'

'One last thing, Mr Kurva. When Varma calls, Mrs Tola should allow the phone to ring several times before she answers it. The more time we get to trace the call, the easier it will be for us to track down the caller. A few additional seconds can make all the difference.'

Chapter 22

A shrill ring shattered the tense silence of the Sunday afternoon as Shashi, Chaaya and Kamna sat nervously in the drawing room, waiting for Varma's call.

They had returned from the Amethyst Financial office an hour back. A careful search of the safe had yielded nothing more, but a scrutiny of the papers in it had deepened the mystery of Vivek's partnership with Navin Gokul.

The Pune firm had been set up a couple of years ago as a fifty-fifty equal partnership, with Navin being given the authority to run the business. The seed capital had been surprisingly large at ₹10 crores. For his share of the seed capital, Navin had borrowed five crores from Vivek, for which they had executed the loan agreement Shashi had seen in the black box.

What had further piqued Shashi's curiosity was that Vivek had taken no collateral for the loan. Why had he lent Navin five crores? Why had he entered into a partnership with the man in the first place, if the latter was not in a position to invest? Further, why had he given Navin full authority to run the company?

Daniel had found out that most of the company's capital, invested in the stock market, had grown handsomely. The firm had acquired a small number of HNI clients in Pune, whose money it managed for a 15 per cent share of the profits.

Shashi had been musing over this when the landline rang. All three of them hurried to the instrument and looked at the caller ID.

'I don't recognize it,' Chaaya whispered.

Shashi quickly keyed the number into a text message and handed his phone to Kamna.

'I'll answer it,' he said. 'If it's Varma, send the message to Ranade and follow it up with a call.'

'Okay.' Kamna took the phone from him and selected Ranade's contact for sending the message.

The phone had rung five times already when Shashi took a deep breath and picked up the cordless phone. Chaaya stepped back a couple of paces, her face a picture of anxiety.

'Hello?' Shashi said.

Silence greeted him.

He listened for a moment and spoke again.

'Hello?'

'Is it Vivek Tola's house?' a gravelly voice asked.

Shashi made the connection at once. The voice was similar to the one he remembered as Varma's, having heard it just 10 days ago. It was slightly muffled now, but still recognizable.

'Yes?' Shashi said.

'Is Mrs Tola there?'

Shashi was now sure about the caller's identity. He nodded vigorously to Kamna. Having already prepared the message for Ranade, she sent it right away. Then she hurried away to another room to call him.

'She isn't available to talk at the moment,' Shashi replied smoothly. 'Can I take a message for her?'

'Call her!' the voice snarled. 'This is urgent.'

'I'm sorry, but she's in bed. She isn't well. I'll ask her to return your call once she gets up.'

'Who is this?' snapped the voice at the other end of the line. 'Shashi Kurva?'

'That's right,' Shashi replied, feigning surprise. 'This is Shashi. May I know to whom I'm speaking?'

'Don't play games with me!' The voice had gone soft, menacing.

Shashi stayed silent, knowing that Varma would continue. He did.

'Did you find the notebook or not?' he asked. 'You accompanied her to the office.'

'It's you!' Shashi exclaimed, bringing his acting skills into play. He laced his voice with surprise and anger, adding a pinch of defiance. 'She's expecting your call on her mobile. What the devil are you up to? First, you murder Vivek. Then you threaten his bereaved widow. She's frightened to death – hasn't slept for three whole nights. She had to be sedated and put to bed.'

'Shut up!' the quietly sinister voice lashed out at him. 'Did you get the notebook or not?'

'No.' Shashi modulated his voice as if he were trying to keep his temper in check. 'There wasn't any notebook there. We emptied the safe and checked the papers, one by one. Are you sure it's supposed to be there?'

'Don't lie to me!'

'I am not lying.' Shashi's voice was now cold and hard.

He glanced at Chaaya sitting on a sofa with her hands tightly clenched in her lap. Kamna had returned to the room after calling Ranade and was standing behind her sister.

'As far as I'm concerned,' Shashi said into the mouthpiece, 'you can take the bloody notebook and go to hell.'

'You son of a – '

'Listen,' Shashi cut in. 'Chaaya herself is desperate to find the notebook and give it to you so that you'll get off her back. By the way, is it a brown leather-bound notebook? She remembers seeing one in the house.'

There was a silence. 'Could be,' Varma finally said.

Good! Varma didn't know how the notebook looked. That would make it easier to deceive him with a forged notebook.

'Chaaya has already begun looking for it in the house,' Shashi went on. 'She'll continue her search once she's able to get out of bed. I can call you as soon as she finds it. Do you have a number where I can reach you?'

'Don't try to be too clever, Kurva. Don't get so sharp that you end up cutting yourself. I'll call again tonight.'

'Give her 24 hours, at least. Chaaya is ill. Nobody else would know where to look for the notebook in this house. Be reasonable; if the notebook is here in the house, it's safe.'

There was a pause. Shashi sensed Varma hesitating. He wondered if Ranade's men had been able to trace the call; he had managed to keep Varma engaged in conversation far longer than he had expected to.

'Okay. I'll give you time till tomorrow morning,' Varma conceded. 'And no tricks. Remember, your precious Chaaya has two small children.'

'You bastard!' Shashi hissed, feigning rage and trying to prolong the conversation. 'Are you a man or a monster? Wasn't killing her husband enough? What more do you want from her?'

A bark of a laugh came through. 'Remember, no tricks. I'll call you in the morning.'

'Okay. But before you go, tell me one thing.'

'What?'

'Why did you kill Vivek?'

Shashi thought he heard a surprised intake of breath. An instant later, the call was disconnected.

'Okay, we've bought some time,' Shashi said, hanging up. 'I wonder if the police have been able to track him down.'

His question was answered five minutes later when Ranade called.

'Varma called you from a shop a kilometre away from the one he had used the last time. It is between Sewri and Wadala. My men couldn't get there in time to catch him.'

'It's a given that he won't be foolish enough to use the same shop twice, inspector.'

'You'll be surprised at the stupid mistakes criminals sometimes make, Mr Kurva. How many have been caught because of just one error! All the police need is a single mistake. We're watching several spots in Sewri. There are whispers that Kashyap was seen there too. We'll extend our watch to Wadala now.'

'That would take a lot of men.'

'It always does. Most cases are solved because of the endless, mundane work our men do. Many dozens of feet and eyes roam the streets, seeking that one elusive break we need. Someone is watching the shop Varma called from the last time. We know full well that the chances of him going there again are remote. But if he does, we'll latch on and follow him.'

'Good luck, inspector. I'll call you once the forged notebook is ready.'

Hardly had he hung up on Ranade, when his phone rang again. It was Tanuja.

'Shashi!' she said in an excited whisper. 'Have you seen the email Daniel forwarded?'

'Not yet. I've had no time. What does it say?'

'It has the profiles of the eight households that traded in Purple Country's shares. There's something fishy going on, Shashi. I think there's a pattern, but I can't find it. You may be able to make more sense of it.'

■

As Chaaya retired to her bedroom to rest after Varma's call, Shashi switched on his laptop and retrieved his mail. 'Profiles,' said the subject line of Daniel's mail. It had nothing but an attachment containing one-page profiles of the eight men whose demat accounts had traded extensively in Purple Country's stock.

Four of them were CFOs, one was a finance director and two were vice-presidents in the finance function. The oldest of the lot had retired as a senior partner from a reputable audit firm. The last person on the list was an officer in a state government department. Seven of the eight men were from the finance functions of different companies. This must be the pattern Tanu had mentioned. But that, by itself, meant little, as men who managed money were prone to play the stock market too.

Shashi went back to the top of the document, made a list of the companies where they were employed and studied it. He recognized three of the names, but was not sure what businesses they were engaged in. He opened the browser and began googling the names of the companies.

Fifteen minutes later, he had established some basic facts.

All seven – medium-sized companies with turnovers ranging from 1,600 to 3,700 crores – were headquartered in Mumbai. Though some were involved in manufacturing and others in service, all of them were listed companies. And finally, all seven seemed to be doing well, with their share price climbing steadily for the past six months.

The eighth man was an oddity in that he was not in the private sector, but in government. He had completed B.Com. and M.Com. from Mumbai University and now held a middling job in the state finance department.

Beyond that, Shashi drew a blank. Try as he might, he could find nothing else in common. The promoters were completely different, the factory locations were different and they seemed to be catering to entirely different customer bases. Two of them – IT companies – catered primarily to overseas markets.

He spent another half an hour trying to find more common threads, but failed. As he sat back, scratching his head in bewilderment, Kamna, who had been watching him on and off, spoke up.

'Look at the profiles of those men again,' she suggested. 'If I'm not mistaken, most of them are in their early forties.'

Shashi went back to the attachment and noted the ages of the eight men. Six of them were between 40 and 43 years of age. One was significantly older at 63 and the last one – the government employee – was 35.

'You're right,' Shashi said. 'But what does that mean?'

'I don't know...Just thought it might lead to something. Are they all chartered accountants?'

'I suppose so. They can't be CFOs and finance directors otherwise. I'll check, anyway.'

All, other than the government employee, were CAs.

'Six CAs of the same age,' Kamna mused, her voice a murmur. 'I wonder if they know each other?'

Shashi's eyes snapped to his wife and he stared at her for a long moment. 'Great idea!' he finally exclaimed, opening the spreadsheet Daniel had given him earlier. It mentioned the eight men's home addresses.

'Got it!' he exclaimed half a minute later. 'Four of them live in Lokhandwala Complex and three others close by, in Andheri West. Only the government employee lives in Matunga.'

'Doesn't someone from your office live in Lokhandwala?' Kamna asked.

'A few do, but it's a huge complex. It's unlikely that they know these guys.'

'Worth a try, isn't it?'

'Yes, but I'll check that later. Now let me first look at their LinkedIn profiles.'

Shashi logged into LinkedIn and searched for the first name. The 41-year-old CFO of an IT company had completed his B.Com. from University of Mumbai 18 years ago and articled at the well-known audit firm, Lucarro & Co. He had worked there for seven years after his articleship before moving to the IT company. His LinkedIn professional network was extensive, with over 500 connections.

Shashi saved the profile in a Word document and searched for the second name on his list of eight.

The second person had done his B.Com. from Nagpur and articled in a small audit firm there. Once he earned his CA degree, he had moved to another audit firm in Mumbai. Two years later, he had left that firm to join Lucarro & Co.

Shashi blinked. Both men had worked at Lucarro & Co. Was it a coincidence or a pattern? He quickly scanned the rest of the man's work history and searched for the third name from the list. As soon as the profile came up, he scrolled down, looking for Lucarro & Co.

He found it. The third man had joined Lucarro & Co. in Pune and then moved to the Mumbai office of the same firm.

In the next five minutes, Shashi looked through the profiles of the seven finance men. All of them had been at Lucarro & Co. between 1999 and 2004. A few had joined earlier and some had stayed longer. But for the five years between 1999 and 2004, all seven of them had been colleagues in Lucarro & Co., Mumbai. The oldest of the seven, the 63-year-old man, had retired as a senior partner from Lucarro & Co. and was now the finance director of a company.

Shashi was on to something.

If these men had been colleagues for five years, they would certainly know each other. And if they were living in close proximity to each other, it was very likely that they were still friends. Perhaps more than just friends? But how were they getting privileged information from Purple Country? None of them worked there. There was one way to find out. Shashi picked up his mobile and dialled a number.

'Carol,' he said, 'I need you to carry out a quiet investigation when you get to office tomorrow. List all CAs in the company as well as the finance people. Get hold of their résumés and see if any of them worked at a firm called Lucarro & Co. between 1999 and 2004.'

'Lucarro & Co…between 1999 and 2004.' He heard Carol's pen scratching on a paper. 'Okay. Anything else?'

'Talk to some of the junior staffers in the accounts department over lunch and find out the names of the people who come to do our audit – the audit partner, manager, anyone else. But first look up our contract with the audit firm; I think it names the partner and manager.'

'By when do you need the information?'

'As soon as you can get it, but be careful; nobody should know what you're doing. Nobody. Not HR either. This is only between you and me.'

'Got it.'

Shashi hung up and sat back. As Barun and Carol had said last week, over two dozen people had access to confidential information in the company and outside. Any one of them could be leaking the information to this ex-Lucarro gang. But not all two dozen would have been at Lucarro & Co.

His mind wandered to the eighth man, the government employee. A finance department employee who was six years younger than the others and lived 20 km away did not fit into the pattern. Who was he? There was nothing on LinkedIn about him. He didn't even have a profile. Googling his name and designation had not yielded anything either. This was one obscure man, but he had profited handsomely from trading in Purple Country shares.

If there was no link between him and the other seven, how did he get his information? Shashi's eyes widened in sudden realization.

What if there were two people leaking information at Purple Country?

Chapter 23

Darkness had long descended on Pune and the quiet of a Sunday night had shrouded it like a blanket. Its residents had retired in preparation for the bustle of a Monday morning that was less than eight hours away. All was dark and quiet in the office complex, save one small office, where two lights glowed. Only one car – a blue Ford Ecosport – stood in the parking lot.

Navin Gokul was alone and hard at work.

The paper shredder had been working as never before, mutilating reams of documents. Navin had emptied it seven times that evening and the pile of paper ribbons in the corner bore mute witness to the amount of work the machine had done.

Having closed client accounts on Saturday and dispatched the closing papers to them the same evening, Navin had spent all Sunday erasing details of the firm's business activities. He had scanned important papers in the morning and uploaded the scanned images to multiple Dropbox accounts on the internet. He had then transferred the contents of his laptop and the other two office desktops to his repositories on the internet before wiping the files in such a way that they couldn't be recovered.

By the time he finished, no details of the firm's clients or financials remained in the office. Even the rolodex on his desk and the visiting-card holders on his secretary's desk had been destroyed.

The day he had been planning for was close at hand. Very close.

He would walk out of the office on Monday evening, never to return. That night, Navin Gokul would vanish from the face of the earth.

While the arrival of that day had been hastened by Vivek's murder, it was, nevertheless, a direct consequence of Navin's own actions. He had begun meticulous planning six months ago. His alternate identity was ready and had already been in existence for a few months now. He even had credit cards and bank accounts in that name. He had vowed not to suffer Vivek Tola and his machinations any longer. He had decided to be free.

He had diverted a portion of the firm's earnings to his bank accounts. The week before Vivek was killed, the two of them had drawn down from the firm a part of their profits and taken back their initial investment. What remained in the firm now was pure profit, none of which would go to Vivek's heirs. They didn't even know it existed and there were no papers to show that it did. The loans he had taken from Vivek and Amethyst Financial would not be repaid either.

Once everything was in place, Navin had called SEBI and tipped them off about Vivek's nefarious dealings. It was an act of pure revenge and calculated recklessness. It would yield no real benefit for him, but would give him the satisfaction of knowing that Vivek was suffering. He didn't care if they tracked down the call or not, for he would soon be untraceable. Though he had not expected matters to move quite so quickly, he was now glad they had. He was also glad that Vivek had been murdered; he had deserved that fate and had brought it upon himself. The only person who knew Navin's secret was now dead.

The last 24 hours of his existence as Navin Gokul had begun. Soon, he would have thwarted the men who were watching him.

It was important that he carried nothing with him when he vanished, that he walked out empty-handed. There should be absolutely no link between his present identity and the future one – not even clothes, phones or watches. All his personal effects would be left behind. The chequebooks for his now-empty bank accounts were no longer worth the paper they were printed on. He would leave behind his mobile phone, now wiped clean of all contacts, messages and logs. As a final act, he would cut his credit cards and leave them at home.

Satisfied with his thoroughness, Navin switched off the lights and locked the office. He climbed into his Ford Ecosport and glanced at his watch as he drove out of the compound for the last time.

It was 10.45 p.m. The 2 km drive would take five minutes at the most. He turned left at the gate and gunned the engine, making the car leap towards the main road a few hundred yards away.

A few moments later, a black car, an old Baleno, its headlights off, slid out of a lane and followed Navin's car.

In an unmarked Qualis parked close by, Abdul spoke softly into a wireless, relaying a message to two police parties – one along the route Navin would take, the other outside his house. As Navin's car slowed to turn right at the main road, the Qualis slid forward.

'Are the Pune policemen ready?' Ranade asked as Abdul got off the wireless.

'Yes sir. The one goon watching Navin's house seems to have got word of him leaving the office.'

'Only one?"

'The others may be waiting on the main road.'

'Then we must hurry.' Ranade tapped the driver on the shoulder. 'Faster!'

Meanwhile, Navin had reached the main road and was speeding through the deserted thoroughfare towards his house. Smog hung low around the yellow street lamps, diluting their dim light into hazy halos that barely reached the road. The Baleno was not far behind, but Ranade's Qualis was.

Suddenly, a van shot out from a side lane to the left and turned right towards a speeding Navin. The van was going the wrong way, its headlights blazing on high beam.

Travelling at close to 100 kmph, Navin slammed on the brakes. In the few moments that seemed to stretch for hours, the blue Ecosport slowed and weaved as the driver of the approaching van also hit the brakes. While the Ecosport held its course under Navin's steady hands, the van skidded. Its rear wheels moved to one side and the van turned a quarter of a circle, its nose pointing towards the barricade that divided the road lengthwise in two.

Navin pressed down harder on the brakes and arched back into his seat, but his car was moving too fast. There was no way he could avoid hitting the van, unless he steered away from it. With a collision moments away, he twisted the steering wheel to the left.

Unfortunately, it was too sudden a manoeuvre for a vehicle travelling at that speed. As the Ecosport's nose swung to the left, Navin felt his car tilt. He tried to spin the steering wheel back the other way, but it was too late. Two of the car's wheels were already in the air. The world he saw through the windscreen spun as the vehicle flipped over violently.

Navin was unaware of what happened in the next few moments, but when the noise and the jolts stopped, the Ecosport was back on its wheels. Battered and with cracked windows, but on its wheels. The engine had fallen silent. Behind him, the Baleno had come to a halt.

Even as an enraged Navin undid his seat belt and climbed out, the men in the Baleno and the van jumped out of their vehicles. Two of them carried pistols and the third held a knife with a long blade. Navin's muddled brain had barely registered that fact when they opened fire. One bullet hit him in the shoulder and spun him around, while the other gouged a furrow in his leg.

Ranade's Qualis, now a hundred feet away, had screeched to

a halt. Out he leapt with Abdul, both men with pistols in hand. While the two of them had their service revolvers, the inspector also carried a pistol with a snout made longer for greater accuracy. This he drew, even as he sprang out of their vehicle.

After his childhood dream of joining the National Defence Academy was shattered by his less-than-perfect eyesight, Ranade had thrown himself wholeheartedly into his police training. To his delight, he had discovered that in addition to his keen mind, he had a steady hand too. Though nature had intended him to wear spectacles, it had not robbed his eyes of their keenness.

Very soon, he realized that marksmanship came to him naturally and with ease. He had hit the bullseye at 50 feet, the very first time he was allowed to handle a gun. Soon, he was able to repeat this feat for much longer distances. Now, in addition to his regular duties, he was occasionally called upon to be a sharpshooter in tight situations.

It was this skill that he proposed to use now.

Seventy feet ahead of him, illuminated by the headlights of his Qualis, were three men intent on attacking Navin Gokul. The one closest to Ranade carried a pistol, as did the man beyond him. Both had already fired at their quarry and scored hits. Ranade judged the third man – the one with a knife – as a threat, but not an immediate one, as he was a good 25 feet from Navin.

Already wounded, Navin was trying to run around his Ecosport and use it as a shield to protect himself from the gunmen. Ranade adopted the classic shooting stance, feet wide apart, knees bent, torso leaning forward and left palm supporting the pistol-wielding right hand.

At that very moment, the two gunmen fired again. Struck by two bullets, Navin collapsed on the road. Two other bullets buried themselves in the body of the Ecosport.

As soon as the men had fired, Ranade cut loose with three shots.

The first bullet struck the man closest to him in the right hand, mangling a finger and flinging the pistol out of his grasp. Even as the man clutched at his injured hand, Ranade's second bullet took him low in the left thigh, making him fall to the ground. Ranade's third bullet missed the target and passed close to the furthest attacker, making him duck and pause.

A moment later, Abdul's revolver boomed twice and the second man spun around, hit in the shoulder. But he still held on to his pistol and Ranade saw him swinging the barrel around to point towards a fallen Navin who was trying to crawl away. With Navin already hit four times, there wasn't a second to lose. Ranade pulled the trigger twice in quick succession, sending two bullets into the gunman's chest. The man fell and his pistol clattered to the road.

Meanwhile, the third man had dropped his knife and taken to his heels. He leapt over the barricade and sprinted into a lane, zigzagging his way across to avoid being shot. Luck stayed with him that night as he disappeared into the dark lane, the very moment that a police jeep drove up from the direction of Navin's house.

Giving no thought to the fleeing attacker, Ranade shouted to Abdul to cover the fallen gunmen and ran to Navin, who had crawled another few feet away, leaving a dark trail of blood in his wake. A quick examination told the inspector that Navin had been hit in the chest and abdomen. The wounds in his leg and shoulder were not serious, but the other two were.

Ranade shouted and waved to the Pune policemen who had just arrived in the jeep, urging them to load Navin into the jeep and take him to a hospital down the road. As two constables did so, the inspector approached the nearest gunman.

The beams from the Qualis's headlights fell on the man's face, revealing his features. It took Ranade no more than an instant to recognize the face.

'So, we meet at last, Mr Kashyap,' he said with more than a hint of grim satisfaction. 'Or whatever your real name is. I'm surprised to see you without a beard or a Frenchie. But you and I will finally have a long talk.'

He watched a constable help Kashyap to his feet and escort the limping man towards the three stationary vehicles. As he watched Kashyap's face, a concern rose in his mind. Kashyap was terrified. The lines on his face and the rapidly darting eyes spoke of the terror he felt.

In Ranade's experience, men like Kashyap seldom feared arrest. It was unlikely that Vivek had been his first victim and still more unlikely that today's incident was his first brush with the law. There was a look of the seasoned killer in him; he was a professional. Such men tended to show defiance rather than fear during arrest. Yet he was terrified. Why?

Ranade frowned. He was missing something. He looked again at Kashyap's eyes, swivelling from one side to the other, as if looking out for something. Such a man feared only one thing: death. Violent death. Why then was he so frightened now? The incident was over and the other thugs had fled.

Or had they?

A sudden thought flashed through the inspector's mind. All such incidents had a getaway car at the ready. Neither the old Baleno nor the van fit the bill, as the possibility had always been there of these vehicles being damaged while intercepting the Ecosport. Where, then, was the getaway car?

Ranade spun around and peered into the darkness behind him. A vehicle could come either from the direction of Navin's office or from the direction of his house. There were no bylanes close by on this side of the barricade and the getaway car would serve no purpose if it came down the other side. He peered into the darkness at both ends of the road. A long moment passed and he decided he could see nothing.

He was mistaken.

Beyond the blazing headlights of the Qualis was a blind spot. Idling in a side lane beyond the Qualis, on the other side of the main road from where they stood, was an SUV. Its engine was purring and its lights were off. Dark rubber sheets, fastened by masking tape, covered the tail-lights. In the SUV were two men.

Ranade turned back to stare at Kashyap and study the terror-stricken look on his face. Why was the man so frightened, he wondered again.

Even as he watched, the situation changed. Abruptly.

A black-rimmed hole appeared in Kashyap's forehead above his left eye and his head snapped backwards. At the same moment, Ranade heard the slap of a bullet passing over his shoulder and, an instant later, the crash of a rifle.

More by instinct than conscious decision, Ranade dived to his left, drawing his pistol as he moved. What he had seen and heard indicated that the shot had come from behind him. He rolled twice and halted in a prone position on his belly, his pistol held in front of his face and pointing towards the source of the rifle shot.

But no more shots came. Instead, a powerful engine roared. Ranade leapt to his feet, shouting to Abdul and the Qualis driver to pursue the fleeing SUV. But before the Qualis could take a U-turn and reach the side lane, the SUV was long gone.

Even as they turned into that lane, unsure as to which road to take at the approaching junction, the SUV was half a mile away and out of earshot. The rear door opened a foot or so and a hand came out to peel away the rubber sheets covering the tail-lights. Soon, it looked like any other SUV travelling on that road.

Back on the main road, Ranade stared in disbelief at Kashyap's lifeless face. Overcome with frustration and a feeling of despondency, he swore colourfully and mentally kicked himself over his lack of foresight. He had apprehended Vivek's killer with great satisfaction, only to lose him in two minutes flat.

Back to square one.

Chapter 24

Shashi stared in amazement at the notebooks in his hands. Had he not known which was the original and which the forgery, he would not have been able to distinguish between the two.

When closed, they did look a little different. Their dimensions were not exactly the same and the bindings were dissimilar in colour and texture. But presuming that Varma – and whoever was behind him – had not seen the notebook before, that didn't matter. What mattered was what lay within.

When the notebooks were opened, they were indistinguishable. Such was the precision of Kamna's forgery that not only were the writing and markings identical, even the colour of the ink and the thickness of the pen strokes were very alike. Kamna had taken care to select the right pen from Vivek's study.

Shashi, who had seen his wife's handiwork from time to time, was astonished at the near perfection of the results. She had occasionally forged his signature when it was urgently required because he was travelling or otherwise unavailable. That had included signatures on cheques as well as on documents. But never had he seen her copy another person's handwriting so well.

Kamna observed her husband's astonishment with a smile, grinning with pleasure as he voiced his praise and admiration.

Shashi now put down the original notebook and examined the copy closely. Ranade had said that a tracking device with a life of a week to ten days would be built into the binding. He inspected the notebook from every angle and ran his fingers over the entire binding, but couldn't see anything out of place. The police too had done an immaculate a job. What remained now was to deliver it to Varma, provided Ranade cleared the forged notebook.

He quickly snapped several photos of the two notebooks – the original and the forged – side by side, and sent them to Ranade. Within ten minutes, he had the inspector's clearance to hand over the forged notebook to Varma.

He glanced at the wall clock. It was 6.32 a.m. He hoped Varma would call soon so that they could be done with the task of planting the fake notebook. He hurried through his morning routine and grabbed a quick breakfast. He wanted to be ready by 7 a.m., should the man call.

Varma didn't disappoint. At 7.07 a.m., Shashi's mobile phone rang. The call was from an unknown mobile number this time. He quickly scribbled the number on a piece of paper and passed it to Kamna, who immediately keyed the number into a message for Ranade. Shashi answered the call on the fifth ring.

'Hello?' he said, adjusting his voice to make it sound sleepy.

'Notebook *mili?*' asked the gravelly voice he remembered from yesterday's call.

'*Mil gayi,*' he answered. '*Ghar mein hi thi.*'

'Are you sure it's the notebook I want?' Varma persisted.

'It seems to be. It has phone numbers disguised as fifteen-digit codes. One page has the name "Zeus" written on it and the first page has the letters "SX" inscribed inside a circle.'

'Good. Pick up that notebook and get into your car. Drive towards Phoenix Mall in Parel. I'll call you soon.'

'Okay. I'm leaving right away.'

'Don't call your inspector friend. Understood?'

'Yes.'

Shashi hung up, briefed Kamna on the call and asked her to inform Ranade.

'He's in Pune,' she told him. 'He's about to start back.'

'Tell him, anyway. Make sure you and Chaaya stay home. We don't want Varma thinking that you're following me or him. We're not taking more risks than necessary. Understand?'

Kamna nodded.

Shashi hurried downstairs and drove out of the apartment compound. He moved quickly through the sparse traffic and made for Phoenix Mall, wondering if Varma or any of his men were following him. As he turned in to Tulsi Pipe Road, his mobile rang again.

'Hello?' he answered using his Bluetooth hands-free, surprised that Varma was calling from a different mobile number this time.

'You're making good time. Now drive past Phoenix Mall and turn right towards Worli Sea Face. I want you to enter the Sea Face Road from the south.'

'From the side where Worli Dairy is located?'

'Yes. You know the way?'

'I do.'

'Get there in ten minutes,' Varma growled. 'I'll call you again. Don't try to get in touch with the inspector or anyone else. You're being watched.'

Shashi threw a glance at the rear-view mirror as Varma hung up. Half a dozen cars were behind him. Was Varma in one of them? He was tempted to call Ranade and tell him what had transpired, but decided against it. If the inspector's tracking device worked as it was meant to, the police should be able to track Varma without following him. There was no sense in jeopardizing the mission by being too adventurous.

Shashi had just turned into the south end of Worli Sea Face Road, when his mobile rang again. The call was from yet another mobile number. Was Varma resorting to single-use 'burn cards' that he destroyed after every call? That would make tracking him well-nigh impossible.

'Yes?' Shashi answered.

'Drive past the dairy and keep going,' Varma directed. 'When the road curves to the right, slow down, but keep going.'

'Okay.'

'Stay on the phone. Don't disconnect.'

Shashi remained silent and kept going at 40 kmph. When the road curved gently to the right, he slowed to 20 kmph and kept to the left lane. Morning walkers thronged the promenade to his left.

'Go another hundred metres further and stop,' Varma continued.

Shashi slowed down to a crawl after about a hundred metres.

'Stop the car.'

Shashi complied.

'Get out of the car.'

'But parking is not allowed here,' Shashi protested.

'It won't take long,' Varma replied. 'There are no policewalas about at this hour. Do it!'

Shashi pulled up at the kerb and got out. He carried the notebook inside an envelope in his right hand and his phone in the left.

'What now?' he asked, speaking into his phone.

'Walk forward, away from the car. Don't look back.'

Shashi did as instructed, wondering what was happening behind him. A minute later, Varma spoke again.

'Slow down. A white Xylo will drive up beside you. Keep the notebook ready. Is it in the envelope?'

'Yes.'

He heard the purr of an engine behind him and tensed. His heart beat faster. The vehicle was here. What would they do now? The bonnet of a large white vehicle appeared to his right at the edge of his vision and matched his speed. He resisted the temptation to turn and look at it.

'The rear window is open a few inches at the top,' Varma said softly. 'Push the envelope in through the gap.'

Shashi stopped and turned to look at the vehicle, his heart thudding away. All the windows were shaded, completely blocking a view of the occupants. The rear window on his side was open a few inches at the top, just as Varma had described.

Shashi stepped across and slid the envelope in through the gap. As he felt an unseen hand grasp it, he stepped back hurriedly. He thought he caught the rasping sound of an envelope being torn open. A few moments later, he heard Varma's voice on his mobile phone.

'Good,' the man said with satisfaction. 'Return to your car and drive back home. Don't attempt to follow the Xylo.'

Without a word, Shashi turned and strode towards his car, a hundred feet away, his heart still thumping madly. A frisson of anticipation filled his being. The shark had taken the bait. Would he swallow it?

■

Every passing hour felt as long as an entire day as Shashi waited impatiently for Carol's call. It seemed as if the hands on his watch were simply refusing to move at the speed they ought to. Every time he looked down at the dial to check, they had progressed no more than a minute or two.

Watching him pace restlessly, Chaaya drew the wrong conclusion.

'There's nothing more we can do, Shashi,' she said. 'Varma has taken your bait and it's up to the police now. I only hope that man doesn't ever call us again.'

Shashi nodded, but chose not to correct her misconception.

Realizing that his restlessness was feeding her own anxiety which might lead to potentially avoidable consequences, he opened his laptop and began working through his mails, trying hard not to think of the ex-Lucarro gang and their mole in Purple Country. It would be some hours before Carol could get the information he needed.

It was, therefore, with surprise that he looked at his mobile when it rang a few minutes short of 9 a.m. It was Ranade.

'Varma has taken the notebook to a godown in Sewri,' he said. 'The building will now be watched round the clock.'

'Who owns the godown?' Shashi asked.

'We haven't found out yet. Meanwhile, I have another bit of news for you. Kashyap was killed last night.'

'What! How?'

Ranade gave him the gist of the previous night's events.

'Please convey the news to Mrs Tola,' the inspector told him before signing off. 'I hope it gives her some consolation. Her husband's killer is now dead. There is no doubt that Kashyap was the one who had disguised himself as a waiter and served the poison-laced chilli cheese toast.'

Shashi and Kamna were in a kind of trance after the call, numbed by the turn of events. Chaaya was in tears. The news that her husband's assassin had been found and killed assuaged some of the outrage that had filled her after Vivek's murder. But it was also as if an emotional dam had burst inside her.

Retribution had been swift, far swifter than the kind the legal system could ever have meted out. The death penalty was satisfying too. But it was still incomplete. Kashyap had merely been the hand that dealt the blow, an instrument wielded by someone else. The brain behind Vivek's murder was still unknown and at large.

The atmosphere in the house changed markedly after Ranade's call. It was as if one chapter had been closed and another opened.

The mission was now to find Zeus and unearth the motive underlying Vivek's murder.

How were Kashyap, Varma and Zeus connected with his brother-in-law, Shashi wondered. Who were Ares, Apollo and Hermes, the other three Greek gods named in the notebook? Did they have anything to do with the ex-Lucarro gang? The latter were company executives, while Kashyap and Zeus were professional killers. They seemed worlds apart.

Shashi's thoughts were in a whirl when his mobile rang again. Carol! Finally! Shashi snatched up the phone.

'Hi Shashi,' she said. Her voice was quiet. 'I've done the investigation you wanted.'

Shashi glanced at the wall clock. It was a little past 11 a.m. Good old Carol! Efficient and quick as ever.

'There is one match; I've sent you his résumé. The auditors are clear. They have no connection with Lucarro.'

'Who is this match, Carol?'

Shashi's heart was thumping. This was the moment he had looked forward to with anticipation as well as dread.

'Amit,' Carol said. 'He was in Lucarro from August 2000 till September 2004.'

The news hit Shashi like a physical blow. Amit? Of all people, Amit Khanna? An outstanding CFO, a star in Purple Country, one of the few to be both liked and respected. How did a man who took immense professional pride in his work come to this? Why?

A part of Shashi rebelled against Carol's finding. Amit's presence in Lucarro during that crucial window only made him a suspect. It was not conclusive. What if it were just a coincidence? Shashi found himself wishing that it were, indeed, so.

But the rational part of him dug up a titbit from the past. Amit, the CFO who was always on top of his work, invariably got his accounts ready a couple of days before board meetings. Was that just efficiency on his part or was there some murky intent behind it?

'Shashi?' Carol asked. 'Are you there?'

'Yes, Carol,' Shashi replied in a choked voice. 'It took me by surprise.'

'Something wrong, Shashi?' Carol's concern for him, never far from the surface, flared.

'I hope not, Carol. Keep this under your hat. Nobody is to know of this. *Nobody*.'

'Of course. But what is this about?'

'Later, Carol. This is too raw now and I may be completely wrong.'

Shashi hung up and turned to Kamna, who had been watching him silently. His eyes looked haunted. He reached out and took her hand, as if seeking comfort.

'Is it Amit?' she asked softly.

Shashi nodded slowly, gazing in surprise at his wife. How had she known? He hadn't mentioned Amit's name during his conversation with Carol.

'I thought it was likely, you know. Amit is in his early forties and lives in Lokhandwala, if I'm not mistaken.'

Shashi blinked in surprise. Of course! Why had he not thought of it himself?

'You don't like thinking ill of your people,' Kamna continued gently, as if reading his thoughts. 'You're particularly fond of Amit and Barun. It could have been Barun too, but he's 10 years older.'

Shashi nodded dumbly, his thoughts tangled and confused. Should he call Amit and ask him if he knew the seven other ex-Lucarro men? Of course not! That would tip them off – if Amit were a part of the gang. Then what should he do? Of course! LinkedIn!

He logged into LinkedIn and went to Amit's profile. After checking that Carol had not been mistaken about him working at Lucarro & Co., he scanned through Amit's connections. Within a minute, he had found four of the other ex-Lucarro men.

Not bothering to look for the remaining three, he called Carol and asked her to send him Amit's PAN number. He would ask SEBI to get hold of Amit's share trades.

He then called Gupta and gave him the news.

An hour later, as Shashi sat dejectedly, his phone rang again. It was Gupta's office, asking him to join a conference call between Gupta, Sudakar and Saldana. The three directors had just had a discussion and wanted Shashi to join them.

'Mr Saldana and Mr Sudakar have been fully apprised of the situation,' Gupta began, as soon as Shashi joined the call. 'We have decided on our course of action, which we wanted you to be aware of. But first, Mr Sudakar would like to say something to you.'

'Good morning, Shashi,' Sudakar said. 'I hope matters are settling down in your sister-in-law's house?'

His tone was friendly, conciliatory, almost concerned. Shashi couldn't help feeling that Sudakar was on the back foot. He was trying to make peace with the CEO he had insulted publicly, the CEO who had upstaged him in the investigation.

'Morning, Mr Sudakar.' He kept his voice flat and even. 'The wound will take a while to heal.' The ambiguity was deliberate, but he went on to answer Sudakar's question. 'It will be months before the household returns to a semblance of normalcy.'

'I can imagine.' Sudakar sounded subdued, suitably empathetic. 'It must have been a huge blow. My deepest sympathies. Now coming to the matter of insider trading in our company, I wanted to congratulate you on the brilliant work you have done.'

'Thank you.'

'You have conducted yourself in an exemplary manner, maintaining the highest standards of professionalism, Shashi. The board is proud of you. You took yourself away from the investigation in the interests of independence and did so despite the malicious rumours personally targeting you.'

Shashi remained silent more out of surprise than an inability to think of a suitable response. The two-faced hypocrite! How blithely he lied when it suited him! His investigation subcommittee had done precious little but put the company at risk and cast aspersions on him of a despicably personal nature. Sudakar was the one who had wanted to suspend Shashi.

'Thanks to your single-minded devotion to the company, we have now cracked the matter of insider trading,' Sudakar went on. 'We can't thank you enough. Now that you have found the culprit, rest easy. The committee will take it to its logical conclusion.'

'What logical conclusion?' Shashi asked. A sense of apprehension had come over him. Sudakar was moving too fast. 'What I have found is by no means conclusive. It may just be a coincidence that Amit was with Lucarro at that time. We have nothing to suggest that he leaked information. We have absolutely no evidence.'

'That's exactly what the committee is doing now – finding evidence. Now that we know who it is, it won't be difficult.'

'What if we are wrong?' Shashi exclaimed. 'We can't accuse an innocent man.'

'The committee will be careful, Shashi. Don't worry.'

Shashi cursed silently. He now wished he had not hastened to inform Gupta. But being a suspect himself, he had to share his findings with someone on the board. There was no one better suited than Gupta; he was the chairman and he was a sensible man. But what on earth had prompted him to inform Sudakar? He was to get his answer immediately.

'Having lost half of our market cap in a week, we must do whatever we can to arrest it,' Gupta said. 'We cannot let the slide continue. I've spoken to Dheerajbhai and Mr Saldana concurs as well.'

'As do the other independent directors,' Sudakar added.

'The board has discussed the matter and is of the opinion that what you have unearthed gives us sufficient grounds for a targeted investigation. It will ease the pressure on the share price.'

'Ease pressure on the share price?' Shashi repeated. He was appalled. 'How? We can't go public with Amit's name! He can sue the pants off us if we are unable to substantiate our allegation against him. *We have no proof yet!* Isn't that so, Mr Saldana?'

'That's right, Shashi,' the lawyer said. 'My advice, therefore, is to not reveal Amit's name. All we plan to say is that it isn't you, but someone else in the company whom we are not at liberty to name.'

'That's worse, Mr Saldana! Pardon me for being forthright, but that will cast aspersions on *everyone* in the company. Every single person! Dozens of upright men and women will be implicitly accused of wrongdoing.'

'Well,' Sudakar interjected, 'the name could be leaked...'

Shashi grew furious. This was getting worse. He had to put his foot down.

'Mr Gupta,' he said, ignoring Sudakar. 'It is the board's prerogative to go ahead with whatever it decides, but I must say that I disagree with this course of action. Strongly disagree! I do not believe that we have adequate grounds for accusing Amit. And to implicate everyone else would be a disaster. It will destroy employee morale to such an extent that the current state of affairs is preferable. From the company's point of view, I strongly advise deferring any action till such time as we find something more conclusive. My second objection is that premature action will jeopardize the larger investigation.'

'What larger investigation?' Sudakar asked.

'The murder investigation of Vivek Tola, for one. And, of course, SEBI's investigation into insider trading. If Amit is indeed a part of the scam, the board's action will tip off those involved.'

There was an uncomfortable pause. Shashi realized that the directors had overlooked this angle.

'You have a point,' Saldana said slowly. 'Employee morale is an issue we must certainly consider. But your second objection raises a different question: to what extent should the company be guided by extraneous considerations? Especially when they are in conflict with the company's needs, which are dire. We will take your objections into account before taking a final call. But the board intends to act today.'

'One last question, Shashi,' Gupta said. 'Is your analysis complete or is there more to come?'

Shashi was on the verge of telling him that Tanuja had begun analysing the stock exchange data, but bit back his words. The board was clear that the company – and by extension, Shashi – should concern itself only with the company's affairs. Extraneous considerations, including the larger investigation, didn't matter. If he told them what Tanuja was up to, they would insist on being kept informed of the findings, with potentially disastrous consequences, as he had just witnessed. Worse, they might wind up the investigation altogether.

Finding Vivek's killer, investigating the firms that had traded in Purple Country's shares and analysing the stock exchange data were all very important for Shashi. He didn't want to give the board a chance to abort them.

He decided to lie.

'It's largely complete,' he said. 'Just a few loose ends to tie up.'

Chapter 25

'These men are clinical, Abdul,' Ranade observed morosely. The fact that Kashyap's assassination had taken place right under his nose and he had been able to do nothing to prevent it still weighed heavily on his mind.

Anger directed at himself had slowly given way to frustration, as he rationalized the events in his mind. It was his foresight that had taken him and Abdul to Pune, armed and ready for a gun battle. It was the same foresight that had made him hasten to follow Navin's car and arrive in the nick of time to save him. Had he been late by half a minute, Navin would be dead now and Kashyap possibly alive and free.

But he had not been prescient enough to anticipate that the enemy would be so meticulous as to have a Plan B and assassinate one of their own men. The assistant commissioner too had consoled Ranade by telling him that he shouldn't blame himself for it. Nevertheless, he did.

'They haven't yet succeeded, sir,' Abdul said. 'Navin is still alive, even though he's in a bad way. Let's not lose hope just yet.'

'What's the latest from the hospital?'

'They performed both the surgeries today. Two of the four bullets hit critical places. One punctured his lungs and another, his stomach.'

'What do the doctors say?'

'Fifty-fifty, but tonight is critical. If he survives the night, his chances of pulling through will be higher.'

'What do we have on Kashyap?'

'He was from Sewri too. He was seen there on at least three occasions and a couple of shopkeepers recognized him from his photo.'

'The shops Varma went to?'

'Yes sir. They say he is an ex-armyman and has seen combat. One man said that he had seen Kashyap with other ex-armymen. But we don't have his real identity yet.'

Ranade nodded. 'There was nothing in his wallet, other than a fake licence and cash. No credit or ATM cards either to make it easy for us. If you can get some details on where he saw combat or where in the army he was, we can zero in on his real identity.'

'What about his mobile, sir?' Abdul suggested. 'That must lead somewhere.'

'Burn cards, Abdul. SIM cards that are used once and destroyed.' Ranade's voice was grim. 'Kashyap had three unused prepaid cards that were procured against false papers. He had been using one in his phone for three hours before his death. The phone too was a cheap one bought in the second-hand market. Everything was for single use.'

'What about the calls he made in those three hours? He must have called his boss or handler.'

'He did. And guess what? That was a burn card too.'

'But the location of that card?'

'Sewri.'

'So that's where their nest is. Kashyap, Varma and their boss – all in Sewri. What about Zeus's number, sir?'

'It seems to come on only two or three days a week, that too for an hour or two each time and mostly late in the evening. We are dealing with a smart man here, Abdul. He doesn't stay in one place when that number is switched on. Yesterday, he was roaming about on the Western Express Highway between 9 p.m. and 10.30 p.m.'

'In a car, I suppose.'

'I'm sure he's nowhere near his home or office whenever he switches on the number.'

'I don't understand why he's using the same number every day when Kashyap and his handler used burn cards.'

'Think, Abdul.' Ranade smiled for the first time that evening. 'There is a good reason for it. Now, here's something interesting I found. The number has been recharged at the same location for the past few months. It's a small shop in Sewri.'

'Then we must watch the shop, sir!'

'It's being watched. The balance is down to under fifty rupees. It will be recharged soon. Zeus cannot recharge it online without exposing his identity and leaving a trail of his credit card or digital wallet.'

'Is the shop near the godown?' Abdul asked.

'Sewri is not a big place. Who owns the godown? You said you had got some information.'

'Dead end, sir. The godown was rented by Kashyap.'

'Not a dead end, Abdul. It may have been rented in his name. But where is the rent being paid from? It can't be in cash; the godown is too big. Get the owner and trace the cheques or bank transfers. It has to lead somewhere.'

'Yes sir.'

'One more thing. It's of no use if the notebook with the tracking device stays at the godown. We must force them to move it closer to where the brain behind this affair lives or works.'

'We can make our surveillance more obvious, sir. That may make them move it out.'

Ranade nodded. 'Let's force their hand. Enter the godown and make enquiries about Kashyap. I wonder if Kashyap's handler and Zeus are the same person.'

'A good chance, I think, sir.'

'What do we have on Varma so far?'

'He left the godown and took a local train. We lost him at VT.'

The desk phone rang, interrupting the conversation. Ranade answered it, listened for half a minute, hung up without saying a word and stood up. A new light of excitement now shone in his eyes.

'Come, Abdul,' he said, as he strode out of the office. 'This is going to be interesting.'

A minute later, they were in a police computer lab, beside an operator with a very large monitor on his desk. On the monitor was a map showing the western suburbs of Mumbai.

'I asked them to map the route Zeus's phone takes during his nocturnal wanderings,' Ranade told Abdul. 'Let's see what it shows.'

The computer operator hit a key and a red dot came up on the screen and began moving, leaving a red worm-like trail in its wake.

'Linking Road in Bandra,' the operator said. 'That's where he switched on the phone yesterday.'

They watched silently as the dot wormed its way south along Linking Road and turned left on to the Western Express Highway. There, it began moving a little faster as it made its way east and then north. The worm lengthened northwards at varying speeds, stopping from time to time, and turned west into Andheri. There, it wandered, sometimes looping back on itself and crossing its earlier path. Finally, it returned to the Western Express Highway, entered Linking Road and vanished.

'He made a long loop north,' Ranade said softly, 'starting and ending in Linking Road. I assume he is taking to the road so that we can't track him down to his house. Agree?'

'Yes sir.'

'Then it is reasonable to assume that, for the same reason, he would travel away from his home, once he switches on the phone, and not towards it. Since he went south, east and then north after leaving home, we can tentatively infer that his house lies to the west of Linking Road.'

'Right.'

'If I assume that he switched on his phone, say, ten minutes after leaving home and extended his route backwards to the west from the starting point, we will get the general area where he lives.'

'But that could be any one of a dozen streets. It will cover a pretty large area, sir.'

'That's right. He could be living anywhere within ten to fifteen minutes' drive from the east of this starting point.'

The operator hit a key and a light pink semicircle sprang up on the screen. The worm's starting point was at the centre of the diameter and the semicircle extended west.

'I've done the same thing from the end point too,' the operator said and hit the key again. A light blue semicircle came up, with the end point of the route at its centre. 'The blue area is ten minutes west of the location where he switched off the phone.'

'That leaves us too large an area to do anything meaningful.' Abdul wasn't impressed.

'That's why we've got hold of the phone's location data for the past three months.' Ranade smiled grimly and nodded to the operator. 'Let's see what we've got.'

The operator hit another key and sat back. A green dot appeared on the screen and wormed its way south from Turner Road, going to Mahim and Dadar before returning to Bandra. An orange dot then appeared and quickly etched an orange worm that traced a path east towards BKC and back.

'Should I display all thirty trips for which we have data?' the operator asked. 'He makes these trips three days a week – usually Monday, Wednesday and Friday.'

Ranade nodded and the operator busied himself with the keyboard. Soon, the map was covered with a jumble of lines of different colours.

'Looks like a plate of multicoloured noodles, doesn't it?' Ranade grinned.

'Yes sir, but the search area hasn't narrowed down much.' Abdul was still not happy. 'Zeus is somewhere to the north of Turner Road and west of Linking Road.'

'Yes, Abdul. For a moment, forget about the routes and look only at the starting and ending points of the past thirty trips. They are in two clusters.'

The operator erased the worms, leaving only dots representing the starting and ending points of the thirty routes. They lay in two clusters: one on Linking Road and the other on Turner Road. Ranade pointed to the cluster on Linking Road and continued.

'This cluster is close to the Bandra Talkies bus stop, where Hegdewar Road meets Linking Road. There is a high probability that Zeus uses Hegdewar Road just before switching on the phone or just after switching it off.'

He pointed to the second cluster and continued.

'Similarly, he seems to use St Theresa Road to enter Turner Road or exit from it. There is a high probability that we will find him passing through one or both of these junctions on the days he switches on his phone.'

Abdul was staring at the screen in awe. His scepticism had vanished.

'That's brilliant, sir!' he exclaimed. 'Have we installed cameras at these two places?'

'Already in place.' Ranade's grin widened. 'There are a few more, deeper in Hegdewar Road and St Theresa Road. It's now a question of watching for a few days and identifying cars that are common. We'll start recording at 8 p.m. and continue for fifteen minutes after Zeus switches off the phone. We start today.'

■

Zeus switched off his regular phone and switched on another one as his inconspicuous grey Tata Indigo Manza passed the Bandra Talkies bus stop. The phone beeped the arrival of two messages.

'*Congrats*,' the first one said. '*You have won £750,000 in the Rover Raffle. Call now to claim your reward. Call 7306417059.*'

He studied the message for a few moments and moved it to a folder.

'*State of the art pest control service at your doorstep*,' said the second message. '*Quick service. 4-month guarantee. AMC available. Call Mohan at 8203315046.*'

This too he studied before moving it to a folder. He sat in thoughtful silence for a few minutes as the car reached the Western Express Highway and turned left. He had already told the driver which route to take. Two critical conversations awaited him today. He glanced at his watch and picked up the mobile again; it was time to initiate the first conversation – with the ex-Lucarro man at Purple Country.

'Good evening,' he began, when the call was answered. 'How are things?'

'Terrible,' was the reply. The voice was tired and despondent. 'What did you want to talk to me about?'

'Matters are not as dire as they may seem,' Zeus said. 'That's what I wanted to tell you – '

'You know what happened today?' the other man snapped. 'They know about the ex-Lucarro circle – both SEBI and the police. We are toast now! History!'

'Don't worry. They don't have a leg to stand on. You haven't traded in your company's shares and there's no proof that you passed information about the company to outsiders.'

'They have analysed all the trades for the past two years! They know everything – '

'Circumstantial evidence,' Zeus interjected. 'Nothing more. Charges will not stick. It won't stand in court.'

'Court?' The man's voice seemed to tremble. 'Screw the court. My name is mud!'

'Don't take it personally. We are all in the corporate world to make money.'

'It's illegal! Don't you get it?'

'Only if they prove it. Besides, it's the law that is wrong; not us. That's why we say it's illegal.'

'What!'

'For a crime to be committed, there must be a victim. Tell me, who is the victim in what the world loftily calls "insider trading"?' Zeus's voice grew passionate. 'The person who sells his shares to you is not the victim – he has already decided to sell and he gets the price he asks for. You are actually helping him! He's not selling because of anything you said or did. He doesn't even know you! He would have sold his shares, anyway, whether you were buying or not.

'Purple Country is not the victim either. Its book value doesn't change; it doesn't matter who holds the shares. It doesn't matter whether *you* own a thousand shares or the person who just sold them. Share price changes because of the company's performance and the market sentiment. As a single share trader, you affect neither.

'Who then, my friend, is the victim? The stock exchange? No! The government? No. Both earn from your share trading. *There is no victim! So, there is no crime!* The insider trading law is just plain stupid.'

There was a palpable silence after Zeus had finished advancing his argument.

'You're mad,' the other man finally declared. 'I wish to God I hadn't ever met you!'

'You can't wish away your actions of the past. You're as much a part of this as I am. If you think you have sinned, you can't wash away your sins.'

'I know.' The other man's voice had grown cold. 'But I can look forward to a better future.'

'The future is uncertain, my friend. But our actions can make it better or worse for ourselves.' Zeus's voice had hardened. 'Before you even *think* of mentioning our arrangement to anyone, remember that I know your wife. I know her relatives and yours. I know where they live.'

Before the other man could respond, Zeus disconnected the call. He fell into deep thought and brooded for the next ten minutes. Matters had taken a turn for the worse. If he did not stem the tide now, there was no telling where it could lead.

It was time for a consultation, which would constitute the evening's second critical conversation. He picked up his phone and dialled a number from memory.

'Good evening,' he said. 'The Pune mission didn't work out as planned.'

'What happened?' the voice at the other end asked. 'I hear you lost your main man?'

'I had to terminate him. Couldn't risk the police getting their hands on him. The police inspector seemed to have anticipated our move on Gokul.'

'What news of Gokul?'

'Critical. May not make it.'

'Okay. What else?'

'I heard from our SEBI source. It appears that they are on to something big, but our source doesn't know what. Kulkarni has put a lid on it and is not allowing anyone into the investigation.'

'What is he investigating?'

'Our source thinks it's stock exchange data.'

There was a long pause.

'That doesn't sound good,' the voice at the other end said. 'Who is conducting the investigation? Kulkarni can't do it himself.'

'A woman SK brought from London. She's carrying out her investigation somewhere else, not at SEBI or Purple Country.'

'She must be staying somewhere.'

'Grand Central.'

'Well, you know what to do.'

'The Lucarro guys have been compromised.'

'Unfortunate. They've become toxic. You must lie low.'

'I don't like this,' Zeus fumed. 'Spice Xchange will have to go underground for months now. I had advised against that visit to SK's office.'

'We had to know if Tola was getting inside information from SK. There was no other way to find out. We had to accuse SK and see how he reacted.'

'He has now brought in this woman,' Zeus said petulantly. 'We should have dealt with Tola the way I had suggested.'

'We eventually did, didn't we? Once you found out that he had deceived you and was running his own little thing. Now deal with the woman your way.'

Zeus sat deep in thought after the call, trying to calibrate the risks Spice Xchange faced.

Firstly, the ex-Lucarro man at Purple Country was weakening. He had been consulting a psychiatrist. What were the chances of him breaking down and going to the police? Were the threats Zeus had made sufficient to keep him in line?

Second, the police inspector was beginning to sniff at his heels. Pune had been a disaster. Only Zeus's habit of expecting the unexpected had saved them from the bigger disaster of Kashyap falling into the inspector's hands. Terminating Kashyap had been a difficult decision, but a necessary one. That left only Varma to do his dirty work. Varma was okay for larceny and thuggery, but not for killing.

The final risk was Shashi's analytics. Never had he expected

SEBI to discover patterns that could threaten Spice Xchange. The analyses they had done in the past had not been deep enough. But Shashi had changed that by bringing in the data scientist woman from London. Damn him! Not knowing what she was up to deepened Zeus's anxiety. There was only one way forward: she had to be eliminated.

Zeus considered his options. He could use the sharpshooter's services again, but that would betray his identity. Ironically, it was Kashyap who had hired him the last time; Zeus had only instructed him over the phone. That left Varma.

Zeus got out of the car and dialled a number. He spoke for five minutes out of the driver's earshot and returned to the car. It had been a difficult conversation.

Some miles away, Varma hung up with sweaty palms and trembling hands, his mind searching for a way out of the predicament. He was to kill a woman. But unlike Kashyap, he had never killed anyone before. He didn't want to start now.

Chapter 26

The soft buzz of the mobile phone intruded upon Shashi's sleep. Conditioned to respond to the familiar sound, he awoke at once, his eyes going instinctively to the luminous digital clock on the table. It was just past 6 a.m.

Who was calling so early? Was it an emergency? He reached for the mobile and looked at it. Carol.

'Shashi,' she said as soon as he answered. 'Something terrible has happened. Amit attempted suicide.'

'What!' His mind cleared in an instant as the last traces of sleep-induced befuddlement vanished.

His shout had woken up Kamna.

'When?' he asked.

'Sometime in the night. Deepika, his wife, called me at four in the morning.'

'Where are you?' Shashi was already out of bed. Kamna was sitting up in bed and staring at him.

'At the hospital.'

'Anyone else with you?'

'I haven't told anyone yet. Thought I should speak to you first.'

'Are you sure it was a suicide attempt, Carol?'

'Well…no. I'm just repeating what Deepika said.'

'Then don't mention it to anyone else. I'm coming right away.'

He quickly briefed Kamna and rushed through his morning

routine. Ten minutes later, they were both in the car, speeding through the deserted Mumbai streets towards Andheri.

Clad in jeans and kurti, Carol was waiting for him when he reached the hospital.

'Some good news, Shashi,' she said. 'His heart is still beating. But his pulse is very faint.'

'Where is Deepika?' Kamna asked.

'Come this way.'

Carol led them through a corridor to a waiting area where a woman in her late thirties sat weeping disconsolately in a chair. On seeing Shashi and Kamna approach, Deepika burst into fresh sobs. Kamna put her arms around the devastated woman and let her weep into her shoulder.

Gradually, the tears abated and Deepika began to speak.

'Amit told me yesterday,' she said haltingly, seemingly unable to look Shashi in the face. 'But I never thought it would come to this…that he would take such a drastic step.'

'Told you what?' Shashi asked softly.

'That thing about Purple Country shares. Sudakar was nasty to him yesterday…said all kinds of things…even insulted his parents.' Her next words were lost in a mumbled blur of uncontrollable sobs. She struggled for composure and continued. 'He said Amit was worthless…a disgrace to his profession and to the company…Is it true, Shashi? Is what Sudakar said about Amit true?'

Shashi's anger had begun to rise as he listened to her outpourings. Yes, Amit might have been guilty of leaking information. But a board member *had* to deal with every issue professionally. Nothing justified personally insulting people in the office. Besides, what evidence did Sudakar have?

'I don't know, Deepika,' he said. 'Amit is the best CFO I've worked with. This insider trading matter is new and still raw. It's being investigated and I can't discuss it. But tell me, what actually happened?'

Deepika opened her handbag and drew out a crumpled piece of paper. '*I'm sorry*,' had been scrawled on it, followed by, '*Forgive me if you can.*'

'Is this all?' Shashi asked. 'He's simply apologizing to you. It doesn't really indicate if suicide was on his mind.'

'There was an empty strip of sedatives lying on the bedside table. He swallowed them all.' Deepika wiped the tears that refused to stop flowing and glanced at Kamna for comfort. 'He was very disturbed after returning from his evening walk yesterday and insisted on sleeping in a different room. He said he was fine when I asked him; said he just needed to get some sleep. He hadn't been able to sleep for a few nights.

'I let him do as he wished, but I looked in on him in the middle of the night. I knew at once from the way he was breathing that something was wrong. And when I touched him, I was certain. I noticed the empty medicine strip when I switched on the light. I called out to him and shook him. When he didn't respond, I called my brother. We brought him here.'

'Listen to me, Deepika.' Shashi sat down beside her and held her gently by the shoulders, forcing her to pay attention to him. 'We don't know for sure if Amit attempted suicide or not. So don't mention it to anyone. Understand? *Anyone*.'

Deepika nodded.

'I'll keep this note for now,' Shashi went on. 'Don't worry about what Sudakar said and don't lose hope. I'll go and speak to the doctors now. Okay?'

Deepika rose to her feet and drew Shashi aside.

'It's so good of you to support Amit, Shashi,' she said in an undertone, the tears creeping into her voice again. 'But he confessed to me last night.'

'What did he say?'

'He said that he did share financial details with outsiders.'

'I see. Did he say how he had gone about it?'

Deepika nodded. 'Through some games on his mobile phone.'

'Where is his mobile now?'

'Here.'

Deepika drew out an iPhone 4s from her handbag and touched a game icon. Shashi stared in fascination at the suite of games that had come up on the phone's screen. It was the same suite he had found on Vivek's second phone. That too was an iPhone 4s.

'Keep it with you now, but don't mention this to anyone, okay?'

Deepika nodded and Carol led Shashi to the doctor on duty, leaving the shattered woman in Kamna's care.

'We were able to pump out his stomach,' the doctor said. 'Fortunately for him, he was brought here within three hours of consuming the medicine.'

'What are his chances?' Shashi asked.

'It's difficult to say. If his pulse becomes stronger in the next 12 to 24 hours, I think he will pull through. Even then, it'll be a while before he wakes up. His wife had the presence of mind to bring the discarded medicine strip along. That helped us act quickly and decisively.'

'Anything we can do, doctor? Let's do whatever we can to save him. The company will pick up the tab. Or I will.'

'There's nothing more we can do, except pray. But tell me something: how did he end up consuming all the tablets in the strip? Was it by accident or…' The doctor left the question hanging.

'I just don't know, doctor,' Shashi replied. 'Neither does his wife. But that's less important for us right now than saving him.'

'I understand.'

'Thank you, doctor.' Shashi rose and left the room.

'You're sure, Shashi?' Carol asked as they walked back to where Deepika and Kamna sat. 'You're sure it isn't a suicide attempt?'

Shashi shook his head. 'No more than you are, Carol. But what could possibly be gained by making it out as a suicide? Deepika won't get insurance money if he dies. And if he survives, he can be prosecuted for attempted suicide. Either way, suicide will pose a problem.'

Carol looked at him in wonder. 'Then we had better impress upon Deepika the seriousness of the matter.'

'She'll have to tell her brother too.' He glanced at his watch. 'I had better call Barun.'

'And the chairman too?' Carol asked.

'He can wait!' Shashi's voice was uncharacteristically harsh.

Carol looked up in surprise.

'He was the one who unleashed Sudakar on Amit.'

An hour later, Shashi sat with Barun in a coffee shop nearby. The latter was furious. He had witnessed the viciousness with which Sudakar had treated Amit the previous evening.

'I wanted to leave the room, but Sudakar wouldn't let me,' Barun told Shashi. 'He wanted to publicly humiliate Amit. I have never come across such crassness in the entire 27 years of my working life. That man is despicable!'

'Did he have any proof that Amit had leaked inside information?'

'Apparently, an analysis of the share registrar data revealed something. Sudakar claimed that Amit and his ex-colleagues from a previous firm were the ones involved in insider trading.'

'Anything else, Barun?' Shashi's voice was shaking with anger. 'Did he offer any other evidence?'

Barun shook his head. So, that had been Sudakar's idea of gathering evidence – accusing Amit without any further investigations.

'Okay,' Shashi said. 'Let me bring you up to speed.'

In the next few minutes, he briefed Barun about the analysis Tanuja had carried out and his subsequent conversation with the board members the previous day. Both men were fuming by the time Shashi had finished.

'The bastard!' Barun cursed. 'If Amit dies, I'll nail Sudakar for abetting suicide. I don't care a fig if he's a director!'

'Don't let's talk of suicide, Barun. Instead, let's take the first step and report him to the chairman. His conduct has been reprehensible, to say the least.'

After lunch, Shashi spoke to Gupta about Sudakar's behaviour. He had just hung up, when his mobile rang. It was Ranade.

'I just heard from Daniel,' he said. 'You remember the last of the eight men – or eight households – who had illicitly traded in Purple Country shares? The government employee?'

'Yes.'

'Daniel has identified him.'

'Excellent!' Shashi was delighted. At last, some progress! 'Who is he?'

'You are not going to believe this, Mr Kurva. He's the son-in-law of one of your board members.'

Shashi was stunned. 'Which board member?' he asked.

'Mr Sudakar.'

'What!'

'It was a simple matter for EOW, once you had identified the demat account. His being a government employee helped us speed up the process.'

'Are you sure of this, inspector?'

Shashi was conscious of the spiteful streak of glee surging through him. After what Sudakar had done to Amit, this was poetic justice, pure and simple!

'No doubt about it,' Ranade said firmly. 'And Daniel has gleaned more from neighbourhood gossip.'

'Tell me.'

'It seems that Sudakar and his daughter have been estranged for over 10 years now. Apparently, she had married without her father's consent. She's been in severe financial difficulty and had to sell off all her jewellery. She has been in touch with her mother for the past three years, but refuses to have anything to do with her father. Daniel suspects that Sudakar is discreetly helping her financially by passing on information to her husband through someone else in the family.'

Shashi's spurt of malicious delight died a quick death. Every man had his problems. Even the mean, cantankerous Sudakar. Gloating over another's misfortune was not the done thing.

'So that's why he was so keen to take on the investigation when I told the board about Varma and Kashyap's visit!' Shashi exclaimed. 'He wanted it under his own control so that he could not only keep tabs on the "investigation", but steer it in the direction that suited him. And when he came to know about Tanuja's analysis and that Amit Khanna was ex-Lucarro, he went hammer and tongs to nail him.'

'Ex-Lucarro?' Ranade asked. 'What's that?'

Shashi gave him a quick, concise account of his investigation into the eight ex-Lucarro men and ended it with his conversation with Gupta and Sudakar.

'So…going after Amit Khanna was Sudakar's way of deflecting the blame,' Ranade concluded. 'If someone else was already leaking information, Sudakar could conceal his own culpability and go scot-free.'

A thought flashed through Shashi's mind.

'It would be interesting to find out which other companies Sudakar is a director in, inspector,' he said. 'You may want to check if his son-in-law has been trading in those shares as well.'

'Daniel is working on that even as we speak. I have a message for you from him, Mr Kurva. He suggests that you focus your analysis on the other seven. He's going after Sudakar and his son-in-law.'

■

Ranade walked into the office to find a glum Abdul staring at a computer monitor.

'Why the long face?' he asked.

'Vivek Tola's notebook, sir. It's useless!'

'The one whose contents were copied and given to Varma?'

'Yes sir. I had high hopes that the phone numbers in it would lead us somewhere. What a let-down!'

'Tell me.'

Ranade pulled up a chair and sat down beside his deputy. Abdul was looking at a spreadsheet filled with phone numbers.

'You remember, sir, that the notebook had a list of 13 phone numbers?'

'Yes, and four more, of Greek gods – Apollo, Ares, Hermes and Zeus.'

'That too, but over 99 per cent of the calls are from or to one of the list of 13 numbers. I've got all the calls marked in this spreadsheet. Now here is the screw-up, sir: there have been *no* calls between any of the 13 mobile phones in the past one year.'

'None?'

'Not a single call. All 13 are heavy corporate users – they make hundreds of calls and run up bills worth thousands of rupees every month. Together, the 13 have made tens of thousands of calls in the past year and received as many.' He gestured towards the spreadsheet on the computer monitor. 'We have well over a lakh and a half calls here, sir. But not a single call has been made from one of the 13 to another on the list. Nor have any been exchanged between these 13 and Zeus or any of the other Greek gods.'

'Sure, Abdul?'

'Yes sir. I've been breaking my head over this for hours now. I have searched for each number four times. This spreadsheet has all the calls made or received by these 13 mobiles in the past one year.'

'I see...Yes, that's surprising all right.' Ranade sat back and frowned. 'That could mean one of two things: either they don't know each other or they're consciously refraining from using these mobiles for communicating with each other.'

'I've thought about that, sir. I suspect they don't know each other. When each of these 13 has called well over a thousand different numbers in the year, why would he hesitate to call the others if he knew them? Lost among thousands of other numbers, these wouldn't draw attention as something out of the ordinary.'

'Hmm...you're right, Abdul.' Ranade produced a cheap ballpoint pen from somewhere and began twirling it around his thumb. 'No calls to or from Zeus either?'

Abdul shook his head.

'What about the other Greek gods? Any calls between them?'

'No. The only calls the other Greek gods exchanged were with Zeus. Not a single call to each other. That's why this is all so disheartening. So much effort for nothing.'

Ranade patted Abdul on the shoulder.

'Don't be discouraged, my friend. I have a hunch that no exchange of calls between the 13 or between any one of them and Zeus means something. We just haven't figured out what. Do you have Vivek's second mobile number?'

'Yes sir.' Abdul rummaged through a drawer and came up with a diary. He leafed through it and paused at a page. 'Here it is.'

'Search for it in your spreadsheet.'

Ranade watched as Abdul brought up the 'Find' window and entered the number of Vivek's second phone. He hit the 'Find All' button and let out a whoop.

'Eighteen matches, sir! There have been eighteen calls between Vivek and one of the 13 people.'

'That's one every three weeks, on an average. Well, don't be so surprised, Abdul. Kurva had found four of these numbers in Vivek's call log.'

'I forgot about that.' Abdul looked sheepish. 'Kurva had mentioned calls to Zeus too. Let me search for them.'

Within a few minutes, he had established that Vivek had spoken to Zeus twenty-seven times in the past year, but not to any of the other Greek gods.

'Okay,' Ranade continued. 'Now check if Zeus has ever called this number or received calls from it,' he directed, pointing to a mobile number in his notebook, which he now held open for his deputy to look at.

Abdul highlighted the cells containing Zeus's calls and searched for the number. There were seven matches.

'The last call was made yesterday evening! Whose number is this, sir?'

'Amit Khanna's. The CFO of Purple Country. Judging by the time of yesterday's call, it was Zeus with whom Amit spoke during his evening walk. Okay, check if Amit has been in touch with Vivek.'

Abdul searched the spreadsheet again and shook his head.

'So this is what we have found,' Ranade summarized, sitting back again in his chair, twirling the pen around. 'Neither the 13 nor the three Greek gods speak to each other. Only Vivek spoke to the 13. Vivek and Amit didn't speak to each other either. But Zeus spoke to Vivek, Amit and the three Greek gods.' Ranade stood up abruptly and slapped the back of his chair in frustration. 'What the bloody hell does it all mean?'

Minutes passed in silence as the inspector paced the floor, brooding on the problem. Abruptly, he stopped and looked up.

'Have you got any more details of the firms that had traded in Purple Country shares?'

'Yes sir. We already knew that two of them were Vivek's firms. That has been confirmed. Four others are Pune-based firms connected to Navin and Vivek's company, Aran Advisors. That leaves 26 demat accounts to be investigated.'

'It's clear that Vivek was getting inside information from Purple Country. And Amit was the insider leaking information. *But there has been no contact between Amit and Vivek!* Then how was Vivek receiving information?'

'This is getting confusing, sir.'

'Vivek had to be getting inside information from Purple Country through *someone*! If Amit was not giving it to him, who was?'

'How about Shashi Kurva...?'

Ranade stared at Abdul for a long moment. 'Hmm...Possible, Abdul.'

'It could be Sudakar too, but I checked for calls between him and Vivek. There were none – '

The phone rang, interrupting Abdul. Ranade answered it, listened in silence for a minute and hung up, his face taut and flushed.

'Navin Gokul wants to talk,' he said softly. 'Let's see if he can throw any light on this matter.'

'Already?' Abdul blinked in surprise. 'Is he in a fit state to talk? Wasn't he operated on only yesterday?'

'Apparently, he insisted on it. He wants police protection.'

Half an hour later, they were in Navin's hospital room. Three chairs stood beside his bed. At the foot of the bed was a camera mounted on a tripod. Navin lay in bed, looking pale and weak. The upper half of his bed had been raised so that he could partially sit up without effort on his part. A foot from his face was a small microphone connected to the camera. At Ranade's nod, the camera began rolling and the cameraman withdrew from the room.

'Are you sure you can talk, Mr Gokul?' Ranade asked gently.

'Yes, inspector, I think it's best that I do.' His voice was low and weak. His breathing was shallow. 'Once I tell you my story, you'll understand why I'm in a hurry. The sooner, the better.'

Ranade turned to the doctor. 'Is it okay for him to talk, doctor?'

The doctor nodded reluctantly. 'As long as it doesn't exceed fifteen minutes. I'll be here too. If talking proves to be too much of a strain for Mr Gokul, I'll ask you to stop.'

'Okay.' Ranade turned to Navin. 'We'll follow the doctor's advice, Mr Gokul. Is that okay?'

Navin nodded. 'But first, let me thank you for saving my life, inspector. And you too, Mr Abdul. Had you not arrived when you did, I wouldn't be here today.'

'Luckily, that didn't happen. And as far as we are concerned, it was our duty.'

'Even so, thank you. Shall I begin? I can't talk for long. It's painful.'

Ranade nodded. 'Please.'

Chapter 27

'My real name is Indranil Dasgupta, a name so common in Bengal that one can find anonymity in it. The events I am going to narrate, though scarcely four years old, seem to have taken place a lifetime ago. It was my great misfortune to have got involved with the worst kind of men in the corporate world.

'I was a software engineer by profession, focusing on web and mobile apps, in addition to data communications. I was enjoying a good run as a freelancer, when I was hired by an online gaming company for a short-term project in Germany.

'I realized only in hindsight that the entire process of my recruitment had been carried out through discussions conducted over the phone or by email. Even though the company had an Indian presence, not once was I asked to meet the client or a representative, until I reached the actual worksite. It was located deep in the German hinterland, half an hour's drive from a small town called Einbeck.

'Even there, I got to meet only one German, a representative of the client. My work was to be done at a data centre that served several companies, including some large European corporations. I was told that excellent connectivity made it possible for data centres to be set up in the German hinterland, where real estate costs were a fraction of what they were in the cities. My client's software system was hosted at the data centre.

'My task was to tweak a suite of game apps they had developed earlier. I was to introduce modifications that would enable a gamer to send cheat codes if he knew the right combination of keys to press. I was neither informed about where the gamers would be nor what gaming devices they would use. All I was shown was how to digitally recognize a cheat code when it arrived at the data centre.

'I was to write software that sniffed out cheat codes from the constant stream of legitimate data traffic between gaming devices and the server at the data centre. Once my software found a cheat code, it was to pluck it from the data stream and send it to another destination.

'What aroused my suspicion was that the cheat codes seemed to achieve nothing as far as I could see. Cheat codes give the gamer an unfair advantage that enables him to win the game. When I asked questions, I was told not to bother about it, as the processing of cheat codes was being handled by another software module.

'But the computer to which I was sending the cheat codes seemed to have nothing to do with the game. It is pertinent to mention here that I'm also an amateur hacker. I was in a position to discover details that my client had not intended for my eyes. Now suspicious, I tried hacking into the computer to which I was sending the cheat codes and made a startling discovery. It was inside a Tor network.

'Tor, which stands for "The Onion Router", is an innovation that strives to ensure anonymity on the internet. It strips away the details of the sender from the data packet and bounces the packet off a large number of Tor nodes before sending it to its intended destination. When the packet eventually reaches the final destination, no trace of the sender remains. The recipient wouldn't know who sent it and neither would anyone watching.

'Crudely put, this is how it works. You send me an envelope with my address as the addressee's and yours as the sender's. The Tor network puts it into twenty or thirty successive envelopes within envelopes, with each envelope carrying the address of a random Tor node. Each node opens the outermost envelope, discovers the address written on the next inner envelope and forwards it to the address it has just discovered.

'This goes on, till only the original envelope remains, but with one difference – the sender's address has now been erased. So I receive your envelope without knowing who sent it or what route it took, as the "post marks" of the twenty or thirty intermediate Tor nodes are no longer available. Anyone watching a Tor node, or even a dozen of them, would also have no way of knowing who sent the message to whom. In effect, the Tor network makes messages anonymous and virtually impossible to trace.

'But there was one key thing I couldn't understand – why would a gaming system want to erase traces? A cheat code wouldn't work if the system didn't know who sent it. Something, it seemed to me, was amiss.

'Meanwhile, something else had begun bothering me. My German companion, who had claimed to be a software guy, was curiously inactive. When I was busy working, he would do precious little, other than watch me surreptitiously. Keyboard sounds hardly came from his desk, which was just behind mine. I concluded that his sole purpose there was to keep an eye on me. But I continued digging between periods of legitimate software coding.

'The more I dug around, the more I discovered. I soon realized that the gaming system was a charade; it concealed something sinister and, most likely, illegal. In the guise of a game, some secret information was being passed in the form of codes – the ostensible cheat codes I was forwarding.

'Mobile phone users, pretending to play a game, would use secret key combinations to open a window inside the game. They would then enter codified information into the window and send it to the server in Germany. There, my software would pick up these pieces of information and send them through a Tor network to another computer.

'When I examined the cheat codes, I couldn't find anything, at first, that made any sense to me; they were just combinations of numbers and letters. But on closer scrutiny, I found that some had a pattern. Some letters – "NP", "GP" and "SL" – were occurring repeatedly. From the work I had done on financial software, I thought I recognized them. We often use such short forms for naming data fields and software routines. I wondered if they stood for "net profit", "gross profit" and "sales".

'To cut a long story short, I discovered that company information was being passed by using mobile phones in India. If that was the case, what was my client doing with the information? Was there a second leg to this?

'There was. Somebody, somewhere on the other side of the Tor network, was looking at this information and using it in some way. But for the life of me, I couldn't figure out who was involved and what he was up to.

'But I did find out that my client had divided the work into four separate pieces and given them to four freelancers. I was one of them. That ensured that no one person ever got to know what the entire system actually did.

'What I did next saved my life. Some kind of divine providence must have prompted me to do it. But for that, I wouldn't be here today. I quickly wrote an additional software code for my own purposes. As my software sent the cheat codes onward into the Tor network, it would secretly send a copy to me. What I would do with it, I didn't know at that time.

'At the end of the project, the client took me on a yacht cruise to the Baltic Sea off the German coast, where I met another representative of my client, an Indian who introduced himself as

Pramod, which I suspected was an assumed name. With him was another Indian freelancer who had worked on one of the other segments of the dubious "gaming" system.

'Within a few hours of leaving the shore, the other freelancer was completely drunk and I was high. But something about Pramod was bothering me. He was up to something nasty. I also realized that the sole crewman, who was supposed to be piloting the hired yacht, was missing. As I picked up more ominous signs, I decided I had to do something about it.

'I went to the washroom and switched on my mobile phone, hoping to connect to some mobile network. But in vain; we were too far out at sea. Just then, I heard the other freelancer cry out. Shortly thereafter, there was a splash, as if someone had been thrown overboard. I wondered if I would be next.

'When I returned to the deck, Pramod held a gun. He had dropped all pretence. He was going to kill me.

'My only chance lay in talking him out of it. But how? That was the providential part. I decided to tell him about the secret software I had inserted into his "gaming" system and added a bluff. If I did not log into the system once a week, I lied, a copy of the cheat codes would be sent to public sites, including those of SEBI and the CBI.

'I spoke in Hindi and said that I had seen through his deceit and had anticipated the danger I might find myself in. I had, therefore, inserted additional software to protect myself. I didn't know to what extent I had managed to convince him, but sheer desperation must have lent authenticity to my bluff, for he ended up buying my story. I was betting on my hunch that he was not the brain behind the scheme and would not risk killing me until he had spoken to his handler.

'He used his satellite phone and, an hour later, another yacht – a much bigger one – drew up beside ours. A rope ladder was dropped and I, followed by Pramod and my German companion, climbed on to the other yacht. The crewman was still missing.

'I was handcuffed and bundled into a cabin below deck, even as the others went about whatever business they had in mind. Presently, I noticed a glow through the porthole and peeped out. The other yacht was in flames. Our own yacht sped away into the darkness of the night. That was the last I saw of Pramod.

'We docked two nights later and I was taken to a cellar where I met Vivek Tola for the first time. I used the same bluff on him that I had fobbed off Pramod with and stuck to it through the interrogation that would last two whole days.

'On the third day, Vivek had news for me. He said that the brain behind the scheme, who went by the name of Zeus, wanted me dead. He had not been taken in by my bluff. But Vivek Tola had suggested that they wait for two weeks to see if I was telling the truth. My blood ran cold. I had just two weeks left to live and I had no other means of bluffing my way through.

'After a terrible 10 days, during which I anticipated the worst, Vivek came to see me again. Zeus had ordered my "termination". But Vivek had an offer to make, a deal to cut with me. If I agreed to share with him the cheat codes I was sending myself, he would allow me to live – and Zeus would be none the wiser. Vivek would fake Indranil Dasgupta's death for Zeus's benefit and I would have to assume a new identity.

'Caught between death and a new life somewhere under a different name – although it meant severing all connections with the past – the choice was obvious. I became Navin Gokul, a financial advisor. Vivek arranged for tickets and a counterfeit passport and I left Europe through a circuitous route that took me to the US, Hong Kong and Malaysia, before I arrived back in India. I landed in Chennai a month after my escape from Pramod, looking different from the way I used to earlier. Not only had I grown a beard, my eyebrows too had been reshaped through selective depilation. From then on, I have always worn my hair long.

'Vivek set me up in Pune and inducted me as a partner into the business. In return for a 50 per cent share in the business, I was to contribute the cheat codes. I soon realized that the cheat codes were privileged information from inside companies, which Vivek used to his advantage and mine.

'I gradually learnt that the client who had hired me for my earlier project in Germany was actually a very small group that called itself Spice Xchange. Zeus, the man who ran it, now believed me to be dead. Vivek, codenamed Poseidon, was a part of Spice Xchange. But all was not well between him and Zeus.'

'The first six months were fine, except for one restriction – I couldn't tell my aged father that I was back in India. To give my family the impression that I was living overseas, I would have to communicate with my father through internet voice calls. Anyway, we began making money and nobody recognized Indranil Dasgupta. But things started changing when Vivek began revealing his true colours.

'Aware of my hacking skills, he forced me to hack into the computers of senior company executives, trawling for privileged information. It suffices to say that I did enjoy a measure of success, which Vivek immediately monetized in the share market. He made me do some other rotten things that I won't go into now.

'Meanwhile, my father had passed away in Kolkata. Vivek had known that he was seriously ill, but had kept the news to himself. He had intercepted messages to me and suppressed them. He knew that I would have flown to Kolkata immediately. By the time I came to know of my father's death, it was too late. Baba had died alone, with no relatives by his side – a fate he didn't deserve, a fate handed to him by Vivek. It was a deliberate act on Vivek's part that screamed for immediate revenge. But I was biding my time.

'Last year, Antwerp Diamond Bank shut down after the deal to sell it to a Chinese group fell through. That hit many diamond merchants hard, including some of Vivek's friends and customers. He pressed me again to hack into banks. I refused point blank; that was not a line I would cross.

'Six months back, matters got worse. Vivek began pressurizing me again to hack into banks. I refused and he threatened to expose me to Zeus. Our tug-of-war continued, as I retaliated by telling him that if he went ahead and exposed me, SEBI and the CBI would learn of his insider trading secrets.

'Knowing that it was only a matter of time before our arrangement collapsed, I began preparing an alternate identity for myself. At an appropriate time, I would vanish and take up my new identity elsewhere.

'Our relationship deteriorated as I continued refusing to help him further his nefarious plans. Things came to a head earlier this month, when he withdrew his capital and went off in a huff. Things had reached breaking point. I made my own plans; I would disappear in a week's time. But before I did, I would pay Vivek back for all that he had done to me. I went to a public phone booth and called SEBI. It was an act of pure revenge, but a calculated one.

'I was well aware of the risk, should my call be traced to Pune immediately. But it didn't matter, as I would be gone within a week. Besides, I was too busy finalizing my arrangements to drive all the way out of Pune to make that one phone call.

'Imagine my surprise a few days later, when I discovered that Vivek had been killed. I had no way of deciding if my tip-off to SEBI had somehow reached Zeus or if it was a natural culmination of the Zeus–Poseidon battle. Realizing that the goons watching me were not Vivek's men as I had first surmised, I panicked. I couldn't think clearly and decided to get away from them immediately. I fled to Bengaluru.

'I didn't know what I'd do next; I'd just given in to my instinct to flee from Pune, where the goons could get me. In Bengaluru, I stayed indoors and thought my plan through. But when Inspector Srinath came to my hotel in plain clothes, I took him to be Zeus's man and fled again.

'While in police custody, I had ample opportunity to reflect on my decisions in a calmer frame of mind. I realized, in hindsight, that I had erred in fleeing from Pune. But what could I have done, inspector? My brain was so scrambled after I'd read the news of Vivek's death that I had done the first thing that came to mind – I had run. When I pondered over the situation in retrospect, I realized that fate had presented me the perfect opportunity to vanish altogether. With Vivek dead, my disappearing act would be that much easier to carry out.

'I returned to Pune to wind up the business and carry through my plan to vanish. All I needed was three or four days. If I managed to evade the men pursuing me for a few days more, I would be free for life.

'This, inspector, is my story. In my defence, all I can say is that the situation I found myself in was not of my own making. I had signed a freelance contract in good faith, but subsequent events forced me into deeds I would not have involved myself in otherwise. I was coerced into the situation. I am not a criminal.'

Navin had lapsed into silence, but the camera continued recording.

'So,' Ranade said softly, breaking the silence, 'privileged information from inside companies is passed using games on a mobile phone. Is it games like chess, Space Invaders, Tertis and Reversi, played on iPhone 4s?'

'That's right. Those were the games being played on the server.'

'Somewhere beyond the Tor network, the inside information is processed. Is that right?'

'Yes. But I don't know who does it or what kind of processing is involved.'

'It would be fair to assume that the processed information is sent to the men of Spice Xchange in some fashion.'

'I suppose so. But I have no idea how it is sent. But I do know it uses the Tor network again.'

'And you said that Vivek's codename in Spice Xchange was Poseidon. Are you sure?'

'Beyond any doubt.'

Ranade smiled grimly; Poseidon was the name of yet another Greek god.

'Did you ever hear Vivek mention the names of any other Greek gods? Apollo, Ares or Hermes, for instance?'

'No. Only Zeus.'

'Do you know who this Zeus is?'

'I wish I did, inspector. He's the one who stalks me now. I would gladly give you his real name if I knew it. I'd give anything to see him behind bars.'

Ranade pulled out a photograph and showed it to Navin.

'Do you know this man?' he asked.

Navin's face paled.

'Yes,' he whispered. 'This is Pramod.' He turned to Ranade. 'Where did you find him?'

'He is one of the men who shot you. We know him as Kashyap.'

'So he did find me!' Navin whispered, almost to himself, trembling visibly and seeming to sink deeper into his bed.

The doctor shot Ranade a warning glance.

'Where is he now, inspector?' Navin asked in a barely audible voice.

'He's dead.'

Conflicting expressions clashed on Navin's face.

'Zeus killed him to prevent my capturing him alive,' the inspector went on.

As Navin fell silent and the doctor began monitoring his pulse, Ranade produced another photograph and showed it to Navin.

'I saw this man on the second yacht,' Navin said. 'He was the one who threw the rope ladder down to us. He was the one who handcuffed me and locked me up in the cabin. Who is he?'

'We know him as Varma. He is alive.'

■

Varma stepped out through the godown's gate and cast furtive glances around him. The policeman lounging across the street could not be missed, even if the plainclothesman at the tea shop could. As the watchman closed the godown gate behind him, Varma hastened towards Sewri station, casting glances over his shoulder to see if any of the surveillance men were following him. They weren't.

Fifteen minutes later, he boarded a southbound local train and stood to one side in the crowded compartment, watching the compartment door and sweeping his eyes over the platform in turn. There were no familiar faces lurking nearby. He allowed himself to relax as the train began moving and remained preoccupied with his thoughts during the fifteen-minute journey to VT.

As the train began pulling into VT station, he moved towards the door, preparing to leave the compartment along with the crowd that provided him welcome anonymity. Even before the train came to a halt, he heard raised voices from the platform; a group of men seemed to be arguing over the placement of some boxes and baskets on the platform.

When the train finally halted, Varma discovered that the quarrel was raging right outside the door of his compartment, obstructing the passengers who were stepping out from the compartment on to the platform. As commuters behind him began pushing forward, the men in front of him tried to shove their way through the crowd on the platform. Squeezed between the two, Varma lost his patience and shouted at the squabbling men on the platform to make way.

Just as the blockage eased, long, nimble fingers dipped into his back pocket and took out his wallet. A moment later, Varma was on the platform, trying to find his way through the jostling crowd. He was not, however, leaving the station, as most others were. Instead, he made his way to another platform to take a northbound train.

Half a minute later, he saw a scrawny lad running pell-mell down the platform, making for the station entrance.

'Someone's pocket has been picked,' he said to himself with a suppressed smile, watching the back of the lad's dirty shirt recede into the distance.

Instinctively, he felt his back pocket to check that his wallet was safe. Shock froze his features as his fingers probed an empty pocket. He stopped and checked again. His wallet was missing. He rummaged through his other pockets to see if he had placed it there. He hadn't.

Varma broke into a run and pursued the lad, knowing full well that he had little chance of catching him. Even as he shouldered his way to the end of the platform, the boy was disappearing through the station's entrance. When Varma finally reached the wide road outside, he was greeted by a sea of humanity and vehicles. The thief was nowhere to be seen.

Half an hour later, the wallet was in Abdul's hands. He let out a bark of satisfaction as he pulled out two ATM cards, an office ID card and a number of bills.

Varma's real identity was no longer a secret. Neither was his address.

Chapter 28

Shashi and Tanuja pored over the analysis results on the desktop computer at the SEBI computer centre. They had recently concluded a long call with Ranade, during which the inspector had briefed them about Spice Xchange and asked them to look out for corroborative evidence in their analysis.

Two days of hectic work by Tanuja had enabled them to set up the stock exchange data in a manner that made it quickly analysable. After a long discussion with Shashi, she had initiated two sets of analysis, the first of which had just finished running.

In the first, Shashi had asked her to analyse the stock exchange data of Purple Country following the same method she had used with the data from the share registrar the previous week. Tanuja had done that and the computer monitor showed the results of share trades before and after the seven events during which Purple Country's share price had jumped.

'I see three findings,' Shashi said. 'First, this analysis confirms your earlier one of the share registrar data. Most of the suspicious trades are the handiwork of the ex-Lucarro gang, Sudakar's son-in-law and the 32 demat accounts owned by private companies.'

'Except that a few more demat accounts seem to have benefited during two or three of the events, albeit to a lesser extent.'

'Correct. Given their lower incidence, let's ignore them for the present.'

Tanuja nodded.

'The second finding is that the derivatives trading reveals a similar pattern: there is a jump in volume just before and after the same seven events. Only the scale is much larger – almost ten times the value of the share trades.'

'Right,' Tanuja concluded. 'And the third finding is that the derivatives trading has been carried out by the same 32 demat accounts.'

'Correct.' Shashi's tone was grim. 'It's now clear – beyond all reasonable doubt – that insider trading in Purple Country shares and derivatives is an organized affair. What remains to be done is for Daniel to identify the people behind these 32 firms. Among them, I would wager, is Zeus.'

'Have all these trades been based on information leaked by just one person, Shashi?'

Shashi nodded slowly. 'It appears so, Tanu. Except for Sudakar's son-in-law, who is not connected with the ex-Lucarro group or the private companies.'

'I ran a check on the son-in-law's demat account. He seems to be trading regularly in three other companies, perhaps companies where Sudakar is a director. The pattern seems similar – buying before a jump and selling soon after. He never seems to hold shares for long.'

'Daniel says that the man is in financial trouble. He probably borrows money to trade and returns it as soon as possible. But that's not for us to investigate; Daniel is doing that. We'll provide the information and leave it to him to follow through.'

'Does that complete the Purple Country investigation, then?' Tanuja asked.

'No, Tanu.' Shashi shook his head sadly. 'I still don't know one key thing – why Amit passed information. How did he benefit? Your analysis confirms that Amit did not trade in Purple Country shares.'

'That's right. He doesn't have a single trade.'

'I'm hoping that your second analysis will throw some light on the matter. Is it done yet?'

Tanuja checked another computer screen and nodded.

'It's done. Let me transfer the results to the other computer so that you can see it.'

The second piece of analysis Shashi had asked for was about the non-Purple Country trades the Lucarro gang had engaged in. He had wanted Tanuja to extract the names of all the companies the gang had traded in, then identify the events for each of the companies, just as she had done for Purple Country. Finally, he had asked her to analyse the extracted trades and see if any pattern emerged.

It had turned out to be far more complex than the first analysis. Formulating and constructing the analysis had taken her the better part of the day.

Soon, Shashi was studying the computer monitor with growing fascination. As he pored over Tanuja's analysis, the pattern he thought he saw became clearer. On the one hand, the scale of what he saw made his heart sink. On the other, he was increasingly captivated by the simplicity and brilliance of the scheme he thought he had deciphered.

Still hesitant and concerned that he might be reading more into the pattern than warranted, he started again at the beginning and went through the analysis slowly and with great deliberation. Fifteen minutes later, he was sure.

'This is fantastic!' he whispered. 'You are brilliant, Tanu! You're going to be a celebrity!'

'Me?' Tanuja was baffled. 'Why?'

'This is going to rock the stock market and corporate India, Tanu. I don't think anything like this has ever been perpetrated before.'

'Oh, get on with it, will you!' Tanuja snapped. 'What are you trying to do, kill me with suspense?'

Shashi grinned. 'Okay, this is how the scheme works. There are eight ex-Lucarro men, including Amit Khanna, working in eight different companies, including Purple Country. They have been passing inside information to each other. The beauty of the scheme is that not one of these men trades in the shares of his own company. But he trades in the shares of the other seven.'

'What!'

'Here it is.' Shashi pointed to the computer monitor. 'Amit, who is a part of the gang and the CFO of Purple Country, has never traded in its shares. However, he has traded in *all the other seven*! The same pattern recurs for the other seven members. That is how they make their money! They must be using mobile phones and Spice Xchange's gaming system to pass information.'

'Devious! But why such a modus operandi?'

'Because that makes it legally very difficult to prove that they are indulging in insider trading! To convict a person of insider trading, you need to prove two things: first, that he leaked privileged information; and second, that he benefited from the leak.

'Now, the use of Spice Xchange's technology makes it almost impossible to prove the first point. That is why they use the Tor network – that makes it impossible to trace the leak back to the insider.'

'And second,' Tanuja concluded, grinning from ear to ear, 'he didn't benefit from the leak at all, because he never traded in the shares about which he leaked information! Brilliant!'

Shashi's manner suddenly turned sombre.

'Even with your analysis,' he said, 'we have – at best – circumstantial evidence. It's going to be difficult for an Indian court to convict these guys.'

'But the US courts did convict high-profile personalities in the Galleon case, Shashi. There too, most of the evidence was circumstantial. Surely, the Indian courts will take cognizance of that?'

'Yes, but the circumstantial evidence used in the US was closer to the Galleon crime. Prosecutors had phone records proving that a company director – the insider in that case – had spoken to the hedge fund manager immediately after a board meeting. Also, the hedge fund bought the company shares within minutes of the call. Thanks to the bloody Tor network here, we have no such evidence in this case.'

'Then…' Tanuja's voice dropped to a whisper. 'Then was all this work for nothing, Shashi?'

'Not at all!' Shashi reached out and squeezed his cousin's hand. 'First, your work will blow Spice Xchange out of the water. They'll never be able to use it again. Second, you've put an end to one of the most ingenious ways of practising insider trading; SEBI and regulators around the world will be that much wiser. And third, I am an ignoramus on legal matters. Maybe, they can still get convictions. Maybe, there is other evidence available to corroborate your findings.'

'Let's hope so, Shashi. But what has all this got to do with Zeus and the other Greek gods? Where do they fit in?'

'My bet is that they are the people behind the 32 demat accounts that traded in derivatives; the ones that your first analysis also unearthed. Ranade just told us that Vivek – or Poseidon – was behind six of these. That leaves twenty-six accounts, which are, in all probability, being used by Zeus and the others of Spice Xchange. That must be how they make money from running Spice Xchange.'

'These 32 demat accounts are the ones to be analysed next, I suppose?'

'Exactly. See what shares and derivatives they had been trading in and look for patterns, the same way you had for Purple Country. That may just lead us to something bigger.'

■

A few miles away, Varma was on the move, carrying out the first of the two instructions he had received from Zeus the previous night. With the Sewri godown under police surveillance, it could no longer serve as the operations centre for Spice Xchange. Zeus could no longer go there and whatever papers lay in the safe there had to be retrieved. Varma was the man to do it.

He crouched in front of the safe, staring at the numbers scrawled on the piece of paper in his hand. He had just used two keys to unlock it; the last step was to rotate the numbered knob exactly the way Zeus had instructed him. If he failed to do so, he would have to start all over again. Kashyap's death and the loss of his wallet had made him edgy and nervous. Unsteady hands, combined with a distracted mind, were hardly the best tools for carrying out work that demanded some degree of finesse.

After three failed attempts that made him increasingly jittery, Varma finally got it right, sweating profusely from the mental concentration the task had demanded. Now he peered inside the safe. There were no valuables in it; just some papers, a spiral-bound volume and two small notebooks, including the one he had taken from Chaaya.

He opened a small grey suitcase he had brought along and transferred the contents of the safe to it. Once he was sure that nothing had been left behind in the safe, he shut it. Then he closed the suitcase. Next, he unlocked the two drawers of the desk and moved their contents into a duffel bag.

Deed done, he made a quick call and went to the entrance of the building. Shortly thereafter, the gate opened and a grey Manza entered the compound. Varma waited until the gate was closed.

When he was sure that no prying eyes outside the compound could see him, he dumped the suitcase and the duffel bag into the boot and got into the car.

The next minute, he was on his way to Wadala.

Varma's actions had caused considerable excitement outside. After more than 24 hours of radio silence, the tracking device in the notebook had suddenly come alive. Trapped within the steel safe, the device's feeble signal had been blocked. But a suitcase's fibreglass exterior was no barrier. Two unmarked cars picked up the trail and followed the grey Manza at a distance.

Within fifteen minutes, Abdul had guessed the car's destination – Varma's flat.

'Don't intercept him,' he instructed the men in the other car. 'We need to know where the suitcase finally goes. If he leaves it in his flat, one of you stay close enough to monitor the signal.'

That was exactly what Varma did. His first – and easier – mission accomplished, he dumped the suitcase in his flat and locked the door. The next mission, the one which he dreaded, had fallen to him in Kashyap's absence. He was to go to Grand Central Hotel, where the woman from London was staying. And kill her. The pick-up car was waiting two lanes away.

When he walked out through his gate towards the spot where the pick-up car was parked, two men stepped into his path. Another came up behind him to cut off his retreat. Abdul and the others were in plain clothes, but the look on their faces was enough to tell Varma that the game was up.

Unlike Kashyap, Varma wasn't proficient with guns – he had never taken to them despite early training. Though he had wielded one when he forced himself into Chaaya's flat, he was inept with firearms and hadn't used one in years. The last time he had fired a round was during mandatory training in the army many years ago. Even in the firm he and Kashyap had run for a while after leaving the army, he had not handled firearms.

The weapon he had chosen today was a dagger, a trusted companion he was very comfortable with. That was the best way to silence the woman. A silent flash of a blade in the night, after which he would make his getaway. No nasty gunshots to attract unwanted attention. But those plans were irrelevant now; he had to first get away from the plainclothesmen in his path.

Hoping that they wouldn't spot it till it was too late, he whipped out his dagger with the blade pointing down. He chose to attack with a downward stab of the weapon, aiming to bury its blade in Abdul's neck. Even if he didn't get the opportunity for a second blow, the first one would be deep enough to incapacitate his victim. Quick as a striking snake, Varma raised his arm and stabbed downwards.

Abdul reacted instinctively. His arms shot up, straight and rigid, crossing each other above his head to form an 'X'. Simultaneously, he bent his knees, arched his spine backwards and threw back his head so that the vertex of the 'X' was a good foot away from his face.

Down came the dagger and entered the 'X' formed by Abdul's arms. As soon as Varma's arm met the unyielding vertex, Abdul responded with an eruption of controlled fury. Even as his right hand seized the knife hand's wrist, his left moved to Varma's elbow and cupped it from below.

Abdul then wrenched his adversary's wrist downwards, twisting it as he pulled it down towards his right. His left hand grasped Varma's elbow and pushed it the other way, creating a twisting force that the other man was unable to counter. Varma had no option but to bend forward towards Abdul's right if he didn't want his arm broken.

Holding the man's wrist in a vice-like grip, Abdul yanked it towards himself and pressed Varma's elbow downwards, twisting the arm even further. A gasp of agony escaped Varma as something in his arm gave way. With his movement completely dictated by the pressure and pain in his trapped arm, he was forced to bend lower.

By now, he had turned half a circle. His arm was behind him and his bent back was facing Abdul.

But Abdul's interest lay elsewhere. As Varma bent low, his face just a couple of feet from the ground, Abdul's right foot lashed out in a swift upward movement. A hard, leather-clad foot, propelled by the thrust of a police officer's vicious kick, crashed into Varma's face, breaking his nose and splitting his lip.

The force of the kick, which had made his torso jerk upwards, put enormous strain on the shoulder connected to Varma's trapped arm and dislocated it with a soft, sickening snap. The knife had long since clattered to the stone pavement.

In desperation, Varma kicked backwards, catching Abdul just above the knee and making him stagger. As the policeman's grip slackened, Varma pulled his injured arm free and staggered towards the getaway car. With his arm useless, his nose broken, his torn lips bleeding and his eyes running from the sting of the kick, the now unarmed man had been effectively defanged. It had lasted all of four seconds.

Varma managed to hobble a distance of three yards before two pairs of strong arms hauled him up.

Chapter 29

On Thursday evening, an unscheduled closed-door meeting was taking place in the secure conference room of a nondescript building, far from the inquisitive eyes and ears of employees at SEBI and EOW and within the police force. The audience comprised just three men – Kulkarni, the head of EOW and the commissioner of police. No assistants, secretaries or serving boys were present. Briefing them were three others – Ranade, Shashi and Tanuja. Even Daniel wasn't there.

It was a big day for Ranade; seldom did a detective inspector get the chance to present a case to the commissioner. Unsurprisingly, he had come neatly turned out and was a little nervous.

It was a big day for another reason too. Tanuja's latest finding was sensational, to say the least. It was sure to send SEBI and other authorities into a tizzy. It was potentially the biggest discovery in the Indian capital markets since the Harshad Mehta scam had come to light in 1992. That particular scam had involved several banks and bankers who had placed their faith in their broker, Mehta. While most of the banks had been duped, two were alleged to have colluded with him to issue fake bank receipts, which the broker had promptly encashed. In addition, he had abused the 'Ready Forward Deal' mechanism of the banking industry to generate illicit cash. With the money, he had manipulated stock prices and raked in huge profits in a bull market. When the scam was finally exposed, the banking system found itself swindled out of thousands of crores.

Like the Harshad Mehta scam, the Spice Xchange one was a pioneer of sorts.

Amit Khanna had asked to see Shashi the previous evening and talked to him alone for half an hour. He had wept and confessed privately, apologizing repeatedly for hurting Purple Country. He had shared everything he knew about Zeus and Spice Xchange, but couldn't decide if he should confess to the police or not. Zeus's threats to harm his wife could not be taken lightly. Unsure about what to do, Shashi had shared a few selective details with Ranade.

Addressing his audience of three, the inspector began by taking them through the facts of the case, starting from Vivek's murder 12 days ago, to Varma's arrest on Tuesday. He gave them the gist of Navin's confession and began explaining the workings of the Spice Xchange's gaming system. He elaborated on the various stages of investigation, touching upon the analysis of the CCTV footage, the identification of Kashyap through the morphed video grab, the mapping of Zeus's routes, the planting of the tracking device on Varma and finally, the strategy that ended in getting his pocket successfully picked.

'The men we know as Kashyap and Varma are ex-armymen,' he said. 'Kashyap's promotion to the rank of Major was blocked because of "conduct unbecoming of an officer". Rumours abound that he was intelligent, but ruthless. And when he finally left the army, he did so under a cloud. We don't yet know what the problem was. He had seen combat in the North East and was proficient with weapons.

'Varma, on the other hand, held the rank of a Captain when he left the army, but was engaged in non-combat support operations. We believe he was in an administrative or technical position and had never been on the front line. After leaving the army, he and Kashyap had set up a security firm.'

'Ex-army, eh?' the police commissioner mused. 'No wonder Kashyap operated with such clinical precision. And boldness.'

'Yes sir. He was no ordinary thug. Vivek Tola's murder was organized like a small covert operation. And the subsequent assault that nearly killed Navin Gokul was meticulously planned as well.'

'It's a pity that Kashyap was killed before we could interrogate him,' the commissioner said, 'but the way he died was in keeping with the kind of man he was. Lived by the gun and died by it. I wonder if the man who killed him was an army sniper. Anyway, go on with your presentation, Ranade.'

'Yes sir. It was clear from Navin's confession that information technology was at the heart of Spice Xchange's modus operandi. To understand it better, we brought in our cybercrime people. Using the information we had gleaned from Navin Gokul and the papers found in Varma's flat, they constructed a schematic of how their technology works.'

Ranade hit a key on the laptop and turned to the diagram on the screen.

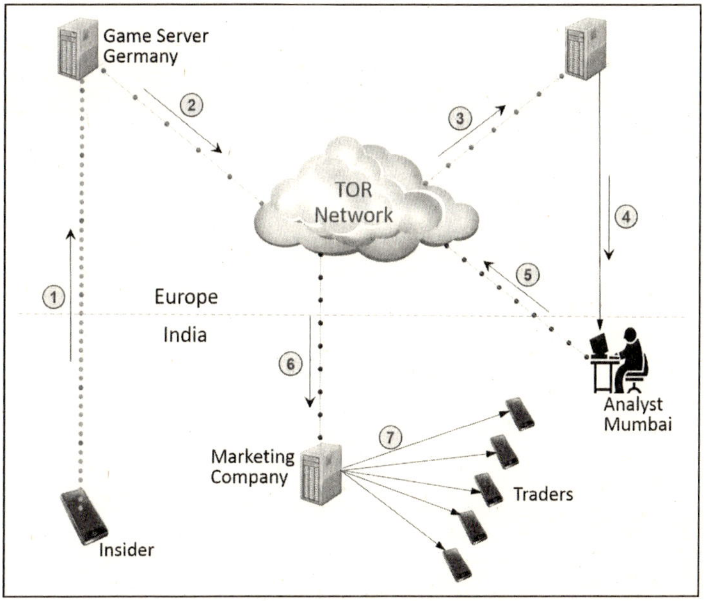

'This is how Spice Xchange's technology works. An insider equipped with an iPhone 4s sends privileged information to a server in Germany under the guise of playing a game. It is usually something as simple as "QNP+21xxx", which means that the quarter's net profit of his company has gone up by 21 per cent. The "xxx" at the end identifies the company where the insider works.

'Navin Gokul's software in Germany plucks this information nugget and sends it through a Tor network that renders it anonymous and makes tracking of the message impossible. On the other side of the Tor network, the nugget reaches another server in Europe, where it is stored.

'Twice a day, analysts from Mumbai log into the server and retrieve these information nuggets. With the knowledge of the Indian stock market they possess, they then gauge the likely impact of the information on the share price. They codify their view in the form of a ten-digit mobile number and send it back into the Tor network.

'On the other side of the Tor network, these anonymous codified messages are received by a computer in India. We traced the digital address of the computer and found that it was owned by a marketing company that sends bulk SMSs. Among the lakhs of SMSs this company sends are the "promotional" messages to traders who are a part of Spice Xchange.'

Ranade hit a key and the graphic on the screen changed. 'This is the structure of the code.

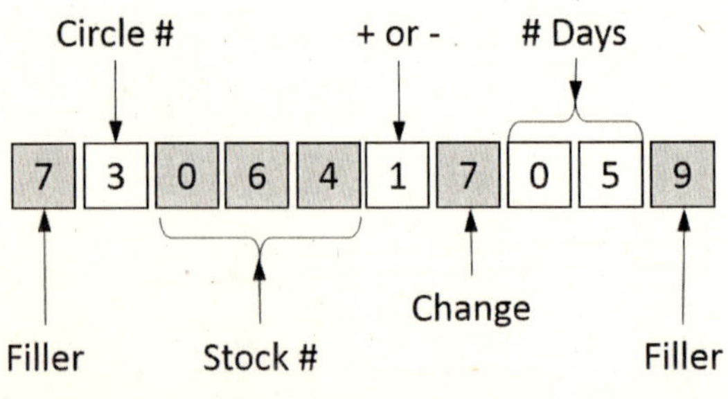

'The first and the last digits of the ostensible mobile number are mere fillers – meaningless random digits added to make the code look like a ten-digit mobile number. The second digit relates to the circle number, which Mr Kurva will explain shortly.

'The next three digits identify the stock. In this case, "064" refers to a midcap infrastructure stock. The sixth digit tells us if the share price will go up or go down. "1" indicates an increase; "0" implies a fall.

'The seventh digit indicates the expected change in the share price expressed on a nine-point scale. "1" means a marginal change and "9" signifies an extraordinary jump or fall. The next two digits provide the number of days in which the share is expected to achieve the increase or fall.

'The number "7306417059" means this: the share price of Stock No. 64 of Circle No. 3 will go up significantly in five days. This ostensible mobile number is added to a random promotional message and sent as an SMS. Here is an example: "*Congrats. You have won £750,000 in the Rover Raffle. Call now to claim your reward. Call 7306417059.*"

'Based on such messages, the Lucarro gang and the owners of Spice Xchange trade in the stock market. Vivek Tola's phone had a number of such messages.'

'Ingenious!' the head of EOW exclaimed. 'Have they been doing this for eight stocks – the companies where the members of the Lucarro gang work?'

'Yes sir. They trade in the stock or in its derivatives.' Ranade gestured towards Shashi. 'But there is more, sir. Mr Kurva will take you through it.'

Shashi stood up and took the floor.

'Before I do that, let me take a minute to summarize how we went about analysing the data. Tanuja here is a data scientist who works for an analytics firm in London and specializes in analytics for the capital markets. It is entirely due to her expertise that we discovered Spice Xchange's scheme.

'She came down last week when we had an inkling that insider trading might well be taking place in Purple Country shares. She began by identifying seven occasions in the past two years when the share price had jumped. She then identified the people who had traded during these seven "events", buying just before each one and selling just after. That is how we zeroed in on the Lucarro gang.

'Two days back, we went a step further. Knowing that they were potential illicit traders, Tanuja extracted all the trades the Lucarro gang had been involved in over the past two years and analysed them. The results were startling. These men, it seemed, were not limiting their trades to Purple Country alone.

'This "circle of eight" was trading in eight stocks. All of them were practising insider trading, but with one crucial difference – none of the insiders traded in his own company's shares. Apart from these eight men, one more person traded in Purple Country shares, though he had no connection with either Spice Xchange or the Lucarro gang. This man happens to be Mr Sudakar's son-in-law. As he has no connection with Zeus or Spice Xchange, let's put his name aside for the time being, while we continue with the analysis.

'In this analysis, we found 32 more demat accounts that had traded extensively in the equity and derivatives of the eight stocks. These 32 accounts, we suspected, belonged to the owners of Spice Xchange. Our next step was to determine how extensive their activities were. Were they limited to the eight companies of the Lucarro gang or was there more?'

Shashi paused dramatically. When he continued, his voice was soft.

'What we found, gentlemen, is going to rock the stock market and corporate India. The holders of these 32 demat accounts not only had access to privileged information from the eight companies where members of the Lucarro gang worked, but also from *36 other companies*. This means that they have insiders in 36 more listed companies. There is a clique that *regularly* practises insider trading of 44 stocks in the NSE and BSE.'

A stunned silence greeted Shashi's revelation. The next moment, exclamations of shock erupted from both Kulkarni and the head of EOW.

'*44* stocks!' Kulkarni said, before the head of EOW could get in a word. 'Are you sure?'

'Absolutely sure. I was just as astonished as you are. We have the proof.'

'What kind of stocks are these?' the head of EOW asked.

'Mostly midcap stocks, but a few large-cap ones too.'

'And who are these men?'

'This clique is run by a group of five men, one of whom – Vivek Tola – is now dead. They go by the names of Greek gods – Ares, Apollo, Hermes, Poseidon and Zeus. The king of these gods, as is the case in Greek mythology, is Zeus.'

'How did you get all this information?' the commissioner asked.

'From the suitcase Inspector Ranade's men confiscated from Varma's flat. It contained all the papers he had removed from the safe in the Sewri warehouse. It's a veritable gold mine. This is what we discovered.'

Shashi hit a key and brought up a new slide.

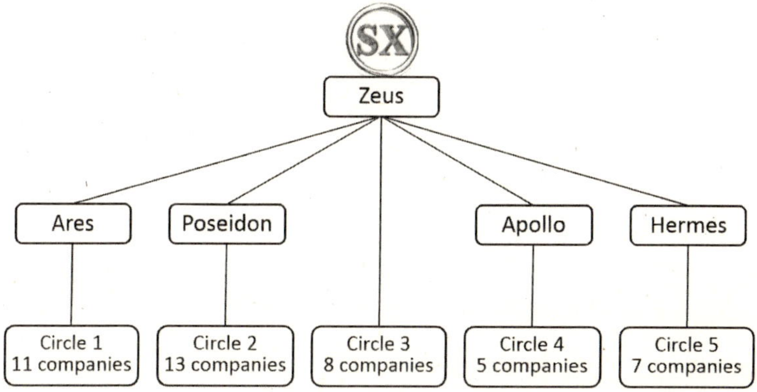

'Each of these five men oversees a "circle" – a small group of insiders like the Lucarro gang. These five circles operate independent of each other and are probably unknown to each other. What is common is their use of Spice Xchange's technology to share privileged information within their circle, which includes their Greek god, who is their ringleader. Zeus and the Lucarro gang are Circle No. 3.

'Each ringleader gets inside information exclusively from the companies in his circle. The only exception is Zeus, who receives information on all 44 companies. This much is clear from the analysis of their trades.

'I suspect that each ringleader is responsible for the recruitment of new insiders. His incentive is clear – the larger his circle, the more money he makes. Vivek Tola was Poseidon, the ringleader of the largest circle.'

'This is astonishing, Mr Kurva,' Kulkarni exclaimed. 'I take it that you have identified all these 44 insiders?'

'Yes, we have,' Shashi smiled. 'With the data access you granted us, identifying them turned out to be a simple matter.'

'Do they all hold senior positions in their companies?'

'Almost two-thirds of them are CFOs, finance directors or vice-presidents in the finance function. This is not unexpected, as the finance function is best placed to obtain reliable market-moving information. The rest are COOs and others who are in the know of things. We also have five board members.'

'How long has this been going on?'

'At least two years. We haven't looked at data prior to 2013. SEBI will have to do that. Tanuja will be more than happy to share her methods with your people.'

'Mr Kurva,' the head of EOW asked, 'what, in your estimate, is the monetary value of all these transactions?'

'We haven't had the time to compute it yet, but I would expect it to be in thousands of crores. These 44 companies, many of which are in the derivatives segment, have a combined market capitalization of between two and three lakh crore.'

'If Vivek Tola was Poseidon,' the police commissioner asked, 'why was he killed?'

'I have a theory, sir,' Ranade replied crisply, stepping forward. 'I will have to see how it can be corroborated.

'As Poseidon, Tola had access to information from the 13 companies in his circle. When he came across Indranil Dasgupta and learnt that he was stealing the inside information from *all* the companies involved in Spice Xchange, he saw an opportunity to make unprecedented profit – he could deal in *all* the 44 companies! By keeping Indranil alive and giving him a new identity as Navin Gokul, he had deceived Zeus.

'Independently, Amit Khanna, the CFO of Purple Country, had been noticing something strange. He spotted large trades taking place in Purple Country shares even *before* the SMS from Spice Xchange arrived. This meant that someone else was playing the insider trading game too. He informed Zeus, who then used his connections to trace the trades and discovered that it was Vivek.

'One obvious possibility was that Vivek was getting inside information from his brother-in-law, who was the CEO of the company. In order to confirm if his suspicions were well founded, he sent Varma and Kashyap to accuse Mr Kurva of the crime and gauge his reaction. What transpired during that meeting must have satisfied him that Mr Kurva was not the one leaking information. That meant Vivek was getting the information from somewhere else.

'His suspicions must have then turned to Vivek's Pune venture. Kashyap must have recognized Navin as Indranil, the man they believed to be dead. Kashyap's phone records show that he had made frequent trips to Pune in the last few weeks. Once Navin's real identity was confirmed, the enormity of Vivek's deceit left no grounds for doubt. Zeus killed him.'

'Good work, Ranade. Your theory rings true. What do you plan next?'

'Thank you, sir. With Navin's help, our cybercrime people have located the server on which the inside information is stored. We then waited for the analysts in Mumbai to log into the server. Once they did, we got their IP address and tracked them down to their penthouse office in Lower Parel. Ironically, it is in the same building that houses Purple Country. We have enough grounds to obtain a search-and-seize warrant.

'Simultaneously, we tracked the promotional SMSs back to the marketing company. There too, we have sufficient cause to obtain a warrant.

'But if we raid these two places, Zeus and the others will be alerted immediately and any chance of trapping them with the evidence will be lost. We, therefore, need to do a simultaneous sweep, not only of those two places, but also of Zeus and the remaining three ringleaders.'

'Okay,' the commissioner said. 'Is there a problem?'

'Yes sir. Our plan to catch Zeus and the ringleaders is a little… er…irregular. I need to discuss it with you.'

'Okay, ride back with me and tell me about it in the car. With Varma already detained, we must move quickly. We don't want Zeus flying the coop.' The commissioner rose and turned to the others. 'Please do nothing that could alert our quarries. Don't even speak of this matter until Ranade gives you clearance.'

He turned to Tanuja and Shashi.

'Your analysis, madam, was brilliant,' he said. 'And thank you, Mr Kurva. We couldn't have achieved this without your help and your wife's. You have helped us to unearth one of the biggest white-collar crimes we have seen in recent years.'

'Come, Ranade,' he said, before turning and striding out of the room.

■

Late that night, a man skulked near a grey Manza parked in a bylane, along with several other cars. Fortunately, the Manza was parked between two dim street lights. Presently, a van came up the lane and stopped near it, blocking the view of the car's rear half from prying eyes.

The man who had been loitering close by darted to the boot of the car with a flexible hose that was equipped with a flat metal nozzle. He inserted the nozzle into the gap between the rear windshield and the lid of the boot and manoeuvred it expertly till the tip had found its way between the rubber beading and the metal of the boot lid. He then pushed the hose through another foot or so.

Taking a small contraption and a canister of compressed air, he blew a cupful of a certain powder through the hose into the boot. Job accomplished, he pulled back the hose and climbed into the van. Half a minute later, the van had disappeared down the lane.

The trap had been sprung.

Chapter 30

The grey Manza threaded its way through the Friday evening traffic in Bandra. In a vehicle following a hundred feet behind, Ranade waited for two things: first, for Zeus to switch on his phone; and second, to see which of the half a dozen routes he would take today.

Once it reached the Western Express Highway, the Manza would slow down as it usually did – time enough for police vehicles to catch up or overtake it. If all went well, this would be the last trip Zeus would be making in the Manza.

'He seems to be taking Route No. 2 or 3,' Abdul said over the mobile phone. 'Shall I give the instruction for both parties to prepare?'

'Yes. All units to converge north. We'll know which route when he turns left off the highway.'

Several groups of policemen had been posted over a wide area so that they covered all the six routes Zeus usually took. In addition, there were three other groups in white vans stationed near three apartment complexes. These were the buildings where Ares, Apollo and Hermes lived. Unlike Zeus, who was always on the move when he switched on his mobile, the other Greek gods made and received calls from their homes. By locating their mobiles, the police had identified the apartment buildings, but didn't know the men's names or which of the flats they lived in.

As the Manza moved slowly northwards, unmarked police cars

raced to the two prearranged interception spots far ahead. Ranade hoped Zeus would take Route No. 2, which led him towards the mangrove beyond Lokhandwala. Near the spot where the car usually turned back was a good place to intercept it.

Forty-five minutes later, the Manza reached the road adjoining the mangrove, a road that didn't see heavy traffic at this time of the evening. As the Manza purred along at a leisurely pace, with Zeus deep in conversation in the rear seat, the driver slowed down at an unexpected roadblock. Four armed policemen stood among movable barricades.

One of the policemen waved a baton-like red light and the Manza pulled over to the left. Two policemen approached the vehicle as the other two stood at a distance, the muzzles of their guns pointing unwaveringly at the car. While one policeman approached the driver's window, Abdul moved up to tap on the wound-up glass of one of the rear windows.

'We need to inspect the car, sir,' Abdul said to Zeus in the rear seat.

The bespectacled, scholarly-looking man nodded absently and continued speaking into the phone. A random police check late in the evening was not unusual in these days of sporadic terrorist activity. Zeus was in his late fifties and mostly bald, except for salt-and-pepper hair on the sides and back of his head. He looked like a leaner version of Gorbachev, except that he didn't have the distinguishing birthmark high on his forehead. The driver had already been asked to step out.

Meanwhile, a fifth man had appeared with a dog on a leash and led it to the driver's open door. As soon as the dog began sniffing, it grew excited and began straining at the leash. The men around the car grew visibly alert. The dog jumped into the driver's seat and tried at once to turn left between the two front seats, sniffing excitedly.

'Please come out, sir,' Abdul said. 'We need to check the back of the car.'

'What is this about?' Zeus asked, as he complied. He put his mobile to his ear and said, 'I'll call you back in a couple of minutes.'

The dog jumped on to the rear seat and immediately tried to push its nose between the base and the backrest. Unable to go further, it gave a short bark and began whining.

At the sound of the bark, six policemen, armed with automatic rifles, emerged from behind a police van that was standing close by and surrounded the car, their weapons trained on its occupants who had just alighted from the vehicle.

'What's happening?' Zeus demanded. 'What are you looking for?'

'Please stand back, sir,' Abdul said. 'Don't approach the car.'

'*Dikki kholo!*' another policeman ordered the driver.

As soon as the boot was opened, the dog, which had been brought around, placed its forepaws on the edge of the boot and sniffed. Apparently, one sniff was enough for the canine to make up its mind. It began barking and wagging its tail furiously.

'Good boy!' its handler said and dragged it away.

As he produced a snack as a reward for the dog, Abdul and another policeman shone torches into the Manza's boot and immediately noticed an irregular patch of white powder. The man beside Abdul picked up a small amount of the powder and examined it. He smelled it, then tasted a pinch. A moment later, he nodded. Another policeman moved in and began taking photos.

'What's going on?' Zeus asked in alarm, as eight gun muzzles were trained on him and the driver. 'What is all this about?'

'Are you the owner of the car, sir?' Abdul asked in a formal tone.

'No.'

'Do you use it regularly?'

Zeus stammered out something incoherent.

'Did you use it on Tuesday and Wednesday?'

'Wednesday, yes. What's going on? I demand to know!'

'Narcotics. I'm afraid you'll have to come with me, sir.'

Abdul took away the mobile phone from Zeus, as another policeman collected a second mobile, a laptop and some papers from the rear seat. Under the papers was a small notebook with the letters 'SX' written on the first page.

'Your name, sir?' Abdul asked, leading Zeus to a police car.

'Saldana. M.A. Saldana. Listen, there's obviously been some mistake…'

▪

Elsewhere, an exhausted Shashi sat deep in discussion with Gupta. On the table in front of them lay a number of papers they had been going through. Gupta was staring at a sheet of paper in his hand. Listed on it were two long columns of company names.

'Are these the companies behind the 26 demat accounts you spoke about, Shashi?' he asked incredulously.

After eliminating the demat accounts used by Vivek Tola, the insiders in the 44 companies and Sudakar's son-in-law, 26 accounts had remained unidentified. Each of these 26 accounts had traded extensively in *all* the 44 stocks. These, Shashi figured, must belong – directly or indirectly – to the people behind Spice Xchange.

'Yes sir. We traced back the ownership of the 26 demat accounts that trade in all the 44 stocks. We believe that the owners of Spice Xchange operate through these accounts. These are different from the accounts used by the insiders in these companies and by Vivek Tola.'

Once he and Ranade began tracing the men behind the twenty-six accounts, they found themselves confronted by a maze of small, privately-owned companies. Ownership was convoluted. In addition to extensive cross-holdings, it was a jumbled mess of subsidiaries and associated companies. The ownership trail went back and forth and, sometimes, ran around in apparent circles.

Often, the trail went overseas, making further tracking impossible for the moment.

After an entire day of non-stop work, Shashi had a brainwave.

In addition to Purple Country, Gupta was associated with a large number of companies and promoters. While some of his associations were formal in nature, like a position on a board or advisory committee, some were not. As a veteran in Indian corporate circles, he knew a large number of promoters and their businesses. If anyone could help Shashi cut through the spaghetti-like mess and arrive at its core, it was he. He had brought his problem to Gupta.

As he looked up at Gupta, he saw the colour drain from his face. His fingers were trembling as he put down the sheet of paper with the company names. Gupta seemed thunderstruck.

'Oh my God!' he groaned and pushed his hair back with a trembling hand. 'It cannot be.'

'What cannot be, sir?' Shashi asked softly.

'There is a pattern here, Shashi…I hope to God I'm wrong.'

'What pattern?' Shashi was on edge, hardly daring to breathe.

'I've seen many of these company names in one man's portfolio. That does not automatically mean that he's guilty, you know. But how else…' Gupta left the sentence hanging.

'Who? Which man?'

'You'll have to trace it properly to be sure, Shashi. It's going to take days, but it can be done. Do it quietly, discreetly. I hope to God it doesn't lead to him.'

'To whom, sir?' Shashi asked again, stumped by Gupta's extreme reaction.

Gupta's lips were trembling as he turned towards him.

'Dheerajbhai.'

■

Miles away, Abdul navigated to the last call Saldana had made from his regular phone – the call Abdul had interrupted when the Manza was flagged down. Stunned, he gaped at the contact's name: Dheerajbhai.

Not wanting to lose any more time, he picked up the prepaid mobile phone Saldana had been using as Zeus and called Ares.

'Ares, this is a message from Zeus,' he said, when the call was answered. 'There is a problem; you need to change your SIM card. Zeus's number has changed too. Go down to the corner of your street. You will see a white van there. Identify yourself as Ares to the driver – he doesn't know you, nor do you know him. Show him your Spice Xchange notebook as ID proof and collect your new SIM card from him. He will ask no questions if he sees the notebook. He will also give you a slip with Zeus's new number. Understood?'

'Yes.'

Abdul cut the call. In the next couple of minutes, he made two more calls – to Apollo and Hermes.

The white van stood at the street corner with its engine running and its side door slid open. A middle-aged man hurried up to it and spoke to the driver.

'I am Ares,' he said, holding up a small notebook with 'SX' written on the first page.

Two uniformed men stepped out of the van and stood behind Ares, while a third man came around the van and spoke up.

'You are under arrest,' he said softly. 'Please come quietly, sir. I don't want to handcuff you in public if I can help it.'

Within the next ten minutes, three vans, carrying Ares, Apollo and Hermes, were on their way to a secure building.

▪

'Why did Dheerajbhai do this to Purple Country, his own company?' Carol asked on Sunday evening.

She, along with Shashi, Tanuja and Kamna, had gathered at what her boss described as 'the best restaurant in Mumbai'. They had spent the better part of an hour with Ranade in the afternoon, during which time the inspector had briefed them on the arrests and asked them to be prepared to give formal testimonies on Monday.

'I'm not sure, but this is what I think,' Shashi replied. 'First, let's keep in mind that Purple Country represents one of Dheerajbhai's minor investments – '

'Minor!' Carol exclaimed. 'He owns almost half the company!'

'I know, but his initial investment was little more than a couple of hundred crore. It's worth a lot more now.'

'It *was* worth a lot more. Not any longer.'

'That's right. Now returning to your question, Dheerajbhai and Saldana knew that Vivek was getting inside information from Purple Country. But they were also sure that he wasn't getting it from *their* insider, Amit. Then who could be leaking the information to him? The obvious answer was Vivek's brother-in-law – me!

'So they sent Varma and Kashyap to verbally shake me down. Perhaps, they didn't expect me to take the matter to the board the way I did. Perhaps, they were confident that they could manage it at the board. If you remember, Saldana had tried to discourage me from taking it to the board meeting. He had said he didn't want it minuted.'

'I remember,' Kamna nodded. 'It made for a stormy meeting.'

'What they hadn't bargained for was Sudakar launching a full-fledged attack on me. He, of course, did it to protect his backside and hide the fact that he was leaking information to his son-in-law. With Dheerajbhai not present at that meeting, Saldana couldn't manoeuvre the proceedings towards the desired outcome.'

'And an investigation subcommittee was set up.'

'Once that happened, they couldn't rein in Sudakar immediately without arousing suspicion. So they let it run for a couple of days, during which time Saldana reasoned with Sudakar in private. But by then, something else was happening – the share price began plummeting.

'Once that happened, Dheerajbhai would have seen an opportunity. If he let matters ride for just a few more days, he could pick up more Purple Country shares as it bottomed out.'

'Which is what he tried to do,' Carol interjected with a nod. 'He said so at the meeting with mutual funds and other institutional investors.'

'Exactly! Two birds with one stone! Dheerajbhai is a very smart man. He knew that there was nothing wrong with the company. Within a month, the share price would return to normal. By that time, he would have increased his stake.'

'What do you think will happen to the share price now?' Tanuja asked.

'It's going to get worse before it gets better, Tanu. The news about Saldana and Dheerajbhai has not yet hit the market. There's going to be more bloodshed once that happens.'

'What do you plan to do, Shashi?'

'Kamna and I discussed it last night. I'm seriously considering a management buyout.'

'You, along with others in the company, plan to buy out Dheerajbhai?'

Shashi nodded. 'And the banks, to the extent they are willing to sell.'

'Where will you raise the money from?'

'I think I can get private equity backing. Kamna has some inheritance and I can raise some funds too.'

Epilogue

The morning after Saldana was arrested, two offices were raided – the marketing company that had sent the 'junk' messages and the office of a private finance company from which analysts had logged into the Spice Xchange server to estimate the impact of each piece of inside information.

Most of the 44 insiders were taken into custody that weekend and their mobile phones seized. The devices all turned out to be of the same model – iPhone 4s. The demat and bank accounts of those insiders were frozen and their passports impounded. The more astute among them had already erased the junk messages they had based their share trades upon.

Within a week, information gleaned from forty-nine phones, the computers in the private finance company and the logs of the marketing company began falling into a revealing pattern. However, the entire body of evidence related only to the last leg of the long trail from India to Europe and back. The Tor network had erased all traces upstream of the marketing company. No investigation was possible. As a result, there was no evidence that could be used to prove that even one of the 44 insiders had leaked inside information. The only proof at hand was of receiving information that was, arguably, privileged.

While the linkages between the 'junk' messages and share trading transactions were clear in a handful of cases, the evidence was entirely circumstantial in others. None of the 44 had retained older messages. Some had preserved no messages at all and only a few had kept the latest ones. Without direct evidence of involvement in insider trading, conviction was going to be tricky. The authorities were entering uncharted legal waters.

It turned out that only four of the 26 demat accounts were operated by Saldana. The remaining 22 were fronts for a maze of shell companies. While some of them cast a shadow on Dheerajbhai, others ran close to powerful men and women belonging to the business–politics nexus. One link pointed to the family of a former finance minister. At least one other cabinet minister of an earlier regime seemed to be involved. Two political families were indicated; they had used their real estate ventures for diverting preferential loans to fund insider trading.

This too was circumstantial.

The case against Dheerajbhai was weak. Forewarned, he had destroyed the phone and the SIM card on which he had been receiving Spice Xchange's messages. The circuitous trail that led to his companies was far from conclusive. He indirectly owned both the marketing company and the private finance company, but mere ownership would not suffice to convict him. Day-to-day operational control would have to be proved.

Amit submitted a formal confession as soon as he had recovered and related how the long-standing friendship between the retired Lucarro partner and Saldana had led to the formation of the Lucarro gang. To make the scheme profitable, all eight members of the gang had then sought employment in well-traded, mid-sized, publicly listed companies.

Unable to bear the acute anxiety, seven more insiders broke down and confessed in the next week. Within days, Amit had received a death threat. It was now anyone's guess whether the confessors would be able to withstand the immense pressure they were likely to be subjected to during the inordinately long period the legal process was certain to drag through.

A fortnight after his arrest, Saldana was out on bail, assiduously preparing a defence aimed at disallowing circumstantial evidence at the trial. His nonchalant manner underscored his optimism. At any rate, the case would take years to be resolved; enough time for the elections to come up and even bring about possible regime changes. And if a new government did come to power, who knew what could happen?

The work of an honest police officer had been done and the matter now rested in the hands of those who were more susceptible to powerful influences. At most, Ranade would be called in as a witness. He did, however, earn an out-of-turn promotion for his work.

All the 44 insiders, most of them CXOs or directors, either resigned or were asked to leave. The few bold ones who had contemplated legal action against their dismissal quietened down and faded into obscurity. It was only a matter of time before SEBI barred them from trading in the stock exchange. Sudakar resigned from all his board positions and was now being openly investigated for insider trading. His career in corporate India was over.

Purple Country's share price tanked further as the news of Saldana, Sudakar and Dheerajbhai's culpability became public. For a brief period, the share price touched ₹52 – the level it had stood at two years ago. Backed by Kamna and the Anjumal Trust, Shashi made full use of it and bought as many shares as he could. Separately, Chaaya bought a sizeable chunk and lent money to Carol as well so that she could do likewise.

The suggestion of a management buyout was received enthusiastically by banks, which agreed to sell half their stake to the management-buyout team and retain the rest. Backed by a private equity firm specializing in turnarounds, Shashi appointed an advisor to guide them through the takeover process.

Unexpectedly, Dheerajbhai offered to sell his stake, an offer that Shashi and his backers gladly accepted. A share was a share; there was no such thing as a tainted share.

Gupta stayed on as chairman and a new chapter opened in the company's history. By the end of November, the share price was steadily climbing back.

▪

'What will happen to Saldana, Shashi?' Chaaya asked, early in December.

'I don't know, Chaaya. This whole matter depends on how much circumstantial evidence will be taken into account. In any case, it isn't going to happen in a hurry.'

'It's not the insider trading thing I'm talking about. I honestly don't care how it turns out.' Chaaya's face was taut. 'I meant Vivek's murder.'

'I wish it were otherwise, Chaaya, but the truth is that the murder charge is still more difficult to prove. Killing Kashyap was a masterstroke. With him eliminated, there's no link at all between Saldana and Vivek's murder. That's why they haven't even filed charges yet.'

'Do you have any doubts that Saldana ordered Vivek's murder?'

'None whatsoever.'

'What does the inspector think?'

'He's in complete agreement with me; he's sure that Saldana ordered the killing.'

'Okay.' Chaaya rose to her feet. Her face was set. 'That's what I wanted to know.'

Ten minutes later, a middle-aged man, clad entirely in white, came to see her. His salt-and-pepper mane was combed back from his forehead. His lips were stained red by the habitual consumption of paan. His eyes were shrewd, watchful, missing nothing. He and

Chaaya retired to the study for ten minutes. He left immediately afterwards.

'Who was that?' Shashi asked Kamna, when her sister was out of earshot.

'Don't you know?' Kamna's surprise was evident.

'Never met him.'

'Oh!' Kamna fell silent for a moment. 'That was Pandey Bhaiya.'

▪

Chaaya called her sister a week later. She was keen on feeding 101 underprivileged people the following day and would also donate new clothes to them. She was dedicating this charitable act to Vivek's memory and wanted Kamna and Shashi by her side.

The next day, a radiant Chaaya, clad in a pristine white sari, stood in the courtyard of a temple and distributed packages to a stream of needy people. In each package were clothes, ₹5,001 and some rice and dal. Outside the temple stood a large tent, where a feast had been organized.

The function lasted for three hours and Chaaya remained quiet and composed all through. By the time it drew to an end, however, her feelings had got the better of her and silent tears were streaming down her face. As the time approached for the function to wind up, Pandey Bhaiya appeared in the distance and greeted her from afar with a deep bow and a 'namaste'. The next moment, he was gone.

Chaaya shut her eyes for a few moments and a shudder passed through her. She went up to the temple's presiding deity and conducted an elaborate puja before the idol.

When she returned, her demeanour had changed. Gone were the tears, the signs of inconsolable grief. For the first time since her husband had died, Chaaya seemed at peace.

She smiled serenely at Kamna and Shashi. It was the beatific smile of the Chaaya of old. She had come to terms with her loss at last. It was as if she had finally accomplished something of paramount importance. Surprised and delighted, Shashi couldn't bring himself to ask her what the reason might be for her unexpected transformation.

The answer came unasked when Ranade called him an hour later.

'I have news for you, Mr Kurva,' the inspector said. 'Saldana was found dead in his bed this morning. He was lying on his back, as if asleep. He had apparently injected himself with krait venom. His fingerprints were found on the syringe and the bottle. There was no sign of a break-in; strangely enough, the front door was not bolted from inside.'

Shashi was stunned. The Saldana he had known was hardly the kind to resort to suicide. He had been too strong-willed, too self-centred, too coldly detached to take such an impulsive step. Just two days ago, he had been overheard arguing vociferously against insider trading being classified as a crime. He was using his favourite line: 'How can there be a crime when there is no victim?'

Shashi said as much to Ranade.

'Who am I to question the investigating officer's conclusion?' the inspector responded. His voice was quiet, but there was a hint of hidden satisfaction in it. 'God has his ways.'

'God?' Shashi asked himself, as he hung up.

His eyes went to Chaaya sitting on a sofa opposite him. She showed a curious lack of curiosity in the call from Ranade. A half-smile still played on her benign face. She was finally at peace.

The image of a man rose unbidden in Shashi's mind; a grizzled man dressed all in white, with red, paan-stained lips.

Pandey Bhaiya.

Author's Note

While the story in this book is entirely a work of fiction, some of the underlying issues are not.

If conviction for involvement in insider trading requires proof that the insider passed privileged information *and* benefited directly from the passing, such convictions are going to be rare. In an increasingly wired world where monetary and economic benefit can be transferred and shared in manifold ways, establishing an irrefutable causal link between the two elements will be difficult.

This is the principle behind Spice Xchange in this story. A person contributes by leaking information about his company, but benefits from trading in shares of unrelated companies. Since information flow gains anonymity as it passes through the Tor network, establishing linkages between sender and receiver becomes well-nigh impossible.

The issue becomes a still more challenging one in India, a country rife with *benami* arrangements, where the rich and well connected wield inordinate influence and it takes decades to deliver justice, if at all.

Circumstantial evidence, therefore, becomes crucial for an investigation to have a fair chance of culminating in conviction. Not only in cases of insider trading, but of other complex financial frauds as well, where the connection between an act and the benefit that accrues from it may not be a direct one. Without such evidence to bring them to justice, fraudsters of the kind described in this novel are likely to get away scot-free.

Finally, there is the question of will or intent. US courts had the courage to convict Wall Street luminaries on the basis of circumstantial evidence. How will our own legal system deal with a potential Spice Xchange, where all available evidence is circumstantial?

Given Indian ingenuity, it's only a matter of time before this question comes up in court, for the technology of Spice Xchange is, by no means, complex.

ALSO AVAILABLE FROM HACHETTE INDIA

Fraudster

RV RAMAN

A YOUNG BANKER is found dead a day after she deposes before a commission investigating large-scale financial fraud…

A DOYEN OF CORPORATE INDIA falls to his death from his south Bombay flat…

A HIGH-SECURITY SERVER ROOM of a multinational accounting firm is hacked, and the hackers aren't just looking for company secrets…

Illicit finance, high-stakes crime and vicious manipulation come together in this story of corruption, greed and treachery among corporate India's black sheep.

Arresting, fast-paced and written by an insider from the corporate world, *Fraudster* will keep you on your toes till the very end.

9789351950318